ISLE OF BRINE AND BONE

Praise for Natalia Macias Lucia's

Isle of Brine and Bone

"The haunting sequel to *Girls of Salt and Sea* is finally here, and it's even more thrilling than the last! Packed with suspense and dripping with atmospheric prose, Lucia draws you in for yet another spine-chilling, seaside adventure!"

—Morgan Hubbard, author of *This Cursed Line*

"A spell-binding, sinister follow-up to *Girls of Salt and Sea*. Lucia once again sucks you into this world with her dazzling prose and descriptions that hit you right in the heart. I experienced ALL the emotions while reading this book, and after that ending, I'm screaming for more!"

—V.B. Lacey, author of *Long Live*

"All. The. Feels. What an ending. I need the next book pronto! I loved the twists and turns of this story, the swoony romance, the spine-tingling ghostly encounters, and the gut-wrenching emotions."

—Rachel L. Schade, author of *Castle of Dusk and Shadows*

"Utterly speechless. This is one of the most beautifully written, hauntingly dark, most BREATHTAKING books I've ever read. Lucia has such an incredible gift…This is masterful storytelling. There are no other words to describe it."

— Emily Schneider, author of *Scales of Ash & Smoke*

Isle of Brine and Bone

HALCYON BAY BOOK TWO

NATALIA MACIAS LUCIA

LIGHTKEEPER
PRESS

Published by Lightkeeper Press LLC
Miami, FL

www.nataliamlucia.com

Cover Design by Maria Spada

ISBN: HB: 979-8-9863441-4-0; PB: 979-8-9863441-0-2; eBook: 979-8-9863441-1-9

Library of Congress Control Number: 2023919406

First Edition: November 2023

For Ryan—
Because you never let me give up.
I love you.

CHAPTER ONE

The winds change in Woodbridge the day the wheelchaired man arrives. I'm surprised to see his shadowy figure on my doorstep, as weeks had slipped into months without a word from him. But now, confronted by that sallow face and inky gaze—those eyes like black pits ignited by a hell-bent inner fire—I know that he's only been biding his time. Waiting for the ideal moment to strike.

Winter had been sharp in Maine, cold and girded with ice, with a blustery air that sliced and jabbed as though it had been wronged and was fighting back. But with my cousin before me, draped in his habitual darkness, paralyzed from the neck down and molded to his chair, the agitated winds at last seem to settle. They grow silent, still, as if in keen anticipation of whatever news he brought with him.

"I've got a lead on my father's whereabouts," Tristen says to me in greeting.

He's flanked by a companion I don't recognize—a muscular man with ash-gray hair and a rigid, military posture, hands firm on the handle grips of my cousin's wheelchair. A valet, I presume, or maybe a bodyguard.

The man appraises me in all of my glorious homebodiness with a sweep of his eyes and a smirk—from my unwashed ponytail to my oversized hoodie to my fuzzy pink Bullwinkle socks with holes in the pinky toes.

"Hi to you too." I wrap my arms around my chest and step aside, allowing them space to wheel through the narrow doorway. "I didn't know you were coming. Much less two of you."

A little heads-up would've been nice. I might've tidied up a bit. Cleared the empty wine bottles from the counter. Swept the dust bunnies from the long-abandoned corners of the apartment.

"We won't be long," Tristen says offhandedly. "You look like hell, by the way."

"Really?" I shut the door. "And here I thought I looked like a ray of sunshine."

Tristen hums in appreciation of my sarcasm as he analyzes the cruddy, disheveled state of my kitchen. His discerning gaze lingers on the mountain of dishes piled in the sink, on the stovetop spattered in days-old marinara sauce, on the loaf of sourdough actively growing mold on the counter.

"How do you live like this, Dell?" he asks, dismayed.

My eyes roll back involuntarily. The last thing I need is Tristen pointing out how bad this looks, or offering up any of his snarky criticisms.

"The lead," I remind him with a testy sigh. "Tell me about the lead."

In the weeks following my departure from Halcyon Bay, Tristen and I had been in steady contact, full steam ahead in our efforts to track down my uncle Florian.

I was limited in what I could accomplish from Woodbridge, chasing breadcrumb trails on the internet—fixating on conspiracy theories I found in blogs and forums hypothesizing as to where Florian might be hiding—while hounding local and state police, as well as anyone known to have been in contact with my uncle in the weeks prior to his disappearance. But every statement I took, every officer I hassled, every scrap of cyber-speculation I dug up, failed to point me toward Florian's trail.

Meanwhile, Tristen—ensconced in his new, sedentary lifestyle—made it his personal mission to question every last one of Florian's business associates, sometimes having them tailed for weeks, hoping they might steer him back to his father. But none ever did.

Tristen also kept watch over Florian's bank accounts—the ones he knew of, anyway—certain that any new transactions would tip him off to his father's whereabouts. But the funds went untouched, the accounts unaccessed.

I even suggested we hire a private detective, someone we could trust to sniff out clues and heat up our ice-frozen investigation. Predictably, Tristen refused, not wanting to entrust this assignment to "some money-grabbing no-name," or concede to the fact that he'd been outwitted by his father.

Before long, our leads dried up and our need for communication dwindled. We hadn't exchanged a message in two long months. For all intents and purposes, we'd failed miserably. All we could do was sit and wait for Florian to emerge from the shadows. It was only a matter of time.

My uncle is not one to bow out quietly, wracked with guilt over his misdeeds. He doesn't have the decency in him to surrender, bereft of the human impulse to atone for his sins. That would be too gracious for a man so brutal. The world just isn't that kind. So I'm not surprised that my cousin kept up the search on his own. I just wish he would've let me know sooner. Wish I could've stopped him before he made this trip.

Tristen pins his black eyes on me, likely contemplating a few clever quips about my unsavory living conditions before deciding it best to let it go. "Right, the lead. Payne?" he beckons.

The ashy-haired valet steps forward, plucking a cell phone from his breast pocket. With a few swift taps, Payne flips the screen to show me a grainy photograph.

I lean in close as he magnifies it, honing in on a bearded man walking through a crumbling alleyway.

He weaves through a tight throng of people, grime crawling up the dingy walls around them—a once-lively yellow weathered by time and neglect. Through all that facial hair, there's something vaguely familiar about him. Something in the sleek wave of his jet-black hair. In the winsome grin slithering up his cheeks.

The quality of the photo isn't great, but it's enough to make me wonder. "Florian?"

"Looks like him," Tristen confirms.

We quiet for a moment, absorbing what this means. My uncle, spotted at long last—alive, on the move, and, worst of all, *smiling*.

"Where?" I ask.

"Cuba, three nights ago, in the heart of La Habana."

I squint at the screen again.

The Florian I knew had been impeccably groomed, donning his charming guise like he would a designer suit. The man in this photo is entirely too grubby—his beard unruly, t-shirt chalky with stains, none of which fits my uncle in the slightest. But that may all be part of his ruse. An effort to blend in with the proletarian masses. To slip by unseen.

His stature is certainly spot on for Florian's. And that fiendish grin is so uncanny, it sends literal shivers through me.

"How do you know for sure that—"

"I don't," Tristen interrupts me, an ever-ready sharpness to his tone. "Normally I'd think a tip like this is bullshit. I mean, why would my father risk keeping so close to home? Why chance it, when he could build a life for himself anywhere else in the world? Live like a king in some far off land, without fear of extradition, or worry over being recognized."

It doesn't make sense to me either. Florian may be arrogant, but a fool he's not. Would he really endanger himself this way? Put his neck on the line—risk imprisonment—after fleeing Halcyon Bay so skillfully? I seriously doubt it.

But then Tristen adds, with sobering gravity, "Except…this isn't the first sighting of him."

Payne swipes at the cell phone screen to show me a second photograph—a map of Caribbean island-nations that comprise the Greater Antilles, just southeast of Florida.

Southeast of Halcyon Bay.

Three red X's are marked across the map. One X over Cuba, another over Haiti, and a third over the Dominican Republic.

"All of these sightings happened within the last month, all of them from trusted sources," Tristen says. "Which tells me that Florian has a vested interest in Halcyon Bay. So much so that he's willing to take a gamble on his own capture if it means remaining nearby."

"Why don't your sources confront him?" I ask. "Turn him over to local police or something?"

If they're able to get close enough to snap his picture, surely they should be able to alert authorities to detain him.

Tristen gapes at me. "You really think it'd be that easy?" he asks. "My father's moving through countries rife with corruption. Local police are more likely to help him than arrest him, especially if he flashes enough money. And even if they did attempt an arrest, don't you think my father would've planned for that? That he wouldn't have an army of men protecting him, or some other ironclad contingency in place? I mean, for goodness' sake, Dell"—he scoffs in frustration—"have you forgotten what he's capable of?"

I grit my teeth against the blow of that question. It stabs into me, a poison-tipped dagger thrust into my ribs.

How could I ever forget?

Dark memories of my last night at Cliffmoor House all but consume me these days, threatening to drown me in a sea of enduring trauma.

They come to me in flashes, in wake and sleep alike.

Flash—Florian stalking us to the attic rafters, his eyes honed on the wolf cane in my hands.

Flash—the splintering echo of Tristen's body hitting the ground, drifting on the wind across the sandy dunes.

Flash—Ambrose's gnarled fingers crushing my windpipe, the wail of emergency sirens dismally far away.

Flash—Bram unloading his pistol on my grandfather, only to be gunned down moments later, drawing his final breath in my arms.

Flash—Blood—a sea of blood—razing the Sandspur shoreline, painting the moon-soaked beach a violent, grisly maroon.

I hadn't forgotten a single second.

Forgetting is a luxury and comfort. A soft, indulgent state of willful ignorance. Forgetting is accepting and moving on.

Laughable.

There would be no forgetting for me, no turning the page. The Klyne brothers branded me for life that evening, like searing-hot iron on livestock hide.

And I know Tristen is treading through his own ocean of miseries—grievances I can only begin to surmise—but he's an arrogant schmuck if he thinks he's the only one marked by the stain of this family.

"My father is circling Halcyon Bay like a shark that smells blood," Tristen comments, his bleak pragmatism ringing through me like a death toll—a portent of sinister things to come. "One can assume it's a matter of time before he manages to sneak in again."

"What does the HBPD have to say about this?"

"They don't know," Tristen replies, "nor do I plan to inform them. Keeping the cops abreast of my findings has proven an utter waste of time, and I'm not in the business of squandering a resource so precious. They can bungle my father's search all on their own, no assistance required from me."

A familiar prickle of heat zips up my spine. The scorch of anger I'd entombed months ago. The swell of resentment over law enforcement's many failures. For what they did and didn't do for my family. For Willow. For Bram.

"So they've just given up?" I ask angrily. "After a few months of shoddy police work?"

"Last I heard, they were following some dead-end trail through New Zealand." Tristen rolls his shadowed eyes. "Who knows if that's even real. Part of me thinks all they've told me is a lie. I don't put an ounce of stock in their intel."

He's right to mistrust the institutions that abandoned him. He'd served the HBPD well as an informant—helping to shutter the next generation of the Brine, delivering information that would wreck the Klynes' repute, ripping back their polished veneer to reveal the heap of crooked parts underneath. He'd saved my life. He'd led them straight to Florian. But then he got hurt, and they tossed him aside like spoiled goods.

"What do you propose?" I ask, aware of how my voice seems to shiver at the edges.

"It doesn't make sense to chase my father across the Caribbean, though I can't exactly wait for him to descend on Halcyon Bay like a plague." Tristen's lip twitches as he thinks out loud. "He's after something, I'm sure of it. Something he left behind. That's the only explanation for why he's sticking around. We just need to figure out what."

We.

The word reverberates in my skull like a ghostly murmur, slams against my chest like a thunderous wave. A reminder that this was all my idea, this endeavor born out of my fiery insistence.

After Palmer's wedding, I'd impressed upon Tristen that—police or not—we should hunt my uncle down. That we should take the lead on this investigation. Put an end to our family's reign of terror once and for all.

I made that declaration months ago, when my blood still boiled in the heat of the moment. Back when I felt invincible, willing to do anything to right the Klynes' myriad of wrongs...

Before I collapsed under this strange spell of disjunction.

Before the ache I'd buried came surging up like lava.

I expected to pursue my uncle across foreign oceans, through foreign cities, but *never* did I think we'd be following his tracks back to Halcyon Bay. Not now...not quite so soon.

These four months away had reinstilled every iota of dread I felt about the island. The thought of returning now—of peeling back the layers on another mystery, trapped on that godforsaken rock—is *gut-wrenching*. I don't feel capable of it. Don't feel strong anymore. Not with this unbearable, crushing weight in my bones, like slow-spreading ice threatening to freeze me over.

It's a feeling I recognize. An old companion.

Fear.

Fear that if I go back, things won't work out for us. Fear of what and who we'll lose in the fray. Fear that the outcome will be bloody, and that it'll be my fault, all over again.

Tristen barely scraped by with his life last time. The fact that he's sitting before me—able to eat, speak, and breathe on his own—is nothing short of a miracle. I might've died if not for Bram, who paid the ultimate price. Willow had been avenged, but the wound of her loss is still raw on my heart, my grief fresh over having to bury a sister I never knew.

I've lost count of all the pains we've had to endure.

How many more have to die at the hands of this family? How much spilled blood will the island demand? Will we ever be free of it, or will it find us nestled in our hiding places, curled up in our shells, and drag us out with the tide?

We've done everything we can, I think stubbornly, battling with myself, my thoughts churning like the wicked sea. *There's nowhere left to follow Florian but…back to Halcyon Bay.*

Yet even with this knowledge—the embers of my former fire attempting to spark up and galvanize me to action—that icy fear gnaws away at me slowly, devouring my spirit, eating up my fight.

Tristen sees the growing conflict on my face, the war entrenched deep in my eyes. His brow furrows with quiet concern, though he doesn't ask questions or push me to speak. He knows enough of fear to recognize it in another.

"I fly out tomorrow morning," he says. "I have a brief layover in Miami. There's someone I want to visit before returning to Halcyon Bay."

The buried scheme in his words brings me pause. "Who?"

"An inmate at a local penitentiary," he says vaguely.

An inmate? I'm almost too afraid to ask.

"Who is it?"

His dark, unflinching eyes level with mine. "Kieran Blackbane."

It takes me a second to process.

Kieran Blackbane.

The Kieran Blackbane.

Cult leader.

Girl killer.

My chest tightens to the point of pain. "No…"

"I know it's a stretch," he's quick to explain, "but Blackbane and my father were old confidants. Who knows what valuable information he might've gathered over the years?"

"You *cannot* be serious."

"I'm very serious. It wouldn't behoove us to overlook this guy. I want to squeeze him a bit, see what he lets slip."

"We're not talking about some harmless vagrant here, Tristen!" An avalanche of unbridled, fearful emotion rumbles through me. "Need I remind you that Kieran Blackbane *created* the Brine? That he and his deranged sheep-followers brainwashed and *killed* countless girls on the island? That sadistic psychopath deserves to rot in jail for the rest of his life—"

"And jail is precisely where he'll stay," Tristen cuts in, infuriatingly calm. "But there's still a chance he's sitting on a wealth of information that no one's thought to tap into yet. We'd be foolish not to capitalize on that."

There's that damned *we* again.

I shake my head, lost for words. Nothing I say is going to change Tristen's mind. He'd devised his plan, and he'd surely see it through. And he'd come here tonight to ask me to tag along. To stand by his side with Blackbane, and return to Halcyon Bay. To do whatever it takes to capture his father, like I promised I would.

But I'm not in the right mind for this task. Something in me has come…dislodged. Broken. Rusty. I'll only be holding Tristen back—a heavy-hearted load he doesn't need to carry with him.

"Look," I say soberly, shutting my eyes to help push the words out. "I know you're trying to make things right, leaving no stone unturned in the search for your father. And I appreciate you traveling all the way up here to include me"—I swallow hard, guilt writhing in my stomach—"but I can't go with you, Tristen. I can't go back to Halcyon Bay. Not right now. I'm sorry."

Silence permeates the room.

I force my eyes open, and like so many times before, Tristen's response is not one I expect. His steely eyes glint at me, but with neither outrage nor contempt. Instead, something like *relief* sweeps over his face.

"Good," he mutters. "I was hoping you'd say that."

"You were?"

His eyebrow quirks. "No sense in both of us plunging off this cliffside."

I wince at the statement, thinking back to the plunge Tristen took last year from the rafters of Cliffmoor House. My uncle had flown at his son in a violent rage, pushed him through the glass window in the attic, and sent him plummeting to what should have been his death.

That was the incident that landed my cousin in a wheelchair, honed his appetite for revenge, and led him to this very mission.

"Why'd you come all this way?" I ask, despising how weak I sound. Grasping at straws, as if his answer might absolve me of my cowardice, or put a stopper in the well of my depression. "If you hoped I wouldn't join you, why not spare yourself the trip and just call?"

Tristen's eyes flit to the countless cracks in my ceiling. Hundreds stretch across it in jarring, zigzag patterns—an ever-present lightning storm looming above my head. "I tire of the sunshine," he admits, giving me a rare glimpse into the man behind the armor. "It's too bright in Halcyon Bay. Too cloudless. Not really preferable for someone like me. I figured I could use a break, even if only for a day or two."

I nod silently. When life is made of perpetual night, you learn to adjust to the darkness. Maybe, along the way, you forget how it feels to live in the light. Maybe you begin to avoid it, and you seek that same darkness in others. Slowly, deliberately, you build a home of the shadows.

Isn't that what Tristen had been doing for years?

Isn't that what you're doing right now?

"Let's go, Payne," Tristen says, and the valet promptly wheels him to my door. "I'm staying at the Antler's Edge Hotel," he calls back to me, "in case you change your mind."

I don't move—don't know how to respond—as Payne opens the door and a brisk air sweeps in.

"Oh, and Dell?" Payne twists the wheelchair so that Tristen's coal-black eyes meet mine. "You may want to think about cleaning up a bit. The place is starting to stink."

CHAPTER TWO

It's after two in the morning when I arrive at Evergreen Hills, a small cemetery hugging the westernmost edge of the Woodbridge city limits. The gates are locked, the sleepy paths quiet, and the night guard is camped inside the security booth, watching *Seinfeld* reruns on a portable television, chuckling to himself while he gorges on a party-sized bag of Cheetos.

I creep along the exterior wall like I've done so many times before, making my way to a covert spot cloaked in thick tree cover and shifting shadows. My gloved fingers curl around the slick, old bricks as I scale the wall, lifting myself to the highest point. I swing a leg over to straddle it, then jump, landing inside the grounds on a shallow snow patch with a thud. I've gotten good at this break-in process. I barely even feel the fall.

Dusting off snowy flecks from my coat, I pick my way along the gravestones, keeping close to the tree-line and away from the slivers of moonlight cutting across the lawn like spotlights primed to expose me. I huff out breaths in time with my steps—staccato puffs of hot air whispered through the frigid night—and shiver deeper into my fleece-lined hood.

Willow's grave is a short distance away, but I don't rush to it, as is usually my custom. Instead, my strides are slow and careful as I let myself sink into the chilly atmosphere, turning over each of Tristen's words in my mind, his revelations making my blood run colder than the icy weather ever could.

Why would Florian insist on staying close to Halcyon Bay? His wealth runs deep and his network spreads far, paving an easy path for him anywhere else in the world. But despite the heightened potential for capture, my uncle is choosing to remain nearby, like a wolf taunting its prey, nipping at its haunches. Something binds him to the island, but what? What could he be after? What's worth losing everything over?

Tristen's tenacity is admirable, and I don't find fault in his quest, one I'd helmed myself until recently, when my entire life began to splinter and slip through my fingers. But I worry about him going at this alone. About the consequences of looking for answers in seedy places. Fraternizing with the likes of Kieran Blackbane. Probing into his father's connections with the Brine. All with no backing from police and no one to come to his aid should he need it.

Then again, I'm in no position to tell Tristen Klyne what to do.

My cousin is a frustratingly level-headed person—determined, methodical, and assertive in every way—whereas I've become decidedly less so, unraveling like a stuffed doll, delicate stitches snapping loose one after another. I've come derailed somehow, rusted by salt, worn down by memory. The albatross of trauma weighs on me like an anchor. Maybe I've broken too far, the wounds in me too deep to patch up. My mind isn't a safe place anymore. More like a cruel prison, and I its willing captive.

Any explanation for what's become of me barely scratches the surface of the truth.

What is the truth? a voice within me asks, begging me to face it, if only for myself. *Try to confront it. To conquer it.*

The truth is, it feels like my sun has permanently eclipsed. Like all the light in my world has been swallowed by a depthless, black sea. I drift through it alone, sightless and afraid, gasping for air that never comes. No matter how desperately I thrash through that darkness, or how far my frozen fingers might stretch out for warmth, for the tiniest glimmer of hope at the surface, I can't reach it.

The truth is…I'm drowning even as I breathe.

Depression's a soul-sucking bitch.

Willow's tombstone rises up ahead. The marble is smooth, that alabaster sheen gleaming white beneath the moon. I tiptoe in close, the soil still clustered from her recent burial, with a melting blanket of snow lying over it.

Silently, I drop to the ground.

Flowers are placed before the stone—a dusty purple kind that hadn't yet wilted under frost. They aren't from my parents. Mom only leaves white flowers for Willow. I don't bother with flowers myself. Knowing they won't last irrevocably squashes their allure. I usually bring Willow letters instead—all of my thoughts and tears and regrets spilled onto paper. I read them aloud at her gravesite, letting the lonely, painful words dissipate into air.

The violet blooms laid here are fresh. Maybe from Tristen, come to pay his respects. I wonder what he thought of the epitaph on her tombstone. Of the fact that, posthumously, Mom conferred a new surname on my sister—*Willow Jane Urban.* The Klynes would never touch her again.

"I don't know what to do," I breathe into the night.

In the daylight, I can confidently say I know better than to dwell on the strange and inexplicable. I know better than to believe in ghosts and spirits, better than to seek direction from beyond the grave. But under the milky moon, it's harder not to wish for more. I often find myself praying that Willow will answer my broken pleas, afford me some much needed clarity, like she did on that still, summer morning in the shallows of Halcyon Bay.

"Should I go back?" I ask, rubbing gloved hands up and down my arms. I should've grabbed a heavier coat, but I'd been in such a hurry to escape my apartment. To flee my bed and the night terrors that kept me from sleep.

For months, I've had to relive the same terrifying dream.

I'm on Sandspur beach.

It's the night of Palmer's wedding.

My grandfather pins me down into the sand, gripping my neck, squeezing the life from me.

Stop! I cry, but no words emerge.

"Just like your sister." Ambrose smiles wickedly. "A small fish in too large a pond."

I twist and writhe. *Stop it, please!*

His face shifts suddenly, shaving off a decade, metamorphosing into someone younger—my uncle Florian. His lip curls up into a menacing sneer.

Stop! I repeat, but he only presses down harder. Mangling my skin, crushing my bones.

Gunshots ring out. Bullet casings fly. Gunpowder singes my nostrils, a metallic taste filling my mouth.

I scream as a torrent of shots pierce Florian's torso. He does a macabre dance in the dark, twitching and jolting with each new rupture, black blood seeping from his wounds and mouth.

When he collapses onto the sea foam, a figure emerges at a distance, rising slowly from the water. At first, it looks like the shape of a man—like Bram, tall and rugged and strong—but when the figure creeps forward, slipping onto the shore, the masculine body shrinks, becoming slight and slender and delicate—feminine.

Willow's face and corn-yellow hair flash at me in the moonlight.

Upon our eyes connecting, I fall into a dark oblivion…

And am lurched from sleep like a corpse from death.

When this dream came to me again tonight, I awoke panting, my cheeks sticky with tears, throat hoarse from screaming. I crawled from bed into the shower where I sat, hugging myself under a stream of hot water until the shivering ceased. I knew sleep would evade me the rest of the night, and I couldn't bear to stay there, in my cocoon of anxiety, squirming in sweaty sheets, desperate for morning.

I decided to go for a walk, and, unsurprisingly, ended up here.

Granted, it's not the smartest idea to walk the outskirts of town alone at night, and with a cloudy mind to boot. But I've always felt safe in Woodbridge. The town is comfortable and boring, and I know the ins and outs of it. Surprises, accidents, and tragedies seem to skip this place entirely. No one's a stranger here. Nothing's a threat.

Mom still believes I can lead a happy life in Woodbridge. And I can admit it has its gentle charms and consolations, the greatest of which are my parents themselves. For the most part, we've forgiven each other for the past, though residual pains still occasionally spark up. Maybe our wounds will never fully go away. Maybe they'll fade to tender scars instead. Maybe we'll love each other in spite of them. Because of them. Through them.

But I know I can never truly be happy here.

Not without Hatch.

He visited Woodbridge late last fall, and then again after Christmastime. Things were getting serious for us, and we knew that his constant flying back and forth wasn't sustainable. Still, he knew better than to suggest I move to Halcyon Bay—knew better than to even bring up the possibility. And maybe he'd been waiting for me to suggest he move to Maine, but I didn't. I skirted the conversation, procrastinated the looming question growing like a wall between us—*what comes next?* That was the beginning of all this weirdness. We'd been so genuinely happy. Soaring. Falling. But now…now I don't even know what to say to him.

Woodbridge feels like exile.

Halcyon Bay, like a strange dreamland.

Neither of which is akin to home.

"I feel like I betray you either way," I admit to the night wind rustling the frostbitten trees. To the moon that listens but never replies. To my sister, wherever she may be. "If I stay here, then I'm not doing everything I can to make things right for you. But if I go…"

I can't complete the thought, my voice smothered along with my breath, ensnared by a cold, unfeeling chill. Tears run in streams down my face.

If I go, then I'll be away from you. Away from Mom and Dad. And I'm scared to my soul. Scared of who I am if I stay. Scared of who I'll become if I leave.

My phone vibrates in my jacket pocket, and I pull it out to find a text message from Hatch. A nervous fluttering comes alive in my stomach. I miss every inch of his sun-drenched skin. The rough inflections of his voice. The teasing smiles meant only for me.

Hatch…

My Hatch.

Guilt and longing wring my heart as I read his message: *Couldn't sleep, so I'm getting an early start on the day. I miss you, love. When can we talk?*

It's incredible how in sync we are, even when we're 1,600 miles apart.

If I go back to Halcyon Bay…

If I abandon Willow and my parents…

If I leave Woodbridge behind, along with this sense of insipid contentedness…

If I heed the call in my heart and embark into uncharted waters with Hatch…

If I dare take up this fight against my uncle…

What awaits me on the other side?

Will I ever truly be able to wrench myself away?

CHAPTER THREE

Something hard bumps me in the ribs. I feel it through my many layers of clothing, down to my ice-frozen skin.

"Rise and shine, kid," drawls a male voice.

I open my eyes and gasp, dry, frigid air whooshing into my lungs. I'm still in the cemetery, curled against Willow's tombstone, as if it might shield me from the bone-chilling cold. The security guard nudges my side with his boot.

I bolt to my feet—my frigid bones aching—while the guard watches on, head tilted to one side like he's deciding what to do with me.

"S-sorry," I say through chattering teeth. How could I be this stupid? How is a *cemetery* the one place I can sleep dreamlessly?

The guard's eyes flick to Willow's tombstone, taking in the clean, unweathered look of it. How new it is. How fresh the pain.

"Someone you know?" he asks.

I cup my gloved fingers, bouncing in place. "M-my s-sister."

"Ah…" A wave of sympathy washes over his burly face. "Can't say I don't understand what you're going through. I've got my mother buried in here too, just a few lanes over." He glances around the grounds, coming to some silent conclusion in his mind. "Listen, kid, I don't want to get you in trouble. Just don't let this happen again, all right?"

I can't tell whether he means I shouldn't break in again, or that I shouldn't let myself get caught next time. Either way, I shudder my thanks, grateful he's letting me go without a fuss.

He offers me a leather-gloved hand. "The name's Monty."

I shake it. "D-dell."

"Well, Dell, you'd better get somewhere warm. Wouldn't want you dying from hypothermia on my watch. Our undertaker's not coming in today, and I'm no good at digging graves." He chuckles at his morbid joke. "You got somewhere to go?"

"Mhm." I pull my beanie down on my forehead, wiggling my toes back to life in my boots.

"I'll walk you out then."

"It's ok-kay. I c-can see m-myself out."

Monty shrugs in his parka, bunching his shoulders around his neck. "It's no trouble, gates don't open for another hour anyway. If the owners show up and see you roaming in here alone outside of operating hours, then old Monty might be out of a job. And with a daughter in college, and two more champing at the bit"—he aims soft, brown eyes at my face— "we can't have that happening."

Despite my full-body shakes, I give him a tightlipped smile, bobbing my head. He's already agreed to cut me loose. The last thing I want to do is test the limits of his patience.

We trudge down the main gravel path in silence. Monty pants a little, the wet-cold air of morning pushing in on us like fog. He's middle-aged and heavyset, with a thick black mustache curling over his lips, and he waddles as he walks, the keys in his pants jingling with every step.

"Hard time sleeping?" he asks.

"How d-did you know?"

"Either you've got a lot on your mind and found some semblance of peace by your sister tonight, or you're narcoleptic." He squints at me, hints of a teasing smile tugging up his lips. "Are you narcoleptic?"

I shake my head and Monty holds his arms out in a *told-you-so* gesture. "Your sister's grave has been getting a lot of attention lately."

"We r-recently r-relocated her here. My p-parents and I t-try to come a few t-times a week."

"Yeah, I've seen 'em around. The lady looks like you, only blonder." He nods to himself, likely recalling the faces he'd seen. "Another bloke in a wheelchair came by yesterday afternoon. Asked to see her site specifically."

"M-my cousin. He's in town v-visiting." I snort a little at how I'd made it sound, as if Tristen's trip to Woodbridge was a run-of-the-mill occurrence. Just two normal, well-adjusted cousins enjoying a nice family visit.

"I see," Monty says, oblivious to my snide inner commentary. "And how about that other fellow? The older gentleman that stopped in a few weeks back?"

I stare Monty dead in the face.

Slowly, he lifts his caterpillar eyebrows.

An older gentleman a few weeks back? Willow had only been reinterred last month. The burial had *just* taken place, and it was a closed event—none but the priest, myself, and my parents present. We'd informed our loved ones, of course—Hatch and June and Tristen all knew—but no one that fits Monty's description.

Unless…

"What did he look like?" I ask, a drip of panic seeping into my brain. "This older man?"

"Oh, uh, well, he was tall and kind of refined, I guess? He had dark hair and a beard. Wore dark clothes too—"

"Black eyes?" Desperation clings to my breath. *Black as bottomless chasms. Hateful, vile, and deadly.*

"If memory serves, yes."

The twinges of warmth that had begun to crawl into my cheeks recede, all the blood draining from my face.

"Hey, you okay, kid?" Monty asks, his hand on my arm as I begin to sway.

Florian isn't just keeping close to Halcyon Bay.

He'd been here.

In Woodbridge.

At the site of Willow's grave.

Proof that he could be anywhere, and none of us would ever be the wiser. That he could get to my sister's remains whenever he damn well pleased. That he could get to my mother. To Tristen. To me.

"Hey, kiddo? You okay?" I hear Monty ask again, though his concerned voice sounds impossibly distant.

The *why* doesn't matter anymore. Questioning my uncle's motives is useless. Florian is all about terror for terror's sake.

I can't put aside this decision any longer. Can't procrastinate what needs doing because I'm feeling sad and adrift and aimless and—

Stop.

I put a pin in my fear, ram it down so I can think clearer.

Florian isn't gone.

Your loved ones aren't safe.

This isn't over.

That leaves me only one choice.

I shove past Payne into Tristen's hotel room. "Where do we start?"

"By all means, Dell, *barge* right in," Tristen snaps at me from his seat at the breakfast table. A bowl of oatmeal and a half-eaten banana rest on the placemat before him, a cigarette smoking in a nearby ash tray. "It's not like it's six in the morning or anything."

I realize I've caught my cousin in a bit of a vulnerable moment. He needs Payne's help to eat, and to puff on his morning smoke. He probably doesn't want me to see him like this.

"When do we leave?" I rasp, winded from my sprint in the cold.

Tristen's dark eyes narrow. "What's with the sudden change of heart?"

"Your sick prick of a father was at Evergreen Hills scoping out my sister's gravesite, that's what." The outrage climbs up and out of me like a volcanic eruption. I know it's not Tristen's doing—the evils perpetrated by his father are far from his fault—but I still can't contain my disgust.

Tristen looks agitated, but strangely unsurprised.

"Did you know?" My voice quivers.

"I speculated," he replies carefully, gauging my reaction. "See, I also went to visit your sister. That's partially why I flew up here—to look for signs that my father had been sniffing around. I figured that, if he'd been willing to stay near Halcyon Bay, he might've used his resources to reenter the country as a fugitive. To get *just* close enough to you and your family—"

"For what?" I croak.

"To prove that he can," Tristen says. "To prove that he'll always be several steps ahead. And, of course, to show me that I'll never measure up."

"So what the hell's stopping him from infiltrating Halcyon Bay?" I fire back. "He's already made it to the mainland without detection. A sleepy island town should be a cakewalk after that."

"The island's too hot right now with law enforcement swarming. It'll be a while before my father tries anything there. But I assure you, he's not afraid. And I think this confirms it."

My mind races at full speed, trying to comprehend what we're supposed to do now. How do we follow Florian's ghostly trail? Where do we even begin?

"I need to buy a plane ticket," I say, running through vague action items in my head. "What time's your flight to Miami?"

His mouth flattens into a tense line. He doesn't speak for a moment, but I can almost hear the clamoring of thought behind his eyes. Always concealing something, always plotting.

"Tristen?"

His jaw pulses.

"*Tristen?*"

"Fine," he growls. "Payne? The tickets, please."

The valet collects several sheets of paper from a laptop bag and hands them to me. Skimming through the pages, I see a set of plane tickets with my name printed on them. First class seats.

"What about my parents?" I ask.

Tristen's eyebrow arches. "You really want them tagging along on our little adventure?"

I absolutely do not. Florian's capture is the last thing I want them involved in—the last thing I want my mother worried over. Not when she'd been doing so well. Not when she was free of the Klynes at last.

"If Florian is ballsy enough to show up at the cemetery, why wouldn't he show up on their doorstep?" I point out. "He could use them as collateral to get to you. Or me."

Tristen's eyes flash with awareness, and I realize my secretive cousin has already thought of this—maybe even already *planned* for this.

"What did you do?" I ask him slowly.

"I have a twenty-four hour surveillance team on retainer," he says matter-of-factly. "They're camped out in the woods outside your parents' cabin. There are others keeping an eye on your place as well. I've been watching out for you all, from a respectful distance, for some time. I can ramp up security now that we know there's a real threat—"

"*Some time?*" I repeat, my blood surging.

Tristen clamps his mouth shut.

"Exactly how long have you been watching us?"

"Not watching you. Watching *out* for you."

"Enough with the technicalities. I asked you a question. How long?"

"Since my father disappeared." His face is flat and unabashed.

Months. He's had security watching us for *months.*

I'm not sure whether to thank him or wring his neck for this.

"Why didn't you tell me?"

"To what end, Dell? To endure your third degree? My father is *my* problem. I did what I saw fit to protect you and your parents."

"So you opted to spy on us rather than be honest?" I retort. "Rather than give us a choice in the matter?"

"For goodness' sake, *it wasn't spying.* They're not a pack of voyeurs. No one's peeking in your windows late at night."

"How the hell would you know what they do? You're barking orders from two thousand miles away. You have no idea what's going on here."

Tristen exhales hard, entirely over my complaints. "Fine. You're right. I should've asked. My apologies."

It couldn't be more obvious that not one bit of him is sorry. And not one bit of *me* believes he wouldn't do it again. If the threat were significant—if he deemed it necessary—there's nothing Tristen wouldn't do.

"Yes, you should have," I snarl. I've worked up a sweat with this conversation. Between talk of Florian's alarming proximity and Tristen's less-than-candid surveillance schemes, my sweater is dampening through to my jacket.

"If we do this, it's a partnership," I insist. "No more making decisions without consulting me. No more acting of your own accord. You run things by me *first,* are we clear?"

"Crystal." Tristen's throat bobs with insincerity. "Now, go round up your belongings and say your goodbyes. Our plane leaves in a few hours."

Sighing, I turn to leave the hotel room, but at the very last second, pivot on my heel. "Why did you buy my tickets if you hoped I wouldn't come?" My cousin's actions don't exactly make sense, and I'm more than a little peeved at him for constantly overstepping.

"Because hopes are just stories we tell ourselves," he says. "Pretty lies to help us get by. They're nice for a minute, when we want to lose ourselves in fiction, or dwell in the realm of infinite possibilities. But inevitably, that illusory castle of hopes will crumble, until all that remains is the dusty rubble of reality." Tristen scoffs out a derisive laugh. "I stupidly hoped you'd keep your distance from this, Dell, but we both know that's nothing more than a pipe dream. Hence, the tickets."

My eyes narrow. "So you knew I'd come."

"Of course," Tristen replies, no pretense in his words. "I knew you'd come."

CHAPTER FOUR

I've learned the hard way not to lie to my parents about my whereabouts. I have to tell them I'm going back to the island—no matter how badly they may take it—on the off-chance that a murderous cult might plot to sacrifice me to their demonic ocean goddess…for a second time.

I pass by their cabin after leaving Tristen's hotel, sitting them side-by-side on the distressed leather sectional I've curled up on since I was a child. I peer into their wide-eyed, apprehensive faces—faces that mean more to me than life itself—momentarily tongue-tied and wondering how on earth I'm ever going to get my thoughts across. How to offer them enough truth to make my plans admissible, but not so much that they might try to stop me.

"You're going back," Dad says without prompting, his knuckles rubbing the gray scruff on his chin.

It's not a question—just unadulterated, dread-induced fact. The prospect of my return to Halcyon Bay is one that forever looms over my parents, like skyscrapers built on restless unease.

Seeing their crushed expressions, an instant wave of remorse slams into me. I know that putting them through this again, after all that happened last year—returning to the place that harbors so much death and tragedy for our family—will only hurt them worse, and I *hate* myself for it.

"Yes," I say, unable to pull my gaze from Mom's. From that entrancing whirlpool-blue that governs so many of my actions and so much of my heart.

Mom's eyes have been significantly lighter as of late. Airing out a lifetime of secrets and moving Willow closer to home seemed to work marvels for her mental state. That is one victory I refuse to jeopardize. I won't subject Mom to *anything* that might derail her progress, or weaken her spirit. The rosy flush is back in her cheeks now. The pill-happy doctors, a distant memory. I intend to keep it that way.

"Is this about Hatch?" Dad asks gently. Almost intuitively.

Even without knowing the full extent of my troubles, he knows how much this particular one weighs on me. The question of what comes next for Hatch and me—what I'm willing to do to make it work between us— is always tugging at my thoughts.

No, it's not about him.

Yes, of course it is.

Can't both be true?

The immediate reason for my return isn't Hatch, but I can't deny that he's the one that matters above all others. The one that will persist beyond Florian's ploys, beyond our family drama, beyond my mixed feelings about the island…

Eventually, Hatch will need to take precedence over everything else, despite however long I try to put "us" on the back burner. Matters of the heart can't go ignored forever. I know it. I'm just avoiding it. Avoiding my own inadequacies and failures. My fears and my childish inclination to run at the first sign of trouble.

Dad senses my hesitancy. "Look, honey, we think Hatch is great. And we know your feelings for him are strong—"

My pulse thrums in my ears, the conversation taking a turn I'm not prepared for.

"—so why don't you see if he'd want to move up here?" he asks, the suggestion one I've considered daily for the past several months. "Give your relationship a real shot, with both of you living in the same place. The guy's crazy about you, Dell. I'm sure he'd do it if you asked."

I believe it, with every melancholy throb of my heart. I just wish I understood *why*. How on earth did I find someone like Hatch? Not just a good guy, but a great one. The best one. Far better than I deserve, considering my less-than-stellar attentiveness to our relationship.

"There are some things we need to work out before he goes uprooting his life for me," I say, my cheeks reddening with the lie.

Truthfully, there's nothing to work out between us. If it means being together, Hatch would do whatever I asked. But is that fair of me, to ask for so much? Do I want him to relocate, leave his family, abandon his lifestyle and his line of work, all to start from the ground up in Woodbridge?

He'd do it for me. Trade the sea for the mountains to be by my side. *Always,* he'd said, and I'm sure that he meant it. But is it right for me to ask for something so big—so permanent—when I feel so uncertain about my own place here? About where and how I fit, or if I might be better off somewhere else?

"Is that why you're going back?" Dad probes again. "To work those things out?"

"Yes," I lie, pushing down that looming pile of questions. "I want to get to know Hatch's family better. And I'd like to spend time with Palmer. It won't be long now until the baby arrives."

I keep the larger reasons for my return to myself, just like I keep Tristen's surveillance a secret too.

You're no better than he is, I think in disgust, doing to my parents what I myself had been furious about moments ago. But that's still not enough of a deterrent. I need to know that they're okay. If I'm not here to watch out for them myself, then I need assurances of their safety. One small omission to serve a greater good…I hope.

"Is that all, Dell?" Mom's voice nearly cracks my heart in two, her maternal instincts reaching out to me like sentient tentacles, infiltrating every buried emotion beating under my skin. "There's nothing else you want to fill us in on?"

Her eyes search mine, trying to puzzle out the rest of this story, to untangle the marshy contents mucking up my chest and mind. But how could she ever understand the fullness of what I feel, or the terrors I constantly have to fight off?

Florian is closing in.

Hatch is abysmally far away.

I don't feel like myself here.

I don't feel like myself anywhere.

Too many worries elbowing for space. Too risky to attempt to mold them into words. "That's all. I promise." I stand to leave before I let anything more slip.

"Where will you be staying?" Dad asks.

Crap. I hadn't thought of that. I can't exactly stay at June's or Palmer's. One call to either of them and my parents would blow this charade wide open. Hatch's place might be an option, but the implications of staying with him are far too vast—too consequential—for me to contemplate along with everything else bogging down my brain.

"The inn, I guess, if it's not too swamped," I say casually. "I don't want to crowd June or Palmer right now. They must be so busy. I'd just be an inconvenience."

I bend down to plant a quick kiss on Mom's cheek, and she grabs for my hand, squeezing it in short bursts. One, two, three quick squeezes. *I love you,* it says, the small but tender gesture making everything I'm doing—everything I'm not being honest about—even worse.

"Don't worry," I reassure them, my gaze flitting between my parents, memorizing the lines in their faces. The way Dad's thinning hair curls up at the edges. How Mom's nose crinkles when she's lost in thought. I smile, making every effort to put their worries at ease. "I'll be fine."

I say a silent prayer that we all will.

Back at the apartment, I move quickly to gather my belongings, switching out my boots and gloves, my down vests and knits, for the lighter wear I'll need on Halcyon Bay.

How long will I be there this time? A couple weeks? A month?

However long it takes.

I rip through my closet like a tornado, haphazardly flinging items into my duffel and a large travel backpack before running through a shower, getting myself ready and packed within the hour. I sit down at my computer and pay next month's rent early. Then, I draft an email to my boss at the agency, apologizing in advance for my unexpected absence for the next few weeks as I tend to *family matters*. I read it back once—knowing this very well could be my final straw at this gig—and hit send.

When Tristen's limousine pulls up to my complex—one of my cousin's more ostentatious predilections, no doubt a product of his luxe upbringing—I'm already sprinting out the door.

Tristen sits in the backseat, with Payne in the front next to the chauffeur. I load my bags in the trunk and join Tristen, dropping into an empty seat and avoiding the poignant glare of his gloomy eyes.

"Save it, okay?" I click on my seatbelt. "You're not changing my mind."

"Wouldn't dream of it," Tristen mutters, low and slippery-smooth.

"So what then? What's with the look?"

"I'm just wondering whether you had a chance to clean up at all. Your place really did stink, you know."

"Shut up."

I spend most of the flight working myself up and down a rollercoaster of emotions, wondering how everything had changed all at once. From one moment to the next, my life spent trudging through the trenches of silent pains—comfortably coexisting with my parents, neighbors, and coworkers, all while missing Hatch almost helplessly, with no actionable way out—had been ripped and transformed into something else. Something fierce and purposeful. Something honed in fire and vengeance.

I wish I knew how to get myself *right* for this undertaking. How to be brave and unflinching as we run headlong into the heart of darkness.

But I'm not that girl.

And yet, here I am, coming face to face with Kieran Blackbane, when

I'd nearly died at the hands of his demented wife and children—his entire legacy of terror tied directly to my blood.

Here I am, tracking down my uncle, who'd conspired to cover up my sister's murder, who'd abused my cousin and attempted to kill him, who'd destroyed the lives of countless others along the way.

Here I am, returning to the island at the core of my grievances, but also at the core of some integral, buried part of me. A part I hadn't wanted, but had earned just the same.

Here I am, confronting my relationship with Hatch, after months of driving myself crazy over where we stood and what might happen. There's no doubt that I want him, that I need him even, but is that enough? Am *I* enough? Will I ever be good and solid enough for him?

How will I handle everything coming my way, when I've been an unconscionable, self-made mess for months?

I don't know how.

I'm not that girl.

Not that strong. Not even close.

Yet here I am, trying like hell to be.

CHAPTER FIVE

That afternoon, we arrive at a maximum security penitentiary that looks every bit how I imagined it would—a monstrous square building with little cutouts for windows, coated in gray cinder block and electrified barbed wire.

Our limo pauses at the security gate, and the chauffeur lowers the window to exchange words with the heavily-armed guard manning the booth. After a moment, the guard nods and a jarring siren blares as the gate grates open. He beckons us forward and onto the grounds.

We approach the prison entrance and my heart twists in my chest, fraught with uncompromising terror. Being here doesn't feel real, like I've been dropped inside some slasher film in the making, compelled to play a starring role I didn't audition for.

What if Tristen is wrong about this? What if his plan to meet with Blackbane is fruitless? Or worse, what if it *isn't*, but the price we pay for Blackbane's insight—for time spent in the company of a monster—outweighs whatever value we might procure?

We roll to a stop and disembark.

Payne accommodates Tristen in his wheelchair while I breathe in my new surroundings. An aura of evil lingers over the prison grounds, in stark contrast to the crisp Miami sky at a distance. As if to torture me, the sun rains warmth upon my skin—an enviable, delicious sensation—but it doesn't sink to my insides, or temper the cold inhabiting my veins.

Puffy clouds drift by overhead, like the white sails of a ship. Sleek royal palms sway to the tune of a light breeze, elegant fronds taunting me with their dance. A citrusy aroma hits me too—the sweet scent of oranges wafting in from far off groves. All quiet reminders of how full the world is. How brimming with beauty, goodness, and peace. Just not here.

Tristen tells Payne to wait in the car. It'll be the two of us facing Blackbane alone.

I maneuver my cousin through the steel-barred doors, past multiple security checkpoints, and down a dim, gray corridor escorted by a guard carrying a baton. We pour into a windowed room with distanced tables bolted to the floor. Armed officers stand like statues at each of the four corners, eyes shifting sharply under fluorescent lights. There are two other inmates present for visitation—one whispering with a haggard-looking lawyer-type, the other sitting in silence across from a woman with a severe expression, so thin she's barely visible in her chair.

Our escort leads us to a vacant table farthest from the rest, and we wait for the guards to bring forth Blackbane—inmate 826—for our allotted ten minutes of conversation.

Tristen seems utterly unperturbed, his eyebrow flexed coolly, his expression one of calm concentration. I, on the other hand, bite and peck at my bottom lip until I gouge the skin and draw blood.

"Remind me again why we're here?" I grit out under my breath. "Why the hell is this a good idea?"

"Everything will be fine, Dell. Try to relax," Tristen replies, his tone obnoxiously even.

"*You* relax," I toss back. "I'd rather imagine all the ways this stupid plan of yours can go off the rails."

Tristen sucks his teeth languidly. "It's just ten minutes, Dell. I'm certain you can make it that long without having a meltdown."

If he wasn't paralyzed, I swear I'd take a swing at his face.

Two gun-clad officers burst inside gripping a scant-faced man between them. My heartbeat drums inside of me as I lock in on that pallid figure.

The man's steps are uneven and twisty, as if the ground beneath him is laced with booby-traps and only he knows the route to avoid them. His orange jumpsuit dangles off his body awkwardly—bony shoulders stretched out like a brittle wire hanger. His dark hair is long and matted, peppered in white flakes.

The guards shuffle him toward our table, force him into the seat across from us, and instruct him to keep his hands flat on the tabletop. "There is to be no physical contact with the inmate," one guard growls at us. "You've got ten minutes."

Blackbane's unkempt head dips low, not quite meeting our eyes. The rest of him looks sickly—cadaver-like—with mysterious violet bruises mottling his wrinkled skin and filth packed under his yellow fingernails.

I gulp hard, wondering what my cousin hopes to extract from him. What could this psychopath possibly offer us, other than endless fuel for our nightmares?

Blackbane's mouth cracks into a sinister grin, and I'm shocked to find a line of straight teeth gleaming at me. Not the rotting, blackened mess I was expecting, but a real smile, convincing and terrifying. A politician's smile, harkening back to years past, before the heyday of the Brine.

"Brother…" Blackbane's cruel eyes lift to Tristen's face. "Come to the big house to see me at last."

I side-eye my cousin. *Brother?*

He looks just as confused as me, but only for a brief second. Then, he forces a strange smile. "It's been far too long, old friend."

Blackbane laughs and leans back in his chair, his shoulders jutting out at odd angles, skin pulled tight over gnarly bones. "To what do I owe the pleasure after all these years, Florian?"

Blackbane thinks Tristen is his father. He's so twisted up in the head—so convoluted by his own sick delusions or the cocktail of drugs he's under— he actually believes he's talking to Florian.

Tristen has his response at the ready, slipping fully into my uncle's identity. "I came to consult with you about a rather concerning matter."

"Trouble with the revival?" Blackbane asks, eyes scanning the room from left to right. "What's happened? Information is hard to come by these days. Greer hasn't sent word in months. But I've heard rumors. Whispers. One of our marks escaped?"

Me, I realize, my neck prickling. I'm the escapee. The one that got away.

"No trouble at all, actually." Tristen's lips stretch to a thin line as he lies. "Everything is on course."

Blackbane's face twists with inhuman darkness. "If one of the girls did evade us, Florian, then you know what must be done. Whomsoever refuses water shall end in fire. That is Mother's will."

"Of course, of course. Mother's will be done," Tristen replies, the words rolling off his tongue like second nature.

Mother's will be done—what the hell does that mean?

"I assure you, the revival is intact," Tristen continues. "I've come to visit for a different reason. You see, I find myself in a bit of a personal quandary."

Blackbane inches forward. "Oh?"

"Discussing details now, while under such scrutiny, would be unwise." Tristen's eyes glide across the room, pausing momentarily on each officer. He drops his voice a tad more. "Suffice it to say, I may need to seek passage out of the country for a time."

"Leave Halcyon Bay?" Blackbane's croak is incredulous. "For how long?"

"A short time. Until it is safe for me back home."

Blackbane tucks his chin, drawing away. "There are graver matters than your safety, brother."

"I'm aware." Tristen's retort is slick. "But it does not change the critical nature of my circumstances. It appears the police have caught wind of some of my…earlier transgressions. I sense a witch-hunt on the rise."

Blackbane chuckles. "And your handsomely-paid moles within the HBPD can't dissuade them?"

Tristen swallows hard beside me.

My skin tingles, ears gone muggy with heat.

Both of us wade through the implications of that statement. The cold truth that Blackbane so casually divulged, and the rippling effect it would have on us moving forward…

Florian has moles within the police force.

No wonder their "investigation" is leading them halfway across the globe. My uncle's operatives are throwing off the search *on purpose.* They don't want to catch him and risk losing their meal ticket. It's all a ploy, a game rigged from the inside. Not too surprising, when I really think about it. Florian was the one to bribe Alan Katz to alter Willow's post-mortem report. The fact that his corruption bled into the police department—that he'd venture to keep a handful of officers on his payroll—isn't particularly shocking.

But these were the same men and women tasked with arresting Florian last year…which begs the question of whether we ever stood a chance at catching him, or if the actions taken by the police were all performative. If they'd ever planned on apprehending him, or if they'd *allowed* him to escape the island unscathed.

Tristen weighs his next words carefully—surely thinking about all this and more—before muttering, "Let's just say a handful of rookies at the department are a bit too virtuous."

"Too indomitable even for you?" Blackbane goads.

Tristen fixes him with a piercing stare. "So it would seem."

"And what do you need from me?"

"Insight," Tristen says shortly. "Should I require assistance, who might be willing to help within your network? Whom of your supporters remains in contact?"

Blackbane's eyes cloud over, a plague of black smoke pushing forth from within. "You ask me to disclose the whereabouts of my people?"

"I ask you to share your resources with your oldest friend, and the man who gave you everything," Tristen retorts, his voice imbued with calculated bitterness.

It strikes me how similar he sounds to his father. How effortlessly he switches on his viciousness. It's a handy skill for moments like this, but it still makes me uneasy. Makes me question which side of Tristen is real, and whether I know anything about the person I've joined forces with.

Blackbane shifts across the table, considering Tristen's statement. "Gave me everything, indeed…then stood by to watch it all crumble. You left me to waste away to nothing, Florian. To grow decrepit within these prison walls, when we both know the kind of influence you wield. I assumed you'd have me freed by the first week's end. But, instead, you made yourself a stranger."

"You know that the rumors surrounding our friendship, if not properly mitigated, would've sunk my reputation and my business," Tristen counters. "Calling in favors would've spelled more trouble than I could weather, and fanned the flames of all manner of public speculation. Surely you didn't expect me to throw my life away in my efforts to have you released?"

Blackbane is unmoved, black eyes flashing. "I expected you to do infinitely more, old friend."

"I must disagree with your assessment, *old friend.*"

I see the quiver of Tristen's Adam's apple in my periphery, can feel his subtle rise in temperature. Blackbane holding a grudge isn't something he'd accounted for.

"Be that as it may," Blackbane says callously, "you come asking for help now, after offering me none for decades? After all I've done to keep your secrets? After the kind of unwavering loyalty I've shown?"

More secrets. I stiffen in my seat, wondering what kind of dirt Blackbane has on my uncle. Inwardly, Tristen must be contemplating the same thing, even if on the surface he has to pretend to know exactly what Blackbane is talking about.

"Well," Tristen says, trying to rein in the conversation, "I intend to put that loyalty to the test. Whom of your followers can I trust, Kieran?"

Blackbane's eyes snap wide upon hearing his first name, like the sudden crack of a whip. His curved frame straightens, eyes brightening. It's terrifying to see him come alive this way—an electric current switched on and buzzing through him. Maybe it's been years since anyone referred to him by name. Maybe it clears some of the fog from his mind.

His attention shoots to me for the first time. "Is this one of your lady friends, Florian?" Blackbane asks my cousin, not pulling his eyes from my face. The question sends waves of nausea coursing down my body.

"Answer me," Tristen repeats, his voice wavering ever so slightly. "Whom can I trust?"

Blackbane ignores him. "She is not one of my consorts, nor is she one of my children. And if she isn't *yours*—isn't privy to our business— then why, pray tell, is she here?"

"She's my assistant," Tristen offers.

"Your assistant?" Blackbane tilts his head this way and that, observing me from every angle. "No, I don't think so. Why, she looks like one of your *family*. Yes, I see it now. Looks quite a lot like the young Klyne girl. The first girl, if I recall…"

The first girl.

Willow.

Tristen's eyes flick to me, as if suddenly nervous, the moment slipping out of his control. "She can be trusted, and that's my final word on the matter. Now, are you willing to help me, or—"

"What's your name, girl?" Blackbane spits at me, his eyes savage and untamed. Saliva drips from the corner of his mouth.

I sink deeper into my chair, adrenaline pouring through my veins. I glimpse sideways at Tristen, trying to catch his eyes, to emphasize that it's *time to go*, but he doesn't look at me.

"I'm warning you, Kieran," Tristen says threateningly.

"Your name, girl?" Blackbane shakes with unquenchable ferocity, his rickety frame trembling like a colored leaf in autumn.

I grab Tristen's sleeve and tug. *Let's go, dammit!* But, of course, he can't feel that. Can't sense the urgency in my touch.

"Leave her be!" Tristen barks, undeterred from his target. "Answer the question."

The guardsmen walking the perimeter of the visitation room take notice. One of them yells at us from the corner, "Pipe down over there!" Another swings his baton in warning.

Blackbane doesn't flinch at their bellowed commands. An aura of malice radiates from his figure. "Your name, girl," he repeats, his voice lower now. *"Your name your name your name your name..."* He curses the words under his breath on a loop, eyes rolling back in his skull. He appears to convulse, hands flailing from the table onto his lap.

Hell no. Game over. I push my chair back to leave. With or without Tristen, I'm getting out of this shithole.

"Fine. We're finished here," Tristen hisses through clenched teeth.

Before I can stand, Blackbane dives across the table, latching onto my arm. I cry out as he yanks it hard toward him.

"The marked will fall," he snarls, pulling a cigarette lighter from his pants.

He flicks it on, and presses the small flame to my skin.

CHAPTER SIX

It all unfolds in slow motion.

Blackbane's blotchy face hovers inches from mine, so close I can smell the stale rot on his breath.

His yellow-tinged eyes are raging mad—wild and quivering in their bony sockets.

He smiles like a ghost while cadaverous fingers grip my forearm, a lit pocket lighter pressed to the soft inner skin.

"What the hell?"

I hear the confused shock in Tristen's voice.

Feel the fiery sear of pain…

A scream bursts from my throat like a detonated bomb.

I fight to pull away, but Blackbane's fingers claw in deeper. The hot metal brands me, the lick of fire blackening the skin.

Two guards pummel into Blackbane, grappling with his distorted limbs, hauling him up roughly by the arms.

The cigarette lighter topples to the floor.

"How did he get that?" Tristen roars at the room, though his eyes—

horrified—are trained on me.

I grip my arm, choking back tears. A small pool of bubbling red ruptures from my forearm, the tiny bits of skin around it peeling back in paper-thin strips.

"How did he get a *goddamn lighter* in here?" Tristen's thundering voice shakes the walls.

Blackbane spits at the floor, thrashing against the guards who restrain him. "If not by the salt and sea, then smoke and sacrifice it shall be," he curses.

A guard knocks him hard across the face, and Blackbane's neck twists, snapping to one side. He howls with laughter at their attempts to silence him, foaming at the mouth, his lip swollen and bloody.

I sink back in my chair, my vision watery and stippled in whorls of black.

"Get him out of here!" shouts the warden to his officers, his cheeks drained of color.

A horn blares to unlock the main door, and the guards drag Blackbane, writhing and squawking, through it.

"There's no running from Halcyon Bay, Florian!" he calls as they lug him into the dark depths of the prison. His voice slithers along the walls back to us—a haunting reverberation. "Remember everything that's on your head. Remember *Sereia*."

A team of medical personnel burst through a set of side doors and rush me to the prison infirmary. In my wake, I hear Tristen shouting at the warden and his guards, "Imbeciles, I'll have your heads on a platter for this! Every last one of you will be penniless by the time my lawyers are through!"

Once in the infirmary, I'm ushered onto a stiff bed. Cold compresses are applied to my arm, and I'm handed two blue pills and a glass of water. "For the pain," a woman in a white lab coat explains. She slathers a salve over the burned area, followed by a loose dressing secured with medical tape.

None of it feels real. The havoc that erupted in a fraction of a second. Blackbane's chaotic attempt on my life. I feel entirely separate from it, despite the persistent sting of pain and the adrenaline rush flooding my bloodstream. It's as if I'm watching the scene at a distance, outside of my body, and at an unsettlingly slow pace.

The medical staff scatters to make room for Tristen to be wheeled forward by a dazed-looking guard. "Leave us," Tristen snaps, and everyone flies out of the room. "Christ, Dell," he mutters as he takes in the sight of me. "Are you okay?"

"Did I pass the test?" I ask, my words long and sluggish.

His eyes are intent on my face. "What test?"

"The one where I make it ten minutes without having a meltdown. Interesting choice of words, by the way, considering the turn of events."

The traces of sarcasm in my voice feel like a lifeline, like a tether back to myself after being so thoroughly rattled.

Tristen sighs, his gaze drooping. "I shouldn't have risked something like this happening."

"I'm fine," I whisper, though we both know I'm not.

"I'll fix it," he insists, "even if it means raining hell on this facility. The lawsuit is going to be *astronomical.* You're about to be supremely rich."

Riches are the last thing I care about, and the last thing I need, considering the inheritance sitting untouched in my bank account. The welfare of my parents, however…

"Do you think you can 'rain hell' without all the fanfare?" I ask. "I'd rather keep this mishap under wraps. Don't want to worry my parents unnecessarily."

One inky eyebrow flicks up sharply on his face, as if he's debating arguing with me on this point, but then seems to think better of it. "I'll see what I can do."

"Great." I nod steadily, collecting my thoughts. "Where's the lighter?"

"I have it. Tangible evidence of this prison staff's utter ineptitude."

"Can I hold onto it?"

Tristen's brow furrows. "Why?"

"Sick sense of humor, I guess. Seems like a fun little memento to commemorate our day together," I say somewhat sourly. Maybe I need that bit of concrete proof to know this is real life. That this absurd situation isn't something I concocted. Maybe I want a reminder that it happened. A reminder of how easy it'd be for something like it to happen again.

He snorts. "Can't say I understand your reasoning, but I think you've earned it." His eyes flick down to his chest. "It's in my breast pocket."

My lashes flutter with exhaustion at the thought of grabbing for the lighter. Even the slightest movement feels next to impossible right now. "I'll get it from you later, when I haven't got quite so much lead in my limbs."

It isn't the pain meds making me feel this way, nor the burning sensation radiating from my arm. It's the sheer weight and wideness of fear in my bones. The magnitude of every unknown hurdle we'll soon face. Blackbane. Florian. Who *else* do we have to look out for? How many more threats await us?

"What did he mean…about smoke and sacrifice?" I ask.

"What?"

"Blackbane. Before they took him away, he said: *if not by the salt and sea, then smoke and sacrifice it shall be.*"

"So?"

I get the feeling Tristen is being purposely obtuse.

"*So* what did he mean by that?"

"Nothing, he's insane," Tristen says deliberately. "You said so yourself, remember?"

I can tell he's being careful not to divulge anything that might upset me further. Trying not to add to the claustrophobic heaviness pressing in on my chest.

"You deemed him worthy of an audience, so he can't be that insane," I argue.

Tristen doesn't offer up an explanation, stewing on some private knowledge he doesn't want to share.

"Tristen." I say his name solemnly, so he understands that I'm not playing. "Be honest with me, please. What does that mean?"

"It's an old tenet held by the Brine, okay?" He huffs out a breath. "Any escaped 'marks' must be terminated by fire, per their refusal of water.

Once Blackbane figured out who you were, I guess he thought he'd get a jump-start on the task."

I hadn't given much thought to the practices of the Brine. Details about what they might've done to me on the fields if Tristen hadn't freed me wasn't something I cared to know. But now, after Blackbane's threats, I don't see another option.

"I don't understand. I thought *Salemorte*"—the word spills from my lips with an indelible shiver—"took place at that giant pyre in the fields? Weren't they planning to kill me with fire anyway? Burn me at the stake or something?"

"No, the pyre was purely ritualistic, like a ceremonial precursor to your drowning. *Salemorte* is a bacchanal of sorts, a drug-fueled celebration of your sacrifice to the island. Once the festivities of *Salemorte* were over, the actual killing would've happened at sea."

"How would they have done it?" I ask, my stomach pretzeling over the real question I'm asking. *If things had gone differently, how would I have died?*

"Far too easily," Tristen replies. "They would've dragged you to the rock wall and forced your head underwater. It would've ended quickly. You wouldn't have had your wits about you to put up much of a fight."

"Why not?"

"The sea trumpets," he explains. "They would've had you so wasted—so utterly terrified—you would've been begging for death."

Begging for death. I don't doubt it, recalling how muddled I'd felt with the tiniest bit of sea trumpet powder Tristen blew in my face last year. It was like my brain was melting in my cranium. Like my veins had been slit open, siphoned of blood, and infused with hot venom instead. The effect was rapid, albeit brief, considering I'd only breathed in a small amount. But it was potent enough to knock me out for several minutes. I'd only come to after Riley decided to use my face as her personal punching bag.

"Once you stopped struggling—once they knew you were dead— they would've staged the scene," Tristen continues. "Wrapped some fishing line around your neck, or slashed your wrists to make it look like a suicide-drowning. Someone would've waded out and dumped you where the seafloor drops and the current picks up. Your body would've washed up on the opposite side of the island the next morning."

"Fantastic," I mutter. He'd painted quite a macabre and vivid picture, one that I wouldn't be able to force out of my mind for weeks. "That's enough honesty for one day. Thanks."

"Nothing like that is ever going to happen to you again," he says. "I promise."

He couldn't promise that, not after what had just transpired with Blackbane. Not after he'd disclosed that any active member of the Brine would willingly *burn me alive* if they learned who I was. Still, I appreciate the sentiment. It's almost sweet.

"Blackbane yelled a name, at the end," I say. "A woman's name. It started with an S. Sarah, or Sierra, or—"

"*Sereia.*" Tristen's gloomy eyes seem to go entirely flat, still and chilling as a frozen black lake.

"Sereia," I repeat, the shape of it soft on my lips. It's a beautiful name, like whispers carried on an ocean wind, but wistful too. Immeasurably sad. "Do you have any idea who she is?"

"Was," my cousin corrects. "And yes. I do."

His gaze moves to his feet, and I know he's about to say something substantial. Something that will potentially change *everything* about our search for his father, and whatever he's after on Halcyon Bay.

Tristen's nostrils flare, every second that passes filling me with dread. Finally, he murmurs, so low I almost don't catch it—

"Sereia was my mother."

CHAPTER SEVEN

After nearly being set on fire, I'm more than ready to leave Miami.

Flying first class is just as glamorous the second time around, though I don't enjoy it one bit. Between the scorching throb of my bandaged arm, my head steeped in a heavy fog, and Tristen seething across the aisle—storm clouds and guilt pressing down on his shoulders—there's little space left for me to kick back and relax. Payne sits beside Tristen, leafing through a magazine, never bothering to remove his sunglasses from his eyes. A screen above my head silently plays an action-adventure flick with subtitles, but I can't bring myself to watch. All I can think of is our encounter with Blackbane. What he'd intimated. What he'd done.

Tristen doesn't offer any more details about his mother, nor does he speculate as to why Blackbane brought her up like a hangman's noose dangling over my uncle's head. Was *she* the secret Blackbane had been holding onto for years?

I can only imagine how Tristen must be feeling, knowing his mother—a subject so delicate—had been spoken of so recklessly. Like she's just another pawn in Blackbane's web, or a game piece in Florian's schemes. It isn't right. Isn't fair.

"We're going to need assistance when we get to Halcyon Bay." Tristen's voice punctures the quiet like the stab of a needle. "People we can trust. I'd like to bring the staff back to maintain that ridiculous house while we—"

"Wait." I freeze as the world seems to tilt around me, almost as if the plane took a sudden nosedive. "Bring the staff *back?*"

"Well, yes. Briggs, of course. Inga and Emery too, and the gatekeepers, and so on." His face expresses tenebrous confusion. "Why's that so surprising? They're innocents, Dell. No way any of them are involved in my father's dealings."

"No, I know they're not, but"—ice spills faster into my veins—"why would we need to bring them *back?*"

I know his answer before he utters the words. I'd just refused to let my mind wander in that direction. Hadn't even wanted to consider the possibility.

"Dell, you have to understand…" Tristen's mouth cracks open a bit, hesitant. Knowing how this might affect me. Knowing what's at stake. "We have to go back to Cliffmoor House."

Heat singes the tip of my nose. *No, I don't understand, you insufferable bastard!* I want to scream it at the top of my lungs. But, tucked beneath all that righteous indignation, I know Cliffmoor House is at the heart of everything. It's the place that bred Florian and Ambrose into monsters. So if my uncle has something to hide—or something to stay close for—it's buried in that house, like the rest of the Klynes' secrets.

After Ambrose died, ownership of the property transferred to Mom and June, but they both refused to claim it, neither one wanting to step foot on the estate again—the fulcrum of their decades-old grief, the pain of it embedded in their chests like a butcher's cleaver. The sisters wanted us all to move on, so they opted to sell and divide the gains among us— between the Klyne daughters and surviving grandchildren—in hopes that we might leave that pain in the past, inching toward a future devoid of generational suffering.

But it soon became obvious that real estate and 'murder houses,' as the papers had so tastefully labeled Cliffmoor House, did not mix well. Every potential buyer pulled back the instant they caught whiff of the scandals surrounding the house and our family. *A risky business investment,* they called it, in about a million different ways.

Then, out of the woodwork, came Finley O'Hare—my grandparents' horse-faced attorney—who directed everyone's attention to my grandfather's will, and a surprising stipulation in regards to Cliffmoor House. It stated that, upon the current owner's intent to sell, Cliffmoor House must first be optioned to the next of kin. Under normal circumstances, that would've been Florian, but in his present condition— as a fugitive at large and under criminal investigation—all his rights to the house were waived. The option to purchase was then conferred onto Tristen, the last viable Klyne buyer.

And, wouldn't you know it, he bought the damn thing.

For whatever reason, my cousin purchased the estate, became its new master and potentate, and assumed all the misery and prestige that went along with it. Perhaps he'd known that keeping Cliffmoor House was important somehow. That it might lead us to Florian. Or perhaps he simply got a kick out of the irony of it all. Owning the house that once swallowed him whole. Possessing that which was always kept from him, held over his head like some unattainable trophy. He was the last Klyne man standing, so to speak.

But Tristen hadn't moved in.

After all this time, over all these months, he still lived out of a penthouse apartment he'd shared with his father downtown. Meaning Cliffmoor House still stands like a relic by the sea, gray and withering and utterly vacant, the ghosts and memories its only inhabitants.

Why would he want to move in now? And why drag me along?

"Are you okay with that, Dell?" Tristen's dark eyes slide to my face. His question is gratuitous, one he doesn't need to ask but knows he should anyway, as a token of our partnership—a sign of cordiality. Testing the waters to see how far I can be pushed.

Is that what this is? A push to see how far I can bend before I snap? An evaluation of my willingness to be here?

Of course, I can refuse him. Keep my distance from Old Town, stay at the inn, or with Hatch, or literally *anywhere* else on that godforsaken island. But, somehow, I know that whatever I'm meant to do there, whatever's left for me to dig up, won't be as easy to accomplish if I'm away from Cliffmoor House.

Maybe Tristen knows it too. Maybe he hates the place as much as I do, and hates the thought of making it his residence, but is strong enough to know that fear won't help him catch his father. Maybe, on some level, this is a sacrifice for him too.

The best thing we can do is to curl up in the belly of the beast, biding our time while we pinpoint its weakness. Then, we'll end it, once and for fucking all.

"Fine," I respond, letting the decision sink into my bones. *Fine.*

And even though it isn't, I vow to make it so.

"Do you mind doing the honors?" Tristen asks when our limo rolls to a stop. We're parked curbside in an unassuming neighborhood, awash in a haze of late afternoon light. "I'm sure he'll be happy to see you," he says. "Besides, you have a *gentler* touch than me."

We'd made it onto Halcyon Bay without trouble, the island welcoming me back almost serenely, as if it had known it was only a matter of time until I returned. It was putting on a show of decency. Playing nice. As soon as I stepped through the airport doors, beams of golden sun reached down, salty sea air swooped in, and I felt at once lighter and heavier in my skin.

Through the car window, I see a pale blue cottage with white shuttered windows—no frills, uncluttered, and spotless, just as I'd expected. Rolling my eyes at Tristen, I get out without responding, slamming the car door behind me, my feet carrying me to the porch faster than my mind can think up a proper greeting.

I knock softly, making out the distant applause of a gameshow broadcast inside.

Briggs is prompt to answer the door, looking the most casual I've ever seen him in a collared pull-over, khaki cargo shorts, and woven leather sandals. His wrinkled mouth gapes wide when he sees me, silver eyes sparkling behind his spectacles.

"Miss Dell!"

"Hi, Briggs." I smile when the old butler steps up and wraps me in a hug—more of a grandfather to me than any I've ever known.

"What a lovely surprise!" he chirps. "I'm so happy to see you!"

"I'm happy to see you too. Sorry to drop in unannounced like this—"

"Nonsense! I'm just watching old *Jeopardy* reruns. Passing the time." He waves a hand in the direction of the television. I like him so much more this way. Easygoing. Relaxed. Out of his stuffy uniform.

"Come on inside," he beckons.

I step into a warm living room, admiring how much it suits Briggs. Practical, simple comforts span the modest space, the scent of a lemony cleaner clinging to the air.

"Can I get you something to drink?" he offers. "Tea or coffee—"

"No, thank you. I'll just be a minute."

Briggs smiles at me for a long, contemplative moment, his eyes swimming, as if ruminating on how far we've come since last summer—on the palpable affection between us, and perhaps the reminders I bring with me. Reminders of the family he once cared for, the young girls he watched grow to womanhood. All of those memories are wrapped up in my eyes, my nose, my lips, all of my features.

"How are you, miss?" he asks.

A dangerous question and a slippery slope.

I force myself to lie. "I'm doing well."

"And your parents?" he asks eagerly. "Laurel?"

This I can be frank about. "She's great. Feeling better than she has in years." I sigh, smiling, overwhelmed with pride that I'd helped my mother. I made her okay again. Liberated her by digging up the truth, even when that truth put us both through hell. But she was good now. It was all worth it.

"I'm so thrilled to hear it!" Briggs' grin puckers his eyes.

"How's your family?" I ask before thinking twice about it.

The house is quiet around us. Only one car is parked in the drive.

Clearly, Briggs lives here alone. I realize too late that I don't know much about his personal life—whether he's married or single, divorced or a widower. Whether he has children, or lives on Halcyon Bay without attachments.

"Oh, it's just me here, miss." His smile fades. "Never really took the time to find myself a wife, or start a family of my own." He shakes his head ruefully. "My loyalty was always to the Klynes."

I've never gotten past the notion that Briggs and my grandmother might've shared an amorous connection, something more than a working relationship. It wouldn't surprise me, knowing the extent of my grandfather's cruelty. Virginia likely felt that she couldn't escape him, but that might not have stopped her from seeking solace in another pair of arms…and another bed.

"I'm sorry," I say, kicking myself for being so thoughtless.

"Nothing to apologize for," Briggs insists. "I get my fill with my sister's family. They visit a few times a year—the whole motley crew, grandkids and all. And, believe me, that is plenty of excitement for this old geezer."

I smile at that. "I'm glad to see you're doing well."

"Oh, well as can be! Strange not to be working, but there are worse things in life than retirement." He sighs almost somberly.

"That's why I stopped by, actually…"

Intrigued, he raises a silver eyebrow.

"I'm moving into Cliffmoor House temporarily with Tristen. We were hoping you might consider coming back?"

Briggs tilts his head. "I see…" He clears his throat, deliberating his answer as he does. "I did inform Master Tristen that I wasn't keen on returning to the estate—"

"You did?" *Why the hell am I here if Tristen had already asked?* "Oh. I'm sorry. I wasn't aware…"

He hums before continuing. "But I suppose I can make an exception, now that I know *you've* returned. It's quite a challenging house to maintain, and I'm sure you two have a lot on your plates as it is."

Tristen must've known Briggs wouldn't refuse me if I asked. *The prick.* I bite down the urge to wrap my fingers around my cousin's neck and squeeze until his face turns blue.

"Name your price," I say confidently. "I'm sure Tristen will be more than willing to pay it."

"Oh, my former stipend is more than enough, miss. I'll try to bring Inga and Emery along as well. I'll have to see what they've gotten up to these past few months, but I'm sure it won't be a problem."

"That would be wonderful, thank you. I do have one condition, though." I make sure to put on a serious face. "There will be no more uniforms. No deferential terms like master and miss. None of that unnecessary submission or formality. You're our *friend*, Briggs. We're grateful to have you back."

He grimaces slightly.

"Do we have a deal?" I ask.

"I suppose. If that's truly what you wish."

"It is." I nod for added emphasis.

"Then I'll be by the house in the morning, Miss Dell—khakis and all—to take stock of what's needed."

"*Just* Dell, Briggs, remember? And great. I expect to see you wearing those leather sandals as well."

He bursts out in an uncharacteristic guffaw, wiggling his toes. "They look rather silly, don't they?"

"Not at all," I reply warmly.

After exchanging quick goodbyes, I trek back to the curb where the limo awaits. Shimmying into the seat beside Tristen, he flits his shadowed eyes in my direction.

"Success?"

Before I can stop myself, my hand whips out to smack him on the shoulder, though I know he can't feel it. "You're a real jerk, you know that?"

He smirks, forever teetering on the tightrope of good and…something else. Not quite bad, but close enough to set me permanently on edge.

"Splendid," he says haughtily. "I knew you could do it, cousin."

CHAPTER EIGHT

Cars and bodies pack White Magnolia Court, the flashing of cameras and squawking voices disorienting even through the closed car windows.

"What a zoo," Tristen mutters, watching with disgust as the hordes press in closer, fingers and cameras pointed our way, peering in through the glass at us like we're fish in an aquarium.

"Vultures, all of them," Payne chimes in. I'm surprised to hear him speak. I've gotten so used to his silence.

"Why are they here?" I ask, trying to mask the startled streak in my voice. I dip my head to avoid being photographed. If my parents happen to see my face in the papers—on my way into Cliffmoor House with Tristen, no less—I'll have way too much explaining to do.

"Some pathetic journalist must've caught wind that I was moving in," Tristen says.

"Why do they care?"

"Are you kidding? Picture the headlines! *Disgraced Invalid Returns to Family Murder House.*" Tristen snorts morbidly. "Sounds like a perfectly scandalous story. Imagine how many copies they'll sell to all the bored housewives and loose-lipped sailors on this trash heap of an island."

After countless honks and hard brakes later, we finally reach the gate and I get my first real look at the estate.

Cliffmoor House is a hulking ghost trapped behind a cage of wrought iron and vine. Eerie wisps of mist crawl over the grounds, engulfing them in heavy, near-constant gloom. The mansion itself seems frozen in time, like its many statued denizens. The sight of it resurrects memories I wish would stay buried forever.

Our driver taps a combination of numbers into the keypad. The gate grates open and we leave the newspeople behind, zipping smoothly up the mossy brick drive—a familiar and crushing approach. I feel my inner panic mounting, as if Ambrose might materialize at the curtained window, or Florian might appear standing watch on the porch.

When we pull to a stop, Payne settles Tristen into his wheelchair. I disembark quietly, drinking in the sight of the manor looming before me, immediately regretting every decision that brought me back.

Damn you to hell, Tristen.

His eyes flick to me and he shoots me a half-smirk, as if he can actually hear the thoughts as they spring up in my head.

In that case, damn you twice.

Payne pushes Tristen up the side ramp to the porch while I shrug on my backpack and grab my duffel, climbing the short steps up to the landing. The mahogany door spreads wide before us—a door to a world of darkness, one I thought I'd never walk through again. Prayed I'd never have to.

I jump when a muffled squeal spills from the overgrown rose bushes flanking the porch.

Payne leaps in front of Tristen and I, assuming a defensive stance, hand poised on a weapon tucked into his waistband.

The three of us peer over the banister as the tangle of bushes shakes violently, paired with more strange noises, like an animal is stuck inside, trying to wriggle free.

Payne growls, "What the—" but stops mid-sentence when a *woman* squirms out on her hands and knees.

I scream, dropping my duffel.

"Who the hell are you?" Tristen barks.

Payne draws his gun.

"Shit!" the woman curses in surprise, scrambling to her feet. Nicks and scrapes coat her face from brawling with the plant. Her sandy hair is bedraggled, confettied with leaves and hunks of mulch. Reading glasses hang precariously from her long, sloping nose. Her peach pantsuit is stained with dirt at the knees, her rumpled button-down damp with sweat.

"I'm…argh…I'm *so* sorry! I didn't think anyone was home yet!" She swats the leaves from her hair, shooting us a shameless smile, her coral lipstick smeared messily up one cheek. A notepad is pressed under her arm, and a black camera dangles from a strap around her neck.

"Sorry doesn't answer my question," Tristen hisses.

"Vultures, boss," Payne grits through his teeth loud enough for the woman to hear.

"I've been called worse!" She laughs unapologetically. "Just trying to sneak a peek inside…" Her blue eyes flick to me, and they light up with recognition. "Whoa! Hold the flipping phone! You're Meridel, aren't you?"

I don't respond, suddenly wishing I could evaporate. Fold myself up in the humid air and fizzle into nothingness.

"Meridel Costa?" A large grin streaks across her face. "It *is* you! Boy, I never thought you'd come back to this island. Not after everything that went down last year. And yet, here you are! The *Near Sea Girl* in the flesh!"

Vicious heat pours over me, fast and searing.

"What did you call me?" I whisper.

The woman's smile turns smug, as if she knows she's just thought up her next eye-catching headliner. "The Near Sea Girl," she repeats slowly, nodding to herself with delight. "That has a nice ring to it…" Her words reverberate in my mind, bouncing from one end of my skull to the other— a ringing torment and gruesome reminder. "Oh, it's perfect!" she trills unfeelingly, making a checkmark in the air with her finger, knocking out an assignment from a mental list.

"You do realize you're trespassing on private property?" Tristen seethes.

"And we're in our right to exterminate you like the pest you are," Payne adds, grip steady on his gun.

The woman's eyes flash. "It's all part of the job. Gotta be willing to do anything for a story!" She grimaces at Payne. "I wasn't expecting to find a woman-hating mall cop with a bad case of trigger finger, though."

"Lady, I'm an equal-opportunity hater," Payne counters, flexing his hand around the gun. "But you're right about that trigger finger."

"Stand down, Payne," Tristen snaps, keeping a cooler head than his valet. Payne lowers his weapon slightly. "Dell, call the police. *Now.*"

Shaking, I grab my phone from my pocket.

The woman smirks, wiping the smear of coral lipstick from her cheek. She wiggles her fingers and, with a pointed "Toodles," bolts in a well-trained sprint toward the gate, where the other newsfolk are still camped out. Within seconds, she scales it and drops to the other side, vanishing into the camera-happy throng. Bulbs flash. Voices roar. I barely process her retreat, consumed by the name she'd bestowed on me…

The Near Sea Girl.

My entire existence whittled down to one terrible moment.

My fingers curl around my cell phone, squeezing until my knuckles go white. With a moniker like that, I'll go down in infamy on this island. Become another one of their many legends. I hadn't died at the hands of the Brine—hadn't been claimed by the sea—but that doesn't matter. I would become a ghost of a different kind. A far worse kind. A *living* ghost.

"What was that?" I rasp.

"A sign," Tristen says, a stern line carved into his brow. "We need to tighten up security. And you"—he growls at Payne—"need to rein it *way* back. Pulling a gun on a woman half your size in front of every camera crew on the island? What were you going to do, shoot her point-blank?"

"She was a threat," Payne responds tightly.

"She was a *twig.* A sea breeze could've knocked her over."

Payne fumes in silence, the muscle in his jaw pulsing.

Meanwhile, I'm frozen in place, the phone affixed to my palm. I can't bring myself to check, but I know I rarely get cell service here. And that's never felt more harrowing or isolating than at this moment.

"Do I still phone the police?" I ask weakly, reaching for the duffel I'd abandoned at my feet.

"No, forget them," Tristen replies. "We're on our own. Let's get inside."

Payne unlocks the front door and pulls it open. The foyer expands before us like an eager, waiting nightmare.

Stepping inside, we're greeted by eerie, vacant-eyed statues, an immense, cobweb-covered chandelier, and shadows dwelling in every dusty corner. The mansion creaks and settles around us, snickering at our unease, at the obvious tension that mars our every move. It seems to whisper at us: *you're back, you're back, you're back.*

"Home, sweet home," Tristen murmurs as Payne flicks on a light switch.

The house hums with malevolence, as if its richly papered walls, displays of gaudy art, and tinselly chandelier have been poisoned for all existence. A latent evil stirs up with the dust motes as we venture deeper inside. For months, that evil has lain dormant. Now, we've arrived to awaken it.

"We should get settled in," Tristen says in a somber tone. "Would you like to take your mother's room, Dell, or would you rather—"

"The guest house."

I don't think twice about it. My memories of Mom's old room are traumatizing enough. I've taken all I need from that place.

Tristen doesn't question me, doesn't push to change my mind. "Right. Well, you know your way around the guest house better than I do."

"I'll manage," I say curtly.

Tristen beckons silent directives at Payne, who immediately pulls a ring of groundskeeper's keys from his jacket pocket. He detaches a key from it and hands it to me. It's not one I recognize. The guest house key I used last summer was tarnished bronze with spiral embellishments. This one is silver and boxy.

I take it, judging the unfamiliar weight in my hand. "New keys?"

"I had them all remade, just in case," Tristen explains. "Would you like to meet us back here for dinner?" He stares at me awkwardly, clearly unaccustomed to extending dinner invitations. Unaccustomed to having company at all, except for that of his hired help. "The kitchen isn't stocked yet, but I can have Payne pick something up. Pizza, maybe?"

Pizza. With Tristen. Now *that'd* be something.

I shake my head, certain I won't be able to stomach much of anything tonight. "I'm just going to turn in early. Try to get some sleep. I'm pretty worn out from the trip, and, you know…" I lift my bandaged arm.

"Fair enough." He presses his lips together. "We'll convene tomorrow morning, then. Lots to discuss. Nine o' clock in the parlor?"

"Sure. Nine o' clock." Tomorrow we can talk, but tonight is *mine*. And I want to spend it alone.

"Payne will see you out," Tristen says.

The valet escorts me down the shadowy corridor, the musty stench of dust replacing what once smelled of brandy, pipe tobacco, and honeyed desserts. I steal tight glances into each of the rooms as we go: the study, the dining hall, the music room, the parlor. Slipping swiftly past, I catch a glimpse of Virginia's portrait in my periphery, her pale face seeming to glow from within its gilded confines.

A habitual shiver worms its way down my spine.

Once we reach the back end of the house, Payne unlocks one of the French doors and accompanies me onto the grounds. The gardens are wild and withered from the lack of maintenance, but I don't focus on that. I'm too preoccupied with the scent of salt on the wind, tickling my face, unearthing my memories.

The salt is unsettling, but then, so is Payne's proximity. He walks in time with me across the lawn, steps synchronized, hovering like a chaperone. There's something in his sinewy swagger that irks me, an almost arrogant smugness on his lip. The longer we take our strides in silence, the more I wish he'd leave me alone.

I stop about fifty feet from the cottage, turning to face him. "I've got it from here," I say, giving him my best *time for you to get lost* eyes.

Payne smirks. "I have to secure the grounds, Dell. Goddamn vultures could be lurking anywhere. We wouldn't want them mistaking you for a field mouse, and trying to pick your bones clean through the night."

Those gross, irreverent words—Payne's personal brand of dark humor—feel vaguely threatening. The image of a vulture ripping limbs from a tiny animal is sick. Violating. It sends a million pinpricks shooting up my neck.

"Let them try," I retort, not wanting to consider that he might be right. Maybe I am more vulnerable out here alone. Maybe I should've thought this out better, planned more thoroughly, brought some means of protection with me. All I have is Blackbane's lighter tucked among my belongings. What am I supposed to do with that? Fling it at peeping reporters? Wave a tiny flame around and hope they stay away?

"Oh, don't worry," Payne replies. "If these gates go unguarded, they will try, little field mouse. They will try."

Little field mouse?

"Excuse me?"

He smiles as though he's enjoying this. "Vultures feed on small rodents when carrion is in short supply. Did you know that?"

I bare my teeth, appalled.

"What?" Payne asks, half-laughing.

I can't tell whether he's trying to insult or scare me, or if this is just an ass-backwards attempt at flirtation. Whatever the motive, I don't have the mental capacity nor the desire to riddle it out. I just want him out of my face.

"If you're locking the gates, I'll need a key," I demand. "And a set for the main house as well. I'm not a prisoner here. If Tristen has a problem with it, he knows where to find me." I hold out my palm, silently cursing the valet with every passing second I'm forced to endure his presence.

"Of course." Payne once again pulls the groundskeeper's keys from his pocket, separating a small silver key and a larger gold one from the ring. When I try to take them from him, he pulls them out of reach. "I'm not your enemy, you know." His eyes glint with dark amusement.

"Maybe not"—I snatch the keys from his grasp—"but call me field mouse again, and I'll certainly become yours."

Turning on my heel, I stomp ahead to the guest house.

"It was a joke," he calls from behind me.

"I liked you better when I thought you were mute," I snap over my shoulder, making a mental note to inform my cousin that he'd do well to keep his guard dog on a tighter leash.

"Remember to lock up, Dell!" he calls in a cheerful tone.

"Remember to piss off, dickbag!" I unlock the door and slam it behind me.

Flicking on the lights, I'm overcome by a white-walled emptiness I wasn't expecting. The art that once filled the house with color, lively brushstrokes, and lush landscapes is gone, each of Virginia's carefully-rendered flowers ripped up by the roots.

They must've been relocated after the will reading, I think. Auctioned off to some high-bidding collector, or an eager fan who'd happily pay an arm and a leg for a Ginnie Gold original. Add in the recent murderous scandals surrounding our family, and my grandmother's artwork had surely amassed even greater allure. And a heftier price tag.

Without Virginia's paintings, the guest house feels lonesome and incomplete. I drop my bags onto the wooden floors and hear an echo skitter back at me. It's like a cave in here…

The light fixture in the bedroom flickers. A low hum sweeps along the walls, as if an invisible presence is zipping down the electric cabling. Silly of me to forget that the guest house comes with a live-in roommate— my distant cousin, Eribeth, the resident broke-necked ghost.

Great. Amid all my worries and fears, Eribeth had never even crossed my mind. But now, all I can think of is the last night I spent here, when an unseen force nearly caused me to drown in the bathtub. After Tristen's revelations about Eribeth's demise—how she'd "fallen" from the guest house roof to a premature death, likely at the hands of the Klyne brothers—I can only assume that force was her. But would I be any better off in Cliffmoor House, lying sleepless in my mother's bed, tormented by God knows how many *other* vindictive forces?

Hell no.

I'll make it work here. Make my peace with playing house with a vengeful spirit. But…no more baths. I'll stick to showers this time, especially since it might mean the difference between life and death.

Unpacking my bags takes all of five minutes, and then I'm out of the house again, eager for wide spaces and ocean air in my lungs. I peer across the property, scanning for Payne, but the valet seems to have made himself scarce. I trudge toward the walkway to the beach, and once I reach the wind-stripped, padlocked gate, I unlock it and let my feet carry me over the footbridge.

Dunes marked by tall grass and sea oats give way to rippling sand. Sandspur Beach stretches ahead of me, the centerfold of all my night terrors. My breath turns shaky as I brace myself. *Better to confront this now than delay it and make it worse.*

The beach darkens as night presses in. There's no one as far as my eyes can see—just miles of white sand kissing infinite sky and water. It's impossibly vast, yet I still feel surrounded. Strangulated. Because I know the brutal truth of this place. The blood at its core, and the hidden skeletons. It's beautiful on the surface, but beauty is the finest of liars. I've lived through too much ugliness, seen too much disaster, to be duped by a lovely façade.

I stumble to the shoreline, to where the sea foam floods. The water rises and recedes with each ensuing wave, and I sink in slowly—first my toes, then my ankles, all the way to my calves. Salt crusts on my lashes, settles into the cracks on my lips. Standing statue-still like this, I feel myself almost becoming part of the beach. An extension of the sea. One with the currents.

A dancing wind caresses my hair, breathes its spirit into my lungs, as if trying to resuscitate me, to bring me back to life. But I've never felt more dead inside.

Memories wring my heart like a ratty mop, pummel and knead it like dough. Scalding tears bubble in the corners of my eyes, though I can't pinpoint why exactly. *Everything,* I guess, is the closest reason to the truth. Every aching, exhausting thing about being back on this island…this house…this beach.

My hands turn to shaking fists at my sides, salty streams running hot and fast down my face now. Something wild and primal surges in my veins, about to spill over, in need of release. I can't keep a lid on this pain any longer. Can't shove it down behind the fear anymore.

You're back, you're back, you're back.

Another tumbling wave sweeps across the shore, crashing rough and cool against my legs, spraying up my thighs, my arms, my face…

The wild in me erupts.

I scream.

Like a banshee wailing across the sea, I scream. Scream until I hurt myself with it. Until my throat runs bloody and my voice breaks in half. Until my ears pop and deafen, my chest compressed from the lack of oxygen.

I scream until I've been depleted. Pour myself over Halcyon Bay until I've half-forgotten who I am and why I'm here and where I'm going.

I scream and scream until there's nothing left of my soul to spill. Only then do I fall to my knees in sobs, shaking in the aftermath of my own brutal emotion.

Minutes pass that feel like hours.

The ocean air that envelops me is tepid, but an unmistakable, inside-out cold pulses within. I pull my oversized cardigan a little tighter around me, but the effort is futile against the deep-rooted winter that inhabits my bones.

My fingertips brush the edges of my mouth, as flashes of my watery encounter with Willow push into my vision. A piercing cold struck through me then—biting and sure as death—that made me doubt whether I'd ever know warmth again. Hatch had even noticed a corpse-like tinge of blue on my lips.

That was the moment that altered me, that muddled my biology. The cold would never leave me now. It's *inside* of me—a living, breathing affliction…

Get up, I command myself, gritting my teeth. *Stop feeling sorry for yourself. You did not come all this way to fall apart now.*

I breathe in as deeply as I can.

Get. Up.

I stand, though my legs wobble unsteadily.

Now move.

My shuffling feet drag the rest of me up the beach to the walkway. And though I move like a mindless zombie…still, I move.

Locking the door to the gate behind me, I take in the sight of the Cliffmoor House gardens, finally giving the bedraggled estate my full attention. Gone are the pristinely manicured gardens of my memories. The grounds have grown unkempt and thorny, with vines and weeds overwhelming the flower beds, overrunning the walking paths, spreading like wildfire across the lawn. The once sparkling pool has developed a thick film of grime, propagating mold in its tiled corners, its murky floor blanketed by leaves and debris. The white gazebo is in shambles, debilitated by rust and salt. Strings of twinkly lights still dangle from it precariously, slapping against the metal structure with each wind gust, causing countless tiny bulbs to shatter. Glass coats the grass around it.

Everything about this place has fallen to neglect, the Klyne family all but collapsing along with it. Yet, somehow, Florian managed to escape that fate, surviving on the periphery, evading the crippling effect he'd helped create.

I hate being back here, but I hate *him* more. So I won't succumb to my worst fears, won't yield to the grief. I'll push past the pain, the cold, and the sadness, and I'll make good on my time here. I won't squander it away with my weeping.

Retreating to the guest house, I lock myself inside and settle into the empty space, seeking comfort where there is none. In the linen closet, I find a set of clean sheets and make the unmade bed. Grabbing a towel, I speed through a shower, remembering Briggs' warning last summer about the wonky faucet and vacillating temperatures.

Just once, out of the corner of my eye, I see a small shadow pace behind the shower curtain, but I suck in a breath and keep going, keep pushing. No reason to pretend I don't know what's—*who's*—there.

Pulling on a fresh t-shirt and underwear, I stumble into the bedroom, flick off the lights, and give in to a restless, fitful sleep.

Tomorrow will arrive soon enough.

CHAPTER NINE

The sea sings to my blood, and so I come.

Drawn to the water's edge by a tugging in my chest—my heartstrings plucked by an invisible minstrel—I search the horizon for that unknown caller. For that ineffable force that summons my soul, dragging me from sleep and back onto this beach.

My toes squirm in the damp sand. A sea breeze coaxes me closer, swirling around my arms and legs, nuzzling my face.

Come, it says.

Why do you call? I respond.

A woman rises from the water, like a ship resurrected from the depths. No, not a woman…a creature. Pure spirit.

She breaches the surface, an eerie glow emanating from her body. I take in her luminescent features as she crosses the span of shallow tide between us. That mane of sable hair, so black it seems imbued with night. That pale, shimmering face, lips parted like two rose-red petals. That slender neck curving out to spindly shoulders, her slim torso draped in a diaphanous garb, so sheer and delicate it's barely there, clinging wet to the soft bends of her body. Her eyes are orb-like, otherworldly and piercing.

When the water meets her hips, she pauses her ascent. Her arms are curled around something small and fragile, wrapped in that same filmy material that coats her skin. Bestowing a kiss upon the bundle, she lays it over the water's surface and, with a push, sets it free.

The parcel floats to shore, cradled by waves, while the woman watches on solemnly at a distance. Within seconds, it knocks against my feet, lapping up on a placid current. Before I can bend down to inspect it, I hear something strange…

A mewl.

A whimper.

Swaddled in that gossamer-thin garb is an infant, its skin milky-white, moonlight reflected on pudgy cheeks, with tufts of inky hair sprouting from an otherwise bald head. Through the cloak of gauzy material, I see that the child is male.

I drop to my knees on the foamy sand, and, gathering my courage, reach out a hand to him. But the abrupt sloshing of water draws my eyes back to that expanse of midnight-blue ocean…

I gasp at the sight materializing before me.

The sea is littered with radiant, ghostly faces, the dark-haired spirit just one of *hundreds*. Scores of them poke up from distant points, blue-black water rippling around their bony shoulders. Females, young and old, with shimmering complexions, skins dark and light, and mystical gazes. Sopping hair of every color drifts like seagrass atop the water. My pulse throbs in my ears as I process what I'm seeing…

A swarm of sea spirits packing the Sandspur shallows.

Devilfish breaching the wall between worlds.

All to deliver this child. This *son*.

I look to him, eager for answers, but the boy just stares up at me with keen, ebony eyes. No traces of a smile, no truths to decode. A temple of secrets.

The female that dispatched him glides forward. She bares a set of razor-sharp teeth, her hands spreading the waters with ease. A mere flutter of her fingers and those long, needle-pointed nails, and the waves quite literally *break* around her, cleaved in two, scattering to pave her way.

As she narrows the gap between us, the other sea spirits move in unison, closing in on the vacant beach.

On me.

Terrified, I abandon the boy and skitter back along onto the sand, digging my elbows and heels in for leverage, frantic to escape their clutches. They press closer, closer…

I scream when the sand beneath me gives way, as if the bedrock of the island had cracked open to swallow me. I fall down a hole of consummate darkness, shrieking my fear into the abyss—a blur of limbs, terror, and thundering heartbeats.

My eyes snap open at the sound of impatient knocking.

Panting, I sit up, baffled to be lying in a foreign bed, wrapped in strange, silky sheets that feel like fingertips and grazing teeth.

It was only a dream, I realize after a second.

A gaping, cream-colored room expands around me. Bright shafts of sunlight drift in through luxurious curtains—morning's kiss pulling me from the clutches of night.

A jolt of inner panic zips across my chest when I remember where I am and what brought me here.

Halcyon Bay.

Cliffmoor House.

Florian.

The knocking at the door doesn't slow or falter for a second.

Frustrated, I swat the pillows and sheets away like flies over a picnic spread. Tristen must've asked Dickbag Payne to come wake me.

I slip from bed slowly, shimmying into a pair of sweatpants, reminded of the derisive pet name the valet used on me last night. *Little field mouse.* The ungodly nerve of him.

My tongue writhes as I pad out of the bedroom, gearing up for another verbal spar. Part of me is glad to have a target for my disdain—a focal point for my abhorrence of this place and all it stands for.

Arms crossed over my chest, I enter the main room, only to find someone *else* pressed to the outside of the breakfast nook window, her fingers wrapped around her eyes like binoculars.

Palmer.

My heart soars at the sight of her.

I nearly throw the door off its hinges.

"You bitch," are the first words out of her mouth.

Her hands are on her hips, which have expanded some since last I saw her, and her skin has a radiant glow to it, blond hair loose and rippling. "You come back to *my* town, and you don't even have the decency to call?"

Before I can mumble a lame apology, my cousin rushes up and flings her arms around my shoulders, her bulging belly pressing into me like a second hug. I cling to her for a long minute, letting all the time that's passed since we'd last seen each other—the months and the stilted texts and the growing sense of disconnection—wash away like rainwater.

"I missed you too, Palmer," I murmur into her hair.

"Not enough, evidently, since you couldn't be bothered to let me know you were coming." She pulls away, her lips curling into a funny little grimace. "Um. What happened to you?"

I glance down at my t-shirt, my sweats. "What do you mean?"

"You look like the living dead."

"*Aw,* so sweet of you to notice." I roll my eyes. "Where's your nicer half?"

"Back at Cliffmoor House, scouring for food. He's gained about as much weight as I have throughout this pregnancy." Palmer sighs happily and puts a hand to her belly.

"How are you feeling?"

"Pretty good, actually. Baby girl's kicking up a storm in there. I feel like I'm incubating a tiny ninja."

I laugh and she laughs back, though a million little questions hang in the air between us, invisible but inescapably *there*, waiting to be uttered by whoever's bravest.

"So, how have you been?" Palmer asks cautiously. "You know, since…well, everything."

I know what she means.

Since the night I'd been caught in a shootout on the beach outside these grounds.

Since the moment I discovered our grandfather killed Willow.

Since Palmer's wedding day. A spectacular event, flawless as sparkling crystal, marred by the greasy fingerprints of death.

"Well…I've been…um…"

Every way I can think to finish that sentence—words that might clear away the cobwebs of awkwardness stretching between us—is lacking in some essential way. There is no *right* word or combination of them to define this new form I've taken. Filtering through my mind for a suitable expression is useless. Eloquence escapes me like sand through my fingers, like wind streaming through my hair.

"I guess I'm just…fine."

"*Just* fine?" Palmer retorts. "What a load of crap."

I blink back in surprise.

"You are not *fine*, Dell," she says. "Anyone with eyeballs can see that."

"I really am though."

Her hands cup my shoulders and squeeze. "Why are you pretending? With *me* of all people?"

I swallow, suddenly wishing I could take off running and never come back. Run out to sea until I'm swept away, free as the fish. Until I'm anywhere but here, having to confront Palmer's pointed questions, my stomach churning with hunger and angst.

"Everything's just kind of…messy right now," I explain.

"Now we're getting somewhere!" Palmer's lips pull into a small, cheeky grin. "As resident Queen of Chaos, messy is my middle name."

"Elizabeth is your middle name."

"Potayto, potahto. The point is, you can talk to me. Keeping secrets and burying emotions is just a recipe for disaster."

True, Palmer had desperately clung to her secrets last year, and they nearly destroyed her. Nearly ruined her relationship with Mojo. The thought of my cousin's shrunken figure in the attic—adrift in a sea of bridal tulle and sadness—sends a pang of remorse running through me.

She stares at me with big, beseeching eyes, vibrant blue as the clear morning sky. "You don't have to shove everything down all the time. Fine isn't a feeling. It's just a stupid filler word for when you're anything *but* fine. For when you don't want to open up about what's really going on."

"What can I say?" I shrug. "It's a bad force of habit."

"So un-force the habit."

We scowl at each other for a few seconds, then both slip into soft fits of laughter.

"When did you get to be so wise?" I ask.

"Just sort of happened. Imminent motherhood, you know?" Palmer crosses her arms, looking an awful lot like Aunt June. "Now—breakfast?"

"If that's why you're here, you'll be sorely disappointed. Inga hasn't stepped foot in the kitchen in months."

"Ugh. If only. I'd kill for a slice of her quiche Lorraine." Palmer leans against the threshold. "I'm here because I was summoned by the heir to Cliffmoor House for 'official family business.' And when he told me you'd come back—without sending so much as a freaking text message—I figured I'd drop in and give you the scolding you deserve."

"You're very good at it," I say. "Scolding, I mean."

"I've been practicing." Her smile grows smug. "Can we go now? There's a lukewarm scone in the parlor with my name on it."

"Give me two minutes."

Palmer steps inside while I run to the bathroom, brushing my teeth and switching my t-shirt for a slightly less rumpled one. She props herself on the arm of an upholstered chair, one hand on her belly, an amused expression on her lips, while I pull on a pair of worn jeans and ram my feet into sneakers. Running my fingers haphazardly through my waves— hoping to tame the wild mass of bed head curling into my face—I catch her appraising eyes in the mirror.

"What?" I ask.

"It's like you never left," she says.

This, oddly, feels all too accurate. It's as if no time has passed at all, despite the months I've been away. Life in Woodbridge had kept me frozen, bound to relive the same unchanging day. But now, upon waking up in Halcyon Bay, my frigid prison bars have begun to melt. Time is moving again. I have purpose.

Palmer links her arm in mine after I lock the door. "Any particular reason you're sleeping in the guest house this time around?"

I shoot her a sidelong glance as we traipse up the path to Cliffmoor House. "Is it not obvious that I despise this place with every fiber of my being?"

"Oh, it's obvious," she laughs. "But you're here now, so why make it more difficult on yourself? Why stay out here all on your own?"

"I like being on my own. You know that."

We walk through the overgrown gardens in synchronized silence, clutching each other like two schoolgirls. I don't know when or how this happened—can't pinpoint the exact moment that took us from hostile strangers to intimate friends—but I'm grateful for it. I'd missed Palmer, sass and all. Missed the bond we shared, and the uncanny way we could cut through each other's crap.

This is what I'm thinking when Palmer asks quietly, "Have you talked to Hatch lately?"

The question blindsides me.

I stiffen slightly. "Of course."

"Did you tell him you're back in town?" she probes.

"I'm going to tell him later." I turn to meet her eyes. "What's with the interrogation? When did you become Hatch's wingwoman?"

"I'm trying to be *your* wingwoman, doofus," she huffs. "I don't want to see you self-destruct and ruin a good thing."

There it is again—her striking ability to see the truth in me.

"You have something great with Hatch, something that makes you truly happy when you're brave enough to let it," she insists. "And as your pushiest, whiniest, most demanding family member, I'd like to see you happy, Dell. Sue me for caring."

"Palmer"—I press a dramatic hand to my chest, the edges of my mouth curling up—"are you actually admitting you care about me?"

"It's the damn hormones! They make me *feel* things." She fakes a shudder. "I was perfectly content with the emotional range of a goldfish. Now I'm a total sap! It's miserable."

I can't help but laugh. "Well, if it counts for anything, I like this Palmer best."

"You do?"

"Sure." I nudge her shoulder. "Mushy-gushy looks good on you."

"Don't get used to it." Palmer bumps me back, tucking herself in closer. "Also, are we not going to talk about whatever the heck happened to your arm?"

I press my lips together, sneaking a glance at my bandaged forearm. "Better off saving that one for later."

Palmer grunts in response.

We reach the house, and she yanks a French door open, dragging me inside with her.

It may have nothing to do with the way the past ten minutes of banter have saturated my heart—may just be the streams of daylight seeping inside the dark corridor—but when we slip into Cliffmoor House arm-in-arm, it doesn't feel quite so bleak.

CHAPTER TEN

Mojo's laughter spills from the parlor, and we chase it swiftly down the hall. We find him reclining on the far sofa, talking to someone across the way in a plush wingback chair. I stop short in the entryway, a gasp caught in my throat when I realize *who* that someone is.

Though I can't see his face from here, that golden-brown hair and muscular build are easy to identify. I've memorized every inch of him. Dreamt of his touch. Counted the days until I'd be in his arms again.

My eyes find Palmer's, and I shoot daggers her way. *You bitch,* I mouth, recycling her own term of endearment. She should've warned me about what I was walking into.

Palmer looks unmoved by the fact that she'd led me into an ambush. She knew I hadn't spoken to Hatch yet—knew I hadn't rallied up the right words—yet she'd still delivered me to the lion's den without a moment's hesitation.

Mushy-gushy, my ass.

She shrugs, pursing her lips primly before stealing away to Mojo's side, leaving me to fend for myself in the spotlight.

"Well, if it isn't my favorite cousin-in-law!" Mojo calls to me, arms wide open, smile brighter than the sun. "What's cooking, *muchacha?*"

Hatch's neck snaps around, his hypnotizing eyes falling over me. He doesn't speak at first, but that piercing look says everything—I came back, and he didn't know. I hadn't reached out to him, hadn't called or bothered to send a text message…

Apparently, Tristen had.

I hold my breath as Hatch stands and approaches, his eyes drawing me into a lush sea of green, all heat and electricity and tenderness between us. He looks so unreasonably good, it's unfair.

When he's close, he weaves warm fingers through mine, brushing his lips over my forehead. I exhale at his touch, a wash of calm gliding over me, closing my eyes as I melt into him.

Together again.

That's enough to make everything right in the world.

"Hi," he breathes low, as if confiding a secret.

When I open my eyes again, it's like waking from a beautiful dream, only to find that the dream is real. Touchable. Alive. His heady gaze pulls at me like the moon moves the tide. I'm helpless—*hopeless*—before him.

"Hi back," I whisper, exerting every ounce of restraint not to reach up and smash my lips against his. I can't give into that temptation. Not with a room full of eager eyes glued to us.

"Am I invisible or something?" Mojo asks Palmer. "Did I not just emphasize that she's my favorite?"

Palmer smacks his arm and gives him an impatient *shush.*

Hatch's gaze trails down my body, examining me in his slow, careful way, eventually landing on the gauze at my forearm. His eyes snap up to my face in silent question.

I swallow hard.

"There you are, cousin. Nice of you to join us," Tristen murmurs as Payne rolls him into the room. He's draped in black this morning, per usual, his eyes rimmed with violet, like sunken half-moons on a pale, scarred canvas.

I glare at him, heat pouring from my nostrils. Where does he get off going behind my back, calling *my* boyfriend without my knowledge or consent?

I know that Tristen harbors a multitude of secrets. That he teeters on an ever-unpredictable moral edge, silently battling the darkness in his blood. But this is too much. I'll have to enlighten him on the importance of boundaries. His surveillance in Woodbridge, his constant lies of omission, the way he'd used me like a chess piece last night with Briggs, scooting me across the gameboard as he saw fit—I've had enough. I'm supposed to be his partner, not his pawn. And I'll be damned if he doesn't start treating me as such.

Someone clears their throat, the gravelly sound pulling me back to the moment.

In another wingback chair, Briggs fidgets uncomfortably. Tightness wrings at his old, wrinkled eyes. He's hooked an ankle over his knee, sitting upright and pin-straight, anxious fingers drumming on his thighs. He's likely never been invited to sit here. To be a guest in this space where he's so accustomed to serving.

Briggs looks at me, his eyes gleaming with questions behind his spectacles, as if I might elucidate on why he finds himself called to this strange meeting. But, of course, I have no clue what Tristen's playing at.

Payne situates my cousin at the heart of the room, before the unlit fireplace, beneath the portrait of my grandmother. Tristen's shadowy eyes wander to each of our faces. "I'm sure you're probably wondering why I called you all here."

"You got that right," Palmer quips.

Tristen's jaw feathers—a small sign of unease. "Some information has come to light regarding my father's whereabouts. I thought it only appropriate that you hear the truth from me. The police haven't exactly been forthcoming with their intel."

"Have they located him?" Briggs asks.

"No," Tristen responds. "And, in the spirit of transparency, we've decided not to work with police for the time being—"

"Who's we?" Palmer asks.

No one speaks, but somehow everyone's eyes still come to land on me. Heat rises in my face, my cheeks ablaze. Hatch's hand twitches in mine. I hadn't told him about this either. That Tristen and I were going after Florian on our own. Not that he would object—at least, not explicitly. He'd never try to keep me from doing what I need to do. But I'm sure he'll feel sorely about not having been informed. I can't really blame him for that.

"Who's we?" Palmer repeats. The question is meant for Tristen, but it's me she fixes with a damning expression. "Dell?"

I shut my eyes briefly, focusing on the in-out pattern of my breath and the thrumming of Hatch's pulse against my palm, using that place of connection to ground me.

"Yes—Dell," Tristen concedes. "We're working together to find my father, apart from the HBPD."

"Why?" Briggs asks, squinting behind his glasses.

"All signs lead us to believe that the cops have either lost Florian's trail, or are purposely derailing the search," Tristen explains, "neither of which inspire confidence that he'll be brought to justice. Leaving my father's fate in their hands would be…irresponsible."

"Isn't interfering in an active police investigation, like, criminal obstruction or something?" Palmer asks sharply.

Mojo mumbles in agreement. "Obstruction-adjacent, at least."

Palmer lifts her eyebrows. "You could go to jail, Dell!"

"We're not interfering," Tristen insists.

"Pick a better word, then," she snaps. "Meddling? Tampering?"

"No, and no. We're not impeding the police, Palmer. We're just seeking new avenues. And we've had some developments I think only fair to share with you."

"What kind of developments?" Hatch's voice is a careful hum.

"It appears that Florian is keeping close to Halcyon Bay," Tristen says. "My contacts have spotted him three times in the last month, on various island-countries near Florida. We think he might try to come back—"

"He wouldn't," Palmer asserts, half-scoffing at the notion. "No way he would *ever* come back here."

None of us speak up to argue or agree with her, the room permeated with that fearful possibility. Would Florian really be so brazen as to attempt it? How would he do it? And how soon?

After a few long seconds, Palmer's confidence seems to wane. Her blue eyes bounce from Tristen to me, and she blurts out a worried, "Seriously?"

"He was in Woodbridge recently, if that tells you anything," I say.

Everyone's eyes go round at the news.

Hatch drops my hand, stunned by my revelation, and the fact that I hadn't deemed it worthy to share sooner. The vacancy between my fingers physically hurts.

"When?" he asks me quietly.

"A few weeks ago, at Willow's grave," I confess, shoving down the sadness threatening to rip me apart. "I only just found out," I add weakly, as if that might stem the pain I'd forced on him, my lack of honesty planting inevitable seeds of doubt in his mind.

"Did you go to the cops about this?" Palmer asks.

"No cops," Tristen and I echo.

"Why would Florian go all the way to Woodbridge?" Mojo asks.

"To taunt us," Tristen deadpans. "To make a mockery of law enforcement's so-called manhunt. To prove that he could be anywhere—"

"Not here," Hatch interrupts.

"Not yet," Tristen amends. "But he will be. Sooner than we think."

Palmer zeroes in on me again. "I cannot believe this is why you're here." There's a quivering anger in her voice. An underlying disappointment. "Of all the reasons in the world, and all the people you left behind, you only came back to track down our thug uncle?"

I clamp my teeth down on my bottom lip, certain that if I speak up now, the delicate leash on my emotions will slip.

"We're searching for something, Palmer," Tristen explains. "Something my father desperately wants. Otherwise, he'd be halfway across the world right now, living in the lap of luxury, with all thought of this island turned to dust in his wake. But he's left something important behind. He won't move on without it."

"What do you suspect it is?" Briggs asks.

"Another mystery," Tristen says, clearly bothered by the fact. "But we paid Kieran Blackbane a visit in Miami, and we have some theories about—"

"You did *what?*" Palmer's eyes turn a vicious red, that clear sky-blue engulfed in fire.

Hatch goes deadly still at my side. I'm too nervous to turn my face to look at him.

"Blackbane?" Briggs rasps, a frown carved deep in his face. "Why on earth would you go see him?"

My fingers worm their way around my wounded forearm, encompassing the chunky bandage and the burn hidden below. I'd done everything I could to ignore the pain that throbbed from that spot, but now, talking about *him* makes the ache unavoidable. I feel like I've been marked by his darkness. Like his sin is part of me now, crawling under my skin. Like I'm a ticking time-bomb waiting to detonate.

Palmer notices the worried movements of my fingers. "Let me guess," she hisses. "Does this visit to Blackbane have anything to do with that injury you're covering up?"

Hatch stares down at my bandaged arm once again. When his eyes lift to mine, they're fiercer than a raging storm. He sucks his teeth, bottling his anger with a tight cap.

I want to scream at Palmer to *shut the hell up*. To stop making this so much worse than it is. But at the same time, I can't find it in me to fight back. I knew going to see Blackbane was a bad idea. I did it anyway. These are the consequences.

"Dell's injury was my fault," Tristen says, his words too smooth to sound remorseful. Maybe he'd already made peace with the incident in Miami. Maybe he'd compartmentalized it, turned the page, and moved on. "She didn't want to go, but I insisted."

"What happened, Dell?" Hatch asks tightly.

"Nothing," I emphasize. "I swear, it was nothing."

"Good God!" Palmer pinches the bridge of her nose.

"Blackbane got hold of a cigarette lighter somehow," Tristen explains. "While we were questioning him in the visitation room, he attacked Dell. He grabbed her arm and—"

"*He set you on fire?*" Mojo's jaw drops like a cartoon character.

If this weren't so bad, it might actually be funny.

I close my eyes and let out a groan, wishing I could slam my fist on a rewind button and start the morning over.

"Can we take a collective breath, please?" I ask no one in particular. "Yes, Blackbane's unhinged. And no, we never should've gone to see him. But we did, and"—I extend my bandaged arm—"*this* happened…but clearly I'm fine, see!" I gesture up and down my body, exhibiting my obvious state of fine-ness. "No permanent damage. Can we please move on now?"

Nobody responds.

I'm about two seconds away from driving my head through the nearest wall. "Tristen," I prompt through my teeth, angrily punctuating each of my words. "Get. To. The. Point."

He sniffs, bristling at my attempts to boss him around. "I believe there are people within the Brine's network—former members, possibly— who are helping Florian move around undetected."

"Oh, goodie!" Palmer snaps.

I watch Tristen machinate around his next words. "Blackbane mentioned my mother as well, as if she might be part of what binds Florian to Halcyon Bay. I haven't figured out how yet…or why."

"Your mother?" Briggs asks, his expression uncertain. "But she's…she's—"

"Dead," Tristen finishes his sentence bluntly. "Yes. That's why it doesn't make sense."

"So what's your plan exactly?" Palmer asks sharply. "While we're all looking over our shoulders, waiting for Florian to show up and terrorize us, what's your plan of attack?"

Tristen's eyes pinch together as though he's struggling to maintain his cool. "I've got security stationed at every public marina and private boat ramp on the island, as well as the airport. Eyes on every conceivable entry point."

News to me, I think. There's so much happening behind the scenes I'm not privy to.

"I've also hired in-house security to guard Cliffmoor House and the grounds," Tristen continues. "I'd like to extend that surveillance to your homes, if you're willing. They won't interfere with your day-to-day lives, they'll just be an added layer of protection, in case my father decides to—"

"No," Mojo says firmly, reaching out a hand to cup Palmer's knee. He looks peeved, all signs of his good-natured charisma vanished. "I'm not letting a bunch of randoms on your payroll *surveil* us and our baby. We live in a safe, gated complex. We're good."

"Suit yourself," Tristen replies coolly, his eyes flicking to Palmer. "I wanted to extend the offer to your mother, but—"

"Mom doesn't want any part of this," Palmer cuts in. "And she certainly doesn't want Leif involved. Our family's been through *enough.*"

"Then I won't push the subject any further. I only ask that you stay vigilant. All of you."

"I must decline your offer, as well, sir," Briggs speaks up. "I'll be here most of the time anyway. No need to have guards assigned to my residence."

"Fair enough."

That leaves Hatch.

"I know you live with your mother, Hatcher," Tristen says, stating his case. "She's there alone quite often, isn't she? While you work long hours at the seaport?"

"Florian has no reason to come after us," Hatch counters. "Hell, I doubt he even knows Dell and I are together."

"You were together at the wedding," Tristen reminds him.

Hatch and I had spent much of the night together, dancing under the candlelit tent, nestled close at the ceremony, the reception. But I can't imagine Florian noticed any of that…

Hatch shakes his head, decision made. "If I change my mind, you'll be the first to know."

"Fine," Tristen agrees.

I can tell it bothers him to have been refused, but I'm also slightly impressed that he even asked. That he'd given the others a choice. Maybe my disgruntled cousin is making small efforts to listen to me after all.

The unfortunate truth of the matter is that Hatch, Palmer, and Briggs don't *trust* Tristen. So I'm not surprised that they don't want to concede to his drastic—and somewhat intrusive—security measures. I'm the only sucker who constantly gives him the benefit of the doubt.

"In addition to ramping up security," Tristen continues, "Dell and I are going to look for whatever's keeping my father close, and what any of it might have to do with my mother. Clues are bound to turn up somewhere—"

"That's your master plan?" Palmer cries. "That's not a plan at all!" She throws a contemptuous, head-to-toe glance at Tristen. "I guess I should expect this level of crazy from *you*, but,"—her gaze flicks to me now—"Dell, really? How is this a good idea?"

"I don't have a choice here, Palmer."

"Sure you do! All you have to do is *choose* not to get wrapped up in Tristen's psychotic schemes. It's that simple!"

My frustrations bubble over. "Actually, it's not that simple, and it's not psychotic! Florian helped Ambrose get away with *murder*. He's just as much to blame for the fact that my sister is…"

A knot lodges in my throat. I inhale deeply, blinking back hot tears from my eyes. When I speak again, it's barely a whisper. "Do you just expect me to forget that Willow's dead?"

Palmer's eyes soften, her fire waning. "Of course not."

"Then, please, try to understand. Bringing Florian to justice is the only way I can make things right for my sister. It's all I have."

She frowns, more sad than angry. "I don't understand why you have to put yourself in this situation. Why you can't just try to live your life in peace. Let the authorities handle it."

"What if someone had hurt Leif?" I ask. Palmer's eyes widen to saucers. "What if they'd taken him from you? Would you sit back and do nothing? Would you accept that a corrupt police force is the best you're ever going to get?"

"But"—her lip trembles, as if the hurt and the fear and the possible guilt for pushing me so hard is beating down on her—"you don't even know what you're looking for, Dell."

I shake my head softly. "I still need to try."

Palmer lowers her gaze to her lap, at a loss for how to convince me otherwise. If our roles were reversed, I know there's nothing she wouldn't do for her only sibling. And she knows it too.

"Where do we start?" Hatch asks, looking past me to Tristen.

I touch his elbow gently, seeking answers in that handsome face, but he doesn't budge, jaw set, lips straight as an arrow.

Where do we start?

That's the same question I'd asked Tristen when I barged into his hotel room, determined to exact retribution on my uncle. We're no closer to an answer now than we were then. We have no idea where to begin. Nothing more than a fiery drive and the impetus to try.

"Why are you encouraging this?" Palmer asks Hatch, dismay painted across her otherwise glowing features.

"Because," he says staunchly, "Dell's mind is already made up. And if it means making sure she's okay, then I'm in. I'm *always* in."

The unwavering loyalty in that statement causes the hairs on my arms to rise.

"Hatch, you don't have to—"

"I have to," he vows, those perfect green eyes piercing mine. "For you, I do."

His words feel too private to be uttered in front of so many people. As does the surge of heat shooting through me, blazing fire-bright across my cheeks, my neck.

The room is quiet, everyone waiting.

Hatch asks again, "Where do we start?"

CHAPTER ELEVEN

Hatch painstakingly peels back my bandage, exposing the mass of welted skin and blisters underneath. I wince against the ache of tugging adhesive against raw skin.

He pauses, fingers tentative. "Sorry," he says in a breathy rasp.

All I want is to hear him say my name that way. To feel him whisper it all over my body. But now's not really the time for that.

He goes to work on the bandage again, heartbreakingly gentle for such rough hands, as if I'm the most precious thing they've ever held. Our closeness is overwhelming—*intoxicating*—yet still not enough to cut through the mess in my head.

I don't know how to begin apologizing to him.

We'd barely exchanged a word since departing from the parlor and swiftly making our way to the guest house. The others, too, had dispersed with haste. Briggs had ventured off to load up on groceries and schedule the rest of the staff's return. Tristen had announced he would be meeting with his new head of security to run through details and expectations. Palmer, just before leaving, had invited us to a birthday dinner she's putting on for Mojo tomorrow. "Our place. Eight o'clock. If you can manage to tear yourself away from your *riveting* detective work," she remarked sourly, before storming off with a shrugging Mojo in tow. That left Hatch and I, and the current of electricity surging between us, thick as the morning mist pouring across the salt-soaked grounds.

My shoulder is pressed to his chest as he holds my arm under a trickle of water in the bathroom sink. At once, it's a soothing and painful release—a necessary evil if I'm to keep the burn from infection. In my periphery, I see him scanning my face for signs of pain. For some physical reaction or indication of how I'm doing. But I divert my gaze, unable to face him, biting back small moans of discomfort.

Hatch applies an ointment to the affected area and covers it again with a clean bandage. When he's done, he takes me by the hand and leads me to the bed, the both of us moving as though in a trance. My heart flips when he sits upon the mattress, easily pulling me up beside him.

We lay flat on our backs there, touching from shoulder to wrist, our fingers entwining lazily at our sides. We stare up at the white ceiling—a blank sky laid out before us—listening to nothing but our quiet breaths.

Say something, I think. *Force yourself to start.*

"I should've told you I was coming," I whisper after several long minutes, my fragile voice cutting through the noiseless house.

Hatch doesn't react, though I know he's hanging on every syllable.

"I planned on going by your place today to surprise you, but Tristen beat me to the punch." I swallow. "I didn't know what to say to you. I thought you'd be disappointed. That I'd come back for *this,* but not for…you know…"

Us.

I'd come back for this search, this problem, this task.

But I hadn't come back for *us.*

"I was just trying to process everything," I explain weakly. "This thing with Tristen snowballed out of nowhere—"

"Snowballed too fast for a phone call?" Hatch asks quietly. "A text message?"

"No, of course not." I could've done either of those things. Any normal person would have. And I hate that I've hurt him—kept him at arm's length. I hate the dejected timbre in his voice.

"Then why didn't you, Dell?" He doesn't sound angry, just genuinely curious, trying to get to the bottom of my hesitance. Trying to help me lower my guards and let him back in.

"Things have been so distant between us lately," I admit. "I was scared of what you'd think. About having me back."

Hatch rolls onto his side, one scruffy cheek propped up on his knuckles. The hem of his t-shirt slides up over his hip, revealing the golden skin and sculpted muscle underneath.

"Do you want to know what I think?" he asks.

I twist my neck to meet his face, my stomach tightening at the intensity of his gaze, the familiar heat of desire unspooling in my core.

"More than anything."

His mouth curves into a wry, lopsided smile. "I think I'm glad you're here, regardless of the reason." He reaches out gently, fingers tangling in a lock of my hair, then moving across my cheek to graze my bottom lip, sliding down the hollows of my neck to my collarbone. "And I think we should really do something about that distance…"

He curls a hand around the back of my neck, drawing me closer. I'm a puddle for him—liquid-soft and desperate—leaning in without thought, without doubt, only to find his mouth waiting…

Then all I am is fire.

With every taste of his lips, every sweep of his tongue, I burn, blazing and radiant and more *me* than I've felt in months. He's a crackling lightning strike. The spark of flint against rock. The electric jolt of a defibrillator. He brings me back to life.

One delicious kiss slips into another, and another, and another—a string of languid touches and panting breaths and hunger the finest meal could never satisfy. I lose myself in Hatch's arms, and find myself there too.

I know that I love him. Deeply. Irreversibly. With everything I am and every scarred bit of my heart. And though I'm still learning what that means, and how I'm shaped by it, and how to live with it…God, do I love this man.

And so a new question forms in my mind, one that seems tantamount to all other things…

Could he love me too?

"Stay," I plea huskily in between kisses, pressing against the length of him, relishing in the responsiveness of his body to mine. "Stay here with me while I'm in town."

It's a selfish request, I know. Hatch has a life here. A home, and people who count on him. I'm transitory—around for days or weeks at a time—while the rest are permanent. But I can't help myself.

Hatch pulls back a little, and the heady, drunken sensation I'd felt rush to my head seems to plunk right down to my toes.

"What is it?" I ask, afraid of the answer I'll get. "You don't want to?

"*Of course* I want to," Hatch says quickly, his hands cupping mine. "But I work really late most nights. A new project came up at the seaport recently, and it's keeping me pretty busy. I don't usually make it home until the early morning."

"What kind of project?"

"I…can't really say," he answers suspiciously. "Not yet, anyway."

I raise my eyebrows. "Why?"

"It's sort of a surprise," he explains.

"'Sort of' a surprise? How is something 'sort of' a surprise?"

Hatch shoots me an inscrutable look. "Fine. It's a surprise."

"For me?"

"Yeah, for you." He smiles again, and warmth consumes my insides.

"When do I get to see this surprise?"

"Soon."

What kind of surprise could Hatch be working on at the seaport?

He'd secured new work for himself crew-hopping between various fishing trawlers—offering an extra pair of hands wherever needed, an able body whenever a boat found itself undermanned. I'd questioned this at first, wondering why he wouldn't want something a little more consistent. But Hatch simply said he didn't want to replace Bram with another captain—a quiet, offhand remark he'd made over the phone one evening. It nearly shattered my glass-fragile heart. Hatch missed Bram more than anyone on this island, felt the heaving absence of his friend every day. So when he said he didn't want to tie himself to another man's ship, I understood the sentiment and promptly let it go.

Hatch also does maintenance on Captain Patton's schooner in his off-hours, making good on the deal he'd struck up with the old seafarer last year—the one that secured me a ride from Prospero Pier, that brought me back to safety after being terrorized on the sea trumpet fields. Free labor was their arrangement, and Cap'n Pat was cashing in.

Does that mean Hatch is making me something between jobs? Planning an excursion, maybe? Could the captain be in on it?

My curiosity gets the better of me. "How soon is soon?"

Hatch presses a deep kiss to my brow. "Soon," he repeats, a secretive twinkle in his eye.

I'll have to wait then. Be patient. Trust him. I can do that.

"So, with all this secret work you're doing under cover of darkness, how do you get any sleep?" I ask.

"I squeeze in a couple of hours here and there. It'll be worth it. You'll see."

"What about dinner?" I probe. "You've still gotta eat, right?"

"That depends." He inches closer, leaving a torturous breath of space between us. It pulses with energy, the pull between our bodies impossible to resist. "Are you asking me out, Dell?"

"Oh, I wouldn't say that," I tease.

"No?" His bottom lip juts out, and all I can think about is how much I want to take it between mine and suck. "That's a shame…" His fingertips trail above the waistband of my shorts, his touch both featherlight and electric against my skin. I'm nearly undone by it. "We could have such a fun time together…"

"It takes more than a pretty face to seduce me," I say, holding back a giggle on the tip of my tongue.

Hatch's fingers pause their clever movements. His eyes narrow playfully. "You think my face is pretty?"

I smack his shoulder, eliciting that crooked smile I love. "Actually, I wanted to see if we could make plans for a dinner with your family…"

"*My* family?" His eyes widen with surprise.

Sudden panic drips through me. Is this too much, too soon? Am I making assumptions? Dragging him into something he's not ready for?

"Only if that's something you want," I'm quick to amend.

"You're kidding, right?" The heat of his eyes is matched only by the blood-rush to my cheeks. "Dell, I've wanted that for *months*. I just didn't know if…well, you hadn't been back, and I didn't want to push—"

"I really want to meet them," I cut in, sorry I ever made him feel like I didn't. Sorry it took me so damn long to get here. Sorry to always be lagging behind, tripping over my feet and weighing us down.

Hatch nods at me, his cheeks lit from within. "All right. I'll talk to Mom and we'll set something up. And I'll make sure Holden and the others are there too."

Holden—his brother. We'd only met once, when I showed up on the Seaborns' doorstep uninvited, begging for Hatch to give me another chance. It wasn't much of an introduction. Or a first impression.

Hatch has gotten to know my parents pretty well over the past few months. He's made efforts to travel and see me, to assimilate to my life, no matter how difficult or distant the road. He even gave me space when I needed it, whether I'd had the courage to ask for it or not.

Meanwhile I've made no efforts to become better acquainted with the ones that know *him* best. So I have to step it up. Get my shit straight. Do whatever it takes to hold onto him. I don't know what would become of me if he were ever gone from my life.

I rest my cheek against his chest. "I missed you, pirate man."

He drops another kiss into my hair, humming contentedly. "Missed you too, love."

Those silky words feel like an intimate caress, like touches we've shared on moonlit nights, sparing but magical. The impetuous, hungry part of me wants to lunge at him this instant—to strip back the clothes and sheets and barriers until all that's left is *us*, body to body, heart to thundering heart. But I don't make a move. I'm too at peace in this moment, in his presence. In the chance to spend more than a couple of days together.

I let myself sink into those eyes that call to my soul. Let myself loosen up in his embrace, soften against the honed muscles of his arms.

He kisses me like nothing else matters, fills up every strained bit of distance we've endured. With barely any effort, he unwinds the thorns that have braided over my heart. Digs up the ones burrowed under my skin.

For a few brief minutes, the rest of the world stills.

And I remember what it is to be happy.

After Hatch leaves for the seaport—promising to pick me up later in the afternoon—I'm eager to make myself useful, so as not to drown in the emptiness left in his wake. I trek back up to Cliffmoor House, wondering what progress Tristen's made on the security front.

Peering inside the parlor, I spot him sitting in his wheelchair by the fireplace. He's engaged in conversation with a woman, perched on the couch facing away from the door. Their voices are hushed, serious in tone, but there's a hint of friendliness there as well, more so than any I've heard from Tristen before.

Strange.

His face doesn't bear its usual surliness either. That sunken, pale countenance is almost alight, the edges of his lips curling up ever so subtly. Not into his habitual smirk, but into something more genuine.

Tristen notices me loitering in the doorway. "Dell, come in. I'd like to introduce you to someone."

The woman across from him stands, pivoting to face me. She's tanned and slender, wearing head-to-toe black—a skin-tight shirt, tactical pants, and combat boots. Her chestnut hair is chopped in a long, blunt bob, with two dyed strips of peachy-pink framing her face. Her eyes are a soft butterscotch-brown. She looks tough, but like it may only be a shell— a hardened exterior to shield a sweet inner filling. I'd say she's about ten years my elder.

"This is Novela Santos," Tristen says.

She offers me her hand. I notice the flash of a gun at her hip. "Nice to meet you, Dell. You can call me Nova."

Masking my discomfort with a nod, I offer her a tight, "Hello," as we shake hands.

Relax, I tell myself. *She's part of Tristen's security detail. Guns are compulsory.*

Truthfully, I don't much like the idea of in-house security—or the lack of privacy that comes with armed guards patrolling the grounds—but I understand why my cousin deems it necessary. His last encounter with Florian left him paralyzed. The next attempt on his life may very well be the last, unless he surrounds himself with the right people.

"Nova's going to be our head of security," Tristen informs me.

It's likely just my trauma talking, but I can't help but wonder whether every stranger I meet intends to maim or murder me. Nothing about Nova screams 'psycho killer' on the surface, with her kind eyes and unthreatening demeanor. She actually seems quite nice, in fact.

Then again, so had Prescott.

"She and her team are very qualified." Tristen shoots Nova a broad smile, and I cough in surprise. *Tristen doesn't smile.* The best you can expect from him is a condescending sneer, but not *this*—not actual teeth. Never this look of satisfaction.

"So how does this work exactly?" I ask warily.

"We'll have five guards on the premises at all times, stationed at various points of entry," Nova says. "One at the main gate, another outside the front door, a third manning the beach entrance, a fourth at the garden gate, and a fifth patrolling inside the house. All of them are highly trained in combat—most are former military—and have been thoroughly vetted by me. I've made sure they have no ties to local police, no reason to run to them about what they may see here. They know how to be discreet."

Clearly Tristen had informed Nova about our beef with the HBPD. They'd certainly proven not to be our allies—not worth trusting when it comes to Florian—but I still can't help but recall what Palmer said earlier about criminal obstruction and jail time.

Is that where we'll end up at the end of this?

"I'll be updating the video security system as well," Nova adds. "There are a few cameras in place already, but the technology is abysmal.

I'd like to add at least six more, and modernize the equipment. Bring in state-of-the-art cameras, night vision, magnified audio, the works. It'll be costly, but—"

"Whatever it takes," Tristen interjects. "Money isn't an issue."

Nova nods, a pretty smile winding its way up her face. "My favorite kind of client."

Like a third wheel, I watch the pair of them grin at each other, realizing I'm painfully unwelcome to whatever private conversation they're having with their eyes. Tristen doesn't look at *anyone* like that—his expression wide open, dark eyes enthralled, mouth slightly agape. It's as if he's caught wind of something in Nova's face he's never seen before. Some magnificent, cosmic phenomenon. A star gleaming brighter than any he's ever witnessed.

"When do you get started?" I ask Nova.

"I'll need a couple days to prepare and order the equipment. After that, just as soon as your cousin gives me the go-ahead, we'll be here." Nova's sweet, toffee eyes are still tangled up in Tristen's as she speaks, captivated by their swirling darkness. Black and gold, oil and honey, like opposite reflections of each other.

"Perfect," Tristen says.

"Perfect," Nova repeats.

I don't know what the hell they're talking about anymore.

"Well"—I stand to go, deciding it imperative that I make myself scarce—"I'll leave you two to keep chatting then."

Nova waves me off, breaking their spell. "I'd better be going too. Lots to arrange. But I very much look forward to working with you…er, *both* of you."

Her eyes dance over me quickly before settling back on Tristen. For a moment, I think she might say something more, but then she just dips her head and strides out of the parlor.

My gaze flits between her back and my cousin's awestruck face, absorbing the full effect of what had just transpired.

Eventually, Tristen catches me staring, and his expression instantly turns foul. "What?" he snaps, black eyes fierce as blades.

There's the Tristen I know.

"You tell me," I laugh. "Seems you've got a lot on your mind."

He doesn't bother to respond. Instead, he barks out for Payne, who quickly enters the room and begins wheeling my cousin into the corridor.

"Hard to process all those fluttery new emotions?" I taunt, thrilled to have something to tease Tristen about for once.

"I have neither the time nor the energy for your badgering," Tristen retorts, cloaked in that heavy sullenness once again. "I'm late for a physical therapy session."

Without another word, the men disappear, leaving me alone in the gaping parlor and to my own devices.

CHAPTER TWELVE

The day stretches like a looming shadow before me, holding nothing but the promise of anxiety and isolation. I decide to go snooping around Cliffmoor House to fill the time, looking for some clue as to what my uncle might want in Halcyon Bay.

I can't begin to imagine what he left behind here—what's so damn irreplaceable that he can't find anywhere else—but one thing is indisputable: all roads lead to this house. I'm certain I haven't uncovered all of its secrets. More exist beneath the surface, waiting to be brought to light.

I start on the second story.

The dark corridors are just as I remember them. Patterned, midnight-blue walls lined with old family photographs. Heavy mahogany doors revealing exquisite rooms. Each one offers up beauty, luxury, comfort, and absolutely nothing else.

Until…

I reach a door at the end of the east corridor—a door leading to my grandparents' quarters. Steeling my nerves, I slip inside.

Before me unfolds a wide sitting room with wingback chairs and glistening tea tables surrounding a magnificent fireplace. This one is fairly smaller than the one in the parlor, but what it lacks in size it makes up for in opulence, caged in by an ornate mantelpiece. A massive portrait of Ambrose and Virginia hangs above it—a beautiful, yet chilling capture in their middle age, my grandfather's hand latched dominantly on my grandmother's shoulder. Muted unhappiness pulls at her features, draining the light from her blue eyes despite the practiced smile she wears. A nauseating flutter comes alive in my stomach. I pull my gaze away from them before I start to retch.

A double door is nestled into the opposing wall, and upon opening it, an elegant bedroom expands before me—a bedroom so vast, it looks like a small ballroom. I expect to see a sumptuous bed at the center of it, but instead, I see *two*. Two immaculate beds with Victorian upholstered headboards, made up with lavish comforters and cushions, the silky fabrics of them exquisite and complimentary.

As I take in the details of the palatial room, my stomach twists and roils. What good is it to live among such superficial beauty if it's only a mask for the horrors within? No amount of money or pedigree or expensive goods can erase what a person buries beneath the skin, in the same way that towering walls and gilded art can never constitute a home—not when the framework, the bones of it, are crooked. Eventually, the cracks in the façade will deepen, the house will crumble, and so too will its inhabitants.

Against the far wall, three arched windows stretch practically to the ceiling. I approach them and look down upon the front side of Cliffmoor House. At the moss-coated driveway, and the lush cul-de-sac, and the peaceful, tree-lined street beyond it.

This is where Ambrose watched me, that first summer night when I walked up the drive. A window had been left open, and I remember the curtains shifting. I told myself then that it was nothing more than a wayward breeze, but an eerie sensation bloomed in my chest just the same. The feeling that someone was observing me—sizing me up from the shadows.

I move on toward the bed closest to the windows, reaching for the bedside table drawer. It's obvious from the instant I open it that this was Ambrose's nightstand. A stack of delicate, lace handkerchiefs stare up at me, pressed and folded into neat rectangles to show off the embroidered *AAK* along one edge. Revolted, I slam the drawer shut and back away.

In Virginia's bedside table, I find a bespoke, leather-bound bible, soft with wear, with a braided cord looped around a gold button. Pulling it from the drawer, I run my fingers over the velvety surface, surprised that my grandmother wouldn't have kept anything more personal in here. I unloop the cord, ignoring the nagging twinge of hesitation in the pit of my stomach that screams, *Drop the bible and run!*

I crack it open anyway.

It isn't a bible at all.

The thin printed pages are hollowed out at the center, and within those pages, burrowed in a hidden crevice, lies a journal.

It's plain and black and small enough to fit in the palm of my hand. I lift it gingerly and begin flipping through the pages, many of them lined with swirling handwritten entries.

It feels inappropriate to read them, intruding on my grandmother's innermost thoughts. These are the words she'd poured out in private, when she might've had no one else in the world to confide in.

But it's too tempting to pass up.

I flip to a random page and start reading an excerpt, quickly discovering that Virginia wasn't using this journal as a diary, but rather, a log of sorts. It chronicles a series of strange moments she experienced at Cliffmoor House. Not with its human inhabitants, but with the *inhuman.*

Guest House:

It was an exceptionally hot day, much too hot for gardening, so I sought out the cool, quiet shelter of the guest house in hopes of making progress on a new landscape. After several hours of work, I went up to the main house to fetch some lemonade. Upon returning, I was dismayed to find that my paints had been splattered all over my canvas. Angry splotches of color covered it from top to bottom, as if someone stood before the easel and hurled paint jars at it. They, along with my brushes, were scattered all over the floor. Aside from my obvious surprise, I couldn't find it in me to be upset. Maybe she simply didn't like what I'd been painting.

The downy hairs on my arms stand on end as I reread that last sentence, one word setting my nerves into a frenzy: *she.*

Virginia had known about Eribeth. Well, maybe not about *her* specifically, but she'd definitely had a feeling about the presence occupying the guest house. Enough to know it was female. Maybe even enough to know she was connected to the Klynes by blood.

I remember Freya mentioning that Virginia had encountered spirits too. That Cliffmoor House was something of a magnet for them, a Mecca for the weird and uncanny. Then again, it's impossible to know when this had all taken place. Virginia's journal entries aren't dated, so there's no easy way to tell how long ago they'd been written.

Perhaps if I read through them, start to finish, I can establish some chronology based on context clues. Maybe I can piece together some sort of timeline—fit her entries to the little bit of family history I know? Would that make a difference? Point me in some new and consequential direction?

I'm not all that confident, but I read on anyway.

Foyer:

I was taking my afternoon tea in the parlor when I heard a scream. Emery had been dusting the statues in the foyer, when she said she saw something move in her periphery. Assuming it was Inga or Colin or myself, she turned, shocked to discover that the statue she'd just dusted had mysteriously shifted out of place. There was no real explanation for how it got that way, angled to one side so that its eyes were aligned with hers. The poor girl swore it wasn't facing that way before. I've told Ambrose hundreds of times, I never liked those damned statues.

I shiver and promptly glance around the quiet room, as if I myself am surrounded by a host of spirits. I'm about to slam the journal shut— spooked over this latest, somewhat disturbing find—but one last journal entry brings me pause, the title of it strange enough to seize my attention completely.

In the Walls:

I find myself pacing more often at night, venturing downstairs to not disturb

Ambrose's sleep, and yesterday, I heard something quite bizarre. Scratching noises, as if there were someone creeping inside the walls, grazing their nails over them, desperate for release. Then, whispers followed. Incoherent murmurs that seemed to evaporate whenever I strained to listen, pressing my ear from place to place, hoping to catch some semblance of what was being uttered in a low stream. I'd like to think it was my imagination, but I know better than that.

Hell. Now I've thoroughly creeped myself out.

Taking the journal with me, I vacate my grandparents' quarters, shelving my read-through of Virginia's journal entries for a rainy day—or perhaps a sunny one, when I'm not quite so alone.

I continue my inspection of the second floor, peering in door after identical door until eventually, I slip through one and a chill courses over me. An ice-cold streak emanates from the sea glass at my chest, my breath hitching, as if my heart is being squeezed by some unknown hand.

Willow's room. It has to be.

The puffy bedding is a burnt orange color, like the streaks left behind by a dying sun at dusk. The walls are a creamy yellow that remind me of a melting ice cream cone. The bronze chandelier is dainty, crystals tarnished with age, the curtains sheer and dripping from a massive window facing the grounds…and the distant sea that claimed my sister. Every last bit of Willow's personality has been ripped away. I peek in the drawers and even under the furniture, wondering if the room's hiding places might offer me something more. But there's nothing tucked in there, nothing special to find. This place doesn't hold her captive anymore. Not like it does me.

I move through to the opposite corridor, reaching the attic door. Cautiously, I climb the spiral staircase up to those lofty rafters—the scene of the crime perpetrated on Tristen last summer.

The space is untouched and dank, the still-broken window covered by a warped piece of plywood. A draft sweeps in through cracks at either side of it, and I notice water damage to the floors beneath the window. The wood is black with decay, eaten up with rot and salt. *Good.* I can only hope that the rest of the house succumbs to the angry whims of nature too.

I make my way back to the first floor. Room after room, I peruse slowly, letting my eyes and fingers wander. Some of what I take note of is familiar—things I'd seen and wondered over last year—but there's a lot I hadn't focused on, or rather, hadn't *wanted* to. I'd been too busy trying to escape the clutches of my family every chance I could. But I'm not running now. I'm fully present, surrendered and submitting myself to whatever may come. Whatever's left to find.

I reenter the parlor, struck as always by my grandmother's mesmerizing portrait. I'd spent more time in this room than any of the others, but now, walking carefully along its edges, fingertips lightly dusting the furniture, walls, and frames, I feel that it's all new to me. There's so much I hadn't bothered to *see* before.

A large model ship sits atop a side table, in similar style to Captain Patton's schooner—regal and elegant, a replica of a ship from a European fleet. An impressive globe mapping out the distant reaches of the ancient world occupies a corner desk. There are books too—an entire case of them—that for some reason find their resting place here, rather than in the study where the others are kept.

I blow the dust away from an eye-level shelf, scanning the titles, dragging a fingertip along their spines, hoping they might speak to me. Offer up some sacrificial speck of knowledge to serve my cause.

If only it were that simple.

I pluck a couple of books from the shelf—two clunky, leather-bound tomes that look more like outdated encyclopedias than diverting reading material. I open them carefully, wary not to break the spines, then scoff at my own idiocy.

Why should you care?

With every step I've taken today, I've been so careful not to disturb the articles of this house. It's as if they hold some lingering power over me, compelling me to behave reverently—submissively—in their presence. As if they're extensions of the Klynes themselves.

That *really* pisses me off.

You don't owe them anything, I think. This house is a hotbed for all manner of evil. A breeding ground for contempt and suffering. Nothing here deserves my respect.

I grip the books harder, my nails curling into the leather, ripping into them, scratching down their covers. I begin to tip the books off the shelves one by one, relishing in every *crash* and *thud* when they hit the floor, their edges undoubtedly bruising.

Normally, the thought of ruining books would make me cringe, but I couldn't give less of a shit right now.

Shelf after shelf, I push each book over and let it drop, until all that remains is one row at the very top, perched high above my head. I reach up on my tippy toes, and with one firm swipe, send three books toppling, dodging them when they fall. I'm about to launch book four off the shelf when my finger hooks into something cool in the wood.

It feels like metal. Some sort of latch?

I pause, tracing the strange contours of the mechanism, finding a space wide enough to fit a finger through. I loop one through it and tug a little…

The wall gives.

Goosebumps rise over every inch of my skin as I step back to analyze what just happened. There's a crevice in the wall where the shelves meet the mantel, large enough to put a hand through and push…so I do.

The wall swings in a few feet, exposing a dark, musty space within.

Holy crap.

Shaking with either excitement or nerves, I peek inside, using my cell phone light to see better. The crevice is vacant, no larger than a broom closet. At the far end, a narrow flight of stairs leads below ground.

Before I can stop myself, I squeeze inside and follow them down, my curiosity far outweighing my unease. Twenty-one steps later, I hit a small landing. There, rising before me, is a tall metal door. I eye the key-hole, not feeling particularly optimistic, but when I try the knob, I'm amazed that it actually opens.

Once inside, I run my hand along the nearest wall, flicking a light switch on when I find it.

The room is furnished as beautifully as the rest of Cliffmoor House. Two recliners and a round coffee table sit atop a plush rug. Slatted wood panels embellish the back wall, spanning the entire width of the space, boasting shelves filled with books and decorative items, and an impressive painting at its center.

On the right, there's a door leading to a small bathroom. In a nearby armoire, I find clothing, blankets, pillows, and towels. There's also a kitchenette—a small stovetop with two gas burners, a microwave, a compact refrigerator, and a pantry. Pulling open the narrow pantry door, I find cans of non-perishables, soft drinks, cases of water, and coffee. On the wall beside the metal door, there's a panel of switches and video screens, as if all the security operations of the house can be manned from within this room.

A safe room, I realize. A place to hide in case of emergencies, equipped with everything one might need…and then some.

Tucked into the shelves of the back wall are all sorts of elegant decor. A heron made of glistening Swarovski crystal. An open mollusk shell—its exterior preserved in a glossy veneer—with a shiny black pearl burrowed into its center. An intricately carved wooden box. A pistol with an elaborate, bone-inlaid design.

The giant painting at the center of it all is of Cliffmoor House, encased in a stunning gold-leaf frame. It depicts the mansion in crisp, vivid strokes, the colors amplified to make it appear larger than life. Objectively speaking, the Victorian beach house *is* beautiful, but the darkness swarming within taints its charms indelibly.

Of course the Klynes would adorn their safe room with extravagant trinkets and artwork.

I poke around the space a while longer before deciding it's time for a break. I've been searching for hours, combing the house for clues, absorbing its surly energy. I feel it rubbing off on me—the dread of being back sinking down deeper, dragging my mind into sinister places.

Abandoning the safe room, I seal the wall behind me, collecting the mess of books I'd left scattered on the floor and leaving them in neat stacks on the tabletop. Marching out the back doors, I inhale a breath of salty air.

Hatch will be here soon. The thought alone carries enough sunshine to chase the darkness away.

CHAPTER THIRTEEN

We're parked at the Overlook, a popular tourist destination with unparalleled views of the island's white-sand beaches, Idyll Point, and the quirky pastel town beyond. It's tucked away from the beaten path, the road up encased in palm trees and flowering plants. Luckily, tonight it's mostly vacant, with only two other vehicles parked at far ends of the lot, both with young couples leaning against their car hoods.

Hatch and I recline in the bed of his old Ford Ranger, watching the sun drop beneath the sea. My back is pressed to his chest, his arms curled tight around me, needy with touch, as if he'd been yearning to hold me this way since the morning.

The days are shorter this time of year, the night quick to push in and wrap Halcyon Bay in a tenebrous blanket, sending it to sleep under a thousand winking stars. But this twilight atmosphere—the brief and brilliant moments before night consumes the day—is pure island magic, so enchanting it nearly takes my breath away. I wish I could capture it somehow. Wish I could seize this rare and fleeting peace, bottle it up like sweet perfume—a cocktail of hazy, golden light, windswept hair, and hungry eyes. *This* is the Halcyon Bay I'd like to keep forever. The love-soaked evenings, the melting sunsets, and Hatch, perfect specimen that he is. If it were always this way, I might be able to think of this place differently. I might even learn to care for it more.

"What'd you do today?" Hatch asks, his breath tickling my ear.

It had been several minutes since we'd last spoken, letting the spectacle before us do the talking, our bodies reconnecting to the tune of crashing waves and crying gulls. Upon hearing Hatch speak, I realize I'd missed the soothing cadence of his voice these past few months. The rough and the soft of it, low and decadent. Hearing it through the phone does not do it justice.

I lean into him, the panes of his chest like solid rock behind me. "I did some exploring in Cliffmoor House."

"Find anything interesting?"

"A hidden safe room. Hidden from me, anyway. It opens up through the bookcase in the parlor."

Hatch hums contemplatively. "How'd you find it?"

"I was just walking the house, inspecting things, and I guess I got ticked off at myself for being so…careful? For treating *their* crap with so much dignity. So I, um, kind of started furiously hurling books off the shelves…" I wince a little at how it sounds, but there's no going back now. "I discovered a latch in the wood, pulled it, and voilà. Hidden safe room."

"Furiously hurling books off the shelves?" Hatch repeats slowly.

I twist my neck to glimpse his expression—his eyebrows arched, the corners of his mouth quirked teasingly. He whistles. "I never thought I'd see the day."

"What day?"

"The day Dell Costa, devout bookworm and bibliophile, commits crimes against literature."

An embarrassed groan escapes my lips.

He laughs, giving my arm a squeeze.

"I picked them all up afterwards," I admit sheepishly. "I knew Briggs wouldn't leave them strewn all over the floor like that, even if I asked him to."

"How hardcore of you."

I elbow him, and he snorts.

"I just feel like that stupid house is always hiding something," I say. "Like no matter how far I dig, I'll never hit bottom."

"Maybe there is no bottom," Hatch says, surely not meaning it to sound so damn ominous, but the notion sends my mind reeling. "Maybe it keeps going on in perpetuity."

Maybe it does. Maybe the Klynes' secrets have a domino effect that way, one crashing into another, until a long and endless line of clandestine truths reveal themselves. A maze of ever-shifting parts. I can't help but wonder whether any of my searching today was even useful. Whether it was all a waste of time, misdirecting my focus from things that truly matter.

I force myself to shake off that gnawing sense of defeat. It's too early for that—too premature to know how the pieces fit. And if there's one thing I've learned about Halcyon Bay, it's that everything is related in one way or another, the strings of one occurrence pulled by another seemingly unaffiliated factor. Even if only to help me put this all in the past, it's worth it. The more I understand about this place, the easier it will be to let go of. To bury.

"Did anything else interesting come up?" Hatch asks.

"I found my grandmother's journal. It's not really a journal, I guess, not in the traditional sense. It's more of a record."

"A record of what?"

"Um…" I clear my throat. "Paranormal encounters?" It comes out sounding like a question, at an irritatingly squeaky pitch.

"Paranormal encounters." Hatch's slow, disbelieving voice sets a torch to my cheeks.

"You know, like, ghost-type-things?"

He snorts, sending a jolt of frustration through me.

"Is that so far-fetched? Considering everything that happened last summer—all your spooky island legends—I figured you'd understand."

Hatch scrunches his nose. "Spooky island legends?"

"Yeah. Reincarnated banyan trees and whatnot." I wiggle my fingers for added creepy effect.

His grin widens. "You remember that?"

I fix him with a hard stare, as if to say, *Seriously?* I remember everything when it comes to Hatch—every whispered word and indulgent touch. But I don't say as much now, holding fast to the matter at hand.

"The point is, pirate man, if ghosts really do haunt this island, you know damn well that Cliffmoor House of Horrors is swarming with them. Virginia wasn't crazy. These things actually happened to her. Hell, they've happened to *me*."

Hatch's smile turns coy and devious, his thoughts concealed behind a dubious expression, eyes swirling with something loaded but secretive.

"What?" I blurt, desperate to know what he's thinking behind those perfectly infuriating eyes.

"Is it wrong of me to admire what I find beautiful?" he asks plainly.

A rush of heat floods my cheeks. I feel those words *everywhere*. Feel them so profoundly across every inch of my body, it's as if he'd been speaking with his hands instead.

I don't usually enjoy compliments. Don't know how to receive them other than with a degree of humiliation, tail tucked between my legs. But this is different. This feels *good*.

He feels good.

I gaze deep in his eyes, challenging myself to bear the full, glorious weight of his stare. To not turn away from him, not back down, no matter that I feel my insides rapidly turning to mush. A quiver of excitement zips from my core to my legs, and I'm immensely grateful to be sitting down, wrapped in his firm, sturdy arms. Otherwise, I think I might disassemble. Unravel at the seams.

My eyes forge a slow, languid trail from his eyes to his lips and back. Claiming him with nothing more than a look. *My Hatch.*

"Beautiful and bold," Hatch says on a breath.

A thrill runs through me at seeing this man as hopelessly affected by me as I am him. I could punch myself in the throat for missing out on this for months. For letting my fear and confusion get in the way of all this goodness.

"You just missed me is all," I murmur.

But then that look in his eyes—like wisps of fire dancing over water—shutters into something softer, more somber than expected.

"I missed you terribly," Hatch confesses, the words too sad for what should be a happy reunion. We're together, at last. We've made our way back again. But he's still unconvinced. Still clinging to that uncertainty I'd lodged like an emotional chasm between us, a volatile ocean he can't chart or navigate.

How had I made such a mess of things?

I turn my face to the distant lighthouse, the rolling sea, the waning sun. Everything is a reminder of Hatch. Of moments we'd stolen and shared—a lovesick swirl of bliss and pain.

He drops his next question like a bomb, and I feel my stomach drop with it. "What's going on, Dell?"

I'm not ready for this. Not prepared for a conversation so much bigger than I'm capable of, deserving of a clearer head and undivided thought. Deserving of a better version of the girl he finds himself with tonight.

I run my tongue across dry lips.

"Is it me?" Hatch rasps, as if he's holding his breath a little. "Are you…not sure about us?" That hoarse voice *hurts*, like a slow twisting knife to my gut.

Distracted, I start to shake my head. Hatch shouldn't have to wonder how I feel about him, or question where my heart truly lies. It's with him— *always* with him. That isn't about to change. Not ever, as far I'm concerned.

"No, you're not sure?" he asks, misunderstanding me. His eyebrows pull tight, as if trying to decipher some alien language etched across my face.

"What? No!" I exclaim, fumbling miserably before I've strung a sentence together.

"No," he repeats.

"No! As in, I'm not *not* sure, Hatch."

The ringing in my ears gives way to the blare of an inner siren—a five-alarm fire set off by my insides. I'm self-destructing, just like Palmer predicted. And every cell in me knows it.

Pull yourself to-freaking-gether.

"You're not not sure," he says, pausing at each word.

"Yes!" I burst out, exasperation clawing at my throat. "Yes, I'm sure! About us. I'm sure about us. More than anything. Okay?"

Let us be okay.

Hatch breathes out a sigh, arms wrapping more snugly around me, reassuring me of his presence. His face drops to my shoulder, chin tucking into the crevice between my neck and collarbone—a space made just for him. My perfect fit.

"Okay," he says.

"Okay," I echo, trying to remember how to breathe normally again.

After a long, still moment, he says gently, "You don't need to talk to me about whatever it is you're going through. But I think you should talk to someone. Shed some of that burden."

I squirm a little, nuzzling deeper into his chest. I'd considered therapy over the last few months, as darkness bled into my days and terror crept into my nights. But my relationship with doctors is a strained one. The mere sight of a hospital makes the acid twist and spiral in my belly. Selfishly, it feels a bit like failure to need what I'd helped my mother overcome. To find myself in that same dreadful place.

"You went through hell last year," Hatch says. "And you're one of the strongest, most unshakable people I know. But asking for help doesn't make you weak. Your struggles are not a defect. You don't have to hide your pain, especially from me."

Seeing those sea green eyes fraught with emotion overwhelms me, filling mine with tears that refuse to fall, a painful tingle radiating from the bridge of my nose.

"I have you back now," he whispers, his gaze ensnared in mine. "I can't stand the thought of losing you. I need to know that you're going to be okay."

I don't know whether I'll ever be okay, don't know anything past my lips brushing against his. I coax him into a kiss that's tentative and desperate, broken up by shaky, ragged breaths. Our noses graze with every careful drawback, barely-there fingers tracing soft lines over skin. It's as if we're asking each other a series of questions with each tender sweep of our lips—

How long can I keep you?

How long will this last?

How do we stretch this flickering moment into forever?

Once night falls, we grab breakfast for dinner at a cramped eatery called Maude's Short Stack, one of Hatch's childhood favorites.

It's a charming, fifties-style diner with grimy yellow awnings, faded photos of antique cars and pinups blanketing the walls, and a black-and-white checkered floor in need of a thorough mopping. Situated on the quiet side of downtown—we'd actually passed Freya's psychic storefront on our way in, her neon *Spiritual Readings* sign blazing purple in the front window—Maude's is invariably low-key and nostalgic, too mellow to lure the tourist crowd in search of cheap liquor and music. Every patron here is a local, and they all seem to know each other, glancing up from their newspapers and chipped coffee mugs to nod amicably at Hatch.

We slide into the same side of an unoccupied vinyl booth, bury our heads in a menu, and order way more than the two of us can consume. The tension between us has faded since our make-out in the truck, slipping away with the setting sun. Hatch's arm is looped around my shoulders, fingers grazing the ribbed collar of my shirt. We can't seem to keep our hands off each other. Every time our eyes catch, the sweet sparks between us deepen to flame, and we're both suddenly on the verge of ripping into each other. Tugging at clothes, smashing mouths, needing more, always more…

Clearly, we're both eager to make up for lost time.

"What's the next move?" Hatch asks with an amused smile, keeping himself from acting on the more indecent activities filling our minds.

"*Hmm?* What do you mean?" I'm not nearly as self-possessed.

He chuckles, curling a lock of my hair around his finger. "I mean, what do you have planned for tomorrow? More exploring?"

"No, I don't think so. I need some distance from Cliffmoor House.

As much as it pains me, I think I might head to the library."

"Feel like vandalizing a few more books?"

"You just never know with me," I tease, rolling my eyes. "Actually, I'd like to see if they have any pertinent information on the Brine. Tristen is hell-bent on their involvement in all of this. Like maybe they're helping his father somehow."

Everything I know about the Brine, I'd been told by Prescott, and what little Tristen had divulged when I'd pressed him on the subject. That's not much to go on. I'd like to do some digging on my own.

"Okay." Hatch nods. "The library, then. I'll pick you up first thing in the morning."

"You will? What about work?"

"I'm taking the day off," he says. "Figured you might have some use for me. And that you'd rather I not show up reeking of fish."

I can't contain my smile at the prospect of spending tomorrow together. I'd been so lonely today, creeping through the rooms and halls of Cliffmoor House, surrounded by memories, ghosts, and cobwebs. Time had trickled by dreadfully slowly. But tomorrow promises something different, something better.

With him, it's always better.

"Oh, please," I chuckle. "You never reek of fish."

"Hate to say it, love, but Palmer's right on this one." Hatch swipes my bottom lip with his thumb, tilting my chin up. "You're a lousy liar."

He presses a soft kiss to my mouth, and I feel the indelible, delicious smile in it…but it's over too soon. He pulls away, and I sigh frustratedly. It's treachery to feel passions so big in a setting so public.

"One of my many flaws," I grumble.

"No, Dell." Waves of honey drip into Hatch's eyes, making me melt, falling deeper with every second. "It isn't."

CHAPTER FOURTEEN

The Halcyon Bay Island Library is the same shining beacon I remember. A brilliant ivory cathedral with sunlight pouring in through long, tapered windows, illuminating a stunning collection of books. It's the kind of place I'd normally adore. A place to lose myself in prose and poetry, escape the island heat and the mind-numbing oppression of my family's estate. If not for all the awful memories.

My heartbeat quickens when I walk through those massive doors, terrified that I might find Greer waiting inside, her smile thin and eyes narrowed, ever-calculating. After last year's raid on the sea trumpet fields, I'm sure the former librarian is holed up in a jail cell somewhere, but that isn't much of a comfort to me now, with flashbacks sifting behind my eyes. The screech of her car brakes. The way she'd had me abducted and drugged. Her sinister sneer as she uttered those final words: *You will die. Best get used to the thought.*

Hatch knowingly slides his hand into mine as we step through the library doors. I honestly don't know that I could do this without him.

"Ah, my first customers of the day!"

A man with a shaved head and black-rimmed glasses emerges from the circulation desk near the entrance. He's middle-aged and quirky, wearing a blue t-shirt that reads *Get Lit-erary* over a pair of cargo shorts and watermelon-pink Sperrys. I assume he's the new—and very laid-back—librarian.

"Do you mind signing in here?" the man asks, sliding a notepad across the counter. "I'm keeping track of how many visitors we get each day. We're really amping up our community outreach efforts. Trying to get folks into libraries and reading again!" His smile is without pretense, his expression welcoming. I'm immediately suspicious, though I have no reason to be.

"Thanks!" he says when Hatch passes the pad back to him. "Is there something I can help you find?"

"We're looking for books about Halcyon Bay," Hatch says while I continue my silent assessment of the man.

"Right-o! That section's over here." The librarian gestures for us to follow him past the computers into a corner area succinctly categorized as *Regional,* with several cozy arm chairs and tables for leisurely reading. "All of our books on the island can be found in these three cases. Looking for any particular subject?"

Neither Hatch nor I speak at first, not knowing how much is safe to disclose. The Brine often falls into two categories among islanders: unspoken taboo, or source of feverish gossip. And since I'm not interested in fueling any wild speculation—or prompting a lecture on the horrors of the Brine when I'd lived through them myself—I'm disinclined to give anything away. Considering how the last librarian was secretly leading the cult's resurgence and wanted me *dead,* this is probably for the best.

Fortunately, Hatch and I share the same thought.

Unfortunately, we both speak up at the exact same time with a decoy answer, only to blurt out vastly different things.

"Popular landmarks."

"Offshore fishing."

We eye each other, both immediately echoing the other's statement.

"Offshore fishing."

"Popular landmarks."

Crap.

The librarian shoots us puzzled eyes. Then he lifts his hands, laughing. "All right, I get it! Feel free to take a gander on your own. If you need any help, just holler. I'll be"—he waves his arms haphazardly—"somewhere over there."

He prances away, and I'm compelled to squint after him.

"Hey, it's okay," Hatch says, touching my arm. "Every single person on this island isn't out to get us."

"That remains to be seen," I mumble.

The small trove of books is easy enough to comb through, many of them centering on the island's founding, its agricultural facets, and the prestige of being one of the finest fishing locales in all of Florida. Skimming book after book, none of them capture my attention, their contents overly academic and edifying, void of any pertinent information about island culture or the Brine.

I pull out one old book in particular, a hardback bound in rich teal cloth, its edges curled in, the title etched in stunning gold foil: *Legends that Built Halcyon Bay.* I wipe the dust from it and set the book down on a table. It certainly doesn't fit the bill for what I came looking for, but it draws me in anyway.

Leafing through its creamy pages, I'm lured into a world reminiscent of a fairytale, chock full of all the mystical tales that lend Halcyon Bay its allure. The island's history is tied inextricably to these elusive stories, making it out to be *more* than the average island—a strange and enchanted world unto itself, fabled to have been home to all manner of mythical creatures.

The ancient legends dwindled as modern life pushed in, and the rich folklore of Halcyon Bay faded to assimilate to present-day culture. But it's rumored that the creatures still exist here, surviving in secret, unseen by a world chained to science, leaving humans to question whether they ever existed…

All of which sounds keenly familiar.

I flip to the next chapter—one centered on the island's pirating history—and gasp when I skim the first few sentences.

"Hatch, take a look at this!"

Hatch glances up, pulling his face from the book in his hand, in a reading fog of his own. The way his eyes catch mine, like two captivating emerald flames, grips at something deep in my core. I have to restrain myself from climbing into his lap.

"What is it?" He leans over the table, one hand planted on the surface of it, the other draped over the back of my chair, the tanned column of his neck exposed as he reads. I barely fight the urge to stretch up and press a kiss to his pulse point, my lips desperate to meet his skin.

Down, girl. You're in a library, for goodness' sake.

"Pirates brought the sea trumpets to Halcyon Bay," I say.

According to *Legends,* pirates traveling the Caribbean brought with them an assortment of plundered treasure and goods. Among those goods was a mysterious stash of seedlings—the first ever sea trumpets.

The story goes that they were gifted to notorious pirate captain Wilhelm Bluebonnet by a Scottish witch in exchange for some coin. The witch insisted that the seedlings would bring Bluebonnet the greatest riches across the Seven Seas, and that his name would go down in infamy. She instructed the pirate captain to travel the world and sow them at the bedrock where the living meet the dead. And Captain Bluebonnet determined that place to be little old Halcyon Bay.

"That's a twist," Hatch mutters, still reading.

Bluebonnet and his crew landed upon Halcyon Bay's shores, and he sought out the help of a prominent local medicine woman, Amoya, to find the proper spot for planting and tending to the crop. Amoya sowed the seedlings onto what later became known as the sea trumpet fields, and she became their caretaker. Bluebonnet—never wanting to part from the seedlings, or the infinite riches they promised—remained on Halcyon Bay, giving up his pirate hat and his adventures at sea.

He married Amoya, and their love became fodder for the ages—the greatest of all riches, just as the witch had promised. As for infamy, Bluebonnet was forever known as "the one who stayed," betraying the oceans for a new dream on land and the woman who captured his heart.

"It's a love story," I say, somewhat amazed.

During her lifetime, Amoya used sea trumpets to treat the ailments of the local people. They were crafted into a miracle drug with incredible benefits when used properly, but there were also attempts to exploit the flower's herbal powers. Some islanders began to regard the crimson flowers as idols. They'd worship and ingest them, coveting them above all else. Over the years, their presence became destructive, doing more harm than good.

"Enter Blackbane," I mutter, filling in the blanks.

The story goes on to describe how and why the sea trumpets thrive on Halcyon Bay. The seawater itself is integral to their growth. Whereas most plants wither under the damaging effects of salt, the sea trumpets flourish.

Hatch points to the next page. "This part's interesting…"

There was another trove of Captain Bluebonnet's seedlings stowed on a second ship, but due to inclement weather, his ships became separated on their voyage and came to land upon vastly different shores. On Halcyon Bay, the sea trumpets boomed, while on the other island, they struggled greatly. A small crop was still able to grow, but they were weaker, lesser models of their sisters across the sea.

Hatch skips ahead, eyes skimming down each page as he flips. "I'm not seeing anything on the Brine. It's almost as if they don't want to keep record of it. They'd rather we just forget."

Perhaps the islanders don't want to be reminded of this chapter in their history. They only want to whisper about it, in the shady corners of their dive bars, between gulps of liquor at their parties. But it's not something they want to shed light on in the day. Not a moment they care to feature in their precious cathedral of books.

"I'll check this one out for you," Hatch offers, tucking *Legends* under his arm. "Anything else?"

I shrug. "Feels like a pointless trip."

"It doesn't have to be." He grins. "We could always turn to almighty Google."

We settle together at a desk and start up a computer. Hatch drags a second chair beside mine, and he scooches in close, his fingers tracing lazy circles over my thigh.

I type in the search bar: *The Brine, Halcyon Bay.*

The page instantly fills with photos of a group of individuals, all of them with hippie-long hair and carefree smiles, heads tossed back in laughter. Among the many faces are two young women, wrapped around each other like the best of friends. One is short with dark hair and sharp eyes; the other is thin with bulbous glasses and a shaggy blond mane. I realize these are younger versions of Greer and Lettie, Prescott's mother.

My stomach twists up, revolted by the sight, and I quickly click away from the photos. It's inevitable that I'll run into Blackbane's face too, and I have no desire to ever look in his sickening eyes again.

"Try that one." Hatch points to a link that reads *Disbanding Evil.*

The article goes into detail about the police investigation into the Brine and the compound built by the members out in the fields, but no names are mentioned outright. We try a couple more websites, but again and again, nothing. Each new link is a new dead end.

"I don't think the list of names can be made public," Hatch says, "or else it might violate privacy laws."

"Wait, this looks promising." I click through to a blog titled *Emerging from the Sea Trumpet Haze: A Former Brine Member's Story.*

This woman, who chronicles her experiences anonymously as "Brine Survivor," does not seem to care one lick about confidentiality. She's utterly forthcoming about her associations with the Brine, including a detailed list of its adherents, and personal accounts about her time with them.

"I don't know how comprehensive this is, but something's better than nothing," I say.

We read through the woman's rambling thoughts. None of them are cohesive, like her mind had never fully recovered from the trauma. I can see how she struggles to translate her feelings into words—the jagged impetuosity of her writing—as if she'd tried to jot everything down she could think of, but then never went back to revise. Spelling errors run rampant. There are next to no punctuation marks. Just a long, reckless stream of consciousness.

"I wonder if we could track her down somehow," Hatch says, his eyes glued to the screen. "It says here that she still lives on the island. Maybe we could schedule a meeting."

"She's got a contact page," I point out. "Let's fill out the form. See if she answers."

I start to populate the text boxes with my information, but Hatch's hand falls over mine. "Why don't we leave your name out of it for now?" he suggests. "Your family got a lot of attention last year. I don't want some weirdo seeking you out for the wrong reasons."

He backspaces my name and starts typing his instead.

"Since when are you more adept at dealing with weirdos?" I ask, not bothering to mask the prickliness in my tone.

He narrows his eyes at me, caring but firm. "Let me take this one, please?"

I don't want to pick a fight with him, and it does feel nice to be taken care of. I fake an exasperated sigh. "*Fine.* But we talk to her together. Deal?"

"Deal."

With that, I feel we've made some semblance of progress, albeit marginal.

"Do you mind if I check my email a sec?" I open up a new internet tab. "I sent my boss a rushed message when I left Woodbridge, and I haven't checked in since…"

"Go for it."

When I log in, there's the email I'd half been expecting, waiting in my inbox with the subject line: *Notice of Termination.*

I don't really need to open it, but I do anyway, like a train wreck I can't tear my eyes away from.

Ms. Costa, Thank you for your time and efforts at Goberman Advertising. We regret to inform you that your employment has been terminated effective immediately. The reasons are as follows: distracted work performance, chronic absence, poor time management—

I quickly exit the tab, not keen on having all my failures laid out before me. I certainly don't need Hatch seeing them either.

A pit forms in my stomach, though I'm not angry or surprised. I'd been waiting for this moment, *wanting* it even. I just hadn't built up the nerve to resign. And now I don't have to.

Done. It's done.

But it still feels crappy as hell. One more sign of my deficiencies.

Hatch says nothing, though I know he saw enough by the way he tenses beside me, the way his fingers twitch against my arm. He glances sideways at me, silently scanning my face.

"Ready to go?" I ask, quick to stand and collect my things.

"Sure," he says softly, picking up on the fact that I clearly don't want to talk about it.

Before I exit out of the blog and shut off the computer, a surname draws my eye among the long list of former Brine members.

Santos.

That's familiar.

I glimpse down the length of the screen, scanning quickly through the woman's wayward rant. Hector and Maxine Santos were a young couple, she describes, recently married when they first joined the Brine. They had a daughter who grew up within the clutches of the cult.

As I keep reading, my blood temperature rises to a boil, spilling an angry heat through me, like a dragon breathing fire straight into my veins.

The girl's name was Novela.

Nova for short.

CHAPTER FIFTEEN

Hatch chases me out the library doors as I storm toward his truck, my hands itching to wring Tristen's neck.

How could he put us in such a vulnerable position? Letting the estate become a breeding ground for Brine activity, putting me at the mercy of Nova and her team? Surrounding us where we sleep, like an enemy army?

They'll have weapons, cameras, twenty-four hour access to the main house, the guest house—*Christ.*

"I can't believe he'd be this blind," I grit out, anger clawing at my chest like a rabid animal.

Having Payne around is one thing—his antics mostly irritating—but *this?* Nova isn't trustworthy. Not by a long shot. How on earth could he make her our head of security?

Over my dead body.

She has to go.

Her entire posse of gun-toting flunkies have to go.

If Tristen refuses to see reason, I'll leave. Secure accommodations for myself somewhere else. Somewhere safe.

But is it too late for that? Won't the Brine track me down just as easily sheltered up in some motel?

"Maybe he doesn't know," Hatch offers.

"He knows," I toss back, approaching the Ranger at full-speed. *"Calculating bastard.* How dare he not tell me about this! He makes these unilateral decisions, then claims it's all for my benefit—"

"Dell…"

Hatch's voice is strange, a streak of dread crackling through it. It makes me stop in my tracks.

"What is it?"

He's staring at the newspaper receptacles. The memory of Callie Oxton's face splashed across these very same bins sweeps over me, the blur of my past clashing with my present. I see *The Halcyon Bay Beacon* in its usual, prominent position, the latest issue occupying three out of the five bins. But that's not the paper Hatch's eyes are fixed on.

I edge in closer to examine the one that's captured his attention, sitting neatly in the compact yellow receptacle furthest to the right, brittle from the relentless island sun. It's a publication called *The Daily Mariner,* which looks more like a tabloid than any newspaper of repute. On the front page are two side-by-side photographs of a dark-haired girl on a beach. The first photograph is a shot of her from behind, kneeling on the shoreline, her shoulders curled inward, the wide expanse of ocean dwarfing her thin figure. The second photograph is a zoomed-in side-shot of the girl's face, a harrowing frown upon her lips. She rubs at one of her cheeks with a hand, her hair swept up in a billow of wind. Caught in an emotional moment. A *private* moment.

"That's me," I croak.

Hatch doesn't respond.

It *is* me, on the evening I arrived, when I ventured to Sandspur Beach—an attempt to face my demons in a preemptive strike. I was certain I was alone out there. Certain no one would hear me scream. Certain I could let myself crumble, break, *feel* with unbridled intensity. Succumb to the weight of this place, in hopes that the weight might fall away.

Shaking with the knowledge that I was being watched, my vision goes momentarily hazy. I'd been probed and dissected from afar. My picture taken—stolen from me—my every emotion twisted into fodder for the rumor mill. A fresh new chapter in my already sensationalized story.

From the look of the photographs, the reporter had been hunkering down in the dunes that span between Cliffmoor House and the beach. Watching…waiting…and along I came to put on an unforgettable show.

The journalist in the rose bushes, I remember. She'd sprinted off before we could stop her. Had she written this? Had she doubled back to gain access to the grounds from the beach?

Seething, I read the headline, the bold typeface searing into my mind.

Called Home to the Bay: The Near Sea Girl Returns

By Moriah Gillies

The Near Sea Girl.
Incredible.
"Dell, wait—"
Hatch tries to stop me, his hands grasping at my arms, but I'm already stabbing coins into the receptacle and snatching out a copy.

I shake the paper open and begin to read aloud, my every word a vicious snarl.

The raid on the sea trumpets fields last October shook our beloved island community to its core, making neighbor look at neighbor with sudden harrowed suspicion.

Before that fateful autumn night, it was believed that the Brine had been entombed in the arcane graves of island history, never to be resurrected again. But the drownings of two young girls called these long-held truths into question, and a sickening reality was soon unveiled.

The Brine had been growing its numbers in secret.

A reckoning was approaching.

More girls would perish.

That is, until the Brine's schemes were thwarted in a covert operation organized by our hometown heroes at the police department.

Now, as we sift through the murky aftermath, we find ourselves wondering—is it *really* over?

For no person is this question more pressing than Meridel Costa, granddaughter of deceased Ambrose and Virginia Klyne, former icons and pillars of Halcyon Bay.

Recent discoveries about the Klynes' sordid past, along with Ms. Costa's abduction by the Brine, and a subsequent altercation with her grandfather which resulted in his death, all seem to have taken a justifiable toll on the young woman's mental state.

Pictured here, Ms. Costa was spotted on Sandspur Beach earlier this week, visibly overcome with grief. She screamed at the ocean, as if to unburden herself of some deep-seated affliction, or the trauma she shares with all the "sea girls" before her.

Whispers of Halcyon Bay's legendary Girls of the Salt—the ghost-like victims of the Brine, more commonly referred to as sea girls or devilfish—have flurried to life in the wake of last year's events. And it seems Ms. Costa, our resident survivor and "Near Sea Girl," is buckling under the pressure.

Despite having lived over twenty years in Woodbridge, Maine, Ms. Costa, a Halcyon Bay native, appears to be setting down roots on the island once more. She currently resides at her family's estate, the landmark Cliffmoor House of Old Town.

One might wonder why Ms. Costa would return to a place engulfed in so much tragedy. But, as most locals would tell you, Halcyon Bay is a near impossible place to relinquish—and even less so for the Near Sea Girl herself.

Perhaps it is the call of the sea which summons her. Or, perhaps, her guilt for having escaped a fate so dark.

What will become of the Near Sea Girl?

Does her return bring tidings of terror for the island?

A portent for renewed Brine activity?

Only time will tell, for both us and Ms. Costa, and we'll be holding our breaths in suspense over what this next chapter may bring.

I lower my hands, those flimsy sheets of paper crumbling in my fingers, the sentences I'd read converging in my mind, blurring out of focus, then melding together.

A justifiable toll.

Deep-seated affliction.

A fate so dark.

The Near Sea Girl.

Next thing I know, I'm kicking the receptacle, the sole of my sneaker connecting hard with the bin. One unflinching strike, and there's a visible dent in the corner, the plastic around it cracking apart.

"Dell, stop!"

Hatch grips my waist and hauls me backward. But I don't want to stop. *I want to break something.* I want to unleash all hell upon this island. There's no reason to keep my shit together anymore. If these people want a spectacle, I'll fucking give them one.

"Dell?"

Hatch is reluctant to let me go.

"I'm fine," I growl, shaking him off.

"I don't think you are," he says, his voice distant, drifting far beyond my reach.

That moniker roars in my mind again and again—the Near Sea Girl.

My ghost. My curse.

"Dell," he tries again.

"I said I'm fine, Hatch!"

Maybe it's for the best that I become that living specter. That I give in to the darkest parts of myself, lean into this persona they want to cage me in anyway. Why fight to come out the other side unscathed, when I could so easily bury myself in the pain that disfigured me? Be the girl made crazy by all she'd endured, another one of Halcyon Bay's many legends. A ghost of a different kind. *The monster they created.*

That would give the citizens of this pathetic island town something *really* scary to talk about.

"It's just a stupid article," Hatch says, stepping closer. "A blatant money grab. This writer is deluded. None of what she says is true."

Except for the parts that are.

I feel the heat of Hatch's gaze on me, but I can't bear to face him. My heart thrums with unruly emotions, my mind clouded in dangerous thoughts, both of which threaten to pull me under for good.

But Hatch refuses to let me drown.

"Hey. Look at me."

I can't do it.

Slowly, so as not to scare me away, he lifts his hands to either side of my neck, calloused thumbs rubbing soft lines over my jaw.

"Look at me, love."

My vision clears a little when I force myself to look up. Hatch's sea green eyes—always so inviting, like waves lapping the shore—are suddenly rougher, sharper. More insistent.

"Do not let them change you," he says, voice low. "You are so much more than they say you are. So much better and stronger than everyone on this island. Never forget that."

My every racing thought quiets as I hone in fully on Hatch. Nothing in the world makes sense except for him. He dips his forehead to mine, grounding me. We breathe in unison.

Do not let them change you, whispers a voice in my mind, fluttering up from the depths where I'd almost buried it.

Not Hatch's voice this time.

Mine.

CHAPTER SIXTEEN

I find Tristen in the study with Payne, poring over detailed maps of Halcyon Bay. Stacks of them blanket the giant mahogany desk, overlapping haphazardly, red lines and coordinates penned messily across them.

The taxidermy wall-mounts keep watchful eyes on the men's progress, their concentrated faces illuminated by dim lamplight. Otherwise, the study is dark, the curtains drawn, consistent with Tristen's disdain for the sun. He might've thrived in Woodbridge, with its ever-gray skies and blustery weather. Maybe, if this search for his father ever ends, he'll pick up and move somewhere more suited to his temperament.

They don't look up when I cross through the doorway, too consumed by their work to take notice.

Without greeting or warning, I ask brusquely, "How dare you?"

Payne snaps to attention. Tristen's sullen gaze swims up to mine, his eyebrows pulling together in a deep V. "How dare I, what?"

"Nova." Her name is joyless on my lips, the way one might spit out a word like 'death.'

"What about her?" he asks, immediately defensive.

That only enrages me more.

"She's one of *them*, isn't she?"

Recognition falls in shadows over Tristen's face. He narrows his eyes slightly, as though he's been dreading this conversation, waiting for the inevitable moment he'd have to address it. Meaning he'd known it was coming. He'd known about Nova all along. *Miserable prick.*

"Leave us for a moment, Payne."

The valet straightens and strides out of the room, tossing me a simpering wink as he departs. I scowl at him before rounding on Tristen again. "What the hell is wrong with you? How could you hire her knowing she's one of them?"

"She's *not* one of them." His expression is flat and unaffected. "Nova was just a child when her parents—"

"That makes no difference!" I snap.

"It absolutely does," Tristen counters sharply. "No one has a choice in what they're born into. Nova may have a past with the Brine, but she's totally disconnected from it now. Her parents' decisions are not her own."

Listening to him rationalize Nova's circumstances sets my teeth on edge. "She can't work here."

"You'd condemn an innocent woman for the sins of her family?"

"In this case, yes," I reiterate, entirely willing to condemn first, ask questions later.

"You're not thinking clearly," Tristen retorts, his paper-thin patience disintegrating before me. "Nova merely understands how the Brine operates, can point out the signs should they present themselves. But she isn't a threat, Dell. Having her here can only benefit us."

I glower at him, at a loss for words. How can he be so obtuse about this matter, yet so astute for all others? Tristen isn't the type to make careless mistakes. Why choose to be so blind about this one? Why see past the obvious truths in front of him?

An awe-struck horror crawls over me as I work out the truth in my mind. "You like her," I say slowly. "You *like her*, like her. As more than a passing fancy."

"I—what?" Tristen falters, flustered.

"You barely know this woman!" I cry, the facts clicking firmly into place. "Yet you're going to let a few hasty *feelings* muddy your judgment?"

"That's preposterous," he snaps.

"Preposterous is hiring someone with every reason to want me dead as our goddamn head of security!" I explode.

Tristen blinks wildly, as if in disbelief over how this situation has spiraled.

"You're really prepared to gamble my life away on the off-chance that she'll be who you hope she is?" It certainly feels that way. Like he's offering me up as the sacrificial lamb, all to get into this strange woman's good graces.

"You're being ridiculous," he says. "We have nothing to fear from Nova. Everything will be fine—"

"*Fine?*" The word sets me off, the scorched skin of my forearm a gripping reminder of the last time Tristen insisted that everything would be 'fine.' "Fine like when we went to pay Blackbane a visit? Fine like *this?*" I stretch out my arm, showing off my bandages.

His mouth clamps shut, struck by my words.

Had he thought I'd forgotten? Tucked away the memory where it could no longer touch me? Suppressed the sear of fire and those maddening eyes for good? No, *hell no.* It had only been a couple days, for goodness' sake.

"Put your feelings for Nova aside, and tell me this one thing," I say. "If it was *you* the Brine wanted—if you'd been the one drugged and dragged onto those fields, you that had been burned by Blackbane—would you be so certain about her? Would you be able to turn a blind eye to her past?"

His Adam's apple bobs as he mulls over the question. "I wouldn't have hired Nova if I didn't think she could do the job properly," he says carefully. "My feelings are not a factor."

"So you do have them."

My cousin goes quiet, neither confirming nor denying my claim, but there is no louder admission. Against all odds, he cares for Nova. He wants to keep her close. And I almost feel bad calling her intentions into question. But not enough to stop.

"You didn't answer me before. Would you trust Nova so readily if *you* were the Brine's target and not me?"

"Yes," he replies solemnly, without a whisper of doubt or a second of pause. "Yes."

The word gnaws at me like salt in a cut. "Your judgment is so far off, it's disgusting."

"You don't have to trust her, Dell." Tristen's tone is reproachful, but pleading. "Trust *me*. I know what I'm doing."

"That's just it! I don't know that I can trust you, Tristen. And if trusting you is something I'm having to doubt, then maybe I shouldn't be here at all."

You could be wrong about her, a hopeful voice rustles within me, deepening the cracks in my anger-fueled theory. *Maybe you're taking this all too far.*

Tristen saved my life once before, and I don't believe he'd knowingly put me in harm's way, but that doesn't mean his judgment isn't flawed. He's a Klyne man after all, one that could easily be clouded by vengeance, pride, or desire. By a need for companionship and love, or just a pretty, smiling face devoid of contempt. Someone willing to overlook the sullied repute of his father, the darkness of our past.

Nova bears a similarly dark past. She wouldn't judge him. She might understand. And maybe she's an exemplary person. Maybe she'd truly guard us with her life. I'm just not open to taking the chance.

Turning on my heel, I make for the hallway, needing some space from Tristen to collect my thoughts.

"Where are you going?" he calls at my back, voice strained, as if he knows that maybe I'm not just walking away from this conversation. Maybe I'm walking away from him too.

The truth is, I don't know what's next for me. Whether to leave Cliffmoor House and find lodging elsewhere, or pack it in altogether. Wash my hands of this and head back to Maine.

And just give up? That small voice floats up again, incredulous and unforgiving.

No. I won't do that. There's too much at stake. Too many people I love here.

I turn to face him again. "I'm going to get ready for Palmer and Mojo's dinner, if that's okay with you."

I'm not sure why that's the excuse that spills from my lips. Maybe because the party—while still hours away—is the only neutral subject I can think of. The only thing that won't kick off another nuclear-level argument.

To my surprise, Tristen's face flashes with lightning-fast emotion—a perfect O on his lips, as though he'd been slapped by my revelation—but he quickly smooths it over, reassembling his features into a careful, practiced mask. Then, once more, he's all hard angles, scorn, and bite.

It's easy to deduce that he isn't going to Palmer's tonight. More likely, that he wasn't invited. Does it bother him to be excluded?

"I won't keep you any longer then," Tristen deadpans, feigning boredom. His eyes flit back to the maps before him, and with that subtle motion, I'm dismissed.

It hits me as I march outside that I'm the only family member that tolerates Tristen. The only one that aims to see past his baggage. The only one offering him a real chance at atonement. Granted, I'm also the one that knows him the least—for the shortest amount of time anyway. But I've also seen parts of him that no one else has. Goodness. Kindness. Bravery beyond measure.

A bond was forged between us that day on the sea trumpet fields. Putting aside his dubious past transgressions—the dim light inside of him that wanes and flickers in the shadows—I'll *always* owe him my life. His darkness can't drive out the truth of what he did for me, or the person he's trying to be now.

That's the man I choose to see, the one with goodness dwelling within, showing its hardened face after a lifetime of neglect.

Maybe I'm not ready to turn my back on him just yet.

CHAPTER SEVENTEEN

I've visited Palmer and Mojo's apartment once before, but it looks entirely different now from the white-walled shell I remember.

They've painted, furnished, and decorated the place, filling it with homey furniture and warm lighting, lush potted-plants and bohemian throw pillows, roomy jute rugs and abstract art splashed across the walls.

"Are we early?" I ask Palmer when she greets me at the door. No other party guests have arrived. It's just Hatch and me for now. "You said eight, right?"

"Sure did," Palmer says. "And no, you're not early. Everyone else just runs on island time."

"Oh, right." I forget the islanders operate on a schedule all their own here, moving to an easy tempo I can't seem to acclimate to.

The truth is, maybe I don't want to get too comfortable. Maybe I prefer the role of hopeless outsider—compelled to stay at the fringes, dipping in and out of strange waters like a pen dipped in ink. Maybe it's part of a larger defense mechanism. My missteps and fumbles might make it all easier when it's time for me to leave again.

"We brought pie," I offer, handing over the box of store-bought dessert—the best we could manage on short notice.

"Yum," Palmer groans, almost indecently. "What kind?"

"Guava and cheese." The most eye-catching flavor at the grocery.

"*Yum*," Palmer repeats, this time with an even deeper—and irrefutably indecent—groan. She lifts the lid and sniffs, tossing her head back in sugary rapture.

When my cousin comes down from her momentary pie-high, she rolls her eyes at us and says, "Well, don't just stand there, weirdos. There are appetizers in the kitchen, and the bar is fully stocked. So come on in. Eat, drink, be merry." She lowers her voice to an aggrieved murmur before adding, "The birthday boy certainly is."

"Oy, *Hatchell!*" Mojo calls from the kitchen. He brandishes a large bottle of tequila in one hand, rotating his pelvis in wide, suggestive circles—a naughty, Jagger-like dance move, decidedly on-brand for a rockstar in the making. "Get in here, you two!"

Hatch and I exchange an amused look as we slip inside the apartment, and Mojo tap dances over.

"Happy birthday!" I say as Hatch hands him a twelve-pack IPA.

Mojo kisses my cheek before shooting coy, half-moon eyes at Hatch. "C'mere, big boy!" He plants a second kiss on Hatch's cheek, eliciting laughter from the both of us.

Mojo wiggles his eyebrows, swinging the handle of tequila around. "Welcome to *Cinco de Mojo!* Who's up for a celebratory shot?"

Hatch and I glance at each other. "No, thanks," I blurt at the exact same time Hatch says, "I'm good, bro."

Mojo's megawatt smile plummets. "Way to kill the freaking vibe. Don't you know this is supposed to be a party?"

I wonder how much of that bottle he's actually consumed tonight. At least half the liquor is missing, the rest sloshing up and back with every enthusiastic jiggle of his arm. For his liver's sake, I hope he didn't drink it all in one go. But, based on the way he's gyrating like a fiend—his purple Hawaiian shirt mostly unbuttoned, showing off his tanned and tattooed chest—I wouldn't doubt it for a second.

"A *dinner* party," Palmer interjects sternly. "Which would imply that food is the main attraction tonight. Not tequila."

"But tequila goes great with food!" Mojo cries. His eyes jump from me to Hatch as he pokes one finger in the air. "Just one teensy-weensy *Cinco de Mojo* shot?"

Hatch catches my eye, chuckling under his breath.

"All right," I concede. "The teensiest."

Mojo takes off like a horse to the races, collecting three shot glasses, lime wedges, and salt, swiftly hustling back to prepare them.

Palmer cocks her hip, crossing her arms above her belly, lips pursed up tighter than a rosebud. Far too comical to be taken seriously. "Tonight's supposed to be low-key," she complains to her husband. "I didn't realize your inner frat boy was invited."

Mojo laughs, unbothered, as he sloppily pours tequila in all three shot glasses. "I believe the term you're looking for is 'dude-bro,' babe. Frat boy is *so* yesterday."

I slap a hand over my mouth. Palmer scoffs, unimpressed.

Mojo passes Hatch and me a glass and a lime wedge each. Then, with glossy eyes, he instructs us to "Lick, drink, suck," before promptly pouring salt on the back of our hands. He raises his glass. We follow suit. "To you, my radiant sweet cheeks!" Mojo proclaims through a hiccup. "You sexy, sassy, beautiful woman! Thanks for putting up with a goober like me. God knows I love you more than life itself."

Palmer rolls her eyes, though her cheeks flush red with pleasure.

"I'll drink to that," I tease, nudging her arm.

"*¡Pa' arriba, pa' abajo, pa'l centro, pa' dentro!*" Mojo chants. We follow the movements of his shot glass, lick our salt, toss back our tequila, and suck our limes. It's all citrus and acid, bitterness and celebration. It sends a fiery tickle racing down my throat.

Mojo makes a satisfied whooping sound when we finish, then slings a dangly arm over his wife's shoulders. "Palm's feeling a wee bit antsy tonight, y'all," he whispers loudly.

"I'm not antsy!" Palmer snaps. "I'm *annoyed*."

"At what?" Mojo's eyes blow wide and innocent. "*Moi?*" He contorts his face into a long, wicked smile—Grinch-like and hilarious—nuzzling playfully into Palmer's neck. She swats him away just as the doorbell rings.

He pops a kiss on my cousin's forehead, collecting our shot glasses and prancing away. We watch on as he yanks open the front door, howling with excitement as a chorus of voices fill the apartment.

"Must be nice," Palmer mutters under her breath.

"What is?" I ask.

"Drinking tequila. Frolicking like a fool. All the luxuries of not having to push out a ten-pound baby in a handful of weeks."

I wince at her words, aware of how much she's going through privately, the joys of becoming a first-time mother constantly doused by looming panic. She could probably use a shot more than anyone.

Her stony expression softens when she meets my eyes. "I don't resent him, Dell. I'm just"—she sighs—"having a weird day."

"You're allowed to have a weird day," I assure her.

She lifts a dismissive shoulder. "I'm tired and cranky," she admits, her voice caught between a whine and a grumble. "This whole birthday dinner thing was my stupid idea, and now I wish I hadn't planned it at all. No one's even here yet, and Mojo's already piss-drunk—probably the baby nerves getting to him. And I'm too pregnant to be social! I look like a freaking beluga."

Hatch coughs to shield a laugh, and I elbow him, not bothering to be subtle about it.

"Guess we all know what Seaborn really thinks of me," Palmer mutters, though I see hints of a smile tugging up her lips.

"Palmer, you're *nothing* like a beluga," I insist. "You look incredible. I mean, come on, you're glowing! And Mojo is…a little hyper right now. But that's only because he's so excited. A lot's happening for both of you."

"Maybe you're right." Palmer tilts her head to one side. "Besides, knowing me, I probably should've said orca. Belugas are *way* too friendly."

"Fine." I take Palmer's hand and squeeze. "Then you're the prettiest orca I've ever seen. Okay?"

Hatch laughs again—louder this time—and I fix him with a condemning, *can you not* stare.

"You realize you're talking about whales, right?" he asks. "I'm not supposed to find that funny?"

"Correct," Palmer and I echo.

"Oh. Cool, cool. Makes perfect sense." Hatch nods. "I think I'll go take another swig of Mojo's tequila. Lord knows I'm going to need it tonight."

Palmer snorts, then bursts into a giggle. I see the tension slipping from her eyes, washed away by our banter. She clamps one hand on my shoulder, and says, "I'm really glad you're here."

I feel every bit of truth wrapped up in that statement as if she'd whispered it straight into my heart, and even more so when Palmer's gaze flicks to Hatch next. She cups his shoulder with her other hand, and says, "Both of you."

Before we know it, she's pulled us into a bear hug, her belly cradled between us like a beach ball. Hatch blinks fast in obvious surprise. I smile as I wrap one arm around my cousin, breathing in her coconut-scented hair, and another around Hatch.

After a moment of baffled pause, he does the same.

I never thought I'd see the day.

The doorbell rings again and Palmer pulls away from us, smoothing down her white eyelet-lace dress. "All right, enough of this sentimental crap. Time to nut up and play hostess." She tosses us a brilliant smile and chirps, "Behave while I'm gone, children," before scurrying off to greet her guests.

"What the heck was that? " Hatch asks, mystified.

"Growth, I think? Let's not question it too much."

"No complaints here. I'll take this version of Palmer over the out-for-blood mean girl any day. At least I can disarm this one with laughter."

He had done that. Had helped Palmer unload the weight of her worries, and afforded us a truly heartfelt moment. I'm so grateful to Hatch, for how he's forgiven Palmer's past mistreatment. For being here, by my side, making my cousin laugh.

"Dell!"

A little boy's voice sends my heart skyrocketing.

Palmer's brother Leif breaks from the crowded entryway. He plows into me, throwing lanky arms around my hips. I bend down to offer him a sideways hug. His golden retriever, Bear, nuzzles against my thighs, tail happily swatting at me left and right.

Leif's golden-blond head smells of apples and sunshine. He'd stretched out so much lately, like a flower poking up among weeds. How is it possible he's only seven years old?

"Hey, Leif!" My heart warms at saying his name again, like I've missed the sweet, natural sound of it.

When the boy smiles up at me, I notice the once toothless gaps in his mouth filling in. His eyeglass-frames look slightly less bulbous on his face too, which is tanned from afternoons spent on the softball field. Palmer had mentioned that Leif had recently retired his coloring books, throwing himself fully into the sport. Aunt June had even enrolled him in a youth league, and he was now the star pitcher for the HB Loggerheads.

Bear stubbornly bumps my knee with his head, intent on being properly greeted. "Hi there, boy!" I press my lips to the space between his eyes, rubbing that spot behind his ear he loves so much.

Aunt June sweeps forward an instant later, wrapping soft arms around me, that familiar scent of cinnamon and baked goods woven into her hair.

"Dell, honey! I'm so happy to see you," she says, gazing at me with my mother's whirlpool eyes. Her hands lift to my face, cupping my cheeks with affection, but then her smile slips downward. "Are you eating, Dell? You look like you've lost some weight."

I force a smile, trying to avoid the shrewd pierce of my aunt's gaze. I've shed a few pounds over these past months. Mom had noticed it back home as well. She'd even shown up at my apartment with arms full of groceries a time or two.

"I'm eating. Promise."

June squints like she doesn't believe me, but is obliged to drop the subject, sparing me any further scrutiny for now. The smile winds its way back onto her face, but this time, it's different. Less nurturing and motherly. More *flirtatious*.

"Dell, there's someone I'd like to introduce you to."

She shifts to the side and beckons forward a middle-aged man. His head is shaved and he wears dark-rimmed glasses, along with a quirky smile and a punny t-shirt.

Get Lit-erary.

The island librarian.

"Meet my boyfriend, Dexter!" June trills.

The librarian—Dexter—shoots me curious eyes as he steps up to shake my hand. "Hey, I recognize you!"

"You do?" June asks.

"She was at the library today," Dexter explains cheerfully. "With him, actually." He points at Hatch now, standing at my back.

"What a small world!" my aunt cries, overjoyed, as if this news is the most splendid thing she's ever heard. She certainly looks like a woman in the throes of new love. When everything is thrilling and dreamy and worth giggling over.

"Hi, again. I'm Hatch." Hatch extends his hand to Dexter, while I continue silently sizing up the man, wondering how well my aunt knows him. "And this is Dell…" Hatch nudges me gently, compelling me to reach out and shake the librarian's outstretched hand. His teasing green eyes encourage me. *Be nice,* they say.

Fine, mine respond begrudgingly. I take Dexter's hand and shake.

"Dell's my niece, Dex," June explains, flinging an arm around my shoulders to squeeze me tight. "My sister Laurel's daughter. They live in Maine, but Dell comes down and surprises us on occasion."

"Ah." Dexter nods his approval. "Who could blame you? It's gorgeous three hundred sixty-fix days a year here! Minus the occasional hurricane, of course."

Dexter's right. Halcyon Bay is deceivingly gorgeous, just like so many of its inhabitants are deceivingly neighborly, disguising sinister intent behind eccentric personalities.

I offer him a tight-lipped, narrow-eyed smile.

"Something to drink, Junebug?" Dexter asks my aunt, grinning.

A girlish flush blooms over June's cheeks. "Oh, yes. I think Palmer might've picked up some Sauvignon Blanc for me—"

"Did somebody say *vino?*"

Everyone turns toward Mojo's eager voice.

He appears behind Hatch, flourishing an uncorked bottle of white wine. The handle of tequila is nowhere in sight. I can only pray that someone pried it from Mojo's fingers, and stowed it away where he wouldn't go looking for it. Like at the bottom of the garbage bin.

"I'll grab us some glasses," Dexter says with a chuckle, making for the kitchen.

"Huzzah!" Mojo shouts at his back. "That's the spirit!"

June puts her hand to her mouth, shielding a laugh.

Based on what Palmer's told me, the relationship between Mojo and her mother has far improved. Maybe Mojo had been right all along— maybe the baby *had* brought everyone together, in all the ways that truly mattered. Even I've come back, for better or worse, as if the island had some invisible lasso over me. If ever I were to stay away too long, all it had to do was tug, and I'd inevitably come running. Albeit kicking and screaming.

Hatch presses in closer, his chest a steadying force at my back. I breathe a sigh of relief at having him there. Already this night is shaping up to be a lot. In a good way, of course. But still overwhelming.

"Only the best for my favorite mother-in-law!" Mojo proudly shows off the wine label, as if it were a treasured, award-winning bottle rather than a two-for-one Winn-Dixie special.

"Seeing as how I'm your only mother-in-law, Moises, I hope you mean that in the most loving way," June counters.

"*Por supuesto.*" He leans over and plants a big kiss on June's cheek— his preferred gesture of affection tonight—with an exaggerated smooching sound, to which my aunt only snickers.

Dexter sweeps forward with several goblets in hand, and Mojo pours into them *generously.* June has to put her hand over her glass to keep Mojo from filling it up to the brim. She shoos him away to Palmer's side, watching as he retreats with a tender smile on her face.

This new dynamic between them tugs at my heartstrings, a muted glow flickering to life inside of me. Amid everything that's gone wrong since last summer, *this* is one that's gone wonderfully right. An upside to the countless downs we've all faced.

"Have you seen the baby's room, Dell?" Leif asks me, blue eyes bright and optimistic.

I shake my head. "Nope, not yet."

His grin magnifies tenfold, as if I've given him a gift. He slips his little hand in mine—though significantly less little than last year—and yanks me down the hall with Hatch trailing behind us.

"Since I'm going to be an uncle soon, I've got special uncle privileges," Leif regales me, tugging me through the doorway of a beige-colored bedroom. "I even got to help Palmer and Mojo pick the theme for the nursery!"

Everything in the room feels cozy and chic—no doubt Palmer's design sense hard at work. Elephants, giraffes, and lions in tones of pastel gray and beige can be found in all corners—stippling the sheets, hanging from an airy mobile over the crib, tucked into a woven toy chest. Green, leafy plants add delicate pops to the room, reinforcing the subtle jungle theme without being too overpowering.

"As you can see," Leif continues smartly, opening his arms wide to show off the space, "I picked jungle animals, but Palmer said they had to fit her *aes-the-tic.* Whatever that means." He glimpses around the room, absorbing the tasteful, yet neutral contents of it, and pinches his lips to one side. "I guess that's a fancy word for 'no fun colors allowed.'"

Hatch snorts at the observation. I almost do too.

"Well, colors or not, you both did an incredible job," I say. Leif beams with pride. "It's a beautiful room for a little girl."

"Mia."

Palmer stands in the doorway with Mojo at her side, his arms curled around her belly, chin perched on her shoulder.

"What?" I ask her, goosebumps rising on my arms.

"The baby's name is Mia," Palmer repeats, a dreamy smile emanating from her face.

A hot prickle of emotion radiates from my nose to my eyes.

Mia.

The name sings through me, featherlight and beautiful. In Spanish, it means *mine.*

"Mia," I say softly, my heart swelling. "It's perfect." My voice is tight, my chest filled with such a sweeping and sudden burst of love, I have to look away to keep them from seeing my eyes well up.

"Our little Mia," Leif croons, his face full of wonder—the purest, goldest stream of sunlight.

I wish I could bask in it, absorb as much of that exuberant childlike marveling as humanly possible. Relish in the palpable love among this growing family, a family I'm genuinely proud to be a part of. A far cry from the disastrous one we'd all inherited.

"That's right, Shrimp," Palmer says softly, her cheeks splotched in pink. "Our little Mia."

Mojo buries his face in Palmer's blond hair, whispering something sweet against her ear.

"Don't cry!" Leif exclaims, seeing his sister on the verge. His clear eyes flick to mine then, mouth gaping when he spots the silent streams running down my cheeks. "No, no, no! Not you too!"

He looks pained by our show of emotion, and we all let out a collective laugh among our tears and sniffles.

Hatch's fingers slip through mine. He gives them a gentle, fortifying squeeze.

Never before have I felt such an irrepressible sense of hope.

CHAPTER EIGHTEEN

On the dinner menu is a steaming seafood paella—a melty saffron-rice dish doused with shrimp, squid, and mussels—the scent of it so luscious, it assaults all my senses before I've taken my first bite.

Guests load up their plates and settle into every corner of the apartment. Hatch and I sink onto one end of the living room couch, and, upon digging in, quickly discover that Palmer's culinary skills are top-notch. Having a chef for a mother afforded my cousin a lifetime pass from cooking duties—never having to suffer through a bad meal—but it's obvious Palmer can hold her own in the kitchen. I'm totally unsurprised. My cousin can do anything she sets her mind to, if only she gets out of her own damn way.

Soon, we're joined by Finch and Leon—Mojo's incessantly-bickering bandmates—looking as unkempt and grungy as I remember.

Finch greets us with a grunted, *"Mmph-harrumph,"* struggling to keep his mouth closed around the massive bite he'd just rammed down his throat.

"Waddup, new girl!" Leon exclaims, shoving past his friend to plop down on the couch beside me. He throws an arm over my shoulders, dragging me in for a hug and humming with deep satisfaction when my cheek presses against his.

I edge away slightly as Finch slumps down next to Leon, proceeding to shovel in another mouthful of paella before properly swallowing the last.

"It's been a hot minute since I've seen your pretty face!" Leon says, his eyes dancing over me. "Still slumming it with my boy, Seaborn, I see." Leon reaches around me to clap Hatch on the shoulder.

The corners of Hatch's lips lift into a tiny smile as he leans into his seat, clothed in quiet confidence. Like he knows exactly who's taking me home without having to show it off, without so much as touching me. No need for spectacle. No need to flaunt our connection.

"Oh, I don't know that I'd call it slumming," I laugh.

If 'slumming' is synonymous with 'utterly, sickeningly in love,' then yes. I'm irrevocably slumming it with Hatcher Seaborn.

"Right, right," Leon intimates, taking a sizable bite of paella. "Mojo told me the two of you are all, like, *written in the stars,* or whatever."

My eyes snap instantly to Hatch's. That billowing sea of green rushes my shore, sweeping me off my proverbial feet and out to an infinite horizon.

Written in the stars.

Is that what we are—eternal as the star-flecked sky? Burning bright as those ancient, celestial bodies?

Would we weave our love into an undying constellation? Look up at the heavens and see the story of our lives, the way anyone else might flip through the weathered pages of a scrapbook?

Yes yes yes. Every drum and patter of my heart echoes that unyielding assent.

Hatch looks at me like maybe he feels the same. Like the earth might slide out of orbit if I leave his side. But maybe that's just my heart talking, convincing me he feels as strongly as I do.

You won't know until you talk to him.

But when's the right time for a discussion so big?

"Mojo's always been nauseatingly sappy about love." Leon swats a hand through the air, as if to suggest he has no use for such matters. "I guess it's easy to be sappy about a thing you locked down so early in life."

"Not a fan?" I ask him.

"Of love? Ha!" Leon chuckles. "Nah. What's the point? *Making love,* on the other hand"—he shoots me a suggestive eyebrow-wiggle—"now there's a pursuit I can get behind."

"Maybe you just haven't found the right person yet," I say.

"Are you volunteering, new girl?" Leon nudges me, a flirty smile creeping up his cheeks. Brazen, considering I'm practically sitting in Hatch's lap.

Finch cackles through his paella-packed mouth. "Bro, you wish!"

Leon ignores him. "Look, I know you've been a bit distracted by ole Green Eyes over there"—he tilts his chin in Hatch's direction—"but if you ever want a taste of something a little different, you can always give the L-train a whirl. All rides are free and guaranteed to impress!" Leon's eyebrows do another wiggle dance. Then he gestures like a train conductor pulling a horn. "*Choo, choo!*"

He looks quite proud of himself for that one. Finch, on the other hand, regards his friend with appall. "You're so sad, dude."

"Shut up, Bird Brain."

"The L-train? That's just embarrassing."

"You wanna see embarrassing? How about you go find a mirror?"

Finch explodes with laughter. "How about *you* go look up the word in the dictionary? Oh, wait, you won't, because you're too afraid to see your ugly ass face staring back!"

"Puh-lease. My face is precious. *Heavenly,* so I've been told."

"By who, your blind grandmother?"

Leon glowers at his friend. "At least I know how to use a dictionary. All that red hair dye has seeped through your skull and melted your brain. Now *back off* so I can woo the new girl in peace."

"You're not wooing anybody!" Finch howls.

"I am too wooing somebody, you melanin-deficient troll!"

Hatch edges forward on the couch, commanding the guys' attention without having to ask for it. The energy shifts around us, ever so slightly—the crackling of quiet tensions coming to a head. Hatch's smile evokes the barest hint of a challenge.

Leon gulps as if he knows he's about to get his butt handed to him.

"What's her name, Leon?" Hatch asks levelly.

Leon lifts his eyebrows as though he didn't hear the question. "Come again?" Buying himself more time to dig up an appropriate answer, I'm sure.

"You keep referring to her as 'new girl,'" Hatch clarifies. "I think it only fair that, if you're inviting a woman to ride you, at the very least you should call her by her name."

Leon's face twists with humiliation.

Hatch turns his gaze on me. "What do you think?" He winks, the gesture unseen by the others.

"Sounds reasonable." I can't suppress my smile.

Leon wrings his hands, scrambling for words. Squirming and wriggling like a worm on a stick.

"You don't remember her name?" Finch cackles, losing his mind.

"You don't either!" Leon snaps back.

"I'm not trying to get in her pants, doofus!"

Leon turns back to me with panic in his eyes. "I do remember, I swear! It's, uh…Da…De…wait, I got this! De…Di…"

"Humpty!"

Lira's rasp slithers through the dinner party crowd.

The hawk-eyed bartender saunters forward in a body-hugging jumper and worn leather jacket. She shoots me a smile, flicking her lip ring with her tongue.

"Humpty?" Leon repeats under his breath. "*That's* not it…"

"Back on the island, I see," Lira purrs, surprising me when she bends down to give me a hug.

"Can't get enough of the good life, I guess," I say with a laugh.

Lira snorts, her dark, perceptive eyes bouncing between myself and Hatch. "Maybe there's something else you can't get enough of. Or, better yet, *someone* else."

She cackles, not waiting for me to respond before turning on Finch and Leon. "Ah, dumb and dumber! How's it shaking, fellas?" An endearing sort of disdain drips from her face. "Try not to send Dell running for the mainland tonight—"

"Dell!" Leon cries triumphantly. He snaps his fingers like he'd had my name on the tip of his tongue. "*Aha!* It's Dell! I totally knew that!"

Lira stares at Leon, looking moderately repulsed. "What?"

"He forgot my name," I explain. "Didn't stop him from propositioning me for sex, but, hey…priorities."

Finch doubles over, smacking his friend's arm repeatedly. "Dude, she totally wrecked you, bro!"

Leon sinks a little deeper into the couch cushions, clenching his teeth. "Remember that I know where you live, Finchy boy," he mutters, his attempt at a threat sounding rather silly. "Where you *sleep*. I'd watch my back if I were you."

The flash of a challenge sparks in Finch's pale eyes. "Bring it on, Simba."

I nearly spit out the wine I'd just sipped.

"Hey, everyone."

A woman's sultry coo summons us to attention.

Sasha hovers nearby, waving her fingers demurely. She looks incredible in a pair of high-waisted jeans and an off-the-shoulder burgundy blouse. Her smoky eyes sweep across us, offering casual nods and bland hellos.

She smiles at Hatch specifically. *Marvelous.*

"Well, hello there, beautiful!" Leon exclaims, rising to his feet to wrap Sasha in an embrace, all signs of his former vexation gone. "Where've you been hiding? We haven't seen you around much lately."

"Yeah, we heard you went all 'mainland' on us," Finch pipes up, taking a hearty swig of his beer.

"I was visiting a friend," Sasha says vaguely, her eyes always seeming to veer back to Hatch.

Hatch makes a point of looking away from her, which tells me he must notice it too.

"A 'friend'?" Leon asks.

"Wait, don't tell me." Lira groans. "*Not* the ghost of spring break past?"

A guilty smile curls across Sasha's lips, but she doesn't offer Lira any more of an answer.

"Oh, brother," Lira and Leon both murmur under their breaths.

I remember Palmer telling me that the guy that got Sasha pregnant a couple years back was a spring breaker. He'd had his fun and then he vanished—right back to the mainland. If *he's* who she'd been visiting, then this is a heightened level of idiocy, even for her.

"How are you all doing?" Sasha asks, her slinky eyes mostly still fixed on Hatch. "Feels like I've missed out on a lot these past few months."

"Same old, same old," Lira says. "Oh! Here's a fun little tidbit. I dumped Austin on Valentine's Day. *Again.*"

Sasha puts a hand to her friend's shoulder—a small show of solidarity.

"I'm not too torn up over it," Lira laughs. "Turns out meatheads aren't all that stimulating. Bangin' body, though, I will give him that. Looked real yummy in that Coast Guard uniform."

Sasha giggles. "Having second thoughts already?"

"Not a chance. I'm an impenetrable fortress," Lira insists.

Sasha, of course, glances over at Hatch again. Then me. "And how are you guys? Everything good?"

My neck crawls with heat but I refuse to let it show, maintaining my careful mask of civility. I don't for a second let the unbothered smile slip from my lips.

Hatch turns his face to mine, like one might turn their face to the blazing sun. "We're really good," he says, as if to no one but me. "Happy to be here for Palmer and Mojo."

Sasha nods in silence before turning to watch Palmer, who's giggling as she cuts into the *tres leches* she'd made for dessert—sponge cake soaked in three types of milk, a sweet and decadent concoction. Palmer looks utterly in her element, wrapped in the love of friends and family, her firstborn child practically knocking at the door, bliss and fulfillment written across her face.

I find myself longing to feel that settled. Firmly rooted where I stand, carving out my place in a world so fickle and evolving. To know where I belong. To build a home.

When I look back at Sasha, I see that same desire reflected in her eyes.

"I can't believe they're about to become parents," Finch muses, his serious tone like a dousing of ice water. Even he—ever the comic relief—can feel the sobering weight of change in the air.

"They're going to do great," I say, knowing it to be true.

Hatch presses a kiss to my shoulder, and with that bare brush of his lips, he's shaken up every last nerve in my body. Everyone else fades to nothing around us, like the volume on a TV turned all the way down, leaving only him and me.

Hatch is my home, I realize. My landing zone and safe haven. The refuge and shelter I've been yearning for for months. Not Woodbridge. Not Halcyon Bay. But *him*. My Hatch. Everything I never knew I needed, but can't exist without.

And I need to tell him that.

Need to say all of this.

Not tonight. But soon.

As the party winds down, June waves me over to join her and Dexter in the kitchen. They've taken it upon themselves to man cleanup efforts while the hosts bid their lingering party guests goodnight.

"Got any fun plans while you're in town, Dell?" June asks, keeping the conversation light, a fact for which I couldn't be more grateful. I'm sure she'd like to prod me more about whether or not I'm eating, or riddle me with questions about what I'm doing here. *Why am I staying at Cliffmoor House? What am I plotting with Tristen? Had I kept my parents in the dark this time?*

I wish I knew how much Palmer had shared.

I shrug in response to June's question. Besides spending every second I possibly can with Hatch, my plans revolve around discovering Florian's motives and anticipating his next move. If I manage to accomplish that without getting myself or anyone else killed, I'll be more than happy.

"Mostly hanging out with Hatch," I say, settling on half-truths. "Getting to know his family better. I'd also like to be around when Mia arrives."

It'll be at least a couple more weeks until then, and I get a nagging sense that I'll need more to fill my days than aimlessly searching for clues about my uncle, or waiting for Hatch to have a free moment to see me.

Now that I've been fired, I also need a way to make money, or else I'll be forced to dip into the inheritance I received from Virginia, something I desperately don't want to do. I haven't decided how, or even *if*, I want to spend it.

Basically, I need a job. And fast.

"I may look for work down here too," I add casually, picking up a dishcloth and helping to dry off plates. "Maybe a part-time to keep myself busy."

"What kind of work?" Dexter asks, inspecting a wine glass for stubborn water marks.

I shrug again. Deciding anything these days is difficult. "I haven't really given it much thought yet."

"What'd you do before?"

"Well, my degree is in communication, and my background is in advertising, but I think I'd like to distance myself from that."

"How come?"

"Not really my cup of tea, I guess. I'm not looking for anything too serious anyway, since I don't know how long I'll actually be around."

Hearing myself say these things out loud puts into grim perspective what a lame candidate I'd be for any job. No passion, no dependability, no desire to even be on this island. I sigh, knowing no one in their right mind would hire me—an unmotivated flight risk from the mainland. Three strikes.

"I could use an extra pair of hands at the library," Dexter says, catching me totally off guard. "Library science doesn't appeal much to the youths these days." He smirks. "Can't imagine why. It's such a riveting field! But, alas, it's nearly impossible to find good help."

I open my mouth, but no words emerge. June jumps in excitedly before I can string a sentence together. "Oh, that'd be wonderful, Dex! You two would get along *swimmingly*."

Her eyes—bubbly-blue and exuberant as champagne—land on me. "Dexter's originally from Halcyon Bay too, Dell. The two of us actually went to school together! Then he moved away for college and settled down in Tennessee—"

"Just outside Nashville," he clarifies. "It was nice, but a bit too 'big city' for my taste. After my divorce was finalized, I was waiting for the right opportunity to move home—"

"And when we found ourselves in need of a new librarian," June interjects, "the stars aligned!"

"Perfect timing," he agrees, beaming at her.

I still don't know whether Dexter can be trusted, but their enthusiasm for each other is infectious. Mildly adorable, even.

"But I really am in desperate need of some assistance," Dexter continues. "I know you're not looking for full-time work, Dell, so maybe we can start with a few hours in the afternoons? If you're interested, of course! I figured since you spent so much of your day there today, you might actually enjoy it. That library truly is a book lover's paradise."

I have to agree. The island library is a stunning visual feast, when it isn't tainted by awful memories. And I *more* than love books—I live and breathe them, clinging to my favorites like priceless treasures, so much so that Virginia's first editions are still sitting in tightly-wrapped boxes in my apartment. I'm too scared to unpack them or display them improperly, failing to afford them their well-deserved due.

"What do you say, Dell?" June prompts me. "Wouldn't that be so much fun?"

She must really like Dexter. Must really want him to connect with her loved ones—even the loved ones as detached as me. And Dex seems nice enough. He hasn't done anything to warrant my suspicions, at least. I'd like to put my faith in June's discernment. The last thing I want is to succumb to the sinister paranoia roaring inside of me. It has to stop. I need to force myself to *stop*.

Before I know it, I'm nodding in acceptance, even as I inwardly clench my teeth. "Sure. That'd be great. Thanks for the offer."

"Oh!" June claps, bouncing with glee. "I'm so thrilled to hear it!"

"Hear, hear!" Dexter agrees, lifting a shiny fork in salute.

"When do I start?" I ask, ignoring the tentative quiver at the back of my throat. To be fair, this all escalated rather quickly, and I'm handling it with far more composure than expected.

"The sooner the better. How about tomorrow?" Dexter suggests. "One to five okay?"

"Sure, that works."

"Good." Dex nods.

"Good!" June chirps.

Good. I drill the word into my brain.

Hatch is sitting on the stoop outside the apartment with a brutally-hammered Mojo, his arm slung loosely over Hatch's shoulders. I have a sneaking suspicion that that point of connection is the only thing keeping Mojo upright anymore. His head bobs and snaps, that mop of dark hair flopping into his eyes, a drunken smile plastered on his lips.

"Oh, h-h-heeey, Dell. Did you have f-ffun tonight?" he slurs.

Hatch tosses me wide *help me!* eyes.

"Oodles of fun," I emphasize, extending my arms to Mojo like a child. "But it's time for us to go now. And time for you to get to bed."

"B-bbed?" Mojo asks, refusing to take my hands. "B-bbut not with"—he grimaces at Hatch—"not with *him.*"

Hatch's eyebrows fly up as he stifles a laugh. "You're not my type, dude."

"Ok-kaaay, good," Mojo breathes. "Where's m-mmy wife?"

"She's waiting for you inside," I assure him.

"She's gonna be s-sso m-mmad…" Mojo swings his head back, knocking it against the doorframe with a sharp *crack*. He breaks into a hiccupping fit of giggles.

"That's gonna hurt tomorrow," Hatch mutters. "Let's stand up, bud. Ready? One, two, three." He heaves Mojo to his feet, propping him up like a marionette at his side. "There you go."

"Sleepy time?" I offer coaxingly.

"W-wwait," Mojo mumbles, closing his eyes as if in deep focus, still clinging to Hatch's neck like a life raft. "I want you b-bboth to know…that you guys are the b-bbest, ok-kaaay? You've always b-bbeen here f-ffor us, even when P-Palmer was awful to you—"

I snort.

"It m-mmeans a lot…knowing you have our b-bback."

"We'll always have your back," I promise.

Mojo's brown eyes gleam bright with tears he can't keep down in his current state. "This is the b-bbig one…" A stream slips down one of his cheeks. He smiles through it. "J-jjust a couple m-mmore weeks, and I'll b-bbe…" Laughter bubbles from his lips. "I'll b-bbe a d-ddad…"

I can't tell how much of this emotion is *him*, and how much is the liquor. Either way, I stay quiet, waiting for him to let it all out.

Mojo's lip twitches as more tears pour forth, and more laughter too. "I've wanted this f-ffor so m-mmany years…b-bbasically f-ffrom the second I m-mmet her…I knew I wanted to d-ddo life with P-Palmer…and n-nnow, it's all happening…" His smile falters for a second. "Is it weird that I'm s-sscared out of m-mmy m-mmind?"

"I'd be concerned if you weren't," I say honestly.

"S-ssooo…what you're s-ssaying is…I'm n-nnot a total s-sscrew up?" Mojo's grin is indomitable, head tilting off to the side.

"No," I reiterate. "You're not."

"S-ssweeeet," he slurs, sinking against Hatch's shoulder. "We want you to b-bbe the g-ggodmother, b-bby the way…" Mojo's eyes flutter shut, drifting to sleep where he stands. "D-ddon't tell P-Palmer I r-rruined the s-ssurprise…I j-jjust wanted to s-ssee your f-fface…"

One second later, he breathes out a snore.

I can't speak as to how my face looks right now, but I feel those embers of love smoldering in my chest—the fortifying sense of family and future—growing into a full-scale blaze, doing all sorts of warm and fuzzy things to my insides.

They want me to be Mia's godmother.

It feels like my feet are floating on air. Like maybe I've drank as much as Mojo, and I too have fallen asleep and been whisked away to dreamland.

And maybe we're all too young and stupid to know what we're doing.

Maybe it's imperfect and messy and strange.

But this family, this glimmer of hope, is ours just the same.

CHAPTER NINETEEN

The next morning, I'm up with the sun, despite how late I'd fallen into bed with a full stomach and a fuller heart.

Six solitary hours stretch ahead of me until I have to be at the library for my first day of work. I have no idea how I'm supposed to fill the time. Hatch is busy at the seaport. I haven't spoken to Tristen since our argument, nor do I have any interest in seeing him today. But I still need to find *something* to do. Make myself useful in some way.

I run through a shower, deciding to head up to the main house for breakfast. Inga hasn't returned yet, but Briggs has surely stocked the pantry by now.

I open the guest house door but it swiftly flies out of my hand, slamming shut, as if something wrenched it from the other side. A gust of wind, maybe?

Peering warily through the window, I see the day outside looks calm—the starburst palms at a distance unmoved, the sky a glassy, cloudless blue.

I pull at the door a second time, only for it to bolt from my fingers and crash back into its frame again.

That's not the wind.

I reach for the knob a third time, but freeze when I see the deadbolt *twitching* before my eyes. It trembles for a moment—mustering up some hidden strength—then latches sharply into place. *Click!*

Goosebumps rise on my arms and neck.

I turn the deadbolt, but it flips again—*click!*—locking me in.

Shit.

Terror seeps like slow poison into my bloodstream. Breathing heavily, I glance over my shoulder, taking in the vacant house at my back. My eyes wander up the walls, over the furniture, across the ceiling, frantic as a skittering spider. Nothing had been touched in here through the night. Nothing is moved or out of place, everything just as I'd left it.

"That's enough, Eribeth," I whisper, trying to imbue my words with a courage I don't feel. I don't expect a response, of course. Just the unfeeling stillness of an empty space…

I certainly don't expect the deadbolt to become *possessed.*

It unlocks and locks, unlocks and locks, over and over again, as if controlled by an unseen entity. As if someone *else* has their invisible hand on it, commanding every jarring movement. Fear roars in my mind with every newly engaged *click!*

"Enough!" I repeat, but to no avail.

The walls hum with crackling energy like they did the night I arrived, ripping the ragged breath from my lungs. Panic drips over me, flooding down my legs. The deadbolt continues its terrifying dance—left to right and back again on a berserk loop.

"Stop!" I shriek.

This time, it does.

I twist the deadbolt, haul open the door, and take a breath of salty air. I don't think I've ever been happier to see the Cliffmoor grounds expanding before me.

Rushing out into the sun, a blur of darkness shoots past my face.

I jerk back, narrowly avoiding a collision, just as something slams against the front window.

Catching my breath, I look down to see what it is.

A black seabird lies near my feet, the window above it smeared and feathery.

Biting down the surge of bile in my throat, I kneel beside the bird, pinned in place by its piercing eye—watchful even as it suffers through its last breaths.

I recognize the shape of it, from times when Hatch had pointed out various wildlife on the island's shores. It's a frigatebird, a majestic creature with pointed wings often seen sailing high above the water, drifting on ocean currents, hunting for a meal. This one's underbelly is soft white—a female.

The tingling tenor of death packs the air when the frigatebird shudders one final time, looses a pained whimper, then goes eerily still.

Briggs insists on disposing of the bird himself. I'd bumped into him inside of Cliffmoor House, mumbling incoherently about the broken, lifeless creature by my window, and he'd instantly jumped into action-mode, shooing me off to the kitchen, promising he'd take care of the rest.

My former hunger had all but vanished, replaced by a vomitous swirling in my belly, threatening to make me sick at any moment. I manage to stomach a few spoonfuls of cereal before deciding it best I quit while I'm ahead.

I remember Hatch telling me of old seafaring superstitions, many of which we'd both laughed off—like how women were thought to bring doom to voyaging ships, or how certain words like "goodbye" and "good luck" were to be avoided on board. I distinctly recall him saying that seabirds were believed to carry the souls of those lost to the ocean. It's fortuitous to spot one, but terrible luck to kill one…and here I had. I'd veered into its path, frightened it, caused it to crash. I feel awful for it.

The bird had rattled me so intensely, I'd barely had a second to process all that came before—the door, the deadbolt, and the feeling of dark energy packing that house. Was it Eribeth's presence, as I'd come to believe? Was everything connected?

I venture back to the safe room, my mind desperate for a distraction. I can't explain why I'm so drawn to it—this secretive place within the walls of Cliffmoor House, concealed from all the rest.

I inspect the contents of the shelves more closely, all the beautiful decorative items and heirlooms that my grandparents thought to keep here, hidden away for safekeeping. The books don't seem any different from those in the study or the parlor, mostly nautical guidebooks and deep-dives into historical shipwrecks. The sort of thing my grandfather was into.

I remember how he'd told me to visit that downtown shop, Twenty-Eight from the Main. How he'd gushed when he said that they carried marine antiques and shipwreck treasures. How he'd peered into me with those monstrous eyes—gray spheres that seemed entirely blind to the world, yet still held such an uncanny awareness. That was the day I knew something was off about him, despite not being able to riddle out what. I couldn't fathom the truth of what festered under those rickety bones. The hunger for power and dominance. The hatred for the women he'd been entrusted to protect.

Shaking off the remnants of that memory, I sink into a recliner and flip open Virginia's journal, stopping on an entry I haven't yet read.

The Paintings:

Like the walls of Cliffmoor House, the paintings hide their secrets too. Sometimes I imagine the faces in the portraits watching me as I pass, though most of them are depictions of us—our family, my daughters, even myself. I still get this sense as if I'm being watched, and sometimes feel the urge to pull all the frames down and turn them around so they can't see me. So I'm not exposed under their unfeeling stare, my movements chased by their preternatural gaze.

I wonder if my grandmother suffered from paranoia too. This house could make anyone paranoid, with its maze of walls that seem to press ever inward, at once massive and claustrophobic.

My eyes land on that colorful painting of Cliffmoor House, rendered like some idyllic paragon by the sea. On the surface, it truly is a place of wild beauty—the architecture and design details finer than any other mansion in the neighborhood, its proximity to the ocean an irreplaceable feature. I wonder who painted it. Whose experience of this place was so magnificent, that *this* is how they chose to depict it.

Was it Virginia herself?

There's a faint signature on the left-hand corner of the canvas. I lean in close to see if I can make out a name, but all I see is a scribble—an illegible insignia. My fingers travel over the swirls of the gilded frame, like endless waves undulating in and out. Maybe there's more information to glean on the backside.

Before I can stop myself, I attempt to heave the frame up and away from the wall. It's too heavy for me to carry on my own, the weight of it sturdy and impossibly firm. Maybe Briggs would help, if I asked. But do I really want to bring him into this?

Okay, one more time, I think to myself, trying to balance out the weight of it by stretching one arm along the side, the other cradling the bottom. *One, two, three!* I heave the painting upward, freeing it from its hook. The frame comes loose, the full weight sagging into my arms. I stagger as it begins to slip from my hands, sliding heavily through my fingers. If I don't do something quick, the painting will fall…break…

Without thinking, I hurl it onto the recliner to keep it from smashing to pieces. It lands haphazardly, and for a moment, I'm terrified that it'll tip forward, crashing to the floor. By some miracle, it sticks in place.

Panting, I drop my hands to my knees, letting the sheer stupidity of what I'd done wash over me. All that work to try to riddle out some signature, as if that would offer me anything of import.

Congratulations, you're officially a moron. The cynical voice in my head sounds a lot like Palmer's.

I huff out a ragged breath, resting against the wood-paneled wall I'd pulled the painting from. But where I think the wall should be—firm and sturdy enough to lean against—it isn't.

It seems to…yawn inward.

I yelp, forcing myself upright, utterly confused.

My gaze flits over those slatted wood panels, not seeing anything strange about them, but I can't shake the feeling that *something* is off.

I'd pulled away fast enough to keep from falling, but I knew it was coming, like jolting from a dream where you're plummeting to your death. There'd been an undeniable shift at my back. The wall *had* moved.

I reach out a hand, two knuckles rapping against one of the panels, but nothing happens. It doesn't so much as budge. I push a little harder—still nothing.

I try the next panel, with two fingers this time. I push in, and feel a slight separation in the wall.

Heart pounding, I press both hands to the panel and push hard. It swings inward, as if on a swivel. Amazed, I peer into the crevice of dark space I'd exposed.

An inky tunnel stretches before me, the sting of salt assailing my nose. *Holy mother-flipping hell.*

I squint into the tunnel, but there's no way to see through the endless darkness. A briny moisture clings to the air, caressing my skin like ghostly fingertips. It beckons me to venture inside, to follow this path wherever it may lead.

My hands fly to my jean pockets in search of my cell phone—in need of a flashlight—but all I find is my credit card holder, a tube of lip balm, a hair tie, and Blackbane's stupid cigarette lighter. I curse myself when I realize I must've left my phone in the guest house.

There's no way I'm going down this tunnel without a light.

Sprinting back up the inky stairwell to the parlor, I scan the room for a portable light source. Something I can carry without too much trouble.

A three-armed candelabra glints at me from the corridor.

I take the heavy weight of it in my hand, pulling the lighter from my back pocket. Each of the three taper candlesticks flickers to life, casting a fiery orange glow over my face.

On my way back through the parlor, I make a split second decision to grab the cobwebby fire poker from the hearth, gripping it tight. Who knows what I might find inside the tunnel? Whether I'll need to ward off bats, or snakes, or God knows what else?

I race back down to the safe room—drawing in a breath—and push through the trick panel, landing in the cool mouth of the tunnel.

Ready as I'll ever be.

My first steps are tentative, testing the ground to make sure it's firm. The space is cramped, large enough for one person to walk through at a time. An old, weathered pipe runs along one side of it, bolted to the rock wall every dozen feet or so.

I hold up the glimmering candelabra, illuminating the dark chasm ahead. I can't see where it leads, nor how far the tunnel goes, but I know deep down I have to follow it.

I begin my slow, sloping descent, dragging the fire poker along with me. The sound of it scraping against the ground is my only companion.

Not far away, two diverging paths soon begin to take shape.

A fork.

I suck back a sharp breath, equally excited and terrified. A chilling, clammy streak zips through me.

Trying not to overthink, I veer to the left instinctively, praying I don't come upon any more forks. The last thing I need is to get lost down here. The darkness itself is impossibly disorienting. I can't so much as tell in which direction I'm headed. All I know is that water holds fast to the air, thick with humidity, damp and coating my skin with a film of salt.

Inklings of terror spring up like goosebumps as I push deeper and deeper into the tunnel. Had the panel in the safe room sealed shut behind me? If I get stuck, how will anyone know where to find me? Should I turn back, and give up on this fool's errand?

Venturing down here alone wasn't the safest idea, but who was around to come with me? Tristen couldn't make the trek. Who would he have sent in his place? Dickbag Payne?

As if I'd allow that.

Truth be told, Tristen likely would've wanted Nova and her team to investigate, boxing me out of this place altogether. I'm not about to sit back and wait for that option. And I don't want to undo all the progress I've made. I drive on, bracing myself for the worst, the shadows ahead never seeming to recede.

The candelabra flickers in my shaky hand, the flames casting shapes along the tunnel walls, dancing with far too much life for a place this barren.

How long have I been walking now? Fifteen minutes? More?

I come upon another branch in the tunnel, only this one doesn't diverge into two separate paths. One continues onward, while the other opens into a wide rotunda. A room.

Grimy tea lights line the curved, rocky edges of it, coated in swaths of dust and filth. At the heart of the room lie a series of items I can't comprehend—things that look like they belong in Freya's collections. Artifacts from some occult practice or ritual.

I venture closer, trying to discern the objects sprawled out before me. Various rocks and fabrics, shell fragments and moldy things eaten up by insects and decay, scraps far beyond recognition.

In the low candlelight, my eyes fall upon something strange at the core of it all. *Some things*, rather, each one brittle and ivory-toned.

Salt air seizes my throat, clenches it in an iron fist.

Bones.

CHAPTER TWENTY

Nestled in the heart of the room are scattered remains.

A decomposed human body.

I startle back in horror when my eyes land on the skull, screaming, dropping the candelabra to the ground. With a whoosh, the flames extinguish, the stand clanging at my feet. Darkness engulfs me. I scream again.

Squeezing the fire poker with all my might—brandishing it like a sword—I ram my other hand in my pocket, flicking at Blackbane's tiny lighter.

Once. Twice. *Dammit!* Three times, and that small lick of flame flares against the pitch-black room.

My eyes zero in on the body again, noticing another detail…

Hair.

Long, black, matted hair.

A woman.

Bile rises in my throat as I stagger backwards into the tunnel. I double over and retch, grasping the rock wall for support.

Why is there a corpse under Cliffmoor House?

I gulp down the acrid taste of vomit in my mouth, barely keeping myself from chucking up another round. To hell with playing Indiana Jones. If I stick around any longer, I'm going to go into cardiac arrest.

Moving quickly, I retrace my steps up the sloping tunnel, with Blackbane's lighter flickering in my fingers.

I realize too late I've left the candelabra behind.

Something feels different as I race back the way I came, a haunting presence affixed to my bones. I swear I hear the echo of *two* sets of footsteps in the distance—mine, and a second one. They follow my rushed cadence, that same pattern of heavy *stomp-stomp-stomps* beating against ground.

I can tell I'm close when I come to the fork, swinging right toward Cliffmoor House in a sprint. But as I pass that intersection, I hear something drift up the other side of the tunnel that I can't fully understand.

Whispers.

Murmured utterings and slithery rasps. Low reverberations and uneven breaths. They glide along the walls to me, crawl like fog wisps over the ground…

My feet sprout wings as I fly back to the safe room, ramming myself through the opening and back to safety. I latch the trick wooden panel into place, catching my breath.

Someone else was down there.

Was it another ghostly resident, doomed to the dark underworld? Was it the spirit of that rotting corpse with the midnight-black hair? Or was it something worse? Worse than any phantom or specter. Worse than the dead…

The living.

I slip from the safe room up into the parlor, sealing the wall behind me, my feet and hands moving on autopilot, my mind bustling with gnawing questions.

Where does the other tunnel lead? Could someone really be lurking down there? Squatting underground for some nefarious purpose? Hell, *of course* it's nefarious.

"Glad to see you stuck around."

I whip my head in the direction of that voice, spotting Tristen in his wheelchair, cloaked in the deep shadows of the doorway.

"I thought you'd be halfway to Woodbridge by now," he mutters.

"Damn you!" I cry, struggling to catch my breath. "What are you trying to do, give me a heart attack?"

"I hear a little birdy already did." Tristen smirks tauntingly. "Briggs told me all about your scare this morning. Perhaps your heart is too fragile a thing."

"And perhaps *you* have a death wish, one I'd happily oblige."

"Aren't we prickly this morning?" Tristen's black eyes gleam with amusement. "I've been looking for you for some time now. Is that dusty old safe room really all that fascinating?"

My jaw drops so fast, it nearly hits the floor. "I wasn't in the damn safe room! A freaking tunnel opens up behind the painting in there! *Multiple tunnels,* Tristen. The entire underside of Cliffmoor House is carved out! Maybe whole chunks of the island as well."

His eyes double in size, as if utterly blindsided by this revelation.

"You didn't know?" I pant.

"Of course I didn't know," he hisses. "You think for a second I wouldn't have had it searched by now? I don't appreciate you gallivanting down there by yourself."

"You don't get a say in what I do," I toss back.

"I brought you back to the island, Dell," he says. "It's my duty to keep you safe. You can't be running off into potentially dangerous situations on your own."

Tristen's right. It was dangerous. Terrifying. I swallow a dry gulp of air, my words caught in the back of my throat.

"What is it?" Tristen asks.

"There's a…corpse down there."

His onyx eyes flash. "What?"

"Bones," I whisper. "Human bones. I got spooked and ran when I saw them. I think it was a woman. There was long, black hair…" The memory swirls up the contents of my belly again. I press my knuckles to my mouth, gagging.

"Okay," Tristen says swiftly, thinking up a plan. "Here's how we'll handle this. Nova and her team will be here early tomorrow morning. I'll inform her of your findings, they'll explore the tunnel, retrieve the body, and—"

"Whoa, excuse me?" I spit through the nausea. "Are you completely deranged? We have to tell the police! They need to collect the remains, run tests—"

"I have people for that," Tristen interjects.

"People for what? Testing corpse DNA? News flash: *no one* has people for that."

Tristen glares at me icily, not saying a word, but it's not a stretch to interpret his silence. This is the side of him that scares me. The tendency toward unsavory measures. The dirty, seedy resources he wields at the snap of his finger.

"This is crazy even for you," I whisper. "We have to report it. If this isn't handled properly, we could get in serious trouble. We're talking about a human being, for goodness' sake. They had a life, a family—"

"I'm aware of what it means to be human, Dell," Tristen retorts.

"Then you should know they deserve to be treated with dignity. They're not some puzzle piece in your search for Florian."

"You don't know that," Tristen growls. "That body down there might be *exactly* what we're looking for!"

He breathes deeply, reaching for those lingering strings of composure, winding himself up in their strangulating embrace. When he speaks again, his voice is lower, calmer. "Look. I'll take the blame for everything, okay? If this operation goes south and someone finds out, I'll say you didn't know—"

"That's not the solution!" I argue.

His pit-black eyes are so razor-sharp, I'm sure they would impale me if I got too close. "You said that whatever we found would stay between us," he reminds me. "That we were done with police interference. That's what you agreed to, so that's what I intend to do."

The atmospheric kiss of death I'd felt earlier with the frigatebird comes right back to me now, dousing me in full-body chills. I had agreed to keep the authorities out of this, but that was before I found a *dead body* disintegrating to dust beneath Cliffmoor House. Before I found a buried tunnel system leading to God knows where, with God knows how many access points. And inhabitants.

"I heard something down there," I add, not quite knowing how to put those slippery breaths into words.

"You'll have to be more specific," Tristen says irritably.

"They were like whispers, only they didn't sound normal. They really creeped me out."

"Ghosts?" he proffers with a derisive lift of his eyebrow.

I fix him with a hard stare. "Do not mock me."

"Fine." His eyes roll. "Like I said before, I'll have Nova investigate tomorrow. For now—and I say this with the utmost gravity, Dell—stay the hell out of there."

"You have a terrible need to be in control all the time," I snap, not bothering to divulge that I'm already planning to go back. Tonight. With Hatch.

"You'll get used to it," Tristen says coolly, as if that would be the final word on the matter.

Not if I have anything to do with it.

CHAPTER TWENTY-ONE

Compared with the wilder happenings of the morning, my first afternoon as library assistant is pleasantly uneventful.

Dexter takes me on an extensive tour of the cathedral-like building, guiding me through its numerous floors and departments. He gives me an overview of how the books and periodicals are cataloged and circulated, and—upon providing me with my own set of computer log-in credentials—gives me a preliminary rundown of the library's management system.

I do my best to be an attentive pupil, trying to focus on Dexter's instruction and *not* on my earlier findings beneath Cliffmoor House, nor the fact that I'm determined to sneak back down there later tonight. But it's an onerous task, all things considered. And though he doesn't say as much, I can tell Dexter feels the haze of distraction on me.

Thirty minutes before quitting time, Dex urges me to get a good night's sleep tonight, promising that tomorrow's training session on operating the circulation desk will be more rigorous. "Dealing with patrons—especially the younger, more ornery ones—is a whole different ball game," he says with a wink, before letting me take off for the day.

Within seconds, I'm out the door, hopping on Virginia's bike and zipping toward the seaport. Hatch had mentioned he'd be working on Cap'n Pat's ship this afternoon, so I know just where to find him.

When the familiar, fishy hub rises before me, crammed with boats of every size and color, with a fiery sun bleeding into the sky beyond it, a smile blooms on my lips. I've had so many heartfelt moments here—cathartic laughs and misguided tears and everything in between. The memories meld together like rich paints on a canvas.

Leaving the bike tied up to a rack, I jog across the docks in search of the captain's slip. Before I know it, I spot his schooner—a proud wooden sailing ship, the finest on Halcyon Bay. She stands, elegant even in her weathered state, with a smiling figurehead at the prow, and two soaring masts grazing the cloud-wisps above.

The name of the ship is a mystery, the once swooping, golden letters worn far past any semblance of legibility. But I've always sort of liked it that way—dwelling in the possibility of what it might be. What past love affair might've inspired the captain? What sea adventure was grand enough to pay tribute to? I'd never ventured to ask him before, too content to swim in the endless potential. Sometimes not knowing is simply more fun.

I spot the captain hobbling across the bow, his periwinkle fishing shirt predictably unbuttoned, burly chest glittering with tarnished chains, head shielded by his favorite yellow bucket hat. He squints his one good eye at the horizon.

"Ahoy, Captain!" I call, one hand wrapped around my mouth.

Do sailors still use 'ahoy' or is that terribly cliché?

The captain redirects now, aiming his crystalline eye my way. Recognition dawns on him, as does a broad grin, the glint of gold in his teeth unmissable. "Delly girl! Back from up north, I see!"

I nod, smiling back. "Permission to come aboard?"

"For you, always," he booms, waving me up.

I sprint up the boarding ramp, recalling all the times I've been here before—with the Klynes the day we released Virginia's ashes to the bay, with Hatch when he convinced Cap'n Pat to scoop me up from Prospero

Pier, and again, when Hatch took me for one final sail around the island. Landing upon the salted wood planks now, the deck seeming to groan with each of my eager footsteps, it feels like I'm revisiting an old friend.

"To what do I owe the pleasure, Delly?" the captain asks. "Looking for Seaborn?"

"Actually, yes. Hatch said he'd be here this afternoon."

"The ole summer fling's still going strong, eh?" he croaks teasingly. "Drag my ass to Davy Jones' locker! I thought for sure Seaborn woulda fudged things up by now."

"Oh, no. Not at all. Hatch is great," I insist through a laugh. "If anything, *I'm* the one doing the fudging."

Cap'n Pat places a hand on my shoulder. "I doubt that very much, sweet girl." He speaks with profound affection, as though he's carved out some coveted real estate on that old, salt-drenched heart of his and set it aside just for me.

"I reckon true love can't never be explained," he muses, "just like deep waters can't never be explored. Neptune knows how Freya still puts up with me! You women are blessed with a rare capacity for love."

I smile as the captain weaves thick fingers through his beard, cackling low to himself, big belly shaking. "I like to yank Seaborn's leg here 'n' there, but, truth be told"—he pulls a whistle from his cargo pocket and blows, emitting a sharp trill through the air—"I think you two make a fine pair."

On command, Hatch appears at the bow of the ship, eyes searching for the captain, then going wide when he spots me. "Dell?"

Captain Patton winks at me, dropping the whistle back in his pocket.

"I've told you before, Cap'n, you don't need a dog-training whistle to get my attention," Hatch says as he approaches. "I'll come if you call."

"What, 'n' strain these precious, virgin vocal chords?" The captain rasps out a laugh rolled into a hacking cough.

Hatch's smile is apprehensive as he presses a kiss to my brow. "What're you doing here? Is everything okay?"

I realize too late that I might've stumbled upon him working on his big surprise. "Everything's fine. Sorry if I interrupted something. I totally blanked on the whole surprise thing."

"It's cool," he says. "I'm always happy to see you."

"I didn't ruin anything, did I?" My eyes wander inquisitively across the ship's deck, prompting Hatch to break into a wry, lopsided smile.

He crosses his arms over his chest, the muscles on his tanned biceps flexing temptingly. I want to lean in and bite one—a completely irrational impulse—but I manage to refrain so as to spare the captain.

"Nice try," Hatch says through his smirk. "How was your first day of library duty?"

"It was very, um…peaceful," I say after a moment, to which Hatch laughs. "I wanted to make sure you were coming over later. My cell service crapped out on me *again,* so I figured—"

"I'm going wherever you are, Dell."

On second thought, I might just bite that bicep after all.

"Ah, young love. Ain't it something?" Captain Patton shakes his head as he waddles a short distance away, busying himself with collecting a pile of tangled rope in his arms.

"What are you up to?" I ask Hatch.

He shrugs. "Waxing the hull. Cap'n's riding me pretty hard today. I got sidetracked earlier and made it here late."

"Why's that?"

"Some guy came by the docks looking for someone to fix a bunch of rusty outboards—"

"Outboards?" I ask. When Hatch gets into boat-talk, I sometimes feel like he's speaking a different language.

"Motors that attach to the outside of a boat," he explains.

"Of course! I totally knew that." I toss him a grin. "So you took the job?"

"Yeah, the pay's good, and the repairs shouldn't take longer than a week. I can fix them in my off-time…" He reaches out to twirl a piece of my hair around his finger. "Whenever you're not keeping me busy."

A rush of heat pours into my cheeks. Hatch smiles with satisfaction. "Speaking of which," I say quietly, "I found something kind of crazy today. I need your help to investigate it later."

Intrigue sparkles in Hatch's eyes, emerald-bright and curious. "What is it?"

"A tunnel hidden beneath Cliffmoor House," I divulge, unable to tamp down my own excitement. "It opens up through the safe room."

"Holy shit," he whispers.

"Right?" The thrill and adrenaline I'd felt earlier surge up all over again, my body practically vibrating with restless anticipation. "I only got to explore a little bit on my own, but it splits off into at least two tunnels. I have no idea where they lead, or how many more there might be. Who knows how much ground they cover? How much of the island is hollowed out? And if that's not enough, I found…"

My voice trails off, the truth almost too morbid to speak aloud.

"Found what?" Hatch prompts.

"Um…bones." My mouth twitches around the word.

"Bones?" he repeats in disbelief.

I nod solemnly.

"This here island's built on bones."

Our faces snap to Captain Patton. The ropes are untangled and looped neatly over his arm. He'd made surprisingly fast work of the task.

"What do you mean?" I ask him.

I'd forgotten the captain's prodigious eavesdropping ability. The man might look every bit his age—might waddle and wheeze and flash yellowed teeth through his wrinkles—but his hearing is impeccable, honed into the drop of a pin or the drone of a mosquito.

"An isle of bones," the captain repeats around that glinting, gold-tinged smile. "If you look hard enough, dig into all the right nooks 'n' crannies, you're sure to find 'em everywhere, tucked away just so."

He coughs again and toddles away, the golden sun warming his slumped back, while his departing words—*an isle of bones*—swirl and sink like an anchor to my core.

CHAPTER TWENTY-TWO

A rap at the guest house door that night has me sprinting to swing it open, giddy at the thought of curling up in Hatch's arms before delving into that dark unknown again.

But Hatch is not alone.

Palmer pokes her head around his shoulder, with fire in her sky-blue eyes and a sneer on her cherry-red lips. "Well, well, well. Hello there, *godmother.*"

Aw, crap.

Mojo shrinks behind them both, shaking his head as if deeply embarrassed. He roughs a hand over his stubbled face.

How on earth do I diffuse this situation? Shrug it off? Act like I have no idea what she's talking about?

"Uh…what?" I ask rather stupidly.

"Don't bother playing dumb," Palmer says with rolled eyes. "Mojo cracked like an egg. I know what he told you. I know everything."

Hatch pinches his lip to the side to keep from laughing.

"Are you sure about that?" I ask Palmer. "He was really, *really* drunk last night. I doubt he remembers much."

With a swish of her braid, Palmer's stony gaze locks on her husband.

He stands up a bit straighter, swallows, and says, "I told you we wanted you to be Mia's godmother. That I wanted to see the look on your face. Then I asked you not to tell Palmer, so I wouldn't get in trouble."

Damn. Palmer should consider a career in criminal interrogation.

She prods a finger into my shoulder. "And you, little miss paragon of truth-telling, didn't"—*poke*—"say"—*poke*—"anything to me!"—*poke.*

"Okay, *ow.*" I jab her right back, though not nearly as hard. I glance at Mojo. "How's the hangover, by the way?"

His smile is feeble. "Cake compared to my wife's tongue-lashing. Thanks for asking."

"Please, you got off easy," Palmer snaps over her shoulder. She crosses her arms expectantly, her cloudless eyes boring holes into my face. "Well?"

Heat falls over me like a curtain. "Well, what?"

She lets out a forced breath. "Well, will you be Mia's godmother?"

Yes! I want to shout. *Unequivocally yes!* But is it selfish of me, considering how little I'm around? Am I too volatile and flighty to assume a responsibility so big? So meaningful?

"Are you sure?" I ask her gently. "I mean, I don't live here. Hell, I don't even visit that often. And we've only really known each other for, like—"

"Less than a year," Palmer says, as though she's accounted for all of this. "We know. And yes, Dell. We're sure."

They're sure.

About me.

Even though I'm not.

"So will you do it?" she asks.

Biting back the swell of emotion in my throat, I say, "Of course. I'd be honored."

Palmer laughs. "Good. You should be." Then, she loops her arms around me, embracing me in a hug. After a second, she calls over her shoulder, "You're allowed to join us, babe. I promise not to go all Dragon

Lady on you."

Mojo lets out a triumphant hoot and rushes up the stoop, wrapping his arms around us both. "Get in here, Hatchy boy!" he calls.

I hear Hatch snort and then another set of arms—these ones warm and familiar—come around us.

"So if you two stay together, that'll make Hatch, like, Mia's godfather-by-proxy," Mojo works out.

"Why wouldn't they stay together?" Palmer snaps, flirting on the edge of irritation.

"Whoa there, Dragon Lady. I'm just hypothesizing here."

"Who's Mia's actual godfather?" I ask.

"My brother," Palmer and Mojo respond at the same time, before shooting each other narrowed eyes.

"Sorry I asked," I mutter.

"Are we going to make this group hug thing a habit?" Hatch asks. "Just so I can mentally prepare myself."

"God, I hope not," Palmer whines, fake-gagging and swatting us away as if we suddenly disgust her. "It's already hot as freaking hell. The last thing I need is you three sweating all over me."

"I'd say godmother celebrations are in order!" Mojo announces. "Who's up for a field trip to Pizzana? It'll be our treat!"

Hatch and I exchange a glance. "Sorry, we can't tonight," I blurt. "We're busy."

Palmer's eyes narrow. "Really? What's on the itinerary?"

Shit.

"Can't say," Hatch chimes in. "It's a surprise. For Dell."

Palmer's hands find their way to her hips. "You're an even worse liar than she is."

Oh, no.

"I'm not lying," Hatch retorts. "I'm just…withholding. For the sake of the surprise."

"Oh, cut the crap, Seaborn! You two are up to something."

"Or," Mojo jumps in, nudging his wife, "maybe they want some *alone time,* and Hatch is trying to be polite instead of just telling us to, you know"—he makes a hitchhiking gesture with his thumb—"get lost."

"No, I don't buy it." Palmer turns on me, a challenge in her eyes. "Fess up, Dell."

I spread my hands wide to prove my innocence. "I don't know what you're talking about."

"Is this about your little investigation?" she asks pointedly.

Great.

"No."

One golden eyebrow flies up Palmer's forehead. "It is, isn't it?"

"What part of me definitively saying 'no' means yes to you?" I ask, exasperated.

Palmer runs her tongue along her top teeth as she thinks. "So this has to do with Florian, then? Did you figure something out?"

I glare at Palmer, not bothering to respond. Denial clearly isn't dissuading her. Maybe silence will do the trick.

"Would you rather I go ask Tristen?" she asks.

"Palmer, you hate Tristen."

"At least he doesn't lie to me! Maybe I should redirect some of that hatred toward more appropriate targets." Her eyes slide menacingly from Hatch to me, as if she might intimidate the truth out of us with that icy stare.

But Hatch and I are unmoved. Deadlocked. Impassable.

"Dell, c'mon!" she cries, breaking her hard-ass, bad cop act. "Tell me what's going on!"

"Howling like that cannot be good for my goddaughter."

"Great! Another person trying to tell me what to do. I swear, if I hear one more 'don't do this' or 'don't do that' with regards to *my* baby, I'm going to scream!"

"You kind of already are," Hatch points out.

"Then I'll scream even *louder,*" Palmer threatens, a streak of madness in her eyes. Hatch takes a concerted step back. "And I'll…I'll…throw a tantrum! Yes! I'll go full-blown Pregzilla on your asses."

"She will, dude," Mojo whispers at Hatch. "I've seen it happen before."

I cross my arms. "Will you huff and puff and blow the guest house down too?"

"Oh, that's real nice. Let's all have a laugh at the pregnant girl's expense." Palmer's face splotches with pink. "I'm just one big joke to you guys, aren't I?"

I see tears filling her eyes, a shiny glaze to them that hurts my heart. "Wait, no…" The tremble on her bottom lip seals the deal. "Palmer, stop!" I'm mortified at having affected her so. "Look, just stop it, please? I'll tell you, all right?"

"You will?" she sniffles.

"Yes. Put Pregzilla back in her cage. I promise I'll tell you everything."

Palmer's face lights up, all pretend-anger melting away. She wipes away the fake tears, bursting into a villainous smile. "Finally! Took you long enough."

Hatch and Mojo snicker in unison.

I glower at her. "You're severely insufferable."

"You mean highly effective." Palmer nudges me impatiently, tapping her toe to help drive home the point. "And I believe I'm owed an explanation. So chop, chop! Let's hear it."

"Fine," I growl. "I found a hidden passageway at Cliffmoor House—"

"*A hidden passageway?*" Palmer's face reminds me of Leif's—all childlike wonder and excitement, like I've handed her a giant rainbow lollipop at the fair. "Through where?"

"The safe room."

"What safe room?"

"Oh, oops. Let me back up. There's a safe room, beneath the parlor—"

Palmer squeals—actually squeals. "*Ehmygod!* Let's go right now!"

"No!" I blurt out quickly. "That's not a good idea."

"Why the heck not?"

"I just don't think we should be going down there. It's really dark, and the steps are steep. It'd be easy for you to fall."

"I'll be careful, Dell, geez. I'm pregnant, not blind."

"No, Palmer, you don't understand—"

"Look." She fixes me with a stern expression. "All I understand is that you're trying to keep me from doing something *fun*. I'm sick of everyone acting like I should be covered in bubble wrap! You all think I'm incapable of doing anything for myself—"

"I found a body down there!" I exclaim, eliciting wide eyes from the others. Hatch shakes his head, lips pressed tight, as though he knows I've made a critical error by letting this detail slip.

"A *dead* body?" Palmer asks, incredulous.

"Obviously," Hatch mutters, garnering a scowl from her.

"A skeleton, technically," I say.

"Um…" Mojo lifts a finger. "I hope I speak for everyone present when I ask, '*What the actual fuck?*'"

I nod. "That pretty much covers it."

"Where are the cops?" Palmer asks. "How are they not swarming this place right now?"

"No cops," I insist. "You know Tristen doesn't want them around." Palmer starts to protest, but I hold up a hand to stop her. "You wanted to be in the know? For me to trust you? Well, there you have it. *No cops.*"

"Fine." She nods, a roguish twinkle in her eyes. "Do you know who it is?"

"We don't know yet, but Tristen has 'people' for that apparently."

"People for what?" Palmer asks slowly.

"Testing bodily remains, I assume."

"How messed up do you have to be to have bone-testers on your payroll?" Mojo says under his breath.

"Tristen-level messed up," Palmer replies succinctly. "So let's go down and take a peek, shall we?"

Mojo gapes at his wife, shock melding with horror.

"Oh, don't look at me like that." She waves him off.

He scoffs. "I'm just wondering when the lobotomy fairy swooped in and scrambled your brain. There is absolutely *no way* we're going down there, Palm."

"I'm with Mojo," I say firmly. The sight of those disintegrating bones, that mass of hair, the ritualistic setup, had me doubling over and emptying my stomach. Palmer doesn't need that kind of stress right now.

"Fine, be babies about it! I'm going with or without you." She marches back onto the lawn, leaving us to chase after her.

"Palmer, this isn't funny, okay?" I call at her back. "It's gross and creepy and it made me sick—"

"So what?" She turns around, eyebrows raised. "You survived."

"That's not—"

"Not what, Dell? I'm going out of my mind here. I want to do something exciting! I can't drink, can't party, can't run, can't overexert myself, can't pick up heavy objects, can't do this, can't do that." Her eyes are beseeching. "Don't push me to the fringes like everyone else. Please."

I wish I shared Palmer's gutsy outlook—the sense of wild abandon flaring like lightning in her eyes—but all I feel on the cusp of our little excursion is deep, foreboding dread. Exploring the tunnel with Hatch is one thing. But the four of us? Quite another.

"Babe, c'mon, I don't like this," Mojo says.

"It'll be fine," Palmer insists, giving his arm a squeeze. "Let's have an adventure together! Make some memories we can share with Mia someday."

She takes off toward Cliffmoor House with a spirited skip in her step. Mojo races after her, with Hatch and I trailing behind.

Memories.

I have a sinking feeling these won't be the kind we'll want to revisit at the dinner table.

CHAPTER TWENTY-THREE

We huddle close together in the dimly-lit parlor, everyone waiting with bated breath for me to make a move.

I'd half-expected Tristen to have the room barricaded, in an effort to keep me out of the tunnel and far from whatever depraved activities took place there. But, to my relief, he's done no such thing. Though now, with Palmer champing at the bit to get inside, I almost, *almost* wish he had.

I brush my hand along the top shelf while the others watch on with wide, anticipating eyes. They remind me of the Mystery Inc. gang on the cusp of a "Jinkies" worthy discovery. The only one missing from our little crew is Scooby.

My fingertips dust over the metal latch embedded in the wood, and my heartbeat skitters. *Here we go.* I hook a finger through it and tug the latch upwards.

The wall spreads apart with a groan, exposing the crevice of standing space beyond it, and the narrow flight of steps descending to an inky abyss.

"Whoa," Palmer breathes, her bright eyes shimmering through the shadows.

"I don't like this," Mojo mutters for the umpteenth time. He's unequivocally the Shaggy of our group.

If Palmer hears him through her slack-jawed astonishment, she doesn't make it known. "I've been in this room *hundreds* of times. I can't believe I never knew this was here!"

"Let's debate our options real quick." Mojo oscillates his hands like weights on a scale. "Creepy underground murder-lair, or melty, cheesy complex carbohydrates? Carbs win by a landslide, right? So why don't we go for that pizza instead?"

"Go ahead, Dell." Palmer nudges me forward, ignoring her husband's fearful ramblings. "Lead the way."

Mojo hangs his head, hissing out a breath through his teeth.

"It's dark down there," I warn them. "I'm talking pitch-black. We'll need plenty of light."

"I've got my cell phone," Palmer says.

"Me too," Hatch says, plucking the device from his pocket.

"There should be a couple flashlights in that drawer as well." Palmer points to a table in the corridor, and Hatch goes to retrieve them.

"I'll take this too." I grab the fire poker from the hearth, clasping it with both hands and hugging it close to my chest. Three pairs of eyes latch onto the iron rod, then slide up to my face in morbid question. "Just in case," I add, with what I hope is a casual shrug.

"You're taking us to a torture chamber, aren't you?" Mojo chokes out.

"Not helping, dude," Hatch mutters, his voice strained and low.

I hadn't asked Hatch what he thought of all of this. Palmer's exasperating tenacity had stolen the show, as had my mounting concern over her wellbeing. But I can tell by the way he barely speaks—his posture stiff, jaw tight—that he's not happy. Not totally on board with the security afforded us by one fire iron and a couple measly flashlights.

"Are you kindergarteners about done stalling yet?" Palmer asks, her eyebrows arched in petulant demand. I'd love to smack them plumb off her forehead.

Mojo flashes me wild eyes, begging me to do or say something discouraging. *Anything* to deter his wife from this ill-conceived mission. But as far as I can tell, there's no undoing this. Palmer is getting into those tunnels, whether we tag along or not.

"Fine," Mojo groans before wrapping a hand in Palmer's. "Let's get this over with."

A tingle of excitement slow-crawls across my limbs.

Creepy tunnels, take two.

Flashlights flick on behind me as I step inside the crevice. We descend in a line—adrenaline-fueled and charged with varying degrees of giddiness and terror. Twenty-one steps later, I hit the landing, turn the door knob, and slip inside the safe room, switching on the overhead light.

Mojo whistles, saucer-eyed, when he enters the space.

"This place is incredible!" Palmer cries out in awe, taking in the expansive room and its countless luxuries. "What's it all for?"

"Emergencies, I guess? A place to keep safe from intruders, or to hunker down in case of some natural disaster—"

"Or to hide in, if you're running from the cops," Hatch suggests, walking across the room to inspect the wood-paneled wall up close.

I stare at the back of his caramel hair, my mind racing in time with the pounding of my heart. "You think Florian came through here?"

"Maybe he used it as a hideout after the wedding, long enough to make some calls, secure a pilot and a plane to get him off the island. Seems like it'd be a good place to hole up until the coast clears." Hatch shrugs. "It's possible, right?"

Where the Klynes are involved, anything is possible. Which only makes this harebrained adventure of ours that much more nerve-wracking.

"Where's the entrance to the tunnel?" Palmer asks, coming to stand by Hatch near the back wall.

Steadying my nerves, I approach it too, running my hand along the slatted panels until I hit the right one and push. It swings inward a few inches, enough to make everyone gasp in unison.

I plant both hands on it and push again, using more force this time to make it swivel. Then I slip inside, swallowed up in thick brine and blackness, the tunnel stretching before me.

Hatch is close at my back—so close I can feel his breath on my hair, smell the clean citrus of soap on his skin. He aims his flashlight down the narrow passage, his hand finding my hip, squeezing it protectively. "Why don't you let me go in front?"

I turn to look at him, though his face is devoured in shadow, his eyes mere reflections of that distant stream of light. "This isn't my first rodeo, remember?"

He grunts in disapproval, but his hand lingers on me still, fingers curled into that sliver of skin between my shirt and jeans, the pressure of them a soothing comfort…and a delicious distraction.

Palmer and Mojo step through behind him, the four of us clustered at the mouth of the domed tunnel.

"It's cramped in here," Palmer comments.

"And it smells like shit," Mojo adds, his flashlight shooting wildly in all directions. "Musty shit."

"Keep to the center," is my only response. That part of the tunnel offers the most standing room, whereas the sides dip unexpectedly into walls—their rocky, curved edges easier to knock against.

"Stay close," Hatch breathes into my ear as we start walking, his hand never leaving my side. "Don't run off on me."

I let myself soften against his chest momentarily, humming in agreement. Close is the only way I'm willing to do this.

We move in silence for several long minutes, walking in a line, adjusting to the darkness, the cold, and the salt. Eventually, Palmer whispers above our crunching footsteps, "Who carved all this out?"

"No idea," I reply honestly.

"Do you think Ambrose is behind it?" she asks.

Our grandfather's name sweeps through the tunnel like smoke, curling up in every shadowy corner, licking up the walls, pooling at our feet.

A shiver runs through me. "Maybe."

Moments later, the flashlights illuminate a fork up ahead. "Which way?" Hatch asks, swinging his light from left to right. Both diverging passages look nearly identical.

"Left," I say confidently.

Soon, we come upon that familiar opening—the ritual room, as I've come to think of it. I hang back in the tunnel, sinking down into a squat position, my back pressed to the far wall, while the others fan out inside. I let them absorb the contents of the strange space on their own, submersed in quiet observations—silent questions to which scarce answers exist.

I don't dare step inside and glimpse those rotting bones again.

"Where are they?" Hatch asks after several minutes, poking his head out of the room.

"What?" I ask.

"The bones," Palmer says from within. "They're not here."

Not here?

Chills cascade down my spine as I will myself to join them inside, eyes scanning for that misshapen form of bone and hair. But Palmer's right. They're gone.

"S-she was right here," I stammer.

"Hold the phone—*she?*" Mojo shakes his head. "Oh, hell no. A woman? Why does that make this feel so much worse?"

"What do you mean she was here, Dell?" Hatch asks me, honing in on the more disturbing point.

"I mean she was literally *right here*, Hatch. Right at the center of all of this." I wave my hands at the collection of macabre items.

"Are you sure?" Palmer asks.

"Yes, I'm sure! The bones were here hours ago. I got so freaked out when I saw them, I even dropped my—"

Every hair on the back of my neck stands erect as the memory unfolds behind my eyes.

When I'd seen the pile of remains and jumped back, I dropped the candelabra before rushing from the room, sick to my stomach. I'd forgotten to retrieve it when I fled back to Cliffmoor House. And now the candelabra is missing. As are the bones.

"Someone's been here," I say in a shaky, echoing voice. "I brought a candelabra down with me this morning. I dropped it right here." I point to the gravelly place where I'm certain it fell. But there's nothing there now, the ground undisturbed. It's as if I'd made the whole thing up. Concocted a horror story.

The men aim their flashlights all across the room, looking for the candelabra, the bones, any bit of what I'd described…to no avail.

"There's no candelabra, Dell," Palmer says, remarking on the obvious.

"Don't you think I see that?" I snap.

"Well, what does it mean?" Mojo asks, a quaky edge to his voice. "Were you just, like, hallucinating or something?"

"Oh, come off it." I can't keep from rolling my eyes. "Hallucinating? Really?"

"I don't know! Maybe you had a few too many of Leon's special brownies last night—"

"No!" I squeal.

"I think we're way past weed brownies, man," Hatch says, his flashlight up by his chin, scanning and squinting into each corner.

"All right, everyone calm down," Palmer interjects. "There must be some logical explanation for this."

"There is," I retort. "Someone came through here after I left. They saw the candelabra, realized someone *else* had been snooping around, and decided to move the disintegrating body and cover up a potential crime scene."

Heavy silence permeates the room.

Mojo whistles low. "Shit just got real dark."

"You really think someone else knows about this place?" Palmer asks.

I don't bother answering her. I can't believe I didn't snatch up that damned candelabra the second it slipped from my fingers. Now, I have nothing. No proof. No bones.

Damn it.

"I'm not trying to change your story here, Dell, but…is it possible that you only *think* you saw a skeleton?" My eyes zero in on Mojo again. "No one would blame you!" he insists. "If I were down here alone, I'm sure I'd conjure up dead bodies too."

"Here we go again…" I fling my hands up, letting them slap hard against my thighs.

"I'm sorry, okay! I'm just trying to understand—"

"Why would I make this up?" I argue. "You think I'd do this for attention?"

"I didn't say it was for attention!" he exclaims. "Maybe it's just the stress of being back?"

"If this is all due to 'stress,' then where's the candelabra?" I ask. "It was one of those giant, three-armed, brass ones from the hall. Where did it go?"

Mojo lifts his shoulders, as if to excuse himself. "I don't know…"

"So there you have it! Someone picked up the candelabra and walked away with it. And I bet that same someone moved the bones too."

We fall silent, no one knowing what to say next, all of us quietly consumed with dread, but no one more than me. I *know* what I saw. And I've learned enough about this house not to ignore signs of the strange and twisted.

We aren't alone down here.

Aren't the only ones that know of this place.

"What now?" Palmer asks. I can sense her need to fill the dead silence that envelops us. To distract from the nauseous swirl in our bellies.

I side eye my cousin, amazed to find her looking relatively calm. *Of course she is.* She didn't see the bones. She hadn't been caught off guard by that tangled nest of raven-black hair.

"Here's an idea—how about we turn back?" Mojo sharply punctuates each word. "As in, back to civilization? That sounds *super* appealing."

"We can't leave yet," Palmer whines. "We haven't even seen anything. What else is down here, Dell?"

"This is as far as I came last time, but we could try walking a little farther that way…"

Mojo bristles, fixing me with a glare.

I don't want my pregnant cousin here any more than he does, but this latest development has prompted a raging fire I can't ignore.

Who found my candelabra and moved those damn bones?

Is someone actively using this tunnel system?

"Dell, if you really believe someone else is down here—someone sick enough to transport corpses—then I don't think we should keep going," Hatch says, his persuasive eyes reaching for me, but I refuse to meet them. I don't want to concede. Despite the horrors we may find, I need answers.

"C'mon, don't be such scaredy cats!" Palmer slips out of the room and back into the tunnel. We file out after her. "Let's peek out a bit further, see if we find anything interesting."

She pushes onward, and Mojo rushes in front, brandishing the flashlight ahead of him like a sword, shooting long streams of white into the overwhelming black, while Hatch and I drag a few paces behind.

"I'm not lying," I say to him over my shoulder, though he didn't ask or question my integrity. I just need him to believe it, more than any of the others. I need him to realize how serious I am. "There *was* a pile of bones in there. I swear it."

"I believe you." His hand settles on my hip again. "But that only makes me more worried about being down here."

"I know, but Palmer—"

"It's not *just* Palmer, Dell. It's you too. This is like a sick repeat of last year."

"What do you mean?"

"You running headlong into dangerous situations. Me trailing after you, scared you'll wind up dead. Desperately needing you not to be."

I put my hand over his, hoping to sound reassuring when I say, "This time's different, Hatch."

He scoffs. "How do you figure?"

"Because we're together. Nothing bad happens when we're together."

It's true. Hatch and I are untouchable together. It's when we separate that things tend to go awry.

"Guys, check this out!" Palmer calls up ahead, as she and Mojo turn into a second small room. The glow of Mojo's flashlight fades as they venture inside, and Hatch and I hasten our steps to catch up.

Shallow shelves are carved into the rock walls of the space.

Rudimentary ledges spanning from ground to ceiling, all of them occupied with little glass jars.

An indistinct memory shakes loose in the back of my mind, like a vague and deeply repressed déjà vu.

"What is this stuff?" Mojo asks, nearing one of the shelves and grabbing a container. He shakes it, and the contents make a trickling sound, like hard candies in a tin.

I approach them too, aiming Hatch's flashlight at the rows of identical jars. I can't make out whatever's inside, their filmy glass exteriors obscuring the contents from view.

I swipe my fingers over one of them—even using some spit and the edge of my shirt to wipe away the filth—but that only smears it worse. Finally, I twist the lid on the jar and pour the contents into my hand.

Tiny round capsules glare up at me, a blood-red color I've only seen once before.

Where they touch, they stain my palms crimson.

A pungent floral scent wafts up in the humid air.

"Are those—" Hatch starts to ask.

"Sea trumpets," I whisper, an ache awakening in my bones I thought I'd put to rest long ago.

CHAPTER TWENTY-FOUR

"Since when are sea trumpet pills a thing?" Mojo asks, coming to stand beside me.

We twist the lids off several more jars. All of them are filled with small, unassuming capsules—every last one a bloody sea trumpet-red.

"I thought the Brine used to eat the sea trumpets whole?" Palmer pipes up nervously. "When did they start making them into *this*?"

I shake my head, completely unprepared for the deluge of memory washing over me. "They've gotten more sophisticated, their methods more varied. I've seen sea trumpets crushed into powders. Melted into liquids. And, yes, even manufactured into pill form. Like this."

I recall the vivid red tablets from the laboratory where Greer and the others held me captive. These little glass containers, though grimy with crud, look *exactly* as those had.

"This supply must be old," Hatch says, as if trying to convince himself. "From before the police arrested Greer and the others. From when they were still cultivating sea trumpets in the fields."

"God, I hope so," I whisper, my insides screaming for release.

Screaming for me to sprint back up to Cliffmoor House, back to open air where I can breathe easier. Or, even better, back to the mainland and *off* this hellish rock.

The tunnels are unnerving enough on their own—a dark domain concealed beneath the sun-soaked one above, another secret to tack onto the Klynes' running list—but paired with the discovery of sea trumpets, it's horrifically worse. Too cruel and mystifying a coincidence that I'm the one to find it.

A nightmarish possibility slams into me, and I suck back a strangled breath.

"What is it?" Hatch asks urgently. He swings his flashlight in a wide circle, looking for whatever might've startled me in the shadows.

"I just remembered something," I rasp. "From when the Brine took me." A painful, primal drumming pulses maddeningly in my ears, as if the very heartbeat of this wretched island has slid inside my body to torture me. "They held me underground in this facility they'd built to keep their operations hidden, and I saw hundreds of jars like these, all lined up in medicine cabinets…" My gut twists at the resurfacing image. "And I was dragged through a tunnel just like this one—a tunnel that seemed to have no conceivable end. I didn't give it much thought then. I was too focused on trying to make it out alive…"

No one speaks as I squirm in place, trying to form clear words of my nebulous thoughts. "What if this tunnel is connected to theirs? What if it's all part of one giant system, stretching from Cliffmoor House all the way to the fields?"

"Tunnels long enough to span half the island?" Hatch's brow furrows.

"Is that so impossible?" I ask. "Considering everything we know about the Brine?"

"Definitely within the realm of possibility," Palmer agrees.

"Building something that massive would've been an undertaking," Mojo says, sniffing from an open pill jar before wrinkling his nose and coughing. "It would've had to have been excavated around the time Blackbane started the Brine, right?"

Palmer snaps her fingers. "Remember how our moms moved to New Orleans with Gram before Willow was born?"

"Yeah…"

"Ambrose stayed behind to oversee renovations at Cliffmoor House! They took nearly a year to complete." She bunches her shoulders around her neck. "What if he contracted workers to carve out these tunnels in secret?"

"For what purpose?" Hatch asks.

"Nothing good," I mutter.

"We already know Florian was involved with the Brine," Palmer says. "It only makes sense that they would—"

Her words cut off sharply as she whips around, ears perked. "Did you guys hear that?"

The rest of us stand at military-attention, holding our breaths as we strain to listen. But there's nothing. No distant voices, nor the shuffle of feet. Not the scrambling pitter-patter of rats, nor the slow drip of water.

"There it is again!" Palmer takes a few hurried steps forward, chasing that inaudible sound down the tunnel. "You don't hear it?"

"Hey!" Mojo calls after her, his tone severe. His hand wraps around her wrist, keeping her from bolting. "What's gotten into you?"

"You really don't hear that?" Palmer looks between the three of us, her eyes finally landing on mine, as if I'm her last hope. "Dell?"

I swallow hard, sure that there must be something I'm missing. "What does it sound like?"

"Whispers," she says softly. "Not words, exactly. More like…breaths? Echoey, whisper-breaths?"

I hadn't mentioned that to Palmer before—the fact that I'd heard the same thing earlier today. Vague breathy sounds, like wisps of fog in the darkness. "I heard them earlier," I confess. "Not now though."

"Whispers?" Mojo repeats, peering into his wife's face.

"Yeah, but it's almost like I'm hearing them in my head." Palmer puts her hands to the sides of her temples. "Like they wormed inside my brain or something."

I hear Mojo's angry exhale, feel the heat radiating from his body.

"*Now* are we all in agreement that it's time to get the hell out of here?"

"Absolutely," I say, wanting nothing more than to get Palmer firmly aboveground.

We trek back in silence, Hatch's hand slipping to my waist again as we trail behind Palmer and Mojo, our feet carrying us swiftly to the fork. We're turning right toward Cliffmoor House when—

"There!" Palmer snaps her neck left and changes direction, speeding down the opposite tunnel. It's as if her movements aren't being controlled by her, but by some silent, sinister puppeteer, tugging strings hewn of darkness and shadow.

"Palmer!" we shout, charging after her.

"It's a woman's voice!" she calls back as she runs. "The whispers…she's crying…"

"Okay, enough of this," Mojo fumes, catching Palmer's hand before she sprints away again. "Babe, listen to me. It's time to go."

I can't tell whether Palmer's listening or not, her attention rapt on that indistinct sound in the distance. The echoes—those whispered cries— have utterly captivated her, flooded her ears like some foreign invader and made a home of her brain.

I'm caught between tending to Palmer and taking in this strange new path, one I haven't yet explored. The domed tunnel itself is much like the one we'd just come from—cool and damp with a briny air, black as the ebony, midnight sky.

In the distance, there's something else, beyond our flashlight beams. Hatch asks, "What's that?"

Our eyes squint into the farthest reaches of the tunnel, where a small light source glows faintly.

"It looks like it's moving," I whisper. The light weaves and bobs, like a flickering candle reflecting over the walls. And whereas I hadn't felt outright scared before, now, with the imminent potential of facing something—or *someone*—down here, my mind stretches and bends like taffy, my heart pounding stampede-wild.

"That's it…" Palmer takes a few steps toward the light, but Mojo slides around her, planting himself in front—a barrier to keep her from going any further.

"Other way, sweet cheeks."

"But Mojo," she breathes softly, peering out at that light like it might hold the answer to every question. "What is that—"

"It doesn't matter. Let's get you home."

Instinctively, I back up a few steps…and slam into a solid mass occupying the very center of the tunnel.

Icy, wrinkled hands catch my arms.

A shriek rips from my throat as I fumble with the fire poker.

Hatch is at my side in a blazing instant, wresting me back from whoever grabbed me in the dark. I hurtle against his chest and we stumble backward, pummeling into Mojo, who's made himself a human shield over Palmer. She squeals from within her husband's arm-cage.

Hatch aims his light down the tunnel while Mojo takes things a step further and *lobs* his flashlight over our heads at the intruder…

Striking Briggs squarely in the chest.

"Oof—" The butler staggers back, groaning from the impact. He crashes against the nearest rock wall.

"Briggs!" I cry in surprise.

He clutches his chest, panting out heavy breaths. "M-miss Dell?" He sounds terrified, and terribly confused.

"What are you doing down here?" My shock rapidly shifts to suspicion.

"I was just…in the parlor…" He still hasn't caught his breath. Usually so eloquent and soft-spoken, he pants out his words in short, throaty spurts. "The wall was open…I went down…into the safe room…noticed the painting…had been moved…heard your voices…through the wall…pressed my ear to listen…it swung in…I nearly fell through…"

"You didn't know about this place?" I ask. My eyes narrow at him, an eerie sensation settling across my skin.

"No," he says emphatically, a hand still splayed over his chest. "I never realized…all this existed beneath Cliffmoor House."

"Then why'd you come down here on your own?" My question sounds like an accusation, and maybe it is.

Briggs doesn't answer right away, so I follow up with another set of questions. "Why didn't you tell Tristen? Get him to send Payne to investigate?"

"Master Tristen...has retired for the evening," Briggs says, trying to recover his normal pattern of breath. "It was an old man's curiosity...forgive me, miss."

I want to believe him—he's certainly never given me any reason to doubt his loyalty before—but I've been manipulated by so many. What do I really know about Briggs, anyway? People don masks all the time on this island. Shielding cruel intentions behind poisonous smiles.

Mojo clears his throat. "We were just leaving."

"Yes, of course...we should all be...getting back." Briggs ducks his head low, seeming truly repentant—humiliated. At himself, and at me. We've never had such a contentious exchange. Never had anything but tender words for each other. I can tell he takes my irritability to heart.

"I'm deeply sorry...for having frightened you, Miss Dell. I hope you trust that I meant you no harm."

Briggs shuffles back the way he came. Hatch cups a hand over my shoulder, urging me up the tunnel behind him, with Palmer and Mojo close at my back.

Before we depart, I turn once more to spy that faint flicker in the distance—the light source that had captivated us, that had set the sweat gliding down my back and clinging fast to the nape of my neck.

But, just like the bones and the candelabra, the bobbing light is inexplicably gone.

"You really think Briggs has something to do with those tunnels?"

Hatch and I are alone, back inside the guest house. Mojo had whisked Palmer home as soon as we made it back to the parlor, and Briggs had disappeared as well, mumbling something about needing to tend to the laundry. That left the two of us, along with all of our tangled thoughts and questions.

"Why else would he go down there on his own?"

"For exactly the reason he told you, Dell—he was curious. That's why you ventured down there all alone too, remember?"

He's right, of course. I got curious and followed an impulse. Briggs' motives might've been just as benign…

Then again, how could he *not* know about the tunnels in the first place? How many times in the last fifty years had Briggs cleaned that very safe room? Had he never moved the painting, or discovered that swinging panel? Had Ambrose never confided in him?

"Don't you trust Briggs?" Hatch asks, pulling me back from the flurry of confusion plaguing my mind. "I don't take him for a liar. Do you?"

"No," I admit. "But I've been wrong before."

Prescott's face swims in that space of air between us—those sleepy eyes like the devil's, so sly and unassuming, concealing his inner depravity from a world that would only see a troubled kid.

Yes, indeed. I'd been *very* wrong before.

Briggs has only ever been a loving, nurturing friend, but that doesn't make him exempt from corruption. His supposed affair with my grandmother is proof-positive of that, though I've never made a point to confirm that story with Tristen. Would my cousin be forthright about it? About *any* of the claims he'd made against the Klynes?

"Tristen is sending Nova and her people down the tunnels tomorrow," I mention absently.

Hatch arches a brow, a sigh dripping from his lips. "Is there any point in me asking you not to go with them?"

I lift a shoulder. "You can ask, but I'm still going."

"Figures," he mutters. "And here I thought you were concerned about Nova's connections with the Brine."

"I am, but Tristen trusts her," is all I can think to reply. "If I want to stay in the know, I need to play nice with his pets." Which means that, against my better judgment, Nova is currently my only chance at uncovering what the heck is going on in those tunnels. "Who knows," I add hopefully, "maybe she'll prove to be useful. Maybe she'll have some notion of what all of this means."

"While we're on the subject of the Brine," Hatch says, "I figured something out you might find interesting. It's about 'Brine Survivor.'"

I feel my eyes grow in anticipation. "She responded to your email?"

"No such luck," he says. "But I think I've zeroed in on where she lives."

"How?"

"She posted a photograph on her blog of this community garden next to her mobile home. I could see the house pretty clearly in the background. It took me a minute, but I recognized the neighborhood. It's in Midtown, in a little trailer park called Shell's Shores. I was thinking we could go tomorrow, after you get off work. It shouldn't be too difficult to find her place. The house is bright orange, with quirky little suns painted on the vinyl siding—"

"Suns?" I can't help but to snort. "That's…crafty."

Hatch shrugs, a pensive sort of empathy swimming in his eyes. "Maybe she's just trying to keep the darkness at bay."

A swift pang of remorse hits me.

"Aren't we all?" I reply, offering him a sheepish smile. It's mostly said in jest, but the rasp of my voice—that audible, strangled bite of emotion—isn't lost on Hatch.

There's a sudden shift, the moment turned sober. I feel my face burn under his probing gaze, my cheeks flushed pink, my neck and palms slick and muggy. The overwhelming truth of my deprecating words, along with every one of the burdens seizing my heart, sweeps over me like a wave.

Not quite knowing why, I drop my gaze to the floor.

Hatch sees my struggles more than anyone else, discerning everything I try to keep hidden. He knows how hard it is for me to rise from the pits of despair each morning. How tendrils of memory coil like serpents around my neck—nooses to smother my joy, my peace. How the torments of my past constantly threaten to snuff out the light.

The fight to keep the darkness at bay is the only life I know.

Tears well in my eyes without warning.

Hatch saunters forward and my gaze snaps up, glimpsing the whispered storm rippling in his sparkling eyes. He keeps the full force of that tempest under wraps—those riotous green seas restrained and quiet—

yet always on the cusp of a fierce unleashing.

Before I know it, his hands are gripping my hips, pushing me gently until the kitchen counter bites into my lower back. "Let me take the darkness away," he pleads, his voice a low, earth-shaking rumble. "I'll steal the sun for you, if that's what you need."

I wrap my arms around his neck, running needy fingers through his hair. "Steal the sun?" A shaky laugh trickles from my lips.

Hatch hums in agreement. "Tell me what you need, and I'll do exactly that."

One lone tear escapes me, a scalding stream gliding down my cheek. Hatch wipes it away with his thumb. "What do you need?" he murmurs, the words hot against my lips.

"All I need is you," I whisper, struck by my own breathless honesty.

All I need is you. A simple, yet vital realization.

In Hatch's presence, my fight against the darkness—the demons— gets infinitely easier. My burdens lighter, wounds staunched of their bleeding. He's the antidote to that soul-crushing pain. The infrangible rope that keeps me from tumbling over the edge.

His returning grin is beautiful—a golden, honey-sweet thing— drenched in light and warmth and desire. "You already have me, love. But what about the sun?"

I smile as widely as I can through the misty film of tears, hoping to convey even a speck of the love I feel for him with the gesture.

"If I have you, Hatcher Seaborn, then that's all the sun I need."

CHAPTER TWENTY-FIVE

I'm up before dawn the following morning, shaking off the gritty remains of last night's escapades. Early morning darkness spills through the curtains of the room, a faint stream of blue-tinged moonlight dripping across the bed. Cool sheets slip from my shoulders when I sit up, with a sickening, flowery scent trapped in the back of my throat.

Sea trumpets.

I peel myself from the bed, throwing my legs over the side of it. Before making for the bathroom, I roll my shoulders, stretch my back, wiggle my toes, and—

What the hell?

Fumbling in the dark, I reach for the lamp on the bedside table, my fingers frantic in their search for the switch. A soft, amber glow fills the room. I stare down at my feet…

Only to find them coated in sand.

I hadn't gone to bed this way. I was wearing sneakers last night, for goodness' sake. I'd even showered after Hatch left—a futile effort to scrub away the lingering vestiges of the sea trumpets and the fear they'd sowed in me. I certainly hadn't been to the beach. At least, not that I remember.

Staggering to the bathroom mirror, I flick on the light and drink in the sight of my reflection. My cheeks are ruddy, eyes puffy from a restless night, but it's my hair that truly captures my attention. My dark waves are a tangled, windblown mess. Knotted. Mussed. But not from sleep…

Like I'd been standing for hours by a gusty ocean.

And I don't recall doing any such thing.

The parlor is night-dark while I wait for Nova to arrive. The door is closed, curtains drawn, the opulent room quiet and waiting for purpose. I sink into the shadows, entrenched in silent debate over how on earth I'd wound up on the beach without knowing it.

My fingers ball into a fist, a rust-red residue *still* marring my palm from those damn pills. Had I been sleepwalking? As far as I know, I've never sleepwalked in my life. Had the sea trumpets triggered a somnambulant reaction in me? Weird, but not impossible, I guess.

Was it delirium? Exhaustion? A dream, maybe, or something worse? Some strange calling to the sea? Back to Willow's watery grave?

Scuffling feet and voices fill the hall—Nova and her team filing in.

She enters the parlor after a few minutes, dressed in her customary tactical garb, and accompanied by a large, burly man donning similar gear and a scowl. The pair of them look like vigilante soldiers—stealthy and capable—entering the room without a sound.

Their eyes come to land on me in the dark.

A light flicks on. "Dell!" Nova's surprised smile is a harsh contrast to her attire. "I didn't expect to see you here."

I stand from my place on the couch, not bothering to return the greeting.

"This is my right-hand man, Tank," she says. Tank nods curtly, looking every bit like his namesake—stocky, muscular, and like he'd steamroll over anyone who'd dare get in his way. "We're about to get our equipment set up. We've got a long day ahead—"

"Enough with the small talk," I say. Nova's eyebrow flicks up at my brusque response. "Did Tristen tell you what I found?"

"Yes. We've been informed about the—"

"Great," I cut her off again. "I'd like to have a chat with you, before we head down."

"We?" Nova asks, her very tone a protest. As suspected, she doesn't want me tagging along.

"Try and stop me," I say, my words snappy as a whip. "I've walked those tunnels twice now. I don't need your permission to do it again." I cross my arms over my chest, unyielding in my position.

"Twice," Nova repeats. "Tristen only mentioned the one time—"

"I went back with reinforcements," I say, filling in the blanks. "The bones are gone, by the way."

"What do you mean they're gone?"

"I'd be happy to fill you in on all the gruesome details. But first, we'll have that talk. Alone."

Nova—sensing my adamance on the matter—asks Tank to step outside so we can speak in private. Her partner grunts before stalking into the hall with one last glance at me, a pointed grimace on his lips. I glower in return. *Keep on walking, pea brain.*

Nova plants herself on the couch across from me, leaning forward attentively, elbows on her knees. Clasping her hands together, she maintains a calm demeanor when she says, "Okay, Dell. What would you like to talk about?"

I sit too, the motion slow as I study the woman before me, mimicking her confident posture—elbows propped on my knees, my body engaged and at the ready. "I know about your history with the Brine." Without even trying, my words come out soft and deadly quiet.

Nova swallows, but doesn't speak. To her credit, silence *is* better than a lie.

"I already bit Tristen's head off about it," I confess. "So I'm not here to do the same to you. But I want you to know, beyond a shadow of a doubt, that I don't trust you for a second." She blinks three times in rapid succession. "You're here solely and exclusively at Tristen's request. And though I don't agree with his choices, this is still his house, and, therefore, his call. But I'd like to get a few things off my chest, in advance."

"Okay." Nova runs her tongue along her top teeth. "What things?"

I lean in closer. "Under no circumstances are you and your team to attempt to access the guest house. There will be no security cameras set up inside, nor will I hand over my keys for you to replicate. In fact, after this morning, it'd be best if you and your guard dogs learn to keep your distance from me. Pretend I'm not even here. Pretend I'm a ghost." A scowl pricks at my mouth, my nose. "You may have charmed my cousin, but you haven't fooled me."

Her mouth falls a bit, working through all I've said.

"Look, Dell"—her eyes are like melted chocolate, rich and earnest—"I know you have every reason to doubt me, but I swear, I have no ill will toward you or your family. My exposure to the Brine was minimal, no more than a few years when I was a baby. I grew up with my grandmother, far away from all of that. I've *never* wanted anything to do with—"

I lift my hand, uninterested in Nova's overflowing excuses. Her exposure to the cult may have been minimal, but those early years are formative. Instrumental. And considering how skillfully Greer had roused Blackbane's children to her cause, I'm certain Nova could easily be swayed to do the same. The Brine's seeds are already planted within her, rooted deep, far beyond unearthing. They wouldn't be difficult to tap back into. To fuel and nurture once again.

"I don't need you to convince me of your innocence," I say. "Let me be perfectly clear: *we are not friends.* Tristen is paying you to do a job, so do it. But you'd also do well to respect my wishes."

"He's paying me to protect what he values," she counters. "That includes you—"

"Tough," I snap. "Tristen's will *cannot* infringe upon my own. If he has a problem with it, he can ask me to leave. That's between me and my cousin. Do you understand?"

"I understand." Nova nods solemnly. "But I truly mean you no harm."

"Unfortunately, I don't have the luxury of believing you."

She sighs. "Regardless of how you feel about me, Dell, you know I can't let you back in those tunnels. Not until we do a thorough sweep."

"Good thing I'm not asking. Let me put it to you this way, Nova—if you try to prevent me from going with you, I'll take that as definitive proof that you're hiding something. If you want me to believe you're not involved with the Brine, here's a starting point. Don't fight me on this. I've been down there before. I can help more than anyone."

Nova doesn't answer, likely weighing the potential outcomes—and dangers—of having me come along.

"I'm going, one way or another," I insist. "That is, unless you plan on physically restraining me, which would do wonders for your image and incur a great deal of trouble for your team." I smile cruelly. "I'm a delight when I want to be."

"Fine. But only to prove to you that I'm trustworthy." She pulls her gun from its holster, holding it up to the light for me to see. "Tank and I have the weapons, so you'll stay between us, all right?"

I shrug off her plea, already making for the break in the wall. "Glad you've come to see things my way."

Nova blows out a frustrated breath.

"Better get Tank back in here pronto," I call over my shoulder. "We're wasting time, and there's a lot of ground to cover."

Not bothering to wait for Nova's response, I forge ahead down the dark flight of stairs for what I hope is the last time.

CHAPTER TWENTY-SIX

"Where exactly did you see the remains?"

Nova, Tank, and I are in the ritual room, scouring the contents of it with our flashlights, scanning all the indefinable items covered in dirt and rot.

"Right here in the center," I say, pointing.

Nova shines her beam of light into the heart of the room, coming to stand directly where the bones had been yesterday. "Here?"

"Yes." I nod for emphasis. "The body—er, skeleton—looked to be intact. And"—I swallow hard, hating how much this next part gets to me—"there was some hair too."

"Tristen mentioned that." Nova bends down, her flashlight up by her face as she inspects the surrounding ground. "I see some strands here," she says quietly.

Pulling a clear baggie and a small brush from her pocket, Nova collects the dust and strands in the bag, then seals it tight. "We'll send these hairs for analysis. Hopefully some will still have the roots attached so they can be tested."

The conversation is enough to violently turn my stomach.

"What do you make of this place?" I ask her.

Glancing around the room once more, Nova grimaces. "Based on these items and the absent corpse, I'd say some sort of ritual sacrifice took place here."

"The Brine's work?" I ask, not caring that Nova might feel sorely after our chat.

"Could be," she replies honestly. "And it likely happened long ago. Decades, from the looks of it."

"Can hair really last that long after death?"

"If kept in dry conditions, hair can last for many years," Nova confirms. "Moisture decomposes hair. So if the body had been properly buried, the hair would've most certainly disintegrated by now. While it's pretty dank down here, it's not wet by any means. Not enough to cause hair to decay at a faster rate. My best guess is that this sacrifice happened a while ago."

"But those bones were moved yesterday," I remind her. "Sometime between ten in the morning and eight at night. Meaning *someone* is still using these passageways. Maybe they're even squatting down here."

Nova slips from the room into the tunnel, with Tank and I following suit. "How far did you get?" she asks, pointing her flashlight into the far distance.

"Just until the next room. Where we found the pills."

We reach it after five minutes of walking in silence, the shelves lined with enough drugs to send my brain into a tailspin.

"Yep, these are definitely sea trumpets," Nova mutters, cautiously sniffing at a jar she'd pried open, then handing it to Tank for him to have a whiff too.

"My cousin Palmer and I both heard something as well," I say. "There were these whisper sounds…"

Nova tilts her head, straining to listen. I do the same, anticipating those incoherent murmurs that slid in echoes through the tunnels yesterday. But all I can hear are the sounds of our shallow breathing and our feet crunching on the gravel. Part of me is glad for it. I've had my fill of inexplicable things. Whatever it was that caused the sounds Palmer and

I heard—whether scurrying critters or dripping water—it seemed to have left the tunnels with us yesterday. Followed us up and abandoned this place for good.

"What do you think?" I ask, for what must be the hundredth time.

"Well, considering all of this"—Nova waves a hand at the stocked shelves—"I'd say we have a good idea of where this tunnel might lead."

The sea trumpet fields. Just as I'd thought.

"Do you want to turn back, Dell?" Nova asks, eyes locked on my face. "You don't have to be here for this."

You'd like that, wouldn't you? the suspicious part of my mind snarls.

I shake my head, determined to see this through. "I'm fine to keep going. I want to know what this means." *Need* to know is more like it, for my own waning sanity.

"Let's push on, then," Nova says hesitantly, a crease carved into her brow.

I steel myself, ramming down my fear. Real or ruse, I don't want Nova's pity. I march past her, too arrogant for my own good—exuding confidence that's only for show—as I push deeper into the dark, musty tunnel ahead.

After another fifteen minutes of walking, the tunnel widens, like a giant mouth yawning open.

"What the hell is this?" I whisper as I take in the view. Or rather, the *lack* of view, our flashlights dwarfed by a vast and oppressive darkness like none I've experienced before.

The narrow tunnel spits us out into a massive, dome-shaped cavern—into a void that spreads far and wide, hungrily devouring every unlucky thing to get caught in its pitch-black maw. We shoot our thin slivers of light across it, the cavern at once colossal and confining.

I gasp at what I see inside, every sound and word exchanged between the others drowned out by the pounding of my heart.

Small aluminum boats—eight of them, as far as I can see—are stacked neatly to one side, two by two. They're smothered in patches of rust and grime, likely unusable in their present condition.

"Jon boats," Nova says, her sharp tone snapping me to attention.

"What?" I ask.

"Flat-bottomed boats," she explains. "See the squared-off shape of their bows? They're super stable. Lightweight."

"How did they get here?"

Nova whips her flashlight to the opposite edge of the cavern, where I can just make out a flight of rough stone steps leading downward.

We creep toward them, a salt-heavy scent bubbling from below.

The opening to the crude stairwell is ample enough to drag a small boat through with ease. But there's just one problem—there's no *accessing* the steps. They're inundated. Flooded. Fully submerged in—

"Water," Nova exhales. She bends down. "We must be close to the beach." I can sense the gears in her mind turning, trying to make sense of this. "Whatever passageway used to exist here—wherever it once emerged onto land—is gone now. The sea completely floods the exit."

"Can tidal patterns really shift that much?" I ask.

"Over time? Absolutely," she answers. "Rising sea level is no joke. Who knows if this whole island will be underwater fifty years from now."

The prospect of a climbing ocean slowly swallowing up an island is terrifying. But selfishly, where Halcyon Bay is concerned, the idea doesn't sound half bad.

"Who do you think used these boats?" I ask, my mind and eyes trained on that small, decrepit convoy. "What were they for?"

"Could've been marauders, or smugglers, or pirates," Tank offers up gruffly. When I turn to see if he's joking, his eyebrows soar. "Modern-day pirates. Not the 'walk the plank' type. More like the 'kidnap you for ransom' type."

I assess the worn condition of the boats, as well as the waterlogged steps at my feet. Years must've passed since pirates smuggled goods through this tunnel, years since this place was anything more than a dead end.

"Wouldn't pirates use bigger boats than this?" I ask, astounded to even be delving into this line of thought. "What would they be smuggling?

And how would it be connected to Cliffmoor House?" I know that neither of them have answers for me, but I can't stop myself from asking. "Were the Klynes ever known to deal with pirates?"

"We'll have to do some digging," Nova says. "This might explain the bones and the ritual room too. Who knows what kinds of sordid activities took place down here years ago."

"Well, clearly, no one's making it in and of the tunnel this way," I point out. "Meaning whoever passed through here yesterday must be entering from the other side."

Nova nods with conviction. "Onto the next."

We travel back in the opposite direction—up the length of one tunnel, across the fork, and down the second—until we reach an area where the passage widens, but not like in the Jon boat cavern. This section opens up to a sort of doorway. A wooden frame marks a shift in the tunnel, and beyond that frame, there are real walls and a ceiling. The domed rock transitions into metal…my surroundings suddenly eerily familiar.

I freaking knew it.

How had the cops not caught on to this? Had they not traced this tunnel back to Cliffmoor House? Had they not conducted a thorough search when they raided the fields last year? Worst of all, had they not incinerated all traces of the sea trumpets? Trashed all the drugs?

You already know the answer to that.

My steps grow angrier, less tentative on the ground. Nova glances over her shoulder, and, though she can't see me, whispers, "You doing okay?"

I don't respond, stewing in my inner fury.

"You recognize this place," she guesses, turning back to face whatever's ahead.

"Don't you?" I snap.

"No," she replies. "Do you remember your childhood before you turned three years old? Does anybody?"

A rush of heat floods me, because *of course I don't.* If I did, I'd remember Willow, and the few, precious moments we'd shared. I wish I could recall that far into my past, but memory doesn't work that way. Memory only takes. Pecks and nibbles away until all that's left are half-bitten morsels. Yet I'm still holding Nova to that unreasonable standard—pinning crimes on a woman who had no say in her parentage.

Nova interprets my silence and doesn't persist.

"I guess we know what that pipe in the tunnel was for," she comments when we reach a laboratory stocked with gas-powered stoves.

"A gas line," I whisper, appalled. A line running from Cliffmoor House to the fields, fueling the manufacture of narcotics.

"It's like *Breaking Bad* island edition," Tank murmurs under his breath.

We move on past the room where they'd kept me in my drug-induced state. Though vacant now, I recognize it just the same—white-walled and sterile and utterly terrifying.

We pass the subterranean greenhouse where Greer informed me of her murderous plot, but the blood-red sea trumpets are long gone, the space awash in charred blacks and moldy browns. At least the police had managed to accomplish this much, ridding the island of that flourishing crop.

We approach a set of stairs ascending to a sprawling metal door overhead, latched with an old, rusty padlock. Tank climbs the steps, pulling his gun from his waistband. He shoots the lock, the sound reverberating like a bomb through my body, my heart stuttering with shock. The lock goes flying. Tank pushes the doors open.

Daylight explodes around us, the stench of scorch and death rushing in on a sea blown breeze.

"Dell, wait—"

Ignoring Nova's warning voice and the pangs of terror in my chest, I stagger clumsily up the steps, wincing against that painful burst of light.

And spill onto the sea trumpet fields.

CHAPTER TWENTY-SEVEN

The Ranger greets me with a grumbling roar when I barge from the library at the end of my shift.

Hatch winks at me through the dusty windshield.

I sigh with deep, resounding relief.

Climbing up into his truck, I plant a quick peck on his cheek before melting into my seat, letting my head drop against the headrest.

Safe. Finally.

For the first time in hours, I can let my guard down. Strip back that cumbersome suit of armor, relinquish my sword, and be present with the one person I don't need to fake anything with.

"How'd it go today?" Hatch asks as he pulls out of the lot, sensing my slow and steady decompression.

"It was all right. Dex taught me to work the circulation desk." I know my answer is lackluster, but I'm struggling to put even those few words together.

"What about this morning with Nova?"

I can't muster the will to respond right away.

Hatch doesn't take his eyes off the road, but I can tell he's trying to fill the gaps of what I'm not saying, the information I'm not yet ready to share.

The truth is, I'd been suffocatingly quiet for much of today, inwardly processing the morning's events—confronting the memory of those wicked fields and the persisting wounds they'd left on me. Talking about it now feels like a monstrous endeavor. But with him—*for* him—I'll always try.

"Did you learn anything new about the tunnels?" he tries again.

"One of them leads to the sea trumpet fields," I drone, the admission plunking like a rock to my stomach, even after all the hours I've had to come to terms with it.

"Just like you suspected."

I nod. "That's what the gas line was for. To fuel the stoves the Brine used to make drugs."

"Wow. Any guesses why?"

"My most compelling theory is that Cliffmoor House is a demonic portal that spawns all sorts of evil shit."

"Makes sense," Hatch replies, humorless. "What about the other tunnel? Where does that one end up?"

"It used to spit out onto the coast somewhere," I say, keenly aware of how jaded and zombie-like I sound, "but it's not a viable pass-through anymore. The exit point is flooded. Nova said something about rising tide—about how it's pretty normal. Craziest thing is there were a bunch of little aluminum boats in this cavern right at the end of the tunnel. Nova thinks they might've been used by pirates or smugglers—"

"Your family has ties to pirates?" he asks.

I stare at him, eyebrows raised.

He smiles apologetically. "Right, right. You wouldn't know, of course. It's just so weird. Hard to wrap my head around."

Join the club, I think cynically. I've been trying to wrap my head around it for hours, and all it's afforded me is a gnarly headache.

We wind our way to the Midtown area, to a part of the island far less luxurious and manicured than Old Town. Out here, dilapidated trailer homes are packed in close, mangy strays populate the streets, and overflowing garbage bins line the crumbling sidewalks. It's wild that such disparate worlds can exist side-by-side on one tiny island.

We pass the Shell's Shores entrance gate—if you can even call the rusted hunk of warped chain-link a "gate." A neon welcome sign buzzes overhead, but I notice it's missing a pivotal *S* in the name.

"Welcome to *Hell's Shores*," I read.

This garners a crooked smile from Hatch.

We drive along the tightly-wound streets, in search of an orange house covered in a mural of suns. My heart twists at the sight of so many derelict, shanty homes. Hurricanes and tropical storms must wreak havoc on neighborhoods like this one. Who knows what the residents of this place have lost? How hard it's been for them to persist through the years?

"There it is." Hatch points out a pop of orange peeking out from between two other houses. When we near it—the very last trailer on the farthest block—we see a small vegetable garden perched beside it.

Bingo.

Hatch parks down the street and we disembark, cautiously approaching the screened door.

"Let me take the lead on this, okay?" I gesture at him to stay behind me. "We don't want to spook her, or appear threatening."

"Do I look particularly threatening today?" he asks, adjusting the backwards baseball cap on his head.

You look particularly delicious today.

An ache rises from my core as I let my eyes wander over his body. I quickly catch myself and shake off the ill-timed feeling. "Not particularly, no. But I'm clearly the least intimidating of us two."

Hatch chuckles. "I wouldn't be too sure about that."

I skip the steps up to the door and knock. After a few moments, it opens, revealing a shocking face inside. An icy rush of horror shoots straight to my head.

"Hi, Dell."

No.

That smile…

Those eyes…

"I was wondering when we might bump into each other again."

No.

He looks so different now, his face markedly less youthful. A striking pink line runs down the side of it, scar tissue cutting from temple to mid-cheek. A permanent effect of Tristen's handiwork with a shovel. His nose is sharper as well, crooked from how it must've healed after I broke it…

"This is such a lovely surprise."

NO.

I'm wrenched right back to last summer, to so many horrible recollections. Of being duped, drugged, and dragged onto the sea trumpet fields. Of being threatened—flirted with—at gunpoint.

Prescott's eyes dance with vicious thrill.

"How is this…how are you…" Coherent words evade me. My knees buckle, caving under my weight.

This can't be happening. I sway in place. *This can't be real life.* I'd just started feeling safe for the first time all day.

Hatch is there to bolster me, keeping me upright.

"Scotty!" screeches a haggard voice from within the trailer. "Who's at the door?"

Lettie—Prescott's mother.

Hatch has me by the elbow now, pulling me down the steps until I'm on solid ground again. I can feel his heartbeat through his t-shirt, like a thousand hooves beating against earth. I feel his muscles contract with rage, the chiseled panes of his body harder than stone. I grab his arm, needing to keep him at my side. To keep him from taking matters into his own hands. To keep this day from devolving into a bloody disaster.

"How are you back here?" I finally rasp at Prescott.

"Scotty! Who's at the damn door?" Lettie appears behind her son— all frazzled, silver hair, and that habitual grimace. Her wrinkled eyes narrow at me, viperous. "What the hell are you doing here?"

"You're 'Brine Survivor?'" I croak, the pieces snapping into place.

"What's it to you?" the woman shrieks.

Holy freaking hell.

Lettie is helming a self-directed anti-Brine movement. All while her son stokes its dying embers, helping to bring the Brine back to life.

And now, he's back. Back on the island. Back from prison. Living under her roof.

"Dell—" Prescott starts, taking a step out of the trailer into broader sunlight.

"Don't come any closer," I grit out at the same time Hatch growls, "Stay away from her," quickly shifting positions to plant himself in front of me.

"Relax, fish boy. I won't touch her." Prescott's voice is calm and emotionless—no longer the pleading liar from last summer, begging me to believe his manipulative stories. This Prescott doesn't twist himself into pretzels. This Prescott speaks plainly, casually, cruelly—the next stage in his psychotic development. Shifting from master actor to unfeeling predator.

"I want you both off my property right now!" Lettie squawks, hobbling inside. "I'm calling the police!"

"Don't, Mother." Prescott's sleepy eyes look bored, as if exhaustion overtakes him. "We're fine here."

"They can't be comin' around to harass you, Scotty!"

"Dell's not harassing me."

He peers into my face, and slivers of the boy I met last summer peek through the clouds of his flat, morose exterior. The boy that found some warped fascination in me. The one that wanted to impress me and show me things no one else could.

But that's also the same boy that shoved a gun into my side, threatened to rip my life from me, fought with me like a feral animal. That boy had drugged me without hesitation. That boy is a devil in disguise.

"How are you back?" I hiss again, unsure whether I'd rather him answer honestly or not at all.

"Good lawyers," Prescott replies without a second's hesitation. "I didn't think it was possible either. Your dear old cousin certainly fought tooth-and-nail to keep me locked up."

The ground seems to tremble beneath me. "My cousin?"

"You didn't know?" Prescott asks.

Everything slams into harsh focus.

Tristen was fighting to keep Prescott behind bars. Which means he knew there was a chance he would be released. That he'd be coming back to the island…

Yet Tristen had chosen to keep me in the dark about it. He'd brought me back here, and didn't say a damn word. More secrets. More omissions. More reasons to doubt his intentions.

"How about you come inside and we'll talk this out?" Prescott offers, his eyes briefly flicking to Hatch. "*He* can wait for you out here."

I gape at him. Come inside? Is he completely insane?

"Not on your life," Hatch growls.

I can tell from his stance that Hatch is itching to hit him—hands curled to fists at his side, knuckles stretched to stark-white. I can already picture them laced in blood, crusty with scabs.

I grab his hand, forcing his fingers to unclench to make room for mine. "Let's go," I breathe in his ear, letting Prescott and his mother and all of Hell's Shores melt from my vision until all that's left is *him*. My Hatch.

But Hatch doesn't budge.

"Hatch, look at me, please." Painfully slowly, he does. "Let's go," I repeat. "Let's go."

"Yeah, get out of here, and don't ever come back!" Lettie shrieks. From the corner of my eye, I catch Prescott gesturing at her to be silent.

Holding Hatch's hand, we walk swiftly to the Ranger, avoiding any and all distractions. That is, until Prescott ominously sneers at my back, "See you soon, Dell."

Those four words are an unleashing for Hatch.

Something in him snaps, like a tether at its breaking point, and there's *nothing* I can do to hold him back.

He turns on his heel, a bull seeing red, wrenching his hand from mine and rushing back to the trailer.

"Hatch, no!"

In a few sweeping steps, he's up the stairs, grabbing Prescott by the throat and slamming him against the trailer wall. Once, twice. All I see is a series of jarring movements—Prescott's neck snapping forward and back, his body swinging under Hatch like a boneless rag doll.

Lettie screams with all her might. "Help! You can't do this!" She runs in a chicken-scramble, searching for her phone. "Help, please! Someone help me! They're hurting my boy!"

"Hatch, stop it!" I claw at his arm, but Hatch doesn't respond, doesn't so much as register my touch. Another grating slam against the wall and Prescott's eyes roll back in his skull.

"Stop it! He's not worth it!"

"You're not going to see her soon, you miserable shit," Hatch growls over Prescott's limp form, their faces inches from each other. "You're not going to see her *ever*. Do you fucking understand?"

Prescott doesn't fight back. He just takes Hatch's battering with an unflinching expression. Even through the haze of multiple hard impacts to the head, a cold, calculated smile slides up Prescott's lip. Like he knew this was coming. Like he'd expected it. Wanted it.

"If I so much as see you sniffing around her, I'll do far worse than this." Hatch's eyes flare wildly, his jaw clenching, anger rippling across every inch of him. "I swear on my life, if there ever is a next time, you're going to wish I'd ended you right now."

"Hatch." I yank his arm with both hands, dragging him back down the stairs along with me.

"You won't get away with this! You attacked my boy!" Lettie continues to scream, while Prescott steadies himself, watchful eyes flitting from Hatch's face to mine.

"You can't stop it, fish boy," Prescott calls. "She'll come back to me eventually."

A cog slips loose in my brain.

She'll come back to me eventually.

The world turns all the way down, as if on mute.

Black clouds seep into my vision.

Hatred rips a hole through my chest.

I see nothing, feel nothing, but Prescott's slippery smile taunting me. Dripping over me like gasoline.

I strike a match, and ignite.

Letting go of Hatch, I bolt up those steps again. Prescott's eyes go wide, as if surprised by my boldness, then flicker with pain when I ram my knee into his groin. He slumps to the floor with a guttural moan.

Before I know what I'm doing, my sneaker is on Prescott's throat, pressing down harder, harder. He chokes, face blanching with fear. Exactly the reaction I'd wanted.

I lean in, applying more pressure, and he trembles beneath me. An electric rush crackles through me at seeing him cower and quake—a violent power settling into my bones. A reckless hunger for *more*.

I offer him a breathless smile, benumbed and out for blood.

Lettie, crying, fumbles to dial nine-one-one.

"Call the cops and I'll crush his windpipe," I bark.

Nobody moves or speaks. Not even Hatch behind me.

The voice that uttered those words is unlike any I've heard before. Cold and unfeeling. Immune to remorse.

Is crushing someone's windpipe even something I'm capable of?

Time drags.

Prescott gasps for air.

Lettie's shoulders shiver with every long, tortured breath.

"Here's what's going to happen," I pant, dipping low over Prescott's face. "You're going to stay the hell away from me and everyone I love, or else I will hunt you down whatever hole you're hiding in and I will fucking kill you."

Prescott's blue eyes look awestruck as he absorbs the sincerity of my threat. His mother whimpers, gnarled hands clenching the phone, but she doesn't dare move.

Hatch touches my wrist, aiming to draw me back from the edge, but it's too late. I've leapt headfirst into a dark oblivion, one there's no coming back or saving me from.

What if I don't want to be saved?

I lower my face even more so Prescott can feel the flames coming off of me. "That's a promise, you sick son of a bitch. Next time we meet, I won't hesitate. If you ever try anything against me or my family, it's over for you. *Over.*" My final threat spills over him in chilling waves. "And I'll take great pleasure in putting you six feet under, right where vermin like you belong."

CHAPTER TWENTY-EIGHT

I don't say a word the whole drive back to Cliffmoor House.

Hatch is silent too, wading through deep waters, caught up in the whirlwind of everything I'd said and done. Likely playing back every syllable of my careful threat. The yearning to hurt. To kill, if necessary.

I'd never felt that way before, never uttered words so vicious. Never wanted to inflict such pain on another person…

Liar, a dark voice inside of me snarls, summoned awake from its inky crevice.

I bury myself in the passenger seat, using my hair like a curtain to shield my burning, shame-filled face.

Last year, I wanted to put a bullet in my uncle. I'd curbed that impulse for the sake of Palmer and Mojo's wedding—so as not to ruin Tristen's careful plans—but there's no denying I was ready to shoot him. Ready to take matters into my own hands.

I was ready to shoot Ambrose too, once I exposed the ugly, festering truth of what he'd done. I'd been reckless to follow him onto the beach. Knowing all I knew—the heinous act he'd committed—I should've been more cautious. But I was distraught and desperate, not thinking past my immediate need for answers. My need to see Ambrose ruined, the way he'd ruined my sister.

You didn't get to kill him, the dark voice whispers, *and part of you still regrets it.*

My good sense won over my need for revenge, in the end. The pain of living through the collapse of one's image is often worse than a swift death—especially for a narcissistic pig like Ambrose. I'd wanted him to feel every bit of that pain. Wanted to slow his agony to something unbearable. Wanted it to last and linger endlessly.

But Bram had stepped in. And that was that.

Then, there was Prescott.

Fucking Prescott.

If I'd had the chance to kill him on the fields, would I have done it?

Yes.

The resounding answer bursts from within, almost too quickly.

I wouldn't have tried to incapacitate the prick. Wouldn't have aimed for the benign tissue of his shoulder if I'd gotten myself free and wrapped my hands around that gun. No. I wanted to strip him fully of his power. To stop him from doing to another girl what he'd done to me. I would've aimed straight for his head, his neck, his heart, or whatever scraggy thing occupies the space where his heart should be.

The truth is, I would've killed any one of those times—any one of those men—given the right circumstances.

How long has my darkness been lurking at the fringes, waiting for me to submit to it willingly?

"Dell…"

Hatch's voice is heavy, a world of trouble laced into my name. A dagger piercing the oppressive tension between us.

I go stiff in my seat, discomfited by his tone and the sudden shift of attention onto me. I don't want to be scrutinized or cornered right now, can't bear the loaded questions behind that worried gaze. If he presses me, I know I'm going to lash out. Going to blurt out something stupid and cruel that I don't really mean.

Maybe Hatch reads something in my posture—in the way I'm coiled up like a cocked snake—that makes him rethink whatever he was going to say, changing course before plunging us down a ravine we can't climb out of.

All Hatch says is, "I'm staying over tonight."

Despite my wayward emotions, I won't ever argue with that.

Hatch drops me off with a sobering promise that he'll be back later. I'm glad to have some time to myself, to process the hurt, reconcile my behavior, and hopefully turn a mental corner from this day.

But first, I have to deal with Tristen.

I slip onto the grounds through the garden gate, bypassing one of Nova's black-clad guards. They recognize me, and though their hand briefly flicks to the gun nestled at the utility belt at their hip, they don't make a move to stop me.

Charging the back doors of Cliffmoor House, I'm stunned to find them locked…and I'd left my key in the guest house.

Before I can stop myself, my fists are slamming against the thick glass, over and over and over.

Briggs appears in the hall and rushes to me, unlocking one of the doors. "Miss Dell…" He backs inside the house, creating a wide berth for me to enter. "I'm sorry about that. Miss Nova insists we keep the doors locked—"

"Where's Tristen?" I ask roughly.

On some level, I'm still peeved at Briggs for last night in the tunnel, though I'm pretty sure it was just a misunderstanding. My demeanor is unkind and unjustified, but I can't find it in me to care.

"Payne's helping him in the bathroom," Nova says, coming into view. She speaks comfortably, easily, as if integral to the inner workings of this house. As if she's been here for years. Made herself right at home. This somehow makes me even more pissed. "Is there something you need, Dell?"

"To talk to Tristen," I repeat through gritted teeth.

"I realize that." Nova keeps a steady tone, detached and calm as a therapist facing an unruly patient. "In the meantime, is there anything I can help you with?"

I feel a blaze ramping up in my chest, bursting up my throat. She's just sparked a fire she won't know how to extinguish.

"Perhaps you can help me, Nova," I say. "It is about your people, after all."

"My people?" Her eyes narrow slightly. "You mean my team?"

"No, I mean your *people*. As in, the Brine."

Nova pauses, the muscle in her jaw winding and unwinding.

Briggs takes a step backward, as if he senses the torrent of fury that's coming. "Please excuse me, ladies. Inga requires my assistance in the kitchen."

I give Briggs a moment to make his escape, then quickly pivot on my heel and storm into the parlor. Nova trails after me, her soft brown eyes searching mine when I face her.

"My boyfriend and I went to visit Leticia Savage today," I say pointedly. "Recognize the name?"

Nova squints, but says nothing.

That's a yes.

"I thought you might. We found this blog online from a self-proclaimed 'Brine Survivor,' a first-hand account of this woman's experience and escape from the cult. We thought she might know something valuable, something that might help us find my uncle. So we tracked her down—and wouldn't you know it?—'Brine Survivor' is none other than crotchety, old Lettie Savage."

I scoff, still dumbfounded by the turn of events. "Small freaking island, isn't it? And, wait, it gets even better! Her psychotic son Prescott is back in town! That's the headcase that drugged me and delivered me to the fields to be sacrificed."

Nova inhales a breath, keeping an infuriatingly calm head about her, which only serves to make me angrier.

"But I bet you know all about him already," I seethe. "Bet you two are *real* close."

"I'm only aware of who Prescott Savage is because I watch the local news," she counters, "and because of stories I've been told by Tristen. I recognize Lettie's name because she was a Brine member at the same time as my parents. The cult was something I was born into, Dell, not a choice I made for myself. So I'd appreciate it if you'd stop crucifying me for something I had no part in."

I know Nova's right. No one has a say in what they're born into, and they shouldn't be judged for it. I didn't ask to be born a Klyne. Yet here I am, having to navigate every filthy, nightmare-inducing repercussion of my bloodline.

Nova asks me, "Are you worried for your safety?"

I wasn't worried when I'd attacked Prescott in his trailer. But now, being back in this house, with only my bleak memories and my inner violence for company, *yes*. I'm afraid.

I don't say as much, not wanting to seem weak, but Nova still nods at me perceptively. She pulls a pistol from the waistband of her pants, racks the slide without a word, and flips it in her hand so the grip faces me. "For you," she says, her gaze insistent. "For your protection, if ever I'm not around."

I stare at it for a long moment. I haven't held a gun since Palmer's wedding night. Since the beach, when I'd faced all that blood and death, the smell of salt forever tinged with metal, smoke, flesh, and gore.

"Take it, Dell." Nova gently places it on the table closest to me. "It's ready to use."

"I don't have a license to carry," I mumble, trying to be rational about something completely irrational, unwinding the stringy threads of my fear.

"We'll work on that. So long as you have a way of defending yourself when you need to—so long as you're alive—we'll figure out the rest. I can take you to the range. Get you comfortable with shooting."

Gingerly, I slip my fingers around the weapon, judging the weight and deadliness of it. Trying to ignore the recollections bubbling up from my core. But there's no ignoring them. No forgetting the last time. It all happened on these same grounds, this same place, after all.

Flashes of memory crash over me like lightning bolts, lashing painfully across my mind.

There's a dark night, a fat moon, an old man, and me.

Slam.

I collapse onto the sand when Ambrose strikes my back.

He tells me his brutal story. Airs a bloody confession. Relishes in it.

Screech.

Sirens wail banshee-wild in the distance, red and blue lights flickering over the dunes.

Snatch.

Ambrose seizes the gun from me, points the barrel square at my face—a black hole sucking me in, in.

Bang, bang, bang!

Gunshots ring out, claiming my grandfather's life.

Bram is there at the water's edge—my savior, my friend.

Bang, bang, bang, bang, bang, bang, bang!

More shots pour in senselessly from every direction.

Bram falls hard.

Gurgle.

A sea of blood spills from his wounds.

The beach burns and burns.

"Smile, and she lives. So smile again."

The last words Bram would ever speak—slicing and jabbing and piercing and wrecking my heart forevermore.

"Find a reason, Dell. Find a reason to always smile again…"

I drop into a nearby chair, fatigue sinking its teeth into me. With shaking fingers, I deposit the gun on the table, tears spilling hot and fast down my face.

Nova doesn't push or try to console me. She just waits, ever patient, as though she knows all about the recurrent shockwaves of trauma. How they can erupt at any given moment. Blindside you anywhere.

She's a quiet companion, an unwavering force, and for the first time ever, I appreciate that about her.

CHAPTER TWENTY-NINE

Anger has replaced my grief by the time Tristen emerges from his shower, his hair wet and slicked to his neck.

Payne wheels him into the parlor where Nova and I sit, then takes several steps back to lean casually against the doorway, plucking a pocket-knife from his jeans to scrape beneath his fingernails.

"Quite the party crowd in here," Tristen comments at the sight of us engulfed in grim silence.

My eyes wane to slits. "You've got a lot of nerve, you know that?"

"Oh, goodie." His eyebrows quirk mockingly. "Please, regale me, cousin. I'm on pins and needles."

My eyes slide down Tristen's arms, and I realize I've never seen them exposed before. Dark, ironed sleeves usually trail to his wrists, concealing the pale skin underneath. But in his black t-shirt, those sinewy arms are bare, almost translucent, as if they haven't seen sun in years. Pink scars span every inch of them—a brutal constellation of untended wounds. I swallow back a gasp at the sight of those countless lacerations. Misshapen gashes and nicks. Jagged cuts, long and deep. Cigarette burns.

Seeing them laid bare in the parlor light brings me pause, roiling up the contents of my stomach. Had Tristen inflicted these wounds on himself, in times of terrible despair? Or, more likely, were they a stamp of his father's abuse? Traceable badges of the lifelong evil he'd endured?

"Well?" Tristen prompts with a taunting expression. "How have I managed to infuriate you this time?"

"Prescott Savage." I croak the name out, and Tristen's face *almost* softens. "You knew he was out of jail, free to roam the island again, didn't you?"

His throat bobs. A dead giveaway.

Nova's gaze flicks between the both of us.

"You knew, and yet you said nothing." My head spins at this, the worst part of all. The fact that he'd been aware and still brought me back anyway, without doing the decent, respectable thing first.

"I did everything I could to keep him locked up," Tristen says succinctly, a glassy, unruffled calmness to his voice that only makes my rage burn brighter. "I attended multiple hearings—"

"That's beside the point!" I shout. "You lied to me, Tristen. You've lied so many times, I can't even keep track anymore!"

"I didn't lie. We never discussed Prescott. Not once."

I can't believe he'd get technical about something as blatantly wrong as this. "You knew he'd be here and you chose not to tell me. *That* is a lie! Plain and simple."

The muscle in his jaw ticks defiantly. "I'm sorry you see it that way."

Bastard. I should've known better. Should've known never to trust a man who wore so many faces. Tristen had shown his true colors before. So why hadn't I believed him?

"The fact that you don't see it that way speaks volumes," I say, the hurt inside spilling over.

"I didn't want to bring up his name without cause," Tristen insists. "I had plans to hire security. I knew you'd be safe. Prescott isn't allowed within eight hundred feet of Cliffmoor House. I had my lawyer draw up stipulations to—"

"Is that why you wanted me to stay here with you?" I ask. "Moving back into Cliffmoor House—did it have anything to do with Florian at all, or was it a means for you to control the situation? To control *me?*"

Tristen exhales loudly. "I wanted us to stay at Cliffmoor House because it's our best chance at finding my father. Prescott wouldn't dare show up here—not with the amount of surveillance and security I've set up. You and I both know this place is at the core of everything. Just look at what you've discovered! It all has to mean something."

"This is the last straw, Tristen," I bite out, trying to keep the quivering emotion from my voice. "The last time you keep something like this from me. No more omitting. No more doing what you think is best. No more pretending we're a team when we're obviously not. If I find out you lied to me again, I'm gone."

It's not much of an ultimatum. I could fly back to Woodbridge tomorrow, extract myself from this affair, and it likely wouldn't make one bit of difference. But I can tell Tristen cares about keeping me in his corner. He doesn't like the idea that I might grow to hate him again. Not when we'd made so much progress. Not when we'd almost started to feel like a real family.

"Understood," he says, his dark eyes flashing.

I can only hope he means it.

When Hatch returns, I'm ready to lose myself in him and forget this maelstrom of a day.

Forget coming face-to-face with Prescott again. Forget the fear that had weaseled up from the grave where I buried it. Forget the frightening violence that followed—the things I'd said that didn't sound like me, matched by swift action I didn't think my clumsy-self capable of.

Forget the accusations I'd flung at Nova, with no real provocation, no truth to support my words. Forget the subdued hurt that swam in her eyes even as she helped me, sat with me, treated me as a friend.

Forget the gun I now have in my possession, locked and loaded for my use, my benefit. Forget the treacherous memories it brings with it.

Forget Tristen and his lies, and the fact that I have one less person in my life I can trust. We'd been on shaky ground to begin with, but this was egregious. This felt like betrayal.

Hatch's solemn face when I open the door is one I'm severely underprepared for.

The sooner I get these lights off, the better.

"Hi," he says, exhaling a breath that seems to shake something out of him—some haunted thought he'd bitten down before.

"Hi back," I answer weakly, stepping aside to let him in.

Hatch doesn't pause to kiss me, or to slip his hand around my waist, or to brush his lips over my brow. He just walks right in, steeling himself for what's sure to be a doozy of a conversation.

Heat stretches across my limbs as I shut the door behind him.

"I'm surprised you didn't have to work tonight," I say, hoping to break the ice.

"Work can wait. I need to talk to you about today," he deadpans.

There it is.

The spell of his sea green eyes swirls around me, pours into me, until I'm powerless against it. This conversation is inevitable.

"Okay."

"Look," he starts, "I don't want you going after Prescott."

That's what he's worried about?

"It doesn't sit right with me, the way he still has the nerve to look at you, after everything he's done…" Hatch roughs a hand over his face, as if he's been coming out of his skin for hours, forcing himself to keep it in check. "It's not safe for you to be around him. You know more than anyone how dangerous he is, the kind of shit he's capable of. So I need to be sure that you won't do anything—"

"Reckless?" I crack a small smile, trying to smooth the tension. "Or, what was it you called me last summer? *Impulsive.* That's way less offensive."

Hatch doesn't return my smile. "I need to know you're going to be careful, Dell," he says earnestly, unmoved by my needling attempts at humor.

"I am being careful," I reply. "And I'm not going after him."

It feels like a lie.

Shame consumes me over things I've not yet done, things that might've crossed my mind in my darkest hour. Terrible things I wouldn't dare admit to Hatch right now.

But he sees past all my shiny promises, my true intentions slipping through the cracks. "See, that's the problem," he rasps. "I'm not sure that's true."

He has every reason to doubt me, but I'm still taken aback that he does. My posture stiffens. "Well, you're just going to have to trust me."

"I'm trying to trust you," he says, exasperated. "And I'm trying to be understanding. Do you think this has been easy for me? I mean, you came back to Halcyon Bay on a whim to find your homicidal uncle. That's not even a little bit normal."

I gulp, internalizing those brutal words. *Not even a little bit normal.* They wedge inside all my broken crevices, tangle up in my DNA.

"And I'm trying to be supportive, because I know what this means to you," Hatch adds, "but I'm worried, okay? I'm *really* worried about you."

My pride riles up like a vicious sea. "I didn't realize I was so hard to deal with."

"You're not hard to deal with." His eyes flash with frustration. "You just have a tendency of going rogue sometimes."

Another tough pill to swallow, even if he's right.

"Going rogue?" I repeat.

"Yes."

I shake my head, too upset to see reason. "If I did something that bothered you, why didn't you say anything before?"

"Because I can't just *say anything* whenever I damn well please."

He's concealing something behind that steady tone.

"Why not?"

"Because," he grits out.

"Because what, Hatch?"

"Just *because,* all right?"

"Tell me," I insist.

His nostrils flare, a twitch on his lip. Trying to keep his cool, and the truth from spilling over. "I can't."

"You can't?"

His shoulders curl forward, head dipped slightly.

"What, you can't talk to me now?" I hurl the question at him like it's on fire. "I thought we could always be honest with each other. *Trust* each other. So why can't you tell me what you're thinking? Why won't you—"

"Because, Dell!" Hatch flings his arms wide, his words explosive. I freeze, barely able to breathe. "Can't you see that I'm terrified to say the wrong thing and send you running? I never know what's going to be 'the thing' that flips the switch for you."

A long, stifled moment crawls by before I'm able to rasp, "What switch?"

"The one that compelled you to leave last summer without a goodbye," he says bitingly. "Or the one that made everything so weird after the holidays. Or the one that brought you back here so abruptly, that you couldn't take a single moment to call me."

I'm stung by his words—fiery and volatile and entirely…right.

"Hell, I had to find out you were back from Tristen," Hatch continues. "Not from my girlfriend, who I'd flown across the country to visit *twice*. Not from the woman I've been in a relationship with *for months*. But from Tristen Klyne. How am I supposed to feel about that?"

"I'm…" Truthfully, I'm at an utter loss for words. "I'm sorry…"

"At this point, I'm hardwired to expect you to bail or freeze up," he says. "I'm just waiting for you to decide this is all too much. To wake up one day and find out you took off in the night."

A throb of fevered emotion rushes down my head to my chest. "You really expect me to leave without letting you know?" Tears betray my anger, debilitating my words. After everything we'd been through, doesn't he think I'd give him this much? Doesn't he comprehend the immeasurable depths of what I feel?

Hatch shakes his head, the hurt evident on his face. But then he shuts his eyes, presses his lips into a line, and composes himself with stoic grace.

All while I'm left in weepy shambles.

"I didn't plan on dumping all of this on you tonight," he mutters.

"And I don't hold your methods of self-preservation against you. Whatever it takes to keep you alive and well is fine by me. But I need to know that—when it comes to Prescott Savage—you're not going to act out, or be irrational. What happened today was…" His words trail off, drifting on the edge of a rocky precipice.

"What?"

"It just…wasn't you."

"What if it was?" I toss back. "*You* got physical with him. Why shouldn't I?"

Hatch's brow creases as he gets worked up again. "Don't you see that, when you got close to him, when you fed into his taunts, you gave the prick exactly what he wanted? Even as you were threatening him, it's like he took pleasure in it—"

"I don't care, Hatch!" I snap. "I meant every word I said. I'll kill him if it comes to it. He'd do well to watch his back."

"It's not his back I'm worried about," Hatch growls. He shakes his head again, exhaling angrily, before spotting the weapon perched atop the wicker coffee table. "Where did that come from?"

My chin lifts. "Nova gave it to me."

I can feel his mind racing, like a steam train careening toward some distant, treacherous point. "To defend yourself?" he asks, testing my promises. I'd already assured him I wasn't going after Prescott.

"In case I ever need it," I answer simply.

"And you're comfortable using it?"

I raise my eyebrows, feeling like I've been slapped. "Do not insult me."

"*I'm not.*" Hatch mimics my dour tone. "I'm just saying it wouldn't hurt to practice. We could go to the shooting range—"

"I'm already going to the range," I bite back. "With Nova."

I'd made no such plans, but I don't want Hatch to see me as vulnerable, or in need of insulating from a twisted world.

And maybe—probably—I'm also being a brat.

"So you're on Team Nova now?" he surmises.

"I'm on Team Whoever Trusts Me to Handle Myself," I counter, not wanting it to come out that way…but it does. I double down, making it worse. "And apparently, right now, that isn't you."

His face turns to cold steel—the antithesis to my turbulent fire. And though I know I'm at least partially wrong here, I refuse to admit it.

Definitely being a brat.

Hatch glances around the shadowy guest house once more, choosing his words carefully. "Should I just leave then, or am I allowed to stay?"

The sting of rejection rings clear in that question. I hate that he even feels the need to ask. That this stupid fight has pushed us to this.

"Why would you want to?" I whisper.

Hatch goes silent, refusing to answer me. And though his temper still rages in those glistering, stormy eyes, he tucks the rest of it down deep, giving nothing away.

Please stay, I want to beg him. *Don't abandon me now.*

Instead, I give him a choice.

"Stay or leave, Hatch. It's up to you."

I toss my shoulder as though I don't care either way. But I know perfectly well that if he leaves me tonight, the tears will come and they won't stop.

CHAPTER THIRTY

Hatch stays, though the bed is cold and wide between us.

We're both stone-still in the unlit room, our silence deafeningly loud. I lay on my side, curled pointedly away from him, while he faces my back, not making a move to touch me. I can't tell whether he's drifted off to sleep, or if he's still stewing on his emotions as I am.

This is not how I imagined our evening going.

To a degree, I know I'm being unfair. Hatch trusts me—I feel that truth in my bones. He's just worried for me, afraid of the magnifying dangers of this place. Afraid that he might lose me to them. That I might vanish again without notice—his worst nightmares come true.

I know I haven't made our relationship easy. I haven't been forthright, haven't asked for his opinions when they deserved to be heard. I've given him reason to doubt me, and for that, I'm deeply ashamed. But I still don't appreciate the double standard. Hatch had unleashed his anger on Prescott. Why should I have to keep mine in check? Prescott's sickening fixation with me aside, I had every right to lash out as I did. Hell, I'd do it again. Even take things one fatal step further…

Anger pulses through me—the desire to hurt as I've been hurt. *Maybe that's what has Hatch so concerned.*

"Why wouldn't I want to?" Hatch asks quietly, his velvet-soft voice cradled in darkness behind me.

It's been over an hour since we last spoke, when I'd slipped into pajamas, brushed my teeth, and flicked the lights off without another word. I'd heard the rustle of clothes over skin—Hatch pulling off his t-shirt—before sliding into bed with me, a tired groan rippling from within the mattress. Time sprawled by lazily since then, every second of roaring silence deepening the hurt…until this unexpected question, like a winking ember in the night.

"What?" I ask, barely venturing to breathe.

"Why wouldn't I want to stay with you, Dell?" Hatch clarifies, answering my question from so long ago.

"You tell me," I mumble. "I've clearly given you plenty of reasons."

He makes a disapproving sound. "Never a reason not to stay."

"Not yet," I whisper, vocalizing the fear creeping up inside, the one I've been harboring ever since Woodbridge. The fear that Hatch is too good, while I'm too *something else.* Too wrecked and broken. Too muddled and sad.

"Not ever," he whispers back.

His calloused hand reaches out in the dark, finding my waist, skimming the soft skin beneath my shirt, tugging me closer. I let him.

"You know I trust you, right?" he asks, his breath caressing the shell of my ear, the perfect weight of his arm settling over me.

You know I love you, right? I want to respond, feeling braver with the lights off. But Hatch deserves more than quiet admissions under cover of darkness. He deserves someone who'll give him her heart in the blazing sun—soul bared and fearless. So that's who I'll be when I say it.

"Yes," I sigh.

"And you know that I'd do anything in the world for you?"

"Yes."

"Even show up on your doorstep and word-vomit a ton of stupid shit that makes you question my intentions, when that's *never* what I meant to do?"

A weary laugh escapes me. "Yes."

"Good." He tucks me in close, my back pressed to his chest so no space remains between us. Our breaths slowly synchronize—my every cell attuned to the in-out rhythm of *us*—as if we're one body drawing and exhaling oxygen. Nothing in the world feels more natural than this.

"I won't go after Prescott," I concede after a long minute, as much a promise to myself as it is to Hatch. "I won't seek him out, or put myself in harm's way. It would be a true mercy to never lay eyes on him again. But if he ever tries anything—"

"Then I'll be standing right next to you, ready to take him on," Hatch says, clutching me so fiercely I doubt he'll ever let go. "You know that too, don't you?"

"Yes." It's an answer to his question, and to the way he holds me.

"I know I can't protect you all the time," he admits. "Can't be with you through every dark night, even though I'd like to. It's not that I don't think you're strong or formidable or capable of handling yourself. You're all that and more. It's just that, if I ever lost you, Dell…" His breath hitches. "If I ever lost you, there'd be nothing left for me. I'd be a shell. Dead inside. Life loses all meaning if you're not in it."

"I feel the same way about you," I whisper, melting over his words, as if they'd sparked a match and lit me up like a fuse. "I'm sorry I ever made you feel like you couldn't speak up. I promise I won't disappear on you…" The echoes of my thundering heartbeat are so loud, I swear they fill up the room. "I'm never leaving you again, Hatch."

He's silent, contemplating my statement. What it implies. What it means for our future. Then, he mutters, "You don't have to say that."

"I know." I turn my face to his, reaching up a hand to run my fingers through his hair. "Stop trying to give me a way out, okay? I'm not looking for one."

Hatch brushes a peal of kisses across my shoulder and collarbone. I sink against the pillow, against him, allowing my eyes to shut and my heart to just *feel*. His fingertips sweep lightly over my belly. A delicious ache builds within me, and I can't ignore it. Don't *want* to ignore it. Twisting my legs in his, I paw at his neck, pulling at him until his mouth finds mine. I coax him with my tongue, savoring every taste. Relishing the way he smells of clean ocean breeze. How his touch is both gentle and rough, sinfully perfect in its contradictions. Living for that sharp intake of breath when I take his bottom lip between mine and bite.

His growl of satisfaction corkscrews my stomach. "If this is what making up is like, maybe we should argue more often."

"You really want that?" I ask between breaths.

He grunts, sprinkling kisses up my neck. "Nah. We should always skip straight to the good part."

Such a guy thing to say.

I turn in his arms to face him fully, exploring his body somewhat drunkenly—smiling and clumsy and grasping, greedy for more of him and everything that feels good. His silky waves. The firm panes of his chest. Those pillow-soft lips. His hands, chapped and rugged and all over me— twisting in my hair, gripping my waist, shoving up beneath my shirt.

Every part of this man is familiar, his form a perfect match for mine. Where I end, he begins. Where he breaks, I persist. When one of us lets go, the other holds on. We're opposites and equals, our connection instinctual, unbreakable, safe. And yet...

Every single touch feels brand new to me, every inch of him uncharted, every satisfied little sound a melody. And I want all of it. The crashing tumult of his sea. The electric crackle of his lightning. The wild roar of his fire. To be utterly consumed by him—part man, part force of nature.

Hatch gazes at me through the inky darkness, his star-bright eyes tense and thick with longing...and something deeper. Truer. Infinite.

A rare and bone-deep love.

I feel it in my soul, and I hope he does too, though neither of us pause long enough to utter the words. Our desire is our compass, the moonlight seeping through the curtains is our beacon, until all we are is entwined limbs and beating hearts and breathlessness.

Hatch's body rolls like the ocean over mine.

The world pales and drowns in the deep love we make.

CHAPTER THIRTY-ONE

"Dell, wake up!" Hatch's voice blares from somewhere above me. Strong hands grip my shoulders, shaking me awake.

I grunt groggily, but don't bother opening my eyes. It's still night out—I can tell by the black shroud encasing me, pressed heavily upon my face. A tingly layer of goosebumps coat my flesh.

"Dell, c'mon." Hatch sounds breathless. "Please. Wake up!"

I jolt awake, and my eyes find his—glossy and brimming with worry.

I'm not in bed. Not wrapped in his arms or swathed in sheets, the way I'd been when I shut my eyes hours ago, utterly spent and happy.

Instead, I'm splayed across cold, damp sand, with a vacant shoreline stretching before me, riddled with slow-creeping mist. Coarse granules prick my skin, scratching the backs of my bare arms and legs, coating my lashes and lips. I can taste it, can feel the grit of it in my mouth.

"Hatch?" I sit up, taking in the foggy beach around us. The sky above is streaked in a faint dusting of pink—the onset of morning. "What are we doing here?"

Hatch's face is as blanched as the rumpled sheets we'd left behind. "I woke up and you were gone."

"Gone?" I don't remember this. Don't remember *anything* past falling asleep beside him, curled up blissfully snug to his chest.

"The front door was open," Hatch says. "And when I went out to look for you, I saw the beach gate was ajar…" He clears his throat, an old pain bleeding into his words—bitter memories of the last time he'd run onto a beach like this one to save me.

"Why didn't one of Nova's guards stop me at the gate?"

"You told her to keep them out of your way. They've probably been warned to leave you alone. Plus, you have a key." He points at something shiny poking out of the sand a few feet away—my key to the gates, tossed aside like rubbish. "You must've used it. Don't you remember?"

I shake my head, trying to recall how on earth I wound up here, reaching for the tiniest slivers of memory. The gate key in my fist. My fingers on the door knob. My careful footsteps over the dewy grass, the wooden pathway, the sand.

But I remember nothing, my mind an eerie blank slate.

"You were sleepwalking," Hatch posits.

I shudder. As crappy as the prospect is, I can't think of a better explanation.

"Has this ever happened to you before?" Hatch asks, his question leadened with concern.

"Just once, I think. Yesterday morning."

First, the nightmares. Now, *this?*

I thought it was the devastating memories ruining my sleep. The guilt over losing Bram, the grief over Willow, the trauma afforded me by Ambrose and Florian, as well as the Brine. But maybe, like a gnawing infection, the truth sinks far deeper. Maybe something is wrong *inside* of me, precipitating these late-night trips to the beach.

Hatch's eyes cloud over, lightning flashes of fear woven into that lush, beautiful green.

"What is it?" I ask, noting something unreadable in his expression.

He exhales a breath that speaks to countless unspoken worries. I wish I could steal them away, one by one.

"You didn't look right. You were shaking, and your skin was frigid. I kept rubbing your arms, but you wouldn't even stir. And then, your eyes…" He scans them desperately, left to right, again and again, as if trying to replace the image of whatever horrors he'd seen in them before.

"What about my eyes?"

"They'd rolled all the way back, and it's like they were stuck that way. All I could see were the whites…" He wraps a hand around the nape of my neck, drawing me closer until our foreheads press together, as if he simply needs to feel me there—needs to ground himself in my touch, my presence. "It was like you were in a trance or something. I couldn't get you to snap out of it."

I could've sworn my eyes were closed. All I'd felt was darkness. Pure, black night pushing hard against my eyelids.

"We should talk to someone about this," he says. "A doctor—"

"No," I say adamantly.

"The psychic, then?"

"You want me to go see Freya?" I hadn't seen or spoken to Freya since returning to the island, and I'm shocked to hear Hatch bring her up now, considering how opposed he'd been to her last summer.

"I don't know," he replies. "Maybe she can put you under hypnosis or something. Get to the root of why this is happening."

Hypnosis? Not an idea I love.

"This is dangerous, Dell," Hatch insists. "You can't go wandering off in the middle of the night. Especially with Prescott on the loose."

I want to tell him not to worry, to assure him I'll be fine, but the truth is, I'm worried too. Paralyzed by a silent fear. By what I might do in my sleep, driven by my subconscious—a version of me wholly outside of my control. I have no idea how to fix this, or who to ask for help.

"What do we do now?" Hatch asks.

"Right now? We sit." I exhale a breath, wiping the film of sand from my arms, shaking more from my hair.

Hatch silently watches me, wary of my lax reaction. I shoot him a tired, pleading look. "Let's table this for a little while, please? Watch the sunrise with me. That's what I really need." I pat the sandy ground, prompting him to sit. "I'm not ready to face another yesterday just yet."

Huddling together in our groove of damp sand, we watch the sun slowly emerge beyond the sea, shooting fiery tendrils of orange-pink into the sky. It's only appropriate we greet the dawn how we spent the night—tangled up in each other.

As we silently contemplate the new day before us, I reflect on the promises I'd made to Hatch last night. That I won't bolt or vanish. That I'm not looking for an exit plan. And with the sun's arrival—the crashing waves drizzled in the luster of morning—I wonder if now's the right time to tell him how I feel. To drop the one word I've been clinging to for dear life, like dangling from rope over a steep cliffside.

Just say it.

Say the word.

Love.

I love you.

I'm *in* love with you.

How hard is that to vocalize?

"So we're all set for dinner tonight with my family," Hatch announces, far too casually.

My stomach—which had finally settled down somewhat—catapults into sudden, violent somersaults. "*Tonight?*" I can't keep the irritating squeal from my voice. "And you didn't think to mention this sooner?"

Hatch shrugs. "I meant to tell you when I came over last night. But we fought, and then"—his mouth twists into a smirk, as if privately delighting in the vivid memories of *us*—"well, then I didn't want any distractions."

"You're impossible," I groan, torn between reprimanding him and smiling like the giddy, love-struck fool I am.

"We can cancel, if you're not up to it," he says, nuzzling my neck.

That would make a truly spectacular impression.

"I'm not canceling on your family."

"We can take a raincheck, then."

"No, it's cool." My heart pounds like a war drum in my ears, attesting to how 'uncool' I really feel. "I'm just nervous, I guess."

"Don't be. They'll adore you."

"And if they don't?"

He chuckles, breathy and warm against my skin. "Everyone's entitled to a wrong opinion now and then."

"I don't think that's how opinions work."

"When it comes to you they do. What do you have to be nervous about anyway?"

About a million things.

How much has Hatch told the Seaborns about me? What have they heard through the island grapevine—about my family and their sordid, vile past? Do they know how badly I almost screwed things up with Hatch? Do they think I'm even remotely worth his time?

"Nothing. Never mind." I shake my head, attempting to shake off my worry too. Better not to breathe life into those fears prematurely. Dinner with the Seaborns is happening at my request. I'm not going to do anything to sabotage it. "Let's head back to the guest house. I've got sand lodged in all sorts of indecent places."

"I can help with that," Hatch volunteers with a mischievous grin. I smack him away, not bothering to quell my laughter.

He loops an arm around my shoulders as we walk off the beach. With every step, I grow a little more comfortable with the thought of meeting his family. Maybe they won't *adore* me right off the bat, but I'm determined not to make them hate me. I'll be polite. Gracious. At the very least, they'll see how much I care about Hatch. That has to count for something.

As we cross into the grounds, I see Nova flanked by two police officers marching toward the guest house—toward us. All the quiet mental progress I'd made evaporates, the sight of them sending me into an anxiety spiral. I can only imagine they're here for one reason.

Nova approaches with the cops in tow, their faces coming into clearer view. It's Officers Parris and Dash—an unwelcome repeat of last summer.

"Miss Costa. Hello again." Dash regards me with a tense smile, looking like he's not a bit pleased to be back here. "And you're"—his gaze jumps to Hatch—"Mr. Seaborn, I presume?"

Hatch nods, gripping me tighter.

"How serendipitous to find you both here together," Parris comments, his pale eyes hard and brimming with spite. "Saves us a trip."

"You're not in trouble, guys," Nova cuts in. I can sense the thinly-veiled annoyance behind her unruffled façade. "I've already informed the officers that without arrest warrants, they have no business showing up here, trying to browbeat you—"

"I assure you, Miss Santos, we're not here to browbeat anyone," Dash interjects. "We just want a few brief minutes of their time."

I level Dash with a sharp, expectant look, doing everything in my power to stand tall and erect despite the tremors crawling down my spine. Palmer's words from days ago echo in my mind like a haunting presage: *You could go to jail...*

"We received a frantic call from Miss Leticia Savage last night," Parris says coolly. "She claims that you two brutally assaulted her son in their home yesterday. Is that correct?"

Neither Hatch nor I respond.

"She also claims that you, Miss Costa, threatened to quote, 'crush Mr. Savage's windpipe,' if she attempted to call nine-one-one. Is that true?"

Again, silence.

Nova snorts. "You can't be so dense as to think they'd answer your questions without legal counsel present?"

Dash sighs. "While we recognize that you have a complicated past with Mr. Savage—"

"*A complicated past?*" Hatch scoffs, revolted. "That's the understatement of the century."

"Be that as it may, if you did attack him in the vicious manner Miss Savage described"—Dash shakes his head, lips pressed tight—"then you're both very lucky he opted not to press charges."

"Officers," Nova snaps, holding up an interrupting hand. "Are you aware that Prescott Savage drugged and abducted Dell last year? He's the one that delivered her to the sea trumpet fields and into the arms of Brine leader Greer Hewitt. This young woman has to live with the wounds he inflicted on her every single day—"

"We're aware, Miss Santos." Parris hisses her name as if it's poison on his tongue. Nova's nostrils flare, clearly repulsed by him too. "But Mr. Savage has undergone due process for his crimes. We will not tolerate flagrant lawlessness on Halcyon Bay."

Flagrant lawlessness?

A cold-hearted laugh bursts from my lips.

Parris' glare falls over me like a sheet of ice. "Do you find the threat of anarchy comical, Miss Costa?"

"I find men like you comical, Officer Parris."

The retort slips from my mouth before I can stop it.

"Men like me?" he repeats slowly.

"Narcissistic men who abuse their power, holding others to a moral code you yourselves don't live up to."

"My moral code comes second to the law." Parris narrows his eyes. "You clearly think yourself entitled to dole out retribution as you see fit."

"Oh, for hell's sake." Nova brushes him off. "She's a frightened young woman, not a vigilante soldier."

"And yet, she seems quite willing to enact vigilante justice," Parris points out bitterly. "Isn't that right, Miss Costa?"

I clamp my mouth shut, refusing to concede to any wrongdoing.

"In my experience, *officers*," Nova snarls, "it's your department and its benefactors that exhibit 'flagrant lawlessness' on this island. These upstanding civilians are just trying to survive in your iniquitous world."

I've never heard Nova speak like this—her words deliberate and calculated, precise on their mark. She reminds me a lot of Tristen, actually.

"Let's roll it back a second," Dash chimes in, turning to me with tired eyes. "Of course we understand your inclination to strike back at someone who wronged you, Miss Costa. But justice has been served. Mr. Savage has been sentenced to eighteen months of community service—"

"On what planet is eighteen months of garbage pickup 'justice?'" I explode.

Parris lifts his eyebrows haughtily, as though my angry question were an admission of guilt, but I don't care. He can speculate to his brittle, black heart's content.

"I agree that his sentence is lenient," Dash concedes, "but it's not our call to make, I'm afraid."

Part of me wants to believe Dash is on my side—the part that remembers how he'd shown me kindness in the past, how he'd been genuinely concerned for my wellbeing after Callie Oxton's suicide. But the greater part *knows* not to believe a word he says.

"You have to trust our justice system," Dash adds, as if reading my mind, trying to convince me to go against my better judgment. "Trust that the HBPD will keep you safe."

"Why would I ever trust any of you?" I bite back. "You bungled my sister's murder investigation. You killed Abraham Urban. You let my uncle Florian escape—"

"That's inflammatory," Parris growls, voice dripping with arrogance.

"Please. I *know* some of you are in his pocket. You let him leave the island. I bet you're covering for him, even now!"

"All right." Dash exhales a weary breath. "We don't want to cause any trouble here, Miss Costa. We're certainly not looking to add to your grief. But I would caution you not to take matters into your own hands where Mr. Savage is concerned. Criminal acts, even those perpetrated by victims, will not be condoned on Halcyon Bay. You won't get a pass next time." His throat bobs with some inner conflict. "We just came by to issue that friendly warning—"

"Friendly, my ass," Hatch mutters loudly.

"I think you've overstayed your welcome, gentlemen," Nova says.

Dash dips his head, almost apologetically. "We'll see ourselves out, then. Thank you for your time."

Parris turns up his nose, pivoting after one last grimace.

The officers stride across the lawn to the garden gate. We watch as their backs grow smaller, until finally, they disappear through the arbor of overgrown vines.

CHAPTER THIRTY-TWO

The afternoon crawls by sedately, and I find myself enjoying the peace afforded me at the library—a small reprieve from the insanity of Cliffmoor House, and a placid precursor to dinner with the Seaborns.

The work is mundane, but I like the routine of it—the consistency and the distraction. Categorizing the books, learning the systems, being surrounded by worlds so far removed from this one. It helps, at least for a little bit.

Until Palmer crashes through the doors.

Dex and I are working the circulation desk when she barges in, looking exceptionally out of sorts, her belly swaddled in a peach mini dress—the kind of outfit only Palmer could pull off at eight and a half months pregnant.

"Hiya, Dex!" she cries, trying a bit too hard to sound excited. "Do you mind if I borrow Dell for a while?"

She doesn't bother to consult me on the matter.

"I can't right now, Palmer," I interject anyway. "I'm literally in the middle of my shift—"

"I know, I know, but I need your help with some baby stuff! It's *really* urgent." She makes a show of cradling her bulging stomach, as if to emphasize her very pregnant condition, tossing Dex big baby-doll eyes. "Do you think that'd be okay, Dexter? Pretty please?"

"Yes, of course. Whatever you need," he answers dutifully.

Palmer flashes him a thousand-watt grin. She knows damn well that Dex would do whatever she asks, if only to keep June happy. "You're the greatest, Dex!" she exclaims, her voice saccharine-sweet. "Cool shirt, by the way!"

He's donning a heather-gray tee that reads *Permanent Book Hangover* with a visibly drunk cartoon man surrounded by stacks of books. It's a very cool shirt, in fact, but Palmer's just buttering him up—all batted lashes and sugar-coated smiles. It irritates me to no end.

Dexter doesn't seem to mind, or maybe doesn't notice. "Thanks," he says with a smile. "I was actually wondering whether I should get into the habit of wearing more 'academic' attire."

"No way. Keep the shirts. You're killing it!" Palmer insists, before grabbing me by the wrist and giving me a tug. "We'll catch you later, Dex. Thanks again!"

We're halfway across the parking lot when I finally manage to pry myself free of her.

"What the heck is going on?"

Palmer sighs heavily, her smile fading now that she's without an audience.

"What is it?"

"Okay, look. This is going to sound crazy, but..." Palmer rubs her palms over her eyes, driving shaky fingers through her golden-blond hair. "It's the whispers, Dell. They don't stop."

"What whispers?" I feel compelled to ask, though I know exactly what she's talking about.

"The ones I heard in the tunnel," she says. "It's like...like they followed me home or something."

"No." I shake my head, negating her words and every racing thought screaming *fire!* in my head. "That's not possible..." It's a lie and I know it.

Wilder things have happened. But I can't allow myself to think that they could happen to her.

"Please, Dell." Her nervous demeanor ramps up to a frustrated fever-pitch. "I know some shit went down last year that you refuse to tell me about."

"Palmer, I've told you everything—"

"No, you haven't! Remember last summer? The bathtub incident? Mojo and I found you basically *drowning,* and you actually had the nerve to say you'd fallen asleep!" She looses a breath. "I've lived on this island all my life, Dell. I know weird when I see it."

"But, Palmer, that was—"

"And how about the morning you left town with your parents? When Hatch dropped you off at our apartment? You looked like you'd seen a ghost! Your skin had this eerie blue tinge to it, and you were ice-cold to the touch, like you'd been trapped in a freezer for hours."

I want to deny it. To fabricate some story and convince my cousin of how wrong she is, listing all the irrefutable, scientific reasons why. But I can't find it in me.

"I know some strange things happened to you last year," she says. "Gram had *encounters* of that kind too. Mom didn't like her talking about them, so she usually kept a pretty tight lid on it. But, on the occasional night when she'd had one too many gimlets, Gram would let little tidbits slip. She told me stories about all the things she'd seen and heard at Cliffmoor House. Things she couldn't tell anyone else, or else they'd think her mad." Palmer's blue eyes beg me for the truth. "Please, Dell. Don't lie to me anymore."

This is how I must've looked to Tristen when I made him swear not to keep me in the dark—determined not to be pushed to the fringes, desperate to maintain some small grasp on circumstances beyond my control or comprehension.

Am I doing the same thing with Palmer? Shutting her out? Omitting truths, under the guise of protecting her?

Crap.

"Okay," I whisper, resigned. "What do you want to know?" Palmer always finds a way to weasel into the deepest parts of me.

"I want to know what the hell's going on at Cliffmoor House," she says solemnly. "What happened to you last summer? And what did you do about it?"

When I pull on the door to Freya's storefront, it opens easily, almost as if she'd been waiting for us to show up.

"Gram's psychic is your secret weapon?" Palmer asks skeptically.

"Look, you wanted to know how I handled last summer, right? This is it. I came here." I'm not sure how to better advocate for Freya's particular aptitudes.

I'd briefly filled Palmer in on some of what had happened last year— the gist of my near-death encounter with Willow, the meaning behind the sea glass I now wear on a chain, my suspicions about Eribeth's presence in the guest house. To Palmer's credit, she nodded studiously through my spiel, internalizing whatever shock she may have felt, not appearing too put-off by my chaotic explanations.

Her eyes lift to the collection of empty bottles hanging over our heads in the doorway. "What's this for?"

"Catching unruly spirits," I repeat from memory, with a meaningful smile Palmer can't understand.

"Thank you, oh wise one. That's super helpful," she mutters.

We shuffle inside the small, amethyst-colored lobby—cramped, dimly lit, and smelling of incense. Palmer snatches up a *Psychic Phenomena for the Average Jane* brochure, shoving it into her cross-body purse with a snarky comment about it being "some light bedtime reading material."

I lead her down the jagged hallway to Freya's back room. We make it to the crimson curtain, which is pulled off to one side, held in place by an ornate brass holder with the face of a screeching bat.

I step carefully over the line of red dust on the floor, pointing down at it so Palmer knows to follow suit. She shoots me a quizzical look but steps cautiously anyway, murmuring under her breath, "I don't even want to know."

"Freya?" I call, scanning the contents of the familiar room—the strange objects displayed on bookcases and tabletops and hanging from old chains from the ceiling. The ancient, dusty jars and the torn-up tomes. The elaborate birdcage and the sleek, jet-black feathers. The animal—or *finger*—bones on prominent display.

"You'd think a psychic would've seen us coming," Palmer whispers, spinning around in a slow circle.

"I did," answers a low, transfixing voice.

We both jump, turning to find Madame Freya Larisse standing in the threshold that we'd just shuffled through, appearing as if from nowhere.

My heart wallops traitorously in my chest, but the sage woman doesn't look flustered in the slightest. She merely smiles back, molten eyes glimmering with secrets, twirling a silver spoon in a piping cup of tea.

"I was merely equipping myself for your visit, Palmer," Freya muses, lifting her cup. "It's wonderful to see you again, Meridel."

"Hello, Freya," I say, surprised by the honey-warmth of my voice, like I'm addressing an old friend I'd somehow missed without realizing it. "How have you been?"

Her bewitching smile widens. "Busy as ever, child. The souls of this island sleep not."

Freya glides around us to her table. "Come, please." She gestures at Palmer to take the velvet seat opposite her, pointing me to a wooden stool in the corner shouldering a stack of books. "Bring that over, Meridel. Gather around."

I haul the books into my arms and stack them neatly on the floor, dragging the stool over to Palmer's side.

"To what do I owe this pleasure?" the psychic asks, her eyes evoking a quiet certainty about the questions we've come to have answered. At least she has the decency to let us ask first. Freya never flaunts her power, nor does she aim to highlight our lack.

"Um, don't you need some kind of payment first?" Palmer asks, reaching for the flap on her bag.

Freya flutters a bejeweled hand in the air, sending a shimmer of scintillating light across the room. "The first consult is always on the house, child. Work of this nature brings me profound joy."

"Oh. Okay." Palmer's restless fingers fidget in her lap.

I decide it best I get the ball rolling. "We have a few questions about a certain *presence* at Cliffmoor House."

Freya smiles serenely, as if to say, *Of course you do.*

Palmer jumps in. "Dell found this underground tunnel system beneath the estate. We ventured down a couple days ago, just being stupid, fooling around…" I shoot her a disapproving look at this. "And I…I heard a voice. A whisper, actually. A breathy-whisper-voice." The last bit spills from her lips in a confused jumble.

"When we surfaced, the whispers…well, they didn't stop. It's almost like they followed me home. They kept me up through the night, and then all the next day too. I hoped they would go away, over time. I figured I just needed a good night's sleep. But last night, it was more of the same, and today as well…"

"What are the whispers telling you, Palmer?" Freya asks.

"Nothing I can make out," she replies. "They aren't coherent words. Just distant fragments, snippets of a female voice. I can even hear her crying sometimes."

"There were bones down in the tunnel, as well," I chime in, thinking it pivotal that Freya know this part. "Human skeletal remains. I saw them earlier in the day, but, that evening, when we returned, they were gone. Moved or stolen, maybe."

"Stolen bones," Freya repeats.

I swallow hard. "Yes."

"Do you think the whispers came from this…person?" Palmer asks. "Like maybe their spirit attached to me somehow?"

She puts a hand to her belly, dwelling on her unborn child, and the choices she'd made that may have accidentally landed them in danger. A threat she'd brought upon them unwittingly.

"It's possible," Freya says.

"But why me?" Palmer contemplates aloud, twinges of regret curling around her breathy question.

Freya only observes her with a quiet, watchful expression.

"I thought, maybe, your tokens could help," I say, recalling the psychic's suitcase of ghostly endowments—broken bits and frayed pieces and hunks of junk beyond repair, all of which lead back to some lingering island spirit. That's how I'd found Willow's sea glass last summer, how I'd procured some answers about our watery encounter. Maybe the same can work for Palmer.

"We can try." Freya nods, but the narrowing of her bronze eyes feels disheartening. "Though in this case, I'm afraid, it may be for naught."

The psychic glides to her old credenza, plucking the battered suitcase from its resting place. I remember this exact moment the last time I was here—flanked by a frustrated Hatch, made tipsy by Captain Patton's drink, my hair dripping like a sodden mop down my back. I remember the unnatural blue that dusted across my lips, fleeting evidence of a life-altering phenomenon. I remember my sister's ethereal touch. The stuff of legends, prayers, and nightmares.

I help Freya haul the case onto the table, then stand back as the psychic unlatches the top and flips it open, exposing a dark foam with hundreds of small impressions—hundreds of items, humming with quiet energy. A glowing power that calls only to their specific chosen one.

Which of these might belong to Palmer's spirit? What poor soul is trapped beneath my family's mansion? Not bound to the sun-soaked island, nor the fathomless depths of the sea, but to the oppressive, inky underworld, with no chance of reprieve from the blackness...

"What is all this?" Palmer asks slowly, her eyes sweeping over those strange odds and ends. "Is this where you found—" She runs a hand over her collarbone, insinuating as to my necklace.

I nod in acknowledgment.

"Palmer, run your hand over the items in the suitcase," Freya directs, "and we may discover whose whispers plague you so."

My cousin does as she's told without question, flattening her palm over the case, the gesture keenly familiar. Hovering inches above the black foam, she runs her hand over the contents, visibly holding her breath.

She does this three times without reaction, and my heart sinks like an anchor. "I have no idea what I'm supposed to be feeling," Palmer says, "but whatever it is, it's not happening."

"I suspected things might go this way," Freya says, a disappointed slope on her plum lips.

"Why?" I ask.

"Because Palmer's spirit companion is trapped underground, and I likely wouldn't have heard his or her—" Freya's eyes briefly roll back in her skull, and her head does a snappy twitch to the left. She blinks a few times suddenly, snapping out of her momentary trance "—*her* call. Yes. Definitely a *her*. I wouldn't have been able to identify her token. I have nothing of hers to point to."

Her. A confirmation of what I knew in my core. The bones belong to a woman.

"So what do I do now?" Palmer asks in a terrified whisper, her eyes turning desperate. "How do I silence the whispers?"

"You are expecting, I see," Freya notes, eyeing Palmer's mid-section over the table. "How far along are you?"

Palmer drags her fingers across her belly. "Two weeks shy of my due date."

"Hmm." Freya's eyes narrow, a contemplative expression painting her face.

"Why?" Palmer asks, a shrill edge to her voice. "Should I be worried for the baby?"

"No, I don't believe the spirit means you any harm," Freya says with a shake of her silk-wrapped head. "This is nothing you cannot handle, child."

"How can you know that?"

"Because there is an aura about you, Palmer. Your soul pulses with life-giving energy, a deep and ever-growing love. It exudes into the world around you, bleeding into the very air we breathe, crossing the realms of living and dead."

Palmer and I glance at each other.

"It is a tenor of softness, but one of strength too, as with so many mothers," Freya explains. "Like an armament of light separates you from the rest. You may feel vulnerable right now, but you are tough and capable and filled with great power."

"If I'm so tough, then why did this *thing* latch onto me?" Palmer asks.

"My theory," Freya offers, "is that the spirit chose you because she is akin to you. You provide a safe landing place for her."

"Meaning?" Palmer asks.

"Perhaps this spirit was with child when she died."

My heart wallops, the revelation like a baseball bat to my chest. Had I really found a pregnant woman's bones beneath Cliffmoor House? And had this woman's spirit affixed to my very pregnant cousin?

"Fabulous," Palmer breathes, letting her head droop. She looks so fragile, delicate as a bird.

"Freya, why do the spirits of the island seek us?" I ask. "Why us more than others? Why Cliffmoor House, and our family?"

The psychic's solemn gaze bores into me. "The *women* of your family, you mean."

I've always believed that the Klynes were plagued. Haunted. But it's true what Freya says—we *women* seem to bear the paranormal burden alone. Tristen has never once complained of ghostly occurrences at Cliffmoor House. Ambrose had been right at home there for years. Florian was unaffected. Even Leif, young and impressionable as he is, is entirely unafraid of the bulky mansion. He'd spent funerals and hurricanes holed up in that place, and the kid never so much as flinched. It's as if the pulsing darkness doesn't reach for its male inhabitants. Doesn't penetrate their bones the way it does ours.

But Virginia, on the other hand…

Her journal details a life teeming with otherworldly brushes— inexplicable terrors hiding around every corner. I've had my own litany of mystifying experiences. And now, Palmer is too.

"Why?" I ask again.

"It began with the Cliffmoors," Freya starts.

"*The* Cliffmoors?" Palmer pipes up.

"The original family of Cliffmoor House," Freya confirms. "After Dresden and Philomena Cliffmoor erected the home and moved in, Philomena struggled greatly to conceive and carry a child to term. It is said that she felt the presence of her unborn children everywhere, despite never having met a single one. Dresden worried over his wife's health. Worried that Philomena would succumb to the wiles of her mind.

"After countless miscarriages, Philomena birthed a child—a son by the name of Isaiah. And for the first time in years, Philomena was happy, filled with purpose and love and pride. She cared for her beloved son so dearly. She coddled and cooked for him, spending every last second tending to his every need, foregoing her responsibilities as lady of the house. She kept Isaiah indoors constantly, rarely letting him out of her sight, for she was deathly afraid she might lose him, as she had lost so many children.

"Dresden became concerned. His only son was weakening greatly in this state. The boy wasn't growing, and he had no friends or social prospects. Though Philomena meant well, she was keeping Isaiah from flourishing. So Dresden insisted on separating them, so that his son might learn to stand on his own. But, one day, there was an accident—a terrible twist of fate. Isaiah was struck and killed by lightning in a sudden storm that rolled in from the sea. And Dresden and Philomena found themselves childless once more, with an ocean of hatred swelling between them.

"After Isaiah's passing, Philomena's life turned empty and senseless. She sought out the presence of her son after death—looked for his ghost among the shining finery of Cliffmoor House, which had become nothing more than a glorified dungeon. Dresden had grown cruel, shut off to the world, buried in his work. He all but abandoned Philomena to herself, forbidding the servants from engaging with her, under threat that they would assume her madness. Her only companions in that house were the spirits. She reached for them constantly, and they reached back. Until one fateful day, when it is said that they convinced her to join them."

Palmer and I hold our breaths, eerily still.

"The servants found Philomena tucked in bed well into the morning. Her black hair had turned frosty-white, her skin gray as rotten meat. She appeared serene, her eyes gently shut, as though she'd only just fallen asleep—a sleep she never woke from. The medical examiner deemed it cardiac arrest, but Philomena left behind a note that called it all into question."

"What did the note say?" I ask, when Freya takes a pause.

She recites Philomena's words from memory, with haunting lyricism: "*A woman's heart is a home kept warm by its inhabitants, and I have found the greatest solace in the ones I cannot see. My most devout prayer is that all the ladies of this house find comfort in the company of dead souls, and carry space for them in the ample rooms of their hearts.*"

We're silent for a long moment afterward, until Palmer cries indignantly, "This Philomena lady *cursed* us?"

"She meant it as a blessing," Freya says.

"Some freaking blessing!" Palmer exclaims.

"So this supernatural link that's hardwired into our brains…it's all because of Philomena's curse?" I ask.

Freya presses her lips together, bobbing her head in agreement. "Before she passed, Philomena opened a door to the realm of the dead. Her attempts to make contact with her son, and her other spirit companions, made Cliffmoor House a hotbed for human-spirit intersection. A stronghold for displaced souls and swarming energy. They spilled into that place, making themselves at home. From the way Philomena appeared at her time of death—the gray-tinged skin, and the icy hair—it was almost as if she'd suffered a great scare. As if she'd seen something indescribable. A vision so real, it altered her physical makeup. It's been theorized that the spirits either whisked Philomena away, or that she went along willingly, choosing to leave her corporeal life behind. And she passed that predilection onto the other ladies of Cliffmoor House."

"Which would explain our grandmother's…gifts," I work out, "but I still don't understand why that would affect us?"

"It's in your blood," Freya says. "The Klynes are Cliffmoor descendants. Your grandfather's great-grandmother was Dresden Cliffmoor's sister, Matilda. When he died, Dresden left the house to Matilda and her husband, Harland Klyne. Dresden had no other living children, no kin. So while you aren't ladies of the house, you are connected by blood."

"That's insane," Palmer says. "I've spent *plenty* of time at Cliffmoor

House over the years. I've never had anything like this happen to me before!"

"Yes, but you are in an altered state now, child. You're more susceptible in this condition, and likely more receptive." Freya's eyes flick to me. "Dell had experiences from the moment she arrived. She was sensitive to the spirits from the start because she was in a heightened state of stress."

"So heightened emotion makes us more attuned to the spirits?"

"More attentive. Observant. Open-hearted." Freya waves a hand in Palmer's direction. "Or, possibly, you were able to connect because of some inherent similarity. Something that joins the two of you on a basic level."

"Like my baby," Palmer says.

"Like your baby," Freya confirms.

"But…how do I make it go away?"

The psychic's expression is a medley of regret and pride, as if she knows well the double-edged sword of otherworldly connection. "You can't, Palmer. You have to learn to live with it."

"Learn to live with voices in my head? With constant shadows at the fringes of my vision?" Palmer's fingers twitch against the hem of her dress.

"For whatever reason, this spirit found a safe place in you. There's a chance she only wants to relay a message, after which, she will release you. She will be free, and you will too."

"So, until then, I'm just stuck like this?"

Freya reaches out, taking my cousin's worried fingers in hers. "She chose you for a reason."

"How am I supposed to receive this message?" Palmer asks. "Assuming the spirit decides to clue me in."

"It may come at a time where you're at your most pliable," Freya explains. "When you've surpassed your human limits, and are at the brink of this world and the next. That is when the spirits speak."

Freya's explanation tracks with what I experienced with Willow. I'd been on the brink of drowning when my sister offered me her kiss, her memories. I was dying in those shallows, floundering for breath.

I'd surpassed my human limits.

"Are the men in our family unaffected by this curse?" Palmer asks. "Please tell me I don't have to worry about my brother getting possessed too?"

Freya's lip twitches, whether with amusement or disapproval, I can't tell. "The men of Cliffmoor House are burdened in their own way."

"How so?"

"As I mentioned, Dresden became callous after his son's death. He was abusive toward Philomena, emotionally at least. In his will, when he conferred Cliffmoor House to Harland Klyne, Dresden decreed a certain legacy for the men in his family. Each one was destined to be more successful than the last, but their home life, their marriages, would be riddled with contempt. Relations with their children would be difficult, but they would hold power beyond measure. They would be rich and stately, the world kneeling at their feet, but they would also be doomed to hatred, weighed down by violence, each generation more so than the last. This was their gift and scourge."

Again, this makes sense. Ambrose and Florian had been aggressors from an early age. Eribeth had died in a suspicious accident while they played together as children. My sister was another one of their shared victims. We suspected that Sereia too had fallen by their hand.

"I don't get it," Palmer says. "How do the words of Dresden and Philomena carry so much power?"

Freya gives us both a knowing glance. "The written word is power, especially when imbued with compelling emotion. It is a singular magic, like none found anywhere else. Halcyon Bay has always been a bastion for magic."

"I should've put more stock in my diary entries as a kid," Palmer gripes under her breath. "If the written word is so damn powerful, maybe I'd have that pony by now."

This elicits a trickling laugh from Freya, and we all seem to take a communal breath to regroup.

"All will be well, Palmer," Freya assures her, reaching over to pat her arm. "You will see. I know you are afraid now, but fear is often a springboard for beautiful things." Her smile is motherly, filled with deep compassion.

We collect our things to go, nodding goodbyes at Freya, but she catches me by the wrist as I'm about to slip through the doorway.

"Before you go, Meridel," the psychic hums, her eyes searching mine intently, "I wanted to ask how you are faring? Being back on the island must stir up many difficult memories."

"I'm okay," I say quickly, eager to get off the subject. "It hasn't been easy, but I'm getting by. I have Hatch. And my family."

"Are you sleeping well?" she asks shrewdly.

I pause at this.

How does she know?

My silence seems to be answer enough.

Freya takes my hands in hers and squeezes. "If you need help, child, don't be afraid to ask for it."

I nod, but still don't bring up the sleepwalking. I don't want to prolong this meeting, or add to Palmer's distress right now.

My thoughts are storm-filled eddies, all centered on the unthinkable—on trapped spirits and inherited curses and disembodied whispers that chase us like the wind.

I need to get myself together before dinner with the Seaborns.

Need to put this behind me for now.

A flicker in Freya's eyes tells me she understands. "I'm here, if you ever need me," she says soothingly, before letting my hands drop and escorting us out.

CHAPTER THIRTY-THREE

"Remember, Dell, say nothing about this to anyone," Palmer repeats when she drops me off at my bike in front of the library. "Especially Mojo. The last thing I need is for him to freak out on me."

"He wouldn't freak out if you'd just be honest," I say in reproach. "Didn't you learn anything from last summer? About keeping secrets from him?"

"Please. You're one to talk."

I flash her a scowl. "What's that supposed to mean?"

"As if you don't keep things from the guy you love," she fires back.

"What are you talking about?" My cheeks flood with heat. "Who said anything about love?"

Palmer shifts in the driver's seat, turning on me with a no-bullshit expression. "Meridel. Roslyn. Costa."

"Did you seriously just middle-name me?"

"Are you seriously going to pretend you're not in love with Hatcher Seaborn?"

Whatever sharp-edged thing I might've thought to retort scampers from my mind like a scared animal.

"You *sooo* are!" she croons. "And the sooner you tell him, the better."

"But…he hasn't said it either," I counter lamely.

"Hello!" Palmer blinks in rapid succession. "That's only because he doesn't know how you're going to react! That boy walks on eggshells around you. He's been goo-goo-eyed for you since the night you freaking met! I was there, remember? So don't even try to shrug it off like it's not true."

I can't get into this with Palmer right now, not on the cusp of meeting Hatch's family. I can't let myself walk into that dinner feeling flustered, or giddy, or stupidly hopeful. Can't allow myself to jump to her silly conclusions.

"Just let Mojo know what's going on with you," I implore, my hand poised on the door handle. "Don't pull a repeat of last summer. Don't shut him out."

"I'll make you a deal," she bargains. "I'll tell Mojo the truth about this, when you tell Hatch that you're in love with him." Her sky-blue eyes steel against mine, like the horns of two stubborn rams locked in battle. "Don't pull a repeat of last summer, Dell!" She wags an irritating finger at me, throwing my own words back in my face. "Don't shut him out!"

In this moment, I swear I could murder her.

Instead, I disembark from the car in gruff silence, making to slam the door loudly behind me…

But then Palmer says, with a smug smile on her lips, "The Knotty Talismen are on the lineup for the Songwriter's Fest at The Oyster tomorrow. It'll be Mojo and the boys' last performance before the baby comes. Soundcheck starts at six. Show's at seven. You and Seaborn can buy tickets at the gate." She slides a pair of reflective pink sunglasses onto her face, looking away from me and into the waning sun. "Don't make me regret inviting you!"

"How was your day?" Hatch asks when he picks me up outside of Cliffmoor House that evening.

Nerves stir up my stomach contents as we wind our way to the Seaborns' for dinner. My leg bounces erratically, my bottom lip raw from my constant pecking.

Hatch rests a hand over my thigh to calm me.

"It was fine," I answer. "I spent most of it with Palmer. She stole me away from the library midway through my shift. Soft-core hostage situation."

"I'm sure Dexter appreciated that."

"He gave her his blessing, but we both know the poor guy didn't have much choice in the matter."

"Is everything all right?"

I shrug, not really sure one way or the other, and not wanting to divulge what Palmer made me vow to keep quiet. "I think so…er, hope so."

"That's reassuring," he mutters sarcastically.

"I wish I could give you details, but I've been sworn to secrecy by a very adamant Pregzilla."

Hatch snorts, shaking his head. "Say no more. I know when I'm out of my depths. Just tell me one thing—should I be worried?"

"I think you're safe."

"Not about me, love."

"Okay, well, I think *I'm* safe."

"Right." Hatch grunts. "We'll work on it."

We pull into the driveway of a modest bungalow painted a vivid green at the corner of Bleaker and Camellia Streets—the Seaborn house.

I draw in a shaky breath.

Meeting my boyfriend's mother for the first time shouldn't be such a terrifying prospect. I've gone through this ritual with a handful of guys before, sitting through awkward dinners and painful small talk. But I hadn't cared nearly as much with those guys. Nothing has *ever* come close to what I have with Hatch.

I want Kara—his mother—to like me, but it's more than that. I want her to like me *for her son*. To think me worthy and good. To see how much I love Hatch, even if I haven't said so out loud.

Admittedly, another small worry throbs in my head. Hatch told me his mother once blamed him for his father's death. They seem to have patched things up since—a fact for which I couldn't be happier—but if she'd been willing to assign that pain to him, to place the burden of his father's death on his shoulders, who knows what she'll think of me. How she'll treat me.

"Ready?" Hatch asks, beaming as we step up to the door.

I inhale sharply. "No." Then exhale. "Let's go."

He gives my hand an encouraging squeeze, as if to remind me that he'll be there when the night's over, no matter how this dinner goes. Come what may, it'll be him and me at the end. And that knowledge wraps me up in an emboldening embrace.

He turns the key and tugs on the door, calling into the house, "We're home!"

A chipper male voice answers, "I was wondering what that smell was!"

It's Hatch's older brother, Holden, coming down the hallway, looking just as I remember him from several months ago—the same thick, brown beard, brilliant smile, and Seaborn eyes. A young boy sits atop Holden's broad shoulders, chubby fingers buried in tufts of his father's hair. The child can't be more than three years old, and as they approach, I see that he's blessed with those same vibrant eyes—the Seaborns' stunning genealogical calling card.

"I thought that smell was you," Hatch shoots back, shutting the door behind us. "It's garbage day, right? Isn't that why you stopped by?"

A jingle chimes from below, and I notice a collared Dachshund with shiny black fur staring up at me, sleek tail wagging like a pendulum.

Holden claps his brother on the back, and Hatch promptly reaches for his nephew. "C'mere, Hairball!" With an adorable giggle, the little boy launches himself off his father's shoulders and cannonballs into Hatch's arms.

"Dell, do you remember my brother, Holden?" Hatch smirks. "It's okay if you don't. He's pretty easy to forget."

"I remember." I smile politely—*please like me*—and stretch out a hand before I can overthink it. "Nice to formally meet—" The rest of my greeting is snuffed out by Holden's shoulder. He's pulled me into a hug.

"We don't do 'formal' in this house, Dell." Holden chuckles as he steps back.

I nod, biting down the threat of elated tears.

"So!" Holden's eyes bounce between us, brewing with mischief. "This little meet-and-greet has been a long time coming. What the heck took you two so long?"

Hatch rolls his eyes at his brother's ribbing, but I can see a wash of pink rise in his stubbled cheeks. "Ignore him," he tells me, still cradling his nephew. "This little guy is Harry, by the way." Hatch tickles the boy's underarm, eliciting a milk-toothed smile from him. "What do we say when we meet a new friend, Harry?"

The toddler shoves the better part of his fist in his mouth, a shy twinkle in his eyes.

I laugh as a dribble of saliva runs down his pudgy chin. "Hi there, Harry. Aren't you a cutie?"

The little boy stares back at me, his fingers fluttering nervously in his mouth.

"C'mon, Hairball," Hatch says encouragingly. "Say hi to Dell."

Harry gurgles a muffled "Hi" around his hand, then hiccups, reddens, and promptly buries his face in Hatch's neck.

Hatch coughs back a laugh. "Don't worry, buddy. If memory serves, that's about as eloquent as I was the first time I met her too. Like nephew, like uncle."

"That's not how the saying goes," Holden quips, frowning in spite of the playful gleam in his eyes.

"It's how it *should* go," Hatch counters.

Watching them bicker is an absolute treat, like a camera lens into Hatch's life growing up. A peek into the moments that made him *him*, the relationships that formed a heart so big.

Holden fixes Hatch with a narrow-eyed expression. "Hey, go make your own kid, all right? This one's accounted for." He wraps his son in his arms, and adds, "Come join us in the kitchen, Dell! Hatch—feel free to stay behind."

"I live here, jackass. It's my kitchen."

"Language around the baby!" a woman hollers from the depths of the house.

"Uh-oh! Beastie's pissed. You've done it now, *Thatcher*," Holden calls over his shoulder, bouncing Harry as he walks toward the kitchen.

Hatch sneaks a glance at me and shakes his head, unable to keep a smile at bay. "I'm sorry about him."

"Thatcher?" I ask, anticipating a funny story.

"Holden's always been weirdly into history. As kids, he used to call me Margaret Thatcher whenever I annoyed him. And since he still has the stunted humor of a ten-year-old…" Hatch rolls his eyes—not with irritation, but amusement. "Hatcher. Thatcher. Whatever the hell."

I snort. "Makes sense, I guess. Who's Beastie?"

"That unfortunate soul would be *Beata*, Holden's wife. I swear, the eighth wonder of this world is how my brother tricked that woman into marrying him."

I feel a wet nose press against my leg, and look down to find big, brown eyes staring up curiously—the small Dachshund, wriggling in place, still waiting eagerly for an introduction.

"How rude of me!" Hatch says suddenly, dropping to his knees to smother the dog in caresses. "Dell, this is Maple, my favorite sibling."

Maple rubs her body along the denim of Hatch's jeans.

When I bend down, Maple squats low, tentative but gentle, her belly grazing the floor. I reach out to scratch her behind the ears, and soon she begins to open up, frolicking and pouncing up into my lap. The dog's sleek black coat has a bluish sheen when the light hits it just right.

"Hi, Maple," I say. She practically leaps when she hears me say her name.

Hatch laughs. "Mom picked her name because she's sweet as syrup. Isn't that right, Maple girl?"

He grabs my hand, helping me to my feet. "Let's get this ordeal over with, shall we?" Despite his less-than-enthusiastic tone, I can feel the excitement pulsing through him, the obvious joy when he gives my fingers a squeeze, his two worlds colliding at long last, and with any luck, melding together as one. It feels official, somehow. Real like never before. Like we're plunging into deeper waters, forever shifting the parameters of our relationship.

Inside the kitchen, two women are huddled together, shoulder to shoulder, whispering by the stove. Holden hovers behind them, doing a silly shoulder jig with Harry still in his arms.

"Mom?" Hatch pipes up.

The older, tawny-haired woman turns around, her short hair in a loose ponytail, wisps the color of leaves in autumn framing her face. Her brown eyes are kind but watchful as she takes me in, wrapping thin arms around herself. "Hello, there."

"Mom, this is Dell." Hatch leads me forward, nodding as he guides me. "Dell, this is my mom, Kara."

"Hi." I force a wide smile, my heart stuttering. "It's really great to meet you."

She nods pleasantly, but otherwise keeps her distance. "Thanks for coming, Dell. We've heard so much about you."

Not the warmest of greetings, but also not the worst.

The younger woman, Holden's wife, has pixie-cut auburn hair and pale blue eyes, the color of Willow's sea glass. Her nose and cheeks are smattered with freckles, and when she smiles, they flush prettily.

"Hi, Dell!" she says with a wave, bouncing a little in her running shoes. "I'm Beata, but everyone calls me Bee."

"Or Beastie," Holden offers.

Bee glares at her husband. "No one calls me that but you."

"And you love it," he purrs.

She hums primly and turns back to the stove.

"We're about ready to eat," Kara says, still drinking me in from head-to-toe, as if I've been served up in a glass with a straw. I wonder what she's thinking, what she sees with those appraising eyes, whether I'm anything like she imagined.

Holden pulls glasses from a cabinet and begins filling them with tap water. "What would you like to drink, Dell?"

"Water's fine, thanks."

Holden wrinkles his nose. "Sure you don't want something with a little more kick? Alcohol might help you get through tonight's interrogation—"

"*There will be no interrogation.*" Hatch's voice cuts across the kitchen like a blade. "Here's a thought. Why don't we let Maple sit at the table with us, and we can put Holden's food in the dog bowl? I'm sure he'd be just as happy eating from the floor."

"Yes!" Bee chirps. "I love that idea."

"I'm the only one looking out for Dell's best interests here," Holden complains, shrugging his innocence.

Hatch turns to me. "Just pretend he's not here, okay? If everyone ignores him, he'll have to leave eventually."

Holden sighs loudly. "The world always wants to silence genius."

Bee snorts.

"I was planning on opening a bottle of rosé," Kara says with a smile, pointedly ignoring the antics unfolding in her kitchen. "Would you like a glass, Dell?"

I nod. "Yes, thank you." At this point, I'll gladly take whatever she offers me.

"We've fried up something really yummy for dinner, Dell," Bee says. "I hope you don't mind trying something a little bit different."

"How different are we talking?" Hatch asks, peering cautiously over Bee's shoulder.

"Well, it's a—*hey!*" Bee shoos Hatch away when she senses him hovering. "Get out of here! You'll ruin the surprise."

"Different's good with me," I insist, wondering if I'm annoying anyone with my excessive agreeability. No one likes a people pleaser, and, certainly, no one respects them. But with Kara still watching me like she hasn't decided what to think, I'm second-guessing every little thing I do— fidgeting over every word I've uttered, questioning why my smile feels so tight on my face, whether the dress I wore tonight is too short.

"Why don't you boys go set the table?" Kara suggests, glaring at Holden and Hatch like they're both on the verge of a well-earned timeout.

"Let us ladies chat for a bit."

Hatch glances at me to make sure I'm fine on my own. I smile, nodding to cover for the wild flip-flopping of my stomach, breathing deeply through the thundering hammer of my heart.

Holden swings Harry onto his shoulders again, grabbing a tablecloth and napkins from a drawer, while Hatch assembles all the plates and utensils. They move in unison toward the dining room, jostling each other as they move down the hall, shoulder colliding against shoulder, muttered curses flying between them.

"Try not to kill each other!" Bee calls at their backs. "Remember, utensils are for eating, not stabbing! And mind your language around Harry, please!" She turns to throw me a conspiratorial look. "*Men*," she says.

I cough out a nervous laugh.

"So, Dell." Kara shoots me a good-natured smile as she uncorks the bottle of rosé. I silently brace myself for whatever's to come, determined to prove to this woman how serious I am about her son. "How long are you planning to be in town?"

Fabulous—a question for which I have no answer.

"I'm not sure yet," I say honestly. "At least a few weeks, but maybe more. My cousin is giving birth soon, so I'd like to be around for that."

"It's nice that your job allows you so much free range," Kara comments. "Hatch tells us you're in advertising?"

Double freaking fabulous. Either I outright lie to this woman, or I divulge the bleak truth about my current employment status and accept her inevitable judgment.

"I was, yes," I say, opting for the latter. I've been told time and again that I'm a godawful liar. The last thing I need is for Kara to see through my half-truths and label me a sham. "But I was recently, um, laid off..." Her brown eyes snap up curiously. I try to ignore how that makes the heat rise in my cheeks. "I'm hoping to find something I'm better suited for. Something I'm really passionate about."

To my surprise, Kara doesn't react negatively. "You're young," she says with an understanding nod. "Far too young to settle for work you don't enjoy. You'll find what you're looking for soon enough. In the meantime, I see no harm in moving around."

I nod, grateful to have scraped through that line of questioning without much trouble. "While I'm here, I'll be working part-time at the island library—"

"Ooh, a job in town? That's exciting!" Bee says, shooting me a smile.

"Yeah. My aunt's dating the new librarian, so it was a good fit."

I immediately want to smack myself for letting the connection slip. I've made it sound like Dexter is doing me a favor. Like I landed the job through nepotism.

Who the hell are you kidding? That's exactly how you landed it.

"Well, it'll certainly be nice having another girl around," Bee adds. It's a kindness I appreciate, words that feel like an olive branch.

"Have you and Hatch discussed what's next for the two of you?" Kara asks, keeping her tone light as she sets five wine glasses on the counter.

I don't have a solid answer about this either. The only thing I know is that I want to spend forever with Hatch. How that comes to be is still a mystery to both of us.

"We're still…figuring that out," I say quietly.

Hatch has been great about giving me time to get my emotions straight. He hasn't pushed at all, but I don't expect his loved ones to be so generous. Understandably, they want to know where we stand and that I'm not wasting his time.

"He's very attached to you," Kara admits, a small confession that cuts to my heart. "I don't think a day goes by where he doesn't mention your name. I've never seen him quite so smitten."

"*Kara,*" Bee sings through a smile. "Your boy is *in love.*"

My insides melt all at once, like the sun crawled out from beyond the sea, pushed the moon right out of the sky, and penetrated my soul with incandescent beams of light.

Is Bee *assuming* Hatch is in love with me? Is she goofing around? Had he actually said something? Used the L-word in front of them?

"It certainly seems like it," Kara agrees with a low chuckle, pouring sparkling pink wine into each goblet, going about her task as if the whole world hadn't just irrefutably quivered around us.

Hatch.

In love.

With me.

It's not the first time I've contemplated it, but every day the potential seems to get realer and realer. And I wonder if ever, in the history of time, there's been another sentiment quite as life-affirming, earth-shaking, and indescribably marvelous as this.

Hatch is in love with me.

Or at least *falling* in love?

Or at least *close* to falling in love?

All of which seem far too dreamlike to be real. Too much like a perfect fairytale.

My smile runs deep, down to my core.

"What about you, Dell?" Kara asks. "Is this relationship something you think you'd like to pursue long-term?"

"Goodness!" Bee tuts. "Don't put her on the spot like that!"

"Oh, chock it up to a mother's curiosity." Kara laughs, but beneath that congenial surface, I can tell she wants answers. To know more about the girl that's captured her son's attention, and whether I'm as enamored as he seems to be.

She offers me a wine-filled glass, and an inquisitive smile along with it. "Tell me, Dell. Tell me how you feel about my Hatcher."

"Kara, are you for real?" Bee exclaims, whipping around to face her mother-in-law, cheeks pink with embarrassment.

Kara swats the air, undeterred.

I want to be truthful, of course, but I'm not willing to throw around those three words just yet, though I feel them singing through my veins. I can't blurt them out now, in a nervous moment. Can't say them for anyone but him. When the time is right.

"I'm very serious about Hatch," I say, the cascade of words breathy and altogether inadequate. "And I'd love nothing more than to be with him long-term. Honestly, I don't know what I'd do without him."

Bee and Kara pause, neither one speaking as they take in my face with eager eyes, hungry for detail.

"He's sweet and wonderful and warm as sunshine. He makes me feel like the world isn't such an awful place." Flames bloom in my cheeks, a lump sticking in my throat. "He's everything to me. Absolutely everything. My whole heart wrapped up in a person—"

"Table's set!"

Holden blows into the kitchen like a tornado, a lopsided smile on his face that's nearly a mirror to Hatch's. He takes in the sight of the three of us donning varying expressions of speechlessness—the air brimming with emotion—and his brow furrows. "Whoa, who died?"

Bee presses her eyes shut, inhaling sharply, as if she can will Holden to disappear using sheer brain power. Her grip tightens on the ladle in her hand. "I think I hear Harry crying, hon. Can you check on him, please?" She prompts Holden with her eyes.

"Harry's with Hatch," her husband counters, oblivious to her hints. "He's totally fine—"

"Just go check, please!" she snaps, and Holden ducks out of the kitchen as though his heels have caught on fire.

Bee's eyebrows fly up in her husband's wake—almost comical in their show of irritation. She barks out another exaggerated, *"Men!"*

I laugh half-heartedly, still overwhelmed by the things I'd shared. The pivotal moment Holden had popped like a balloon.

"Well," Kara says, her delicate voice filling the silence, "that's very nice to hear, Dell. Incredibly nice…"

I nod, not quite knowing why, as I take in Kara's face. Her smile is gentler than before—soft in a way that reminds me of Mom's. She looks genuinely happy, as if I'd somehow answered her every question correctly. As if she can see the love radiating through me. As if that's all the peace of mind she needed.

When Kara says, "You're welcome here anytime," her brown eyes fill with heartfelt meaning, like she's offering me a coveted prize.

Without a doubt, I feel like I've won.

CHAPTER THIRTY-FOUR

Bee's culinary surprise—fried gator doused in homemade 'swamp sauce'—is one for the memory books. Despite sounding like roadkill, it tastes utterly delicious. "Like chicken, but better!" Bee chuckles proudly, popping another beer-battered chunk in her mouth.

Throughout dinner, Kara is keenly observant of Hatch and me, and the subtle ways we orbit each other. The easy touches we share. The way our gazes pull to one another, aligned by an inner magnetism.

My former tension has all but washed away now that I've procured her quiet approval, and I find myself truly enjoying my time with the Seaborns. Seeing how I might fit into their family. Hoping they deem me worthy of a forever-seat at the table.

"Dear Lord, Holden, spare us the dramatics!" Bee gripes.

They're discussing an apparent shortage of French fries on Halcyon Bay—a matter that has Holden quite concerned.

"It's scary!" he shoots back. "I mean, what if we have another Potato Famine on our hands?"

Bee groans, exasperated. "How about you leave Irish history out of this, and take the shortage as a sign to eat a *real* vegetable once in a while?"

I snort, loving every second of their bickering.

Hatch chimes in for my benefit. "Holden teaches history at the high school, and he has a habit of relating all things to obscure historical events. Usually pretty unsuccessfully."

"My eleventh grade students would beg to differ," Holden quips. "They're kicking ass on their AP History exams, *Thatcher*, all thanks to my so-called 'unsuccessful' tutelage."

"The more you call me that, the less it makes sense," Hatch deadpans.

"What kind of history do you teach?" I ask Holden.

"World history," he says enthusiastically. "We start in Ancient Civilizations and run all the way through the Modern Age. Right now, I'm teaching European Imperialism and the Opium Wars. Riveting stuff!"

"That sounds really cool."

"Does it?" Holden laughs. "That's not usually the reaction I get from this crowd."

"Well, I like history," I say earnestly. "Plus, my dad's really into it. We used to binge all these History Channel shows together. Didn't matter the subject. Whether it was about World War II or the Vikings or Ancient Egypt, we watched them all."

Holden nods. "I used to do that with my dad too."

The table suddenly falls quiet. I feel Hatch stiffen at my side.

I know he doesn't mind talking about his father—in fact, I think he'd like to speak about him *more,* letting the memories come up for air—but I also know it begets a great deal of tension with his mother. More often than not, Hatch refrains from bringing his dad up so he doesn't have to face the melancholy in her eyes. He says he can't bear it, can't stand to add to her pain. I share the same compulsion with my mother.

Holden, apparently, does not.

"A love of history is one of the few things Dad and I had in common," he prattles on. "He rarely managed to get me out on a boat. I've never been a huge fan of large bodies of water." A chuckle burbles from his lips. "Surprised the old man didn't disown me for that."

"So am I," Hatch quips between bites.

"Hatch and Dad were always more similar that way," Holden says. "They both had this unshakeable love of the sea. Fishing and boating was always a family affair, really. I was the only oddball."

"Not true," Kara interjects. "I have no interest in boating. As far as I see it, the best boat is a sold one."

There's no hostility in Kara's statement, but there's also no room for discussion—a definitive line drawn in the sand. There'd be no convincing her otherwise.

"Well, that may be the case *now*," Holden doubles down, "but there was a time when you loved being on the water, almost as much as Hatch or Dad. It's okay to admit it."

Kara and Hatch are both silent. Frozen.

"People change, Holden," Bee says, her words too gentle for the severity in her eyes.

"Sure they do," he agrees imperviously. "Just not me, though. I never liked it, never will. Too many unknowns and shifting variables. Too many risks. Just look what happened to Da—"

His words cut off with a jolt, and he stares at his wife in horror, as though she'd taken her fork and jabbed him with it under the table.

Bee flares her nostrils, fixing him a withering glare.

Wasn't she the one that said utensils aren't for stabbing?

"Sorry," Holden mumbles, truly looking the part. "That was insensitive of me. I didn't mean to go there."

For a long, uncomfortable minute, no one speaks, until Hatch finally coughs, attempting to cut the tension. "Holden's mouth always had a tendency of getting away from him."

"That must be why he became a teacher," Bee chimes in, clearly still peeved by her husband's blunder. "So he can ramble and rant for hours on end to people who are legally compelled to listen."

"Those poor, poor children," Hatch mutters under his breath. Catching his brother's eye, he shoots him a teasing wink.

Holden's returning smile is sheepish, but he still avoids his mother's gaze. Bee's too, for good measure.

An uncomfortable weight looms over the table, broken up by Harry's squeals of joy as he mashes handfuls of puffed cereal in his mouth, as well as Maple's soft whimpers at Hatch's side, soliciting dinner scraps.

Surprisingly, Kara is the one to shatter the silence. She hums to herself, chuckling softly under her breath. "Holden's a lot like Hugh in that way…"

We all collectively gape at her, taken aback.

"Overly chatty, I mean," Kara continues, winking at her eldest son. "Both gregarious and friendly, sometimes too much for their own good. But they always meant well. Always saw the best in people."

Kara leans back in her seat, lifting her eyes—glistening with heartfelt memory—to the pendant light dangling over the table. She sighs deeply, and it sounds like release. *Relief.* Like finding tranquility after years of chaos.

"To remember Hugh is to honor him," she says, her words at once gentle and firm. "You boys don't talk about your father much, and I know you do that for my benefit. But I'd like us to change that. I want to feel Hugh here, at this table, among family again."

Hatch's throat bobs when he swallows, every inch of him thrumming with heightened sentiment. He catches his bottom lip in his teeth.

I reach over, slipping my hand over his leg, and immediately, his hand meets mine, entwining our fingers.

"Hugh and Holden had twin personalities, but Hatch was always more like me," Kara continues. "More reserved. More guarded with his heart. At least, until now, that is." Her smile brightens her eyes. Her whole face, really.

Hatch doesn't blush or cower under the implications of her words. He just looks from his mother to me, exuding confidence and a sense of pride, his hands cradling mine like a gift.

Kara's gaze jumps from us to something beyond, as if peering into the depths of our future. Into whatever life we might build for ourselves, past the hardships of today and tomorrow.

I wish I could peek into whatever she sees, wish I knew now everything that's to come. But sometimes, it's the not-knowing that makes it all worth it. Sometimes, you have to trust the undeniable gut feeling within—beating in your heart, fluttering butterfly-wild in your stomach. It's intuitive. Instinctual. As natural as drawing breath.

That's exactly how I know that being with Hatch—calling him mine, forever and always—is my privilege. My honor. My destiny.

"That went well," Hatch says through a smile, spinning me round and round as we drift to the Ranger.

The cool night unfolds like infinity before us, winking stars and a dripping moon showering our bodies in ethereal light. The cozy island neighborhood has turned in for the evening—the streetside atmosphere utterly dim and quiet, still but for the whispering wind rustling the palms.

"I think so," I reply, filled with a sense of belonging. "Your mom told me I was welcome anytime."

"You already knew that," Hatch says, tucking me close.

"It still meant a lot, hearing it from her."

"The only problem I see with you hanging out with my family more"—Hatch twirls me again, then backs me up against the truck, removing all manner of space between us—"is that it means I have to share you." He leans over me, his forearm on the truck, dipping down to steal a kiss. "And I don't like sharing."

I giggle, reaching for his frayed baseball cap. I sweep it off his head and slap it on mine, living for the wide-eyed reaction it elicits from him. "If that's the worst of our problems, pirate man, then I'd say we're in a pretty good spot."

Hatch grins at me like a little kid, green eyes sparkling. "A perfect fit," he says meaningfully, adjusting the brim of the cap before burying his fingers in my hair. "Keep it. It looks way better on you."

It's just a stupid baseball cap, but it might as well be a diamond ring for how those simple words make me feel.

I love you I love you I love you.

I have to say it.

Okay, go time. Deep breaths. You can do this.

"Hatch," I start, at the exact same time he says, "Your surprise is almost ready."

I blink wildly, thrown for a loop. "It is?"

His slow, crooked smile is contagious—I can't contain my own in response. "I really think you're going to love it."

"Then why wait? Let's go right now."

Hatch shakes his head. "Aren't we greedy?"

I lift up to brush my nose against his, whispering brazenly, "Maybe I just know what I want."

His hands slip around me, lifting me up until my feet leave the ground, my back pressed fast to the truck, legs hoisted up around his hips. I gasp a little, gripping him tightly. If anyone walks out and sees this…

"As enticing as that sounds," he murmurs, wholly focused on me and my quiet pants of excitement, "I said it was *almost* ready."

"Careful, or your mother's going to revoke that open invitation," I rasp, though I have half a mind to ignore that and give in to his advances.

Hatch frowns a little. "I seriously doubt that." But he slides me down the length of him anyway—achingly slow—until I'm back on solid ground, atop legs like jelly. I clutch at his arms, not trusting myself to stand on my own just yet. "Why don't we go somewhere a bit more private then?"

"Now who's the greedy one?"

He shrugs a shoulder nonchalantly, but those seagrass eyes tell a different story. They're intent—consumed with passion—blazing a fire to my core, my heart.

"Like I said, love," he replies, "I'm not fond of sharing. When it comes to you, I'm *very* greedy. It's compulsory, I can't help it. And I don't want to."

I grin, relishing in Hatch's reaction when I suddenly slip my hand in the front pocket of his jeans. He cocks his head to one side. A distinctly male smile crawls over his lips.

I take my time pulling the truck keys out.

"I'll drive," I whisper temptingly, dangling them in the air.

CHAPTER THIRTY-FIVE

If Cliffmoor House is my own personal hell, Idyll Point is my heaven.

To anyone else, it's only a lighthouse. An old, crumbling structure, like so many sprinkled across this island. A defunct time capsule, left to wither and wear, long stripped of its purpose of guiding sailors to shore. Drained of its light, swallowed up by modernity, abandoned to darkness…

But not for me.

Everything good about Halcyon Bay is wrapped up in that lighthouse. In its old-fashioned beauty, and its quiet, secluded charms. In the memories it rouses, and the promise of more.

Hatch and I settle on the wrap-around balcony, his arms curled over me as we soak in the hazy glow of the city, the watercolor smears of night-life at a distance, and the sounds of crashing waves tumbling onto the beach.

"I wish we could stay here," I say quietly, letting my head drop back to his shoulder, taking in the expanse of star-flecked sky above. "Just you and me, in our own little bubble, far away from everything and everyone."

"We could move in," he jokes, nipping at my ear. "Squat up here till the cops get wise and arrest us. Or at least until the city decides to bulldoze the place."

"They wouldn't."

"They would."

"But you said it was going to be turned into a museum?"

"There's been talk of that, but I've also heard rumors they might demolish it to make way for more beachfront real estate." He sighs, the very thought of it defeating. "Either that or a luxury hotel. Nothing good lasts forever, right?"

They should demolish Cliffmoor House instead, I think. *Convert that massive waste of land into a hotel.*

"I won't let them do it," I say determinedly.

I can sense the smirk on Hatch's lips when he asks, "Are you going to chain yourself to the door in protest?"

"If that's what it takes to save this place."

Hatch chuckles behind me, and before I know it, his lips are on my shoulder, dropping kisses like snowflakes.

"Why's that funny?" I ask, struggling to stay firm, to not let myself fall into the trap of desire. But it's hard—*so hard*—with him touching me this way, folded up in his arms, in the lighthouse of my dreams.

"Because you're adorable when you get riled up."

"Oh, really?" I start pulling away, but he cages me in his arms.

"I love it," he says.

I stop struggling.

Do you love me? I desperately want to ask him. *Tell me you love me, Hatch. Tell me...*

For whatever reason, he doesn't.

Maybe he needs more time, more assurances that I won't leave.

Maybe he can't love a wild, flighty thing.

Maybe I'm too skittish, too prone to retreat...or at least I was.

Even if Hatch does love parts of me—the jagged little bits and pieces—maybe he still struggles to make sense of the whole.

I can't really blame him for that.

"What are you thinking about?" he asks after several minutes of unbroken silence.

"I'm thinking you're wrong." I turn my head to face him, slipping a hand around his neck, pulling his mouth to mine. "Some good things do last forever."

My place in this world is with him.

And that's exactly what I'll prove.

However long it takes.

When I make it back to the guest house later that night, there's a note taped to the front door.

I have news.
Meet me in the parlor.
-T

Crisp and ominous, just as I'd expect of Tristen.

I'm exhausted, but far too curious to spurn his request and head to bed. I march across the night-dark grounds, using my key to enter Cliffmoor House through the back.

Tank grunts at me in greeting from his post inside the door. I nod back and slip through the shadows down the hall.

Tristen and Nova await in the parlor. She's perched on the couch, leaning over the armrest, her chestnut hair cascading like a curtain, those streaks of peachy-pink glistening in the dim light. Tristen is seated on the other side of her, his face aimed at hers like a sunflower trails the sun. Soft, breathy laughter falls in whispers between them, their smiles eager and nervous, like two kids falling in love.

I cough and Nova straightens up, her eyes half-mast when they meet mine at a distance.

"Aren't we cozy?" I comment, slinking inside.

Admittedly, I've somewhat softened toward Nova. How could I not, after she'd come to my aid with Dash and Parris, and provided me a weapon to defend myself with? But I still can't help but remain hesitant.

Trusting her could spell disaster.

Considering how closely she and my cousin are nestled together—and the dusky, bedroom eyes the both of them are currently donning—it seems I'm the only one with lingering doubts.

"I'm shocked that you and your indelible snark decided to make an appearance," Tristen drawls.

I plop down on the couch across from them. "What's so urgent it couldn't wait until morning?"

Tristen's smirk holds an air of mystery. "Notice anything different?"

My eyes sweep over him, up and down, searching intently, but nothing looks amiss. I do the same with Nova, and then around the parlor.

"No?" I reply uncertainly.

"Look closer, Dell," Tristen implores. A secretive little smile blooms on Nova's face.

Whatever game this is, I'm not interested in playing.

"What are you—" My voice cracks, giving way to a gasp when I see it.

Tristen wiggling his fingers.

"Tristen! Y-your…your hands are…moving!"

His smirk grows into a real, bonafide smile. "I've regained some of my motor skills in therapy."

"That's incredible!"

"The doctors don't know how much more I'll recover," he says quickly, as if to not get his hopes up, "but this is promising, at least."

"It's a miracle," Nova chimes in, her voice fraught with emotion. I'm struck by how deeply she seems to care.

"I likely won't retain any function in my legs," Tristen warns, "but if…if my arms work at least…" He sighs heavily, the words falling away as a wave of relief and hope wash over him.

I beam at him, tears rising to my eyes. "I'm so happy for you."

I have half a mind to cross the room and throw my arms around him, but swiftly decide against it. We're not the hugging kind. Hell, one of us might spontaneously combust at first contact.

"I'm glad to hear that," Tristen says. "Glad you're in such good spirits, before I tell you this next thing."

Just like that, I'm on high alert again.

"I'll leave you to it," Nova says, excusing herself and gliding stealthily from the room.

"What's going on?" I ask, all the sympathy and softness I'd just felt draining away like rainwater.

"I want to inform you about something I've been planning," Tristen says, "so you can't accuse me of keeping you out of the loop. I'd hate to be on the receiving end of another one of your tantrums."

"If you wouldn't comport yourself like such a tyrannical prick, there'd be no need for tantrums." I force a thin smile at him, bitterly sweet.

Tristen stifles another smirk, deriving some strange satisfaction over our repartee. "There's something for you on the table there."

My eyes flit to the coffee table, spotting an elegant envelope laid atop it. I grab for it, and once up close, see that it's addressed to *Miss Meridel Costa* in lovely, swooping calligraphy.

The sight of it launches space rockets in my stomach.

"What is this?" I ask, dreading his answer.

"Take a look," Tristen says inscrutably.

I slip a finger across the flap and pull out the card within. An iridescent, midnight-blue card stock stares up at me, sprinkled in flecks and swirls of foiled silver and gold. It's an invitation, equal parts exquisite and unnerving.

You are cordially invited to the inaugural
Stars at Sea Charity Ball
Benefitting the Stand Against Paralysis Foundation
Hosted by Mr. Tristen Rolf Klyne
At Cliffmoor House Estate

My eyes snap up at him, not bothering to read on. "What the hell is this?" I ask, repeating my previous question with more force.

"Dell," he says slowly, regarding me like a child. "In a little over a week, I'll be hosting a charity ball at Cliffmoor House."

My brain doesn't register the words. "You're *what?*"

"A charity ball. You have heard of those, haven't you? A formal fundraising event, usually with music, dinner, dancing, and copious amounts of champagne."

"Are you out of your mind?"

"Think of it as a peace offering to the islanders," he explains. "Given the opportunity to see me—see *us*, rather—in a different light, we may finally emerge from the dregs of scandal. All the gossip and the vilification and the slanders can be put to rest. We don't have to be the ostracized, perpetually-wounded Klyne descendants any longer. We can form a united front, do some real damage control, and combat our reputation, once and for all."

"So you want to put on a dog and pony show for the locals?" I ask, audibly disgusted.

Tristen doesn't reply.

"Since when do you care what they say about you?" I press.

"What I care about is breaking from the shadow of my father," he replies. "Divorcing myself from his legacy, and Ambrose's too. I thought you'd be on board with that. Besides, it'd be good to keep our ears open. Townies talk, and they're never more loose-lipped than at a party while gorging themselves on liquor. You know more than anyone that whispered rumors always carry some truth. I'd like to hear what they're saying about our family. What they suspect about my father—"

"So go plant yourself at a bar or something!" I snap. "You'll hear all the scandalous townie gossip you want downtown! Hosting a ball is *insane*, Tristen. It's *ridiculous*. It's…it's—"

"Far more suited to my predilections," he says. "I'd rather do this on my turf, my way."

I shake my head. "It's a bad idea."

"Like it or not, Dell, there are certain expectations that come with owning this house—"

"To hell with expectations! Who cares about that?"

Tristen's mouth goes flat and severe, and it hits me suddenly. My cousin—who'd always been deprived of the pleasures of this home and its sparkling affairs, always trapped under the thumb of his snake-like father—might be the one person who cares. Deep down, he might not only crave this house, but everything it stands for. The respect, the splendor, the lofty expectations. All the grandeur and pride that go hand-in-hand with this place.

Tristen wants this ball to be a coming-out party for a new era of Klynes, with him at the helm.

"This is all to stroke your ego," I work out. "To show everybody what the new overlord of Cliffmoor House is made of."

Again, silence.

"You're better than this, Tristen! Who on earth are you trying to impress?"

His face is blank—as good as dead—but it's not a stretch for me to surmise the truth.

"I assume Nova and her team will be hard at work that evening?" I ask.

Tristen's jaw ticks. "The team will be working, yes. But I've invited Nova to the ball as my..." He hesitates.

"As your date?" I ask.

"My guest."

Incredible.

"Look, I came back to help you find your father," I say, a simmering anger sliding under my skin. "Not to act as your doting underling while you climb the Halcyon Bay social ranks. I don't care about a stupid ball! If we're not looking for Florian, then I don't need to be here."

"Stop using Florian as an excuse for why you're here," Tristen seethes. "Don't act like I'm holding you hostage. You wanted this. And with every day you're here, every second you spend with Hatcher, and every speck of clarity you gain as to the blackhole that is our family, *you want more.* You're insatiable when it comes to these people. So don't blame me for veering our plans off course. This was always part of my plan. And I deserve to see it through."

"Why do you think you deserve anything?" I snarl. "Let's not forget that you made my mother's life a living hell for years. You blackmailed her about Willow and threatened to destroy my sister's innocence. All the good you've done since does not erase what you did then. So don't try to rewrite history. Don't try to paint yourself as some all-deserving white knight. You're no hero."

His twisted roots haven't shriveled up and disappeared. They're still there, buried, strengthening in the darkness even as he blossoms and shoots to the sky.

"I deserve *something* from all of this grief," he growls.

"Why?"

"Because he took everything from me!" Tristen bellows through his teeth, his face shaking, evoking more emotion than I've ever seen in him. "For fuck's sake, Dell, look at me!"

"I do look at you!" I yell back. "All I ever do is try to see beyond your past, try to make myself believe that you're a good person. So don't tell me to look at you! I do look, Tristen. I look every single day. And I never flinch."

His wild eyes flash at me, treacherous and stark black.

"You think that, just because you're in that chair, you're *entitled* to something?" I ask. "You knew full well what your father was capable of. You knew there were risks, but you went after him anyway! And I'm sorry for what he did to you. I'm sorry that your life has been so difficult. You didn't deserve Florian's abuse, but that still doesn't give you the right to look at the world like it owes you something. Look at all you *do* have! Against all odds, you've even found a woman who might actually be falling in love with you. So why are you clinging to these antiquated expectations? Why are you so obsessed with the past?"

"Why are you?" he growls.

That shuts me up.

"You discovered the truth about your sister long ago, Meridel." His use of my full name makes me shiver, like nails being dragged along a chalkboard. "This family has wounded you in more ways than you can count. Yet, you're still here. Searching, questioning, unappeasable in your need to understand them. Just a poor, overlooked little girl, desperate to connect to the family that abandoned you."

I glare at him, hating myself for the hot tears spilling down my cheeks.

Tristen grimaces. "You think I'm the only one brimming with hatred? The only one that sees the world through rage-filled eyes, acting like I'm owed something for what's been taken from me? Well, I've got some cold, hard news for you, cousin." His pitch-black eyes turn icy—a deadly sharpness to them that reminds me all too much of his father. "Look in the goddamn mirror."

CHAPTER THIRTY-SIX

After my blow up with Tristen, I storm back to the guest house. It crawls with a sinister darkness—too cramped to breathe, too vacant in the night, each shadowy corner harboring monsters and secrets.

I'm too antsy to stay here, prickly in my skin, so I burst back onto the grounds, needing to fill my stifled lungs with fresh air. But the estate at a distance is far too oppressive, the midnight sky dripping low, the island atmosphere muggy and suffocating.

I feel my lungs constricting, crushed by claustrophobic waves, my heartbeat ramping up and up. A tsunami of panic slams into me, flooding my senses. I can't breathe, can't think.

Need to run. Need to escape.

Chest tight, I make for the beach, bounding past the guard, the gate, bullet-fast down the walkway, all the words Tristen spat at me replaying like a broken record in my head.

You wanted this.

Insatiable. Unappeasable. Overlooked little girl.

Look in the goddamn mirror.

I don't stop when my feet hit the sand. They move on autopilot toward that span of black ocean—the only place I might procure some relief from this aching within.

I push past what feels like miles of damp shoreline, desperate to feel the sea on my skin. It calls to me on the breeze—a lilting, tempting siren song that promises respite, release, and resuscitation.

Salt air whisks my hair from my shoulders, caresses my face like an old lover, gathering me up in a brisk embrace. The breakneck gallop of my heart grows erratic, as unstable as my clumsy, staggering footsteps.

Clutching my chest over my sea glass, tears spill from my eyes…and I'm afraid. Afraid I've lost myself to the island, once and for all. Afraid that my lungs will collapse if I don't touch water soon.

What is happening to me?

My knees buckle and I catapult forward, slamming into the sand. It sprays up into my face, my mouth, but even then, I don't stop. I crawl like an animal, feet and elbows and fingers propelling me to the shore, groveling in my approach.

And then, I'm there, amid the gurgling sea foam. The lapping water nips my skin, and I roll onto my back, gasping for breath like a fish. Wave after wave spills over and against me, and I lay there through it, reduced to a puddle of salty tears and saltwater.

The storm of anxiety blows through me, and the crashing sea responds in time. I count as the seconds spill into minutes, slowly recovering my breath, my discernment.

Why did I come here in my moment of need? Why do I seek this reprieve at the sea? At the scene of my nightmares, and my sister's murder?

The sea glass runs ice-cold against my chest, and when I look down at it, the pale blue stone seems to *glow*.

None of this makes any sense…

But I can breathe again. I can think. The cool rush of water did that for me. Put the steady rhythm back in my heart, supplied life-giving air to my lungs.

Sitting up and soaked to the bone, Tristen's words trickle in again. This time, I'm able to face them without panicking. Without feeling like my organs are crumbling under the weight.

I was right in everything I'd said to him, and I don't feel guilty for laying it all on the line. But, I can't deny that he's right about me too. My outlook *isn't* all that different from his. We both cling to our respective traumas, wearing masks to cover up the unhealed hurt. We refuse to let those wounds scab over, continuing to pick at them until they rip open and bleed.

We're gluttons for pain and punishment.

We don't know how to move on.

Maybe we're more alike than I care to admit.

Slogging back onto the grounds, I spot Tristen's wheelchaired form beside the swimming pool.

My instincts tell me to avoid him. To get back inside the guest house, huddle in the shower, and spare myself the grief of yet another gut-wrenching exchange. But my feet find their way to his side anyway, and soon we're both looking out at that murky green pool, making shapes of the swirling filth and the clustered leaves and the clouds of debris.

"What are you doing out here?" I rasp, the effects of the salty wind heavy on my voice. I spot Payne idling at a distance, cloaked in the shadows of a looming tree, ever-watchful of my cousin.

"Getting some air," Tristen replies dourly. "Wishing I were anywhere but on this damn island. Wishing I were anybody but myself."

My eyes snap to his face, struck by the bitter self-loathing in his words.

"I wanted to finish our conversation," he says.

"I thought we were finished."

The night is so calm around us, I can hear Tristen swallow carefully. "Let me have this, Dell…" His voice cracks—a shred of his quiet, inner pain escaping its cage. No amount of sullenness or dripping sarcasm can mask it tonight. Tristen is bared open, the scars on his heart as exposed as the ones that cover his arms. "Please…"

This ill-timed ball means more to him than I can fathom.

"You don't need my permission, Tristen."

"I know," he says, albeit unconvincingly.

"Nor do you need my approval."

"I know that too."

Tristen's milk-white hands, settled at the ends of their armrests, ball into two shaking fists, as if testing his mettle, his fortitude—a gesture so simple, but loaded with meaning. It drags a fresh stream of tears from my eyes.

This man—my cunning and formidable cousin, who diverged from the evil that raised him, who climbs each day from the darkness that swallows him—has been through *so damn much*. Yet here he sits outside my door, begging for acceptance he's never received from anyone.

Gone is the arrogant, princely lord of Cliffmoor House.

All I see before me is a man in need of family.

You owe him, I think. *You'll always owe him.*

"I have nothing to wear," I whisper, my resolve breaking like the distant surf.

"I'll take care of that," Tristen says swiftly, as if to seal the deal on this before I change my mind. "I've sent Hatcher an invitation as well. You two have earned a night of indulgence."

"Why does this matter so much to you?" I ask.

"I can't demand respect from the islanders if I haven't procured that of my own flesh and blood," he explains. "I don't want you to hate me like the others. I know that ship has sailed with your mother and June. Maybe Palmer too. But, with you, I hope there's a chance…" A discouraged laugh spills from his lips. "But we've already discussed the perils of hoping, haven't we?"

My heart breaks a little more for my cousin, who's spent his entire life wondering whether anyone could ever care for him, questioning whether he deserves love at all.

I don't hate Tristen. I never will.

The best way I can think to show him is with my support.

CHAPTER THIRTY-SEVEN

I sleep in uncharacteristically late the next morning, with no indication that I'd done any sleepwalking—my skin free of sand, still smelling of soap from last night's shower. That's a small win in my book.

I don't venture up to Cliffmoor House for breakfast, desperate to shield myself from more emotional turmoil. These past five days on the island had rattled me, but last night's heated exchange with Tristen—and the full-blown panic attack I'd suffered afterward—had tipped the scales and left my nerves in shambles.

I laze around the guest house, doing everything in my power to ignore the slew of worries niggling my mind, but it's a hopeless cause. There's too much going on. The stolen bones in the tunnel. The brewing threat of my uncle. Prescott's unwanted presence. My alarming new sleepwalking habit. Palmer being *haunted* days before she's due to give birth. And now, a charity ball on the horizon…

I'm cracking under the pressure.

I decide to read a few chapters from *Legends,* the library book Hatch and I borrowed, hoping that the tale of Captain Bluebonnet's lost vessel—

the one carrying the second stash of sea trumpet seedlings—will be a somewhat diverting distraction.

According to urban myth, Bluebonnet's second ship took a mighty battering in a tempest, and wrecked upon the shores of a mountainous island near the Caymans called Ula Cove. Less than half the crew survived, but those who did were able to salvage some treasure, wares, and, most significantly, the trove of sea trumpet seedlings.

In an effort to honor Bluebonnet's orders that they be "sowed at the bedrock where the living meet the dead," the pirates planted them in a remote region of Ula Cove called the Vale of Azurine. As recounted by local villagers, Azurine is cursed land—an ancient valley wedged between steep, treacherous mountains, governed by the vengeful death goddess Lanrete. It's believed that many of Bluebonnet's remaining crewmen died while on the journey through Azurine. The few survivors settled in various villages on Ula Cove, while others found new patronage on the high seas— new ships, captains, and colors to sail under.

Over the years, as the sea trumpets of Ula Cove grew, one major difference set them apart from their flourishing sisters on Halcyon Bay…

The Ulan sea trumpets were a vibrant cobalt blue.

No one fully understood why this crop took on such a color, though it's rumored that the blue was due to a surplus of salt in the soil, and a lack of oxygenation. Others claim it was Lanrete who imbued them with their mystical hue—a color so rare, it could only be manifested from the gods.

The blue sea trumpets of Ula Cove were drastically sensitive to disease and weather, and, eventually, they seemed to disappear altogether. The crop had not been spotted in decades, its existence lost to island myth.

Some believe that Lanrete hid the sea trumpets and maintains them in secret, coveting their exotic beauty for herself. Most believe that the sea trumpets were ravaged by hurricanes—uprooted and mangled until they were beyond reviving. And with the later eradication of the sea trumpets on Halcyon Bay, it was assumed that the species had long gone extinct.

If only, I think, shutting the book and tossing it across the bed.

I flop onto my back, focusing on my breath. Reading was meant to be an escape from my problems, a way for me to break from the dregs of reality. But the effect of this story is not nearly so soothing.

I putz around the guest house for another hour before heading to the library for my shift, arriving much earlier than I'm expected. Dex doesn't complain. He grins appreciatively when he sees me, promptly offloading stacks of books into my arms in need of cataloging.

Work is a better distraction. Now that my training is over, Dex trusts me to handle more on my own, and we work in tandem for the next few hours—quietly, diligently.

Before I know it, my shift is over and I'm biking back down the tree-lined streets of Old Town in the slowest, most meandering way possible. Hatch is supposed to pick me up for Mojo's show at The Oyster, so I should be rushing to get ready for the outing. I should be excited to let loose and have some fun…but I'm not.

I pause to give my parents a call along the way. We've spoken a handful of times since I got back to the island, mainly so I can reassure them that I'm still alive and "having a great time." Despite my lie, it's always comforting to hear their voices. To know that, at least, they're safe and spared from this mess. But today, our brief conversation—light and breezy as it is—doesn't do nearly enough to smooth my fraying nerves.

Once I get back to Cliffmoor House, I dump my bike on the grass near the guest house and make my way to Sandspur Beach. I can't seem to keep away from it, like a horrible, masochistic tendency. A wormhole to memory I force myself through, no matter the damage it may inflict.

People are scattered along the beach, lounging on their striped towels under fluttering umbrellas, the sounds of their laughter and reggae music matched by the rolling surf. I dig my toes in when I make it to the shore, grounding myself in the puddling water, the mushy sand, and the hum of the sea. Strands of my hair lash out in the wind, sticking to my salt-sprayed face.

What keeps dragging me out here, like a rope affixed to my chest, summoning me to the seaside at all hours? What am I looking for? Why can't I let go?

Tears line my eyes as a kernel of hard truth surfaces.

Maybe I want to see that disembodied shimmer of silver in the water again, a symbol of my sister's presence. Maybe I want her to seek me out, the way she did last summer. Maybe—selfishly—I wish she were still here. Wish I didn't feel so thoroughly alone without her.

I haven't been right since the morning I swam out and met Willow in these waters. Since the morning she kissed me, and emptied her memories into my brain. The sea claimed me that day, hooked me by the heart, and I don't know how to handle the parts of me that belong to it. I fear that I'll never fully be myself again.

Lost. I'm so lost...

"Found you!"

Hatch's voice carries across the beach.

I turn to see him bounding toward me, the sight of him stoking the dying fire in my heart. Found me, indeed. He always does.

"What're you doing out here?" he asks when he reaches me, cupping my cheek with a warm hand. "I thought you'd be getting ready for the concert?"

I shrug, unable to form the words to answer him, but my eyes speak to that restless fear within—fear over what will become of me the longer I stay on this island. Fear over the inner demons that stalk me like prey, itching to drag me back into their cave of despair. Every time I think I'm doing better, they latch on like vampires, sucking me dry. Every time things start looking up, the fear and sadness creep in again. I hate that I'm like this. And I'm tired of waiting not to be this way anymore.

"Dell, what's wrong?" Hatch's expression shifts as he reads my face. His twinkling eyes soften, melting me to my core, swaddling me in sea green waves that rock and lull and soothe me.

He's the sun that crests over the surf each morning.

He combats my darkness with the promise of light.

I tear my eyes from him and rest them on the horizon, biting back the threat of tears and the tangled knot in my throat.

"Dell?" he tries again.

"I just...feel so lost sometimes," I rasp out quietly.

His hands are on my arms then, pulling me firmly against him, our chests colliding. "Listen to me." He tilts my chin up with a knuckle, his eyes fierce and unyielding. "You are not lost. You're right here, okay? Right here, with me."

A sigh escapes me as I let my head fall to his shoulder.

"I've got you, Dell." Hatch holds me as the sea foam curls around our feet. "I've got you. Always."

With this man, I can do anything, can get through anything.

And with his hand in mine, I muster the strength I need to move along.

On our way to Mojo's show, Hatch takes the scenic route down a jaw-dropping stretch of coastal road I've never driven before. The drive runs parallel to miles of uninterrupted white-sand beaches and the expanse of shimmering ocean beyond.

There comes a point where the sandy coast dips into a series of rock formations. Not cliffs exactly, more like a string of elevated bluffs and sea caves, vastly different from the rest of the island's prevailing flat topography.

"What is this place?" I ask, amazed.

"We call them Whispering Rocks," Hatch says as we speed along the road. "Our very own limestone shoreline. There aren't too many places in the world where you can see something like this. Pretty cool, huh?"

"It's stunning."

Before I know it, the rocks peter out, and once more, there's only sand. I whip my head around, keeping them in my sights. "Can you pull over a minute? I want to see them up close."

Hatch pulls the truck onto the curb and parks it, and I bound outside, headed for the beach.

The tide is high as I approach the rocks from the sandy embankment, watching as the water floods in, pouring forcefully through each hole and crevice, hissing and shooting up in places like a geyser. It's an incredible display. A testament to the untamable beauty and power of nature.

Hatch reaches me, smiling a weightless smile that reminds me of a time when sadness and grief hadn't made a mess of my heart. When I was lighter too. More innocent.

I don't realize I'm smiling back until Hatch says, "You're breathtaking."

His eyes sparkle with meaning, two emerald reflections of a perfect soul. His grin is wild, his hair and clothes windblown—completely stripped back to expose only bare honesty.

"Me?" I ask, slightly embarrassed.

"Yeah, you," he says with utter confidence. "Always, but especially in moments like this. You look so *alive*. Completely vibrant and beautiful. I love it when you let yourself *be* like this. Happy. Free. Uncompromisingly you."

My cheeks hurt from the smile he's coaxed from me, and all I can think of is my need to be close to him.

"You're breathtaking, Dell. I hope you see that when you look in the mirror. I hope beautiful things happen to you every day, and I hope each one puts that brilliant smile on your face. You deserve that."

My heart swells in the bony confines of my chest, attempting to break free. Doesn't Hatch know that he's the most beautiful thing—the greatest thing—that has ever and will ever happen to me?

"Swim with me."

My request is reckless. Breathless.

Hatch's lips inch up. "Like this? Fully clothed?"

"I suppose you could undress." I shrug, downplaying the heat behind my words. "I don't think anyone would mind."

His eyes flash bright with understanding—a swirling, mesmerizing sea storm that nearly knocks me off my feet. "You're the only other person out here."

"And, like I said, I wouldn't mind."

Lord knows when I became this impulsive, lusty girl. Probably the moment I laid eyes on *him*, if I'm honest.

"Okay," Hatch says, a challenge in his gaze. "But only if we strip down together."

My heart palpitates.

"Sound fair?" Hatch lifts a roguish eyebrow.

I reach slowly for the button on my shorts, unwilling to back down from an unspoken dare.

Hatch promptly catches me by the wrists. "I didn't say we should undress ourselves…" He lowers my hands to my sides and his fingers go to work on my button, my zipper, those lush eyes never leaving my face. I feel every sliver of movement as he shimmies my shorts down my legs, a roaring fire radiating up from my core.

He steps back and I kick the shorts aside, standing on the beach in only my underwear.

I grab Hatch's shirt and pull it up over his head, leaving his hair disheveled, his eyes dusky. He pulls me into a long, slow kiss, and somewhere along the way, we lose the rest of our clothes—my top, his jeans, my bra, our underwear—and then we're half-stumbling, half-bolting into the sea.

The water is cool, nipping my exposed skin, covering me in head-to-toe goosebumps. We fall through the surf together, laughing, until we're shoulder-deep. Hatch's hands cup my face as he brings my mouth to his. Our breaths become one, hair dripping over our faces.

I love him so much, I think I might burst.

My legs wrap instinctively around him and I feel the muscles of his body tighten. One of his hands rushes down to grip me. My chest grazes his, skin slipping over skin. It nearly undoes me.

I love you I love you I love you.

Can it always be this way? Just us and an ocean that feels like an extension of our bodies, our souls?

"We're already late for Mojo's soundcheck," I murmur as his lips trail down my neck.

Hatch snorts against my salty skin, and I can't help but to laugh, surprised at the pretty, airy sound of it. It feels so good, the rumbling in my chest like firecrackers popping on the Fourth of July. Hatch does that to me. Puts me in a dizzy-happy, head-in-the-clouds state.

I'd do anything—give anything—to spend my life with this man.

I love you, Hatcher Seaborn.

Say it.

Say it.

Just freaking say it!

"Palmer will kill us if we don't show up soon," I whisper, twisting my fingers through his silky hair.

"I'm going to kill Palmer if she manages to ruin this without even being here," Hatch grumbles.

That makes me laugh all over again.

His arms suddenly come around me and he pulls me underwater, extracting a high-pitched squeal from my lips. Then, everything is a haze of blue-green and him.

We share breaths between kisses, hands woven in each other's hair, mapping across our skin, exploring our every desire.

I swear on my life it's magic.

We breach the surface, and he wipes the water from his eyes. His fingers move teasingly along my shoulder, behind my neck, gripping my hair. "We can afford to be a little late, don't you think?"

I'm nodding without meaning to, my eyes closing to better feel him curled around me. Whatever he's saying makes perfect sense, his words my religion.

I sigh in agreement as his mouth consumes mine, a fresh wave lapping up to embrace us as our bodies melt together.

Suddenly these aren't the same dark waters of my nightmares—the source of every fear and every horrible memory. This is a new sea. A thrilling sea of love and promise and release.

Hatch and me.

That's all there is.

CHAPTER THIRTY-EIGHT

The backdrop to The Oyster—a large, seaside amphitheater, the only major concert venue on Halcyon Bay—is the sea wall, rough ocean, and an orange-tinged sky. A swaddle of cotton candy-pink clouds hang above it, dripping like ornaments over the festivities unfolding below.

We find Palmer, Mojo, Finch, and Leon congregated by the stage, which is shaped, unsurprisingly, like an open oyster shell.

Palmer looks like a pregnant hippie goddess, decked out in a sundress and a fringe seventies vest. She waves us over with fluttering fingers. "Finally, they make an appearance!"

She plucks the oversized sunglasses from her face. Smudges of violet puddle beneath her eyes, as though she hasn't gotten much sleep lately. "You're almost two hours late. And you show up with wet hair, sandy clothes, *and* looking flushed to boot?" Her eyebrows lift suspiciously.

Hatch and I share a sidelong glance, and I can't help the way my heart seems to soar when his hand wraps around mine, aglow with indefinable happiness. I see that bliss matched in him, in the grin that never seems to slip from his face.

Everyone else must notice it too.

"Remember, you two," Palmer coos irritatingly, "it's all fun and games till *this* happens!" She rubs her belly from top to bottom.

"Really?" I shake my head, mortified.

"We're up next!" Mojo announces, rallying the guys. He kisses Palmer's forehead before throwing his long arms over Finch and Leon. "Last one for a while, boys! Let's make it count."

They disappear backstage, and Hatch's fingers graze my elbow. "I'll grab you a drink," he offers, the private look in his eyes melting me all over again.

"I'll take a frozen lemonade!" Palmer chirps. "You're a pal, Seaborn."

Hatch sighs, shooting Palmer a look before trudging off to the concessions.

The second he's out of earshot, Palmer latches onto my arm. "So!" she squeals. "Did you tell him yet?"

"Not yet."

Why didn't I tell him? Am I waiting for him to say it first? Hoping he'll cushion my free fall, make me feel less vulnerable?

"Come on," Palmer groans in frustration. "Get with the program! From the way you two were eye-shagging just now, I would've thought you'd spent all afternoon saying it…again and again and again."

Her innuendo fills my cheeks with heat. "For goodness' sake."

She offers me a diabolical, glossy-pink smirk. "Hey, no judgment here! Mojo and I eye-shag all the time."

I rub a hand over my face, this conversation too ridiculous to warrant a real response. "Did *you* talk to Mojo about you-know-what?"

Palmer flicks a speck of lint off her vest, feigning disinterest. "I have no idea what you're talking about."

"You know perfectly well what I'm—"

"They stopped, okay?" she interrupts me, her blue eyes blazing with solemnity. "Right after we left Freya's, the whispers just…stopped. I don't know what kind of witchery she worked on me, but it looks like we have nothing to worry about anymore."

I know she's only lying to get me off her back, but she's so resolute in that lie, I don't want to poke holes in it.

The strum of a guitar blares through the speaker system, and the festival attendees all start to cheer.

"Waddup, waddup, Songwriter's Fest!" Mojo purrs into his mic. The crowd around us explodes. "If you don't already know, we're The *very* Knotty Talismen, and we're so stoked to be partying with you this evening! Does it get any more majestic than this?" Mojo gestures at the brilliant scenery behind him—the fiery, cloud-puff sky above, and the white-capped seas crashing against the breakwater.

The crowd screams in roaring approval as the band breaks into their first song.

Every word's been said and every poem's been recited.
Every song's been sung and every story's been recounted.
So there's no new way to tell you that my love is like the wind.
I'd sail across the endless blue of sea and sky just for a tiny glimpse...
Of you.

Sometimes I may stumble, or I'll stutter, or I'll slip.
You're like a dream I cannot grasp—I'm so inadequate.
And there's no new way to tell you that my love's a satellite.
Orbiting your sunshine like it's mine, to feel the fire burn...
In you.

How can I be lyrical about this simple miracle?
You've given yourself to me like a gift.
And tell me, please, who can I be?
To measure up, so you believe
I'll always be here waiting faithfully...
For you.

"Ugh," Palmer complains midway through the song. "I really have to pee."

"Now?" I ask. "But they just started."

Palmer glowers at me. "Do *you* have a fully-formed infant using your bladder as a punching bag?"

"Um, no."

"Didn't think so. In case you missed the memo, we're not working with the same urinary capacity these days."

I nod, sorry I ever dared to question Pregzilla. "Say no more. Let's go pee."

Palmer sighs impatiently. "No, it's fine. You stay here, cheer them on. I'll be back in a few."

I start to protest, but she holds up a hand to stop me. "If you so much as try to imply that I need a chaperone to escort me to the bathroom," she hisses, "*so help me God.*"

I clamp my mouth shut.

Palmer takes off without another word, shuffling along the perimeter of the rowdy crowd. I watch her as she weaves and bobs, keeping her in my sights for as long as I can, all the way up until her golden hair is swallowed up in the distance.

The overprotective streak I usually reserve for my mother has clearly extended to my cousin too.

The band breaks into another song, and Hatch is there a second later, slipping a fruity sangria concoction into my hand. When he holds up Palmer's frozen lemonade, I shrug. "Bathroom break."

Sliding his free hand around my back, he tucks me in close, and a mischievous smile steals across his face. I quite nearly forget the fact that we're surrounded by scores of sweaty, writhing people.

"I haven't danced with you in months," Hatch says against my ear, his eyes deepening, swirling with tenderness. "It's about time we remedy that."

We haven't danced since Palmer's wedding night, doused in neon light under that crisp, white tent, claiming our place on a packed dance floor, wrapped in a moment that felt like infinity. Before it all turned to hellish chaos, of course.

And while the chaos of my past has a habit of bleeding into my present, Hatch's carefree smile staunches it somehow. Dims it, makes it all fade into the background. He's the sea of golden light meeting my fragile, barren shore. He's the life and spirit and vigor that drives out the pain and darkness and grief.

His free hand paws my back greedily, as if he'd like to peel back the thin barrier of my blouse. As if he wants all that lies beneath, to connect with everything that makes me me, his yearning deeper than carnal.

I understand. I feel the same way. I want Hatch in full—heart, mind, and body. I want what no one else sees, what no one else can have, and I want to give him mine. All of me, even the broken bits.

Tell him.

He pulls me in close, his fingers tracing rivers up and down my spine, as we create a slow rhythm all our own. A swaying so natural, it's like being rocked by waves.

Tell him.

"I'm happy to be here with you," I whisper.

"You're happy?" he repeats, smiling.

I nod. And though I've yet to utter those three magic words, every one I've said echoes the sentiment.

Tell him.

"Hatch—"

"Your surprise is ready," he says, derailing my train of thought.

"It is?"

"Mhm. I've been wanting to give it to you for a long time." He reaches his hand up to graze my jaw with his knuckle, the rough and soft of it making me weak in the knees. "And I think now, the moment's finally right."

Finally right.

I don't know what Hatch has up his sleeve, but I know I trust him implicitly. And not just because we're draped around each other like cling wrap.

"Tonight, then?" I ask.

"Tonight. The big reveal."

Mojo sings out the last notes of the song and the guys immediately jump into a third. I like the sound of it—uptempo with a beat that makes me want to swing my hips. And with Hatch's hands on me, I find myself loosening up, grinding against him, my hair rippling around me. I sip from my sangria. I feel *good*.

Running my fingers through his hair, I draw Hatch closer and kiss him deeply, hungry to taste him, to live in this place of euphoric happiness and possibility for as long as I'm allowed.

But one swift glance away from Hatch's face—out toward the horizon, where lingering wisps of dusky-pink kiss the sky—and I see something that rips the moment out from under me.

A fiery orange motorbike leans against the sea wall.

Prescott.

The world begins to spin around me, and I squeeze Hatch's arm. From the way he tenses, he can tell something's wrong.

"Hatch," I croak. That's all it takes—his name on my lips in that small, fear-stricken voice, like my world is caving in on itself—and he's on high alert, eyes scanning our perimeter.

His gaze lands on the motorbike. "Is that..."

"Yes," I confirm. "It's his. I'm positive."

Of course Prescott would be here. Who knows whether he's been following me for days, tracking my movements like he did last summer. Violating me in more ways than one.

But then, something else becomes far more important than locating Prescott...

"Palmer's been gone a long time, hasn't she?" I ask, unable to ignore the feeling of my heart sinking to my stomach. I shouldn't have let her go off alone.

"You said she was in the bathroom, right?"

"Yeah, but she left a while ago—"

A woman's scream perforates the night.

It's her.

"Palmer!" I yell, whipping my head around in hopes of catching a glimpse of her. "Palmer! Where are you?"

Without exchanging a word, Hatch and I are running, pushing past confused crowds to get to her. Another ear-piercing scream erupts from my left, and I'm barreling toward the sound, ignoring the yelps and cries spilling from whoever I'm shoving to get there. All I can think about is getting past the swarms, finding her, making sure she's okay…

"Palmer!"

She's not in the field, not by the concessions, not by the bathrooms. I stop and spin in a wide circle, my eyes scanning, searching…

"Palmer!"

My screams are shrill and frantic as fear crawls across my limbs.

"Over there!" Hatch pants.

Under the branches of an old banyan tree stands a circle of paramedics. From a distance, I see a blonde girl reclining on the ground among them.

I race to her.

"Dell!" Palmer screams when she spots me.

The paramedics separate to let us through, and I'm on my knees before her, my eyes scanning my cousin from top to bottom, looking for any signs of injury or distress. She's not bruised or bleeding. Just pale as a ghost, trembling like a dying leaf.

"What is it?" I ask her. "Are you hurt?"

"I s-saw her," Palmer says, the words half-sobbed. She's working herself into a panic, her heaving belly shaking uncontrollably.

"Saw who?" My heart thunders in my chest. "Who, Palmer?"

"The s-spirit," she moans through her tears. "She's *here*."

"How far along is she?" a medic asks me urgently.

"Eight and a half months," I say.

"Ma'am, I'm going to need you to take a few deep breaths, okay?" The medic presses cool compresses to Palmer's forehead and neck. "You need to calm down, or else you could induce early labor."

This only sends Palmer into even more of a panic. Her breathing grows rapid, her eyes like wide, glassy bulbs. She can't stop the ocean of fear that's slowly drowning her.

"She's hyperventilating," I hear someone say behind me.

I take her by the shoulders. "Palmer," I grit through my teeth. "Breathe for me. Deep breath in through your nose, out through your mouth. Come on."

She inhales, but the sound is tight, like an asthmatic in crisis.

"Breathe."

Again, that same sharp wheezing sound—like the air she's gasping can't find its way to her lungs. Like the oxygen is caught in the rigid fist of her desperation.

"Breathe!"

I remember what she'd said to me last year, when she'd wrenched me from the bathtub and likely saved my life. I repeat the words to her now: *"Do not make me slap you, Palmer. I swear I will."*

They snap something awake in her—a memory from months ago to anchor her, to bring her back. I see the tense, gaping fear in her eyes lessen, her attention more focused, her mind more alert.

Palmer's breath steadies.

"You're okay," I say soothingly. "I'm right here."

I wrap my hands around hers—cold and slender and devoid of warmth—gripping them tightly.

She blinks a couple of times, slowly coming back to herself.

"That's right. You're all right," I assure her.

"We need to get her to the hospital," a medic informs me. "Her heart rate is alarmingly high. We need to run some tests, make sure everything's okay…"

"Get Mojo!" Palmer begs Hatch, and with a quick nod, he takes off in a sprint.

The paramedics get my cousin to her feet and usher her swiftly onto a wheelchair. I stay by her side as they roll her to the exit, where a flickering ambulance awaits.

"Dell, don't leave me!" Palmer pleads, her eyes afraid, fingers desperately wrapped around my wrist.

"I'm not leaving you. I'm going to be right here until Mojo arrives."

"Dell…" Palmer's voice chokes as she begins to eye the area surrounding us, as if in search of that otherworldly whisper—a calling only she can hear.

"Palmer, what—"

I see her face contort when her eyes lock on something beyond my right shoulder. I turn slowly, my skin crawling…but no one's there. Just vacant space, green grass. I glance back at my petrified cousin, her mouth gaping open as terror grips her. She lets out another sorrowful moan.

"Ma'am, let's get you into the ambulance, okay?" a medic says, and the team moves Palmer onto a gurney, lifting her into the back of the vehicle. She squeezes her eyes tight, braced against whatever sickening vision appears before her—a ghostly torment that has trailed her for days.

Next thing I know, Mojo and Hatch are there, breathless. Without asking questions, Mojo jumps up onto the ambulance. One of the medics tries to stop him and he zeroes in on them with a quiet fury I've never seen in him before. "She's my wife," he growls fiercely. The medic takes a step back.

"We'll follow you to the hospital!" I call as they shut the back door. "We're right behind you, Palmer, I promise!"

The driver slams into the front seat and the truck careens off, zipping down the street, leaving Hatch and I behind, swathed in clouds of dust and terrified silence.

CHAPTER THIRTY-NINE

Halcyon Bay General is a dreary sight, one that invokes a deluge of unwelcome memories. Memories of Tristen lying immobilized on a hospital bed, his head freshly shaved and covered in wires. Memories of my skin mottled in purple bruises, a cast on my wrist, soreness in my throat. The freshness of death looming over me. The blood on my hands I never could scrub clean.

I don't want to see Palmer here, at least not outside of the maternity ward.

A nurse directs us to Palmer's room but implores that we wait outside while tests are run. Hatch and I sink down against the wall, shoulder to shoulder, exchanging nervous stares under fluorescent bulbs. Neither of us ventures to speak.

Soon, June flies through the swinging doors with Leif's hand wrapped in her own, and rushes toward us. We hasten to our feet. "Is the doctor in there with her?" she asks frantically.

"Yes," I say.

Without another word, June releases Leif, leaving him with us while she enters Palmer's room.

"Is Palmer going to be okay?" Leif asks, blue eyes wide behind his black-rimmed glasses. He nibbles the corner of his lip.

"Of course." I nod to further soothe his worries. "She's just a little anxious right now."

"About having the baby?" he asks. He stretches up to his toes to peer through the window in the door, trying to catch a glimpse of the goings-on inside.

"I think so," I say, my face reddening. It's not an outright lie, but still doesn't quite cover being plagued by a ghost. I figure Leif doesn't need to know that much.

"Palmer doesn't realize what a tough cookie she is," Leif says confidently, his words cutting quick to my heart. "She can do anything."

"Yep," I agree. "She sure can."

"Mia's one lucky baby," Leif continues, a hopeful little smile looping up his face. "Don't you think so, to have Palmer and Mojo for parents?"

I swallow, for some reason getting choked up.

Hatch's hand finds my shoulder. He speaks for the both of us when he says, "The luckiest."

A half hour later, Mojo bursts into the hallway, and when his eyes catch mine, his worried expression darkens. "Can I have a word?"

I exchange a look with Hatch.

"Go ahead. I'll watch Leif," he offers.

I follow Mojo down the corridor, turning off into a separate wing before coming to a stop in a vacant stretch, far from any prying ears. He paces, mussing his hair, a sense of panicked urgency in him. I wish I could quell that desperation. Wish I could help dispel whatever monsters he's grappling with.

"What's going on?" I ask hesitantly.

"Palmer says she's seeing this ghost thing now," he says quietly. "She's having visions. Hallucinating. First it was the whispers, but now…" He raises his brown eyes to mine, normally so gentle, but they've hardened drastically over the last few hours. "She says you knew about this? That you took her to see the town psychic?"

I hear the accusation swimming in his voice—the need to protect the woman he loves, and his unborn child. "I was trying to help…"

"Telling me would've helped," he snaps.

"I wanted to tell you. I asked Palmer so many times to—"

"You had no right to drag her off to see some kook, Dell!" I'm taken aback by his volume, his hostility. "*Especially* without me knowing about it."

"I'm sorry. Palmer insisted…" My words trail off pitifully. It's clear that any counterargument is futile.

"You should've known better."

I lower my eyes, deciding it best not to respond. If Mojo needs a place to pour out his anger, if he needs that place to be me, I'll weather it. If he needs to make me the bad guy, needs someone to take the blame, I will.

"What's going on here?"

An icy voice slithers in from the opposite side of the hall. Tristen approaches with Payne at his back, guiding him toward us in his wheelchair.

"What are you doing here?" Mojo snaps.

"June called Briggs and told him Palmer was at the hospital. How is she?" Tristen asks.

"Like you give a shit," Mojo tosses back.

"Well, well." My cousin lifts a dark eyebrow, his black-pit eyes flashing testily. "Look who finally decided to grow a pair."

"Tristen!" I say sharply. "What's the matter with you?"

"Would I be here if I wasn't concerned?" he growls.

"You probably came to make this all about you," Mojo quips. "Seems like the perfect opportunity to scare us all with your latest scheme. Catch us in a moment of weakness—"

"Mojo, please," I say futilely.

"Why would I want to do that?" Tristen asks.

"Because there's always something in it for you," Mojo says. "That's the only reason you do anything."

Tristen smiles wickedly, the darkness he keeps tucked below the skin threatening to surface. "Bravo, Mojo—a pair *and* a brain. All in one day? I didn't think you had it in you."

Tristen knows how to twist the knife at the worst possible moment.

Mojo's jaw feathers as he makes a fist, moving toward the wheelchair, but I plant myself in front of him, palms on his chest.

Payne mimics Mojo's stance, coming to Tristen's aid. The three men collectively look like they're ready to draw blood.

"Will you stop it?" I snap. My words are meant for all of them, but my eyes are only on Tristen. "How the hell are you helping matters? If you came here to antagonize, you've succeeded tenfold."

Tristen doesn't respond, allowing the anger-packed atmosphere to settle. We stay that way, suspended in awkward tension, until Mojo exhales a huffy breath and slumps back against the wall, letting his head fall against it—utterly depleted.

"I have news about the bones you found in the tunnel," Tristen mutters, his dark shadow-eyes on me.

Mojo spits out an angry laugh. "See, I knew you had an ulterior motive for coming."

"No one will tell me how Palmer's doing, so I may as well make something of the trip," Tristen says, a snarl on his lip. "I sent my forensics guy the hair samples Nova collected—"

"I don't need to listen to this!" Mojo throws his hands up as he backs away. I want to ask him not to leave, not until we smooth things over, but I know it's useless. "I'm going inside to be with Palmer," he gripes, stomping away.

"Really?" I ask angrily, rounding on Tristen. "I hope you're pleased with yourself."

"As I was saying," he replies, ignoring my reprimand, "the hair samples are currently being analyzed to see if viable DNA can be extracted. There were also small bone fragments collected amid the rubble that are being tested as well. I should hear back about everything shortly. From my contact's initial probes, he estimates the woman died anywhere between twenty-five and forty years ago."

"So definitely a woman, then?"

"It looks that way, yes."

I'd known it the moment I saw that long, matted black hair—thick as a wig—surrounding those brittle bones. Freya confirmed it too. Not scientifically, but the psychic's knowledge always seems to supersede science.

How did this woman end up under Cliffmoor House?

Tristen seems to be asking himself the same question, because he says, "This has to have something to do with my father."

My thoughts exactly. At least one of the Klyne brothers is undeniably tied to this gruesome discovery.

"Has he been spotted again?"

"Not for over a week," Tristen says soberly, and I feel a ringing ramping up in my eardrums.

Florian could be anywhere. Could be setting plans into motion *right now* for his return, while we're none the wiser. Mindless sheep destined for the slaughterhouse.

I know he's coming back here to exact revenge, to take back the kingdom we've usurped.

Cliffmoor House.

"If Florian gets back on the island, he's coming for us," I say.

Tristen's eyes flash with steely acknowledgment, and it makes me question whether my cousin has his own set of plans—plans to lure my uncle back at an opportune moment.

All Tristen has to do is set a trap and dangle some bait.

Stage an evening where Florian thinks he can slip by unnoticed.

I'm beginning to wonder whether this is the real reason Tristen wants to host that damned charity ball.

CHAPTER FORTY

The doctors insist on keeping Palmer overnight for observation. They kick the rest of us out around ten o'clock, all except Mojo, in compliance with the hospital's "quiet hours."

I'm content to see Palmer calm and tucked safely in bed—drifting to sleep to a lulling rush of IV fluids—but I'm discouraged that we're no closer to helping her thwart her visions. No closer to dispelling whatever spirit latched onto her.

If Palmer endures another episode like today's, the stress alone could put her and the baby at risk. And if her panic gets bad enough to induce early labor…

I don't even want to consider the prospect.

It all reminds me too keenly of my mother. Of the years she'd spent plagued by visions of Lo—the terrors of her closeted past bleeding into her present, forever blurring the lines of real and imagined. There was nothing I could do to help her either, other than simply to crack open the door and shed light on the secrets she'd cast into darkness. At least then I could understand what sort of monster she was fighting.

But it's different with Palmer. She's not burdened by age-old torments, a haunted past, or skeletons left half-buried in the sand. This specter *forced* itself on my cousin, by no direct fault of her own. And in the most vulnerable moment of her life—on the cusp of giving birth—Palmer is having to manage as best she can.

I can't help but feel that it's all my fault, for having brought her to the tunnels in the first place.

Mojo, I'm sure, would vehemently agree.

He has good reason to be pissed, though I never thought he'd make *me* the target of his ire. Some of his anger may be misdirected, but I'll take the brunt of it without complaint. I recognize sadness and fear when I see it. I can empathize with the hopeless desperation in his eyes—utterly at a loss for how to save the one he loves. I'd be remiss if I didn't help him carry the load.

Hatch opts to save his surprise reveal for tomorrow, once we've shed some of the lingering dread of this evening. We can still hear the echoes of Palmer's blood-curdling screams in our ears, can sense the heavy, antiseptic hospital-smell perfuming our bodies. It's gut-churning, and not the least bit romantic. I don't mind waiting one more day.

I'd even brought *Legends* with me to read Hatch some notable passages, but I decide it best we shelve that too, tossing the book in his backseat for a lighter moment.

He drops me off at Cliffmoor House with a slow kiss and a secretive smile. I wave as he drives off into the night, his headlights cutting sharply through the Halcyon Bay fog.

Slipping through the garden gate, I'm surprised to find Nova standing outside the guest house, staring vigilantly across the grounds. I approach her quietly, assessing the situation. I haven't so much as cleared the tree cover when she says, "Hi, Dell," not bothering to turn her head.

"How'd you know it was me?"

"Your gait," she answers simply, my very footsteps betraying me. "I recognize the sound of it."

"That's a pretty impressive skill," I reply, stepping from the murky shadows into the moonlight.

She shrugs. "Comes with the territory."

"What are you doing out here?"

"We had a security breach earlier tonight," she says, her voice hollow, distant. My heart skips into my throat. "Some journalist was poking around the grounds. We caught her peeking through your windows. Snapping photos, scribbling in a notepad. She must've snuck in from the beach-side. Did you leave the gate unlocked this afternoon?"

Shit. After Hatch came out and found me on Sandspur, I could've sworn I'd locked up on our way back in, but it's possible I didn't. I wasn't exactly thinking clearly.

"Maybe," I admit. "Sorry about that. I was…distracted."

Nova nods. "Just trying to keep you safe," she says tightly, in a way that makes me want to believe her. "I have no clue how the woman slipped past Tank. Usually he's so attentive."

I recall the journalist from the day I arrived at Cliffmoor House—a scrappy, slick, spitfire of a woman who wouldn't bat an eye over trespassing if it meant landing a juicy story. "Well, if it's who I think it is, she's one hell of a runner," I say.

Nova shoots me narrowed eyes. "That's exactly what Tank said when I questioned him. You've seen her around?"

"Unfortunately, yes. On the day we got here, we found her hiding in the rose bushes out front. She ran off when Tristen asked me to call the police. Then, she snuck around to the beach, took photos of me without my consent, and put me on blast in this messed-up article."

"What'd she'd say?"

"She called me the *Near Sea Girl*—you know, since I almost died like one. She suggested that my presence here was a dark omen for the island. Like I'm some kind of bad luck charm or something." I snort, not entirely confident that I'm not. "It made for a scandalous headliner, no matter who she trampled on to get there."

"That is messed up," Nova agrees. "I'm sorry."

"You didn't write it."

"No, but I'm sorry anyway. That's a horrible thing to carry with you, and even worse to be reminded of so callously. You don't deserve it."

My face prickles with heat, Nova's thoughtful remarks like a flaming arrow to my skin. She makes it exasperatingly difficult to hate her. Especially when she continually treats me as a friend.

"I, um…" Nova drops her eyes to her feet, struggling to summon the appropriate words. "I've also been meaning to say that…I'm sorry for the pain it causes you to have me here. I know my past is a sore spot, but I never meant to make you feel uncomfortable. This is your home, and—"

"It's not." My voice goes hard to impress the fact.

"Well, as close to a home as you have here, I mean."

Also untrue, but I don't correct her.

"I know having me here has put a strain on you," Nova goes on. "I don't mean to add to your troubles. For what it's worth, I wish I'd had no part in it. No association to the Brine whatsoever. All I've done ever since childhood is run from it."

I squint my eyes at her. "Run from it?"

"I left the island for years with my grandmother, but this place is like a magnet. It has a sick grasp on me. A chokehold, really. I realize that doesn't quite make sense, but that's the only way I can think to describe it. It calls to me when I'm gone. It lures me back, even when I'd rather leave it behind."

This does make sense, actually. Far more than she knows.

"I want to leave it better than I found it," Nova confesses. "I want to keep future generations from suffering at the hands of the Brine. Keep others from this burden of stigma. I think that's why Tristen took me on for this job. He understands my motives. They reflect his own, like a mirror."

I can't bite my tongue any longer.

"Is there something going on between you and Tristen?"

Nova's head snaps up, her brown eyes wide and startled. "He's my employer." She says it hesitantly, as if she's also had to question the extent of their relationship.

"So?" I counter.

"I don't know. We're a lot alike, I suppose. Running like hell from the choices of our parents. Rejecting the darkness, yet endlessly drawn back toward it. Pursued by the very things we'd rather forget. It's like we both want better for our lives, but we can't seem to apprehend it. We can't…escape."

"It's impossible to fully escape where you come from," I say. "Running from the past is like running from part of yourself. It'll always be there to some degree, trailing your steps like a phantom limb."

"Are you saying I should just give up?" she asks, a sad smile dusting across her lips.

"Never," I say adamantly. "There are always places the darkness can't reach us—places where the pains of our past shrink and fade. So we don't give up, Nova. Not until we find ours."

Her laugh is wistful. "Do you really think I'll ever find such a place?"

"I think, maybe, you already have."

Nova's cheeks flush with understanding. Tristen could very well be that place for her, if she'll accept him.

"Nothing combats the darkness like love," I say, feeling the truth of that statement to my core. "Love is like pointing your face to the sun, letting the shadows fall at your back. It's the closest we ever get to the light. The only place we find solace from the despair in our souls."

Nova presses her lips together, eyes shiny as glass, but she doesn't respond.

"Life wrecks us. Love saves us." A small, fragile smile nudges up the corners of my lips. "So the question you have to ask yourself is, what's stopping you from letting the light in?"

And with those words, I make a silent decision, one that has nothing to do with Nova or Tristen, but everything to do with Hatch.

Tomorrow.

Tomorrow, I'll tell him how I feel. Tomorrow, I'll yield and bask and relish in the light. Tomorrow, I'll stop doubting, questioning, fighting our love—and instead start fighting for it with my full heart.

I love Hatcher Seaborn.

For too long, I've clung to those words like a secret.

Tomorrow, I'll finally set them free.

CHAPTER FORTY-ONE

A sharp pain barrels up my foot, jolting me from sleep with a disoriented wail.

I feel myself falling for a long second, then—*slam!* My ass collides hard with the ground.

Sprawling onto my back with a groan, I splay starfish-wide over the cold floor. Throbbing pain courses up my body, fanning out to my limbs like traveling fire. I grit my teeth through it, breathing deeply through my nose as I try to piece together what just happened in the dark.

When my eyes adjust, I realize I'm lying in the bedroom doorway, at least ten feet from the mattress. Midnight-blue slivers drip over me through the curtains, the sun still hours from showing its face. I must've been sleepwalking again. Must've stubbed my toe on the door frame.

Good to know I'm no less clumsy when I'm unconscious.

I force myself to sit up, my palms grasping for purchase on the floor. But as I'm about to stand, a spine-chilling sensation trickles over me.

My breath falls in shivers from the subtle shift in energy—the innate gut feeling that *something unnatural* is watching me. That I'm being dissected by inhuman eyes. That I'm not alone in this house.

I know better than to look, but the gripping fear is too much.

I squint up, and up, and up…my eyes landing on an inky figure hovering above me, the silhouette of them just visible against the night-dark house.

Eribeth.

The breath rips from my lungs, leaving me gasping for air, rooted like a tree to my spot on the floor.

The figure's head rolls off slowly to one side. Ever so gradually, that slender neck bends, the head tilting beyond any reasonable angle, until nearly parallel with its bony shoulder. When it seems it cannot bend any farther, a disturbing *crack!* reverberates across the guest house.

I recoil from the sound, scrambling back toward the nightstand, reaching for my cell phone, the table lamp, any source of light…

Wrapping a hand around my phone, I fumble frantically to locate the flashlight feature, aiming it at the doorway.

No one is there.

No bent-necked figures or ghostly faces.

Only deep shadows and a blanket of quiet.

Yet I still feel that invisible, unearthly tingle in the air. Still feel those dead, emotionless eyes on my skin.

Trembling and breathless, I drag myself into bed, flicking on the table lamp. I'll be leaving it on the rest of the night.

I sink back against my headboard and stare into the murky corners of the house. So many spirits are caged to this estate. So many tragedies without a just end. And there's no way to free them. No path toward eternal rest. No way to offer them lasting peace.

Or to secure any for myself.

When I venture outside in the morning, I find a familiar wicker basket perched outside my door. The note pinned to it reads:

Miss Dell—my sincerest apologies, once again.

Bundled inside an ivory cloth are fresh scones, orange muffins, and buttery croissants, all still oven-warm…

Briggs.

If anyone should be apologizing here, it's me.

I'd been unduly short with Briggs ever since our brush in the tunnels days ago, when I'd been so quick to cast suspicion on him, allowing my paranoia to get the better of me. It's time I make amends for that.

Using my key, I slip in the backdoors of Cliffmoor House and silently pick my way down the hall, searching each room as I go. Crossing the foyer, I poke into the opposite corridor, headed for the kitchen, when I notice the doors to the ballroom swung open. Tristen is there, alone in his wheelchair, his bent, sullen figure dwarfed by the glittering splendor of the room.

"Tristen?"

I choose to interpret his pointed cough as an acknowledgment of my presence.

Approaching him, I'm mesmerized by the lavish three-tiered chandeliers drooping from the soaring coffered ceiling. Their glistening effect on the space makes me think of honey drizzled over a decadent cake.

"Hello, earth to Tristen? Do you copy?" I try again.

I glance around the ornate ballroom, surprised not to find Payne— my cousin's constant shadow—lurking nearby. Or Nova, for that matter.

"Where is everyone?"

"I needed a private moment," Tristen musters through his teeth. It's anguish, not annoyance, I hear in his tone. His avoidant eyes are misty. Heavy as storm clouds.

"Oh, sorry." I start backing away again. "I was just looking for Briggs—"

"I got the results back," he says in a gravelly croak, "for the hair and bone fragments."

"Already?"

His jaw ticks, the angles of his face harsh and shadowed. "The DNA extraction was successful. They found a match."

A match.

My heartbeat turns to a funeral drum in my chest. "How did they manage that so quickly?"

"I had a hunch and offered up my DNA for comparison. Turns out I was right."

The world lurches beneath my feet, tilting like a carnival ride. I grab onto one of Tristen's wheelchair handles to steady me.

"The skeletal remains…" He clears his throat, though it does nothing to soften the pained rasp in his voice. "It was Sereia, my mother."

My knees weaken. "Your mother?"

"All these years," Tristen murmurs sadly, "I thought she'd been properly laid to rest. I thought she'd finally found some semblance of peace. But no. Of course not." His fingers tremble, slow-curling to fists.

Is Sereia the spirit plaguing Palmer? The one bound to that underground maze of darkness?

Does that mean that…when Sereia died, she was…

Oh, no.

"There were skeletal indicators in a piece of pubic bone that suggest my mother was pregnant," Tristen says.

No no no.

The prickling heat of emotion slithers up my neck, threatening to unravel me. Whoever did this to Sereia—had they known? Had they killed her because of it?

Was it Florian?

Every cell in my body hums with certainty.

"Tristen—"

"Stop it," he says cuttingly. "I don't want your sympathies. I don't want…" His voice catches, a raw whimper erupting from his lips that can only be described as pure agony. "I can't bear it…" Waves of pain overwhelm his face, as if some unseen blade had been launched from a distance, piercing his heart. "I'm not worth the effort it takes to form a consoling thought, anyway."

"Why would you say that?"

He shuts his eyes when the first tear wells, slipping out and over his pale cheek. All at once, I want to cry too. With him. For him.

"Tristen, I'm so—"

"Don't, Dell," he warns.

"But—"

"Stop it! Don't you dare say you're sorry," he cries hoarsely. I've never seen him overcome this way. "There's only one person on this earth who will be made sorry for what happened to my mother."

The grief padding those vengeful words grips me. I don't know how to act, what to say to the person before me—a man utterly gutted by the information he's procured. I don't recognize this Tristen. I don't know how to help him.

"It's fortuitous that I should regain function of my hands," he says. I watch him splay his thin fingers on the hand rests, then curl them in slowly—again, again—strengthening with each consequent stretch and squeeze. "Because when my father does come back…" His jaw pulls tight, mouth twisting into a grim expression. "I'm going to pry the dying breath from his lungs." His dark eyes flick to me, pulsing with visceral, insatiable hatred. "I'm going to carve that fucker to the bone."

His words linger over the ballroom like a spell—a curse. Violent energy packs the space, creeping into every gilded crevice and corner, whispers of impending doom winding between the chandelier crystals. It paralyzes me. Steals away my every thought, my ability to speak…

Tristen quiets too, but his vicious expression remains.

We stay like that for several minutes, reeling from his outburst, until he finally asks me, "Did you say something to Nova last night?"

My mind races to recall our conversation. "Why? Did something happen?"

"Did you mention something about me?" he asks again, more specifically this time.

"I asked her if something was going on between you two," I reply honestly, extra mindful of what I say. Tristen is exceptionally volatile right now. There's no telling what might set him off.

"And?"

"She pointed out your similarities. The dark things in your past that you two seem to share. I told her what I thought about that. That love is the greatest antidote for darkness. That love saves us, and brings light where none can be found."

I try to gauge what Tristen thinks about this. His coal-black eyes still hold that steely viciousness, but the rest of him looks calmer. Less rattled. So I take a chance.

"I also told Nova that, maybe, the two of you can find it together," I add. "A reprieve from the darkness…in each other."

"That would imply that I'm capable of love," Tristen mutters.

"And you don't believe you are?"

"I don't know one way or the other," he says. "And isn't that somehow worse? To not know whether you're built for loving another person? To not think yourself worthy of receiving love in return?"

This brings me back to the words he spat earlier—*I'm not worth the effort*. They hadn't made sense in the moment, but now they do.

"You are," I say resolutely. "In fact, I think you love deeper than most. I think you love so hard that you don't know what to do with it, and it twists you up inside, and you lash out in destructive ways. But you are built for love, Tristen. We all are. And you're worthy of receiving it, no matter what you've been led to believe."

"Well." He swallows tightly. "I may never get the chance with Nova."

"Why not?"

"She approached me late last night, wondering if she was…misreading things. If my sentiments towards her surpassed that of a platonic, working relationship. And I…"

"You, what?"

"I insinuated that she was making more of my feelings than was there," Tristen says. "I made it sound like I didn't care for her. I wanted to spare her from seeing all my deficits. But I regret it now. I regret it more than anything."

"Where is she?"

"Somewhere on the grounds. She believed my lie wholeheartedly. Said she wouldn't misunderstand me again. She actually apologized *to me*. And I sat back and let her." His brow twitches, his eyes afflicted. "I let her walk away thinking I felt nothing, when that's the furthest thing from the truth."

"So find her," I encourage him. "Find her and tell her how you feel. Right now."

"Is there even a point?" he asks. "What can I really offer her? Why should I allow her to settle for someone like me?"

"You don't *allow* her to do anything. That's her decision to make. Don't strip her of that power."

"Even if I know she'd be better off elsewhere?"

"Even then," I say firmly. "You offer her your truth, and you let her do the same. You treat her as your equal."

"She's more than that, Dell," he rasps. "She's…monumental. Far greater than my equal."

I place my hand over his, a shock of ice rushing through me.

Tristen's eyes go round with surprise.

"Then see to it that she knows."

I find Briggs holed up in the kitchen. By the looks of the neatly-penned lists scattered like confetti over the massive center island, he and Inga are making plans to feed a small army…or scores of ravenous guests for a ball.

"Good morning, Miss Dell," Briggs greets me politely when I poke my head inside.

"Ah, Miss Meridel!" Inga chimes in. "'Ello, again! You sleep good?"

Like hell, actually.

"Very good, thanks," I lie through a smile. "How are you?"

Inga chuckles, her short white curls brushing against her cheeks. "Sun shines. Inga cooks. Morning is good."

"I'm happy to hear that."

"Is there something we can do for you, miss?" Briggs asks, attentive as ever. I notice that he's begun to phase in his traditional butler's uniform again—the crisp, tailored blazer and shiny dress shoes. Even those immaculate white gloves. Old habits really do die hard.

"Could we step outside and talk for a minute?" I ask him.

"Of course." Briggs nods and follows me into the hall.

"Is everything all right?" he asks urgently, his silver eyes narrowing with worry.

"No, it's not." I shake my head, peering into his wrinkled face. "I saw the note on your basket of treats this morning—"

"I didn't mean to overstep with the pastries, miss. I haven't seen you around much, and wanted to make sure you were eating."

"Briggs, you have absolutely no reason to apologize. *I'm* the one who owes *you* an apology for how hard I came down on you in the tunnels. And for how rude I've been ever since."

"Nonsense!" He clicks his tongue. "You owe me no such thing."

"You've only ever been a loyal friend," I insist. "I shouldn't have insinuated anything different."

"You've had a turbulent week," he replies kindly. "Anyone else would've buckled under that kind of stress."

"That doesn't give me a free pass to act like a…shrew." I almost say 'bitch,' but decide against it at the last second. I can't imagine cursing in front of Briggs. He's too dignified a person. Too decent. "I truly am sorry for how I've acted."

"Water under the bridge, Miss Dell." He lifts a gloved hand, pinching my chin between his thumb and forefinger—a grandfatherly gesture.

"Briggs, will you ever stop calling me *Miss* Dell?"

"Afraid not, Miss Dell," he replies with a sheepish laugh.

"But we are friends, aren't we?"

Briggs' smile and watery eyes speak to years of dedication to my family. A life lived in service. A life lived for others. "We will always be great friends."

CHAPTER FORTY-TWO

I arrive at the seaport with the sun dipped low over the ocean—the boats, docks, and fishermen doused in a hazy, golden-hour glow.

Everything about this day has catapulted me toward this moment. I spent my shift at the library collecting my scattered thoughts like seashells, navigating my feelings like a ship roams the seas. There's a lot to sift through, emotionally. A lot of self-imposed pressure and tangled-up nerves, submitting to a deep vulnerability I'd normally run like hell from. But for Hatch, I'll dismantle every painstaking wall until all that's left is my wide-open heart, soft and unguarded and ripe for the taking.

I secure Virginia's bike in the parking lot and weave through the bustling marina, locating Captain Patton's schooner with ease, its towering masts soaring high above the rest. Hatch is nowhere to be seen aboard the ship.

I'm about to walk up the boarding ramp, when strong arms slide around my waist from behind, spinning me in place.

"Hi, you."

Hatch plants a kiss on my open mouth, my shock melting into pure thrill at seeing him.

"Hi back," I say, already bursting into a smile.

He laces his fingers in mine. "Ready for your surprise?"

"Is that even a question?"

Hatch chuckles as he drags me forward, zigzagging us through the busy maze of docks, past scores of boats getting hosed off by sailors with liquored-up expressions. Soon, we break into a run, laughing stupidly. I take mental snapshots of *everything*, the camera in my mind clicking away. I don't want to miss a single sun-drenched detail.

Hatch tosses squinty eyes at me over his shoulder, a mischievous smile edging up one dimpled cheek—*click*.

The flaming sun brushes the ruffled surface of the sea, encasing our bodies in radiant halos of light—*click*.

The untied laces of my Chuck Taylors slap carefreely over the puddling, salt-soaked docks—*click*.

My hair, wild and windswept, whips in every direction; Hatch's falls in caramel waves over his tanned face—*click*.

A colony of rowdy seagulls scatter when we swoop in too closely, flying all around us like a movie scene—*click*.

When we reach the far end of the marina, still laughing like fools, Hatch slows his steps and points up ahead.

There, beside a lonely stretch of dock, a classic wooden fishing boat is moored.

I come to a stop, my breath hitching when I see it, the boat's gentle rocking like a friendly wave. I scan the vessel from tip to tip, only to land on a familiar smear of letters etched along the side of it.

This must be a mirage. A byproduct of my giddiness, combined with the glowy twilight atmosphere. I must be punch-drunk off my own excitement. Off my adrenaline. Off my love for Hatch.

But when he pulls me toward the boat, my feet tripping over themselves, it becomes abundantly clear—this is no mirage.

"Hatch," I whisper. "Is that..."

He smiles. "The *Willow's Wind.*"

So it is.

The last time I'd seen the *Willow* was last summer, before Bram sold the boat and his fishing business. I thought I'd never lay eyes on her again. Thought she would only live on in my memories.

"How?"

"I tracked down Bram's buyer months ago," Hatch explains. "The guy was planning to strip the boat for parts, but I made him a hefty offer. Insisted I wouldn't take no for an answer." His fingertips trace absent lines down the back of my arm, but he may as well be injecting me with tiny lightning bolts. Electricity—*magic*—hums in my veins. "She's yours, if you want her."

"Mine?"

"Yours."

Hatch has given me so much in the time I've known him, but *this*—this incredible, mind-boggling gift—far surpasses any I could ever imagine.

"This is what you've been working on all this time?" I ask, my voice soft and incredulous. "All the late nights?"

"Mhm. I've been sprucing her up. Making renovations." Hatch pulls a folded-up sheet of paper from his back pocket. "I even made it official. Here's the title. It's got your name on it and everything."

I'm utterly amazed by him. I never considered that we might be able to salvage the *Willow*. Never dreamed I could feel so connected again to not one, but two people who'd left profound marks on my life.

"I can't believe you did this," I muster.

His answering smile is brilliant. "I did it for you."

We walk up to the *Willow*, and when we reach it, I drag my hand over the polished outer wall, letting an ocean of memories flood in.

I remember my anger when I first met Bram here—when I wrongly accused him of so much harm.

I remember the pain when I crawled back a second time, and the unexpected joy of our fishing day at sea—our wild laughter under the rainy, gray deluge.

I remember the gentle understanding only we could share, our love for Willow forever tinged with grief.

This boat is mine. This precious tribute to my sister—Bram's most prized possession—is mine. An ode to love in all its forms.

I look at Hatch, breathless.

All mine.

I'm so full of love for him, I think I might sprout wings and shoot to the skies. Maybe I already have.

I know it's now or never.

Now *and* forever.

So I take a breath…

And fall.

"I love you."

It spills out with ease, the plainest truth in the world.

Hatch freezes, his sea green eyes round as sand dollars, pupils blown wide.

"I've loved you for a long time," I admit, smiling through the tears lining my eyes. "I've been kicking myself for days, desperate to tell you but not knowing how…"

I want Hatch to understand every bit of what I feel. It's the most important thing to me—this man and this love and all the words I'm about to trip over. I laugh a little, not because I'm nervous, but because I'm so incandescently happy. My vulnerability feels like a *superpower*. Like spilling the contents of my heart, exposing everything I've been holding inside, makes me braver than ever. Untouchable. Fearless.

"After all this time, I still haven't perfected everything I'd like to say. But the gist of it is, I never want to live another day without you."

Hatch takes two slow steps forward, reaching out to pull me into his arms. But then he pauses, swallows, takes his bottom lip between his teeth—visibly holding himself back. Letting me speak.

"You came into my life when I was at my loneliest. When I had no safe place to turn to. I was so scared, even though I refused to acknowledge it. I didn't know how much I needed you. But, somehow, you did. You knew, and you barreled into my heart. You completely disarmed me…" A sob wrapped in a smile escapes my lips. "You punched a hole in my smoggy gray sky and let the light in. You swooped in like an angel, like you were sent to save me. To show me that good things still exist in the world."

Waves of emotion swell in the space between us, begging to be crossed. Blinking back tears, I bridge that gap, my hands sliding slowly up his chest.

"Sometimes I think I dreamt you into existence. That you dwelled within me long before we ever met, in *here*." My hand flies to my chest, my heart. "You're every wish I've ever made on birthday candles or falling stars. I'm often overwhelmed by the mere fact that you're real. And that you're mine."

I look deeply into his eyes, then let my gaze wander to that delectable mouth. "I'm so in love with you. And I would be incomparably lucky to get to call you mine forever." His forehead drops to mine, and I sigh happily. "I am yours, Hatcher Seaborn, and I always will be. For as long as you want me, and as long as I live."

We breathe against each other, hearts melting with the setting sun, as if we're standing on a gleaming precipice, knocking down the walls of mere mortality. Aspiring to something greater. Eternal. Invincible.

"Why don't we climb up into your boat, Dell?" Hatch murmurs. I hear the satisfied smile on his lips before I see it. "I've got a few things I'd like to get off my chest too."

My heartbeat skips into my throat. *Can this really be happening?*

Hatch jumps aboard, then helps me in too, his warm hands wrapping around both of mine. I slide onto the familiar deck, rife with memories—but I'm too preoccupied with the reckless abandon in Hatch's eyes to pay any real attention to my surroundings.

His crooked smile speaks to a quiet longing, the dip in his chin almost teasing. But it's those eyes that threaten to undo me, thread by blessed thread. Those eyes are a raging, tantalizing sea. The heat of them quite nearly makes my heart burst from its confines.

"It's funny you should mention how long you've wanted to say these things, because *I've* been struggling with the same problem for months," Hatch confesses. "Planning for an opportune moment. Waiting to pin down the perfect combination of words. But, truth be told, there is no perfect way to tell you that I can't live without you, is there?"

I swallow, flames licking fast up my neck.

"Or that I don't know how I got through life until this point without you? Or that the thought of being apart from you *physically* hurts?" Now he swallows, eyes burning, fathoms-deep and pure as the ocean around us. "And, imperfect or not, I still have to say it—"

I can't breathe I can't breathe I can't breathe.

"I love you, Dell Costa," Hatch says, unshakably. "I have from the first night I saw you at 'Cuda's, with that stubborn pout on your lips. All I could think about was kissing you, even then, with your eyes dancing like liquid gold in the bar light. I never knew a pair of eyes could feel so much like home."

He steps forward, cupping my face, his electric touch sending pinpricks racing through me. "You pierced every bit of my heart that night. It's been yours ever since. Yours to keep. Yours to break. And I need you to know that—no matter how messy or imperfect the circumstances, no matter the distance or the obstacles that stand in our way—I'm not going anywhere. If there's a breath left in me, I want to spend it with you. I've been searching for you all my life, whether I knew it or not, and I'm never, ever letting you go."

Hatch glances around the *Willow's Wind,* taking in the contents of the old fishing boat. *Our* fishing boat. "This is a start," he says determinedly. "I'm going to give you the world, Dell. This is just a start."

I shake my head in disbelief. As if buying and fixing up Bram's boat for me is an inadequate expression of his love. As if this surprise isn't magnanimous and wonderful and perfect. As if Hatch doesn't mean absolutely *everything* to me. My universe narrowed down to one single person, wrapped up in sun-coated, summer-warm packaging.

"Hatch, I don't need the world," I laugh softly. "I don't care about anything but *this.*" I place a hand over his heart, relishing in the strong drum beneath my palm. "This is my world, right here. You and me, together, until the very last sunset."

And I realize that no matter how much I claim to hate Halcyon Bay— no matter how painful the memories—this island has given me so much more than it's taken away.

"Until the very last sunset," Hatch repeats, tilting his head, gazing into my eyes. And I wonder if my heart will give out from just that look. If I do die in his arms tonight, it will all have been worth it.

"God, I love you," he breathes. "And I love telling you that I love you. *Finally.*"

"And I love hearing you say it," I respond, fully aware of how obnoxious we sound. But I don't care. I adore this man. And we'll live happily ever after, just like this. End of story.

"I've always loved you," Hatch reiterates, closing the breath of space between us. "And I always, always will."

"Maybe you should show me," I whisper.

His eyes darken at my request, his mouth colliding with mine, and—*yes.* He pushes me against the wheelhouse wall, pressing into me with such ferocity, there's no way for me to question his need.

"Forever," he vows against my lips.

"Until the very last sunset," I promise between tastes of his mouth.

I feel the weight of those breathy words rattle my bones, saturate my heart, mark my skin eternally. And as night crawls in, our professions of love loop and twirl among the stars, forming a dazzling constellation.

Written in the stars.

I'm certain that we are.

CHAPTER FORTY-THREE

In the wee hours of morning, I slip back inside the guest house, still floating on a puffy love-cloud of infinite dreams.

The house greets me with eerie silence and a heaving, oppressive darkness. Any other night, that would put me in a mood. But not tonight.

Tonight, I'm all smiles.

Because I'm in love.

Head over heels, balls to the wall, off the deep end, *in love*.

And Hatch loves me too.

Hatcher Seaborn is mine.

Perhaps love is too small a word for what we share. Love can't encapsulate the soaring feeling inside of me, altering my make up at a chemical level. What we have feels too vast and boundless and remarkable to whittle down to one measly four-letter word.

The best things in life really do render you speechless.

And turn you into a babbling idiot.

But I don't care.

Hatch is mine. And the *Willow* is ours.

A map of brilliant possibilities unfolds behind my eyes. Trips we could plan. Places we could see. Lives we could live. All of it, together.

I hum absently as I shut the door behind me, flicking on the light switch.

A crisp, white box awaits me on the coffee table.

How did this get in here?

It's clearly been opened. A midnight-blue ribbon is tossed to one side, as is a cream-colored note card that reads: *As promised.* The lid to the box is shoddily slapped over top.

I approach hesitantly, venturing to lift it.

A gossamer gown that same rich midnight-blue, drizzled with countless sparkling beads made to look like twinkling stars, is folded inside the box, untouched and immaculate.

I lift the dress gingerly. It's the single most exquisite garment I've ever laid eyes on, fit for a queen, but with a plunging neckline and a thigh-high slit far more daring than any royal tradition would permit.

Tristen, I think. He must've spent a small fortune on this.

But that doesn't explain how the box ended up inside.

I know my cousin likely has a spare key to the guest house somewhere, but he and Briggs always respect my privacy, leaving notes and packages for me outside. I'd also warned Nova never to come in here, and after getting to know her better, I don't believe she would.

Why would someone open a box that's clearly meant for me?

I return the gown to its resting place, a sinking sensation dragging across my veins, plunking into my stomach, as I take in the strange, careless scene before me.

Someone's been in here. And I have no idea why.

Shit.

The gun.

Where had I left Nova's gun?

I hadn't worked up the nerve to carry the weapon with me, stowing it in the guest house for when I'm alone and at my most vulnerable. But my mind is frozen, fearful…I don't remember where I put it.

My eyes skitter toward the dark bedroom, shadows spilling from it like a nightborne plague, but I don't dare turn my neck. What if the intruder is still in here?

Where is that damn gun?

Bedside table, bottom drawer, the scared voice in my head reminds me.

I need to get to it, right now…

A large hand clamps roughly over my mouth from behind, muffling my explosive screams. My panic spikes when an arm grips me around the shoulders, pinning me fast to a tall body.

I writhe against my captor, stomping my feet in hopes of connecting with his, digging my nails blood-deep into the arm that restrains me, but it's no use. He jostles me forward and shoves me face-first onto the couch, releasing me from his iron grasp.

Gasping, I lift up onto my elbows, preparing to scream again, to run for my life…

"Ah, ah, ah," a smooth voice taunts, velvet-edged and laced with poison. "Scream and it'll be the last thing you do."

No…

I turn my face to meet his, sucking in a sharp breath.

Florian lifts a revolver to my forehead, the cold barrel grazing the skin beneath my hairline.

His cheeks and neck are covered in a thick, burly mane, his clothes rumpled and worn. But beneath that fraudulent, humble-looking exterior, I know *exactly* who he is. A man materialized from my nightmares, come to terrorize me as I wake.

Tutting under his breath, Florian eyes the mangled skin of his forearm, his shirt sleeves folded up to the elbows. Angry red scratches tear across his arm—little half-moons from my nails impressed down deep, each tiny wound tinged with drops of blood.

"Is this any way to greet your dear old uncle?" he asks. "Hissing and clawing like a feral alley cat? After I was kind enough to bring in your parcel for you?" He practically spits the word *parcel* at me.

My fingers grip the edges of the couch as I fantasize about tearing Florian's eyes from their sockets. Cleaving that smug smile from his face.

He cocks back the hammer on his revolver. "Simmer down, Meridel.

Take a calming breath.”

Nausea climbs its way up my throat. My evening under the stars with Hatch—lying on the deck of our boat, mapping out a future as bright as the moon—all feels like a distant dream. Like something I'd conjured to distract me from a brutal reality. Vanished like smoke. I'd let myself forget that Halcyon Bay will *never* let me be happy for long.

“How did you get in here?” I ask quietly.

Florian sinks onto an armchair, the gun still trained on me. “The front door, of course.”

“Tristen had the locks and keys to every door on the property remade…”

“I have a friend on the inside,” Florian quips. “Copies of those keys were made long ago.”

“Who?” I ask, desperate for a name.

“That's privileged information.” My uncle's grim smile spells disaster. “I don't see much reason for your shock, honestly. You knew full well this day was coming. I hear you and my weaseling son have made tremendous efforts to find me.” Florian flourishes an elegant hand. “And, here I am! Wish granted.”

I glare at him, my mind racing against time.

“Did he not warn you?” Florian asks with feigned curiosity. “I would've thought he'd have the sense to know I'd return *sometime*. But perhaps I was wrong?” He hums, unimpressed. “Tristen remains an unequivocal failure to the end.”

“*Don't*,” I warn.

“Don't, what?”

“Don't you dare utter his name.”

“Oh, I see! You've grown to care for the sniveling weasel. You're trying to protect him! How quaint.” Florian chuckles. “Tell me, Meridel, how is paralysis treating him?”

My tongue writhes in anger. “You could have killed him.”

“Believe me, I meant to,” Florian affirms with a nod, no smidge of remorse to be found in his words. “Disabling him was merely an accident. Traitors deserve far worse.”

"Bastard."

"Careful, darling. You aren't facing my decrepit old brother this time. I won't tolerate your insolence."

"If you were going to kill me, you'd have done it by now," I spit.

"Very perceptive! Yes, Meridel, you're still alive precisely because I have some use for you yet. But—a word of caution—it won't take much convincing for me to change my mind. So I suggest you tread very, *very* carefully."

"What do you want?" I ask.

"As I'm sure you've seen from your little escapades beneath Cliffmoor House, I have product that needs to be moved off the island."

Product?

Florian's eyes narrow. "I know you've been in the tunnels. You've seen what's stored down there. And yet, you've opted *not* to take that information to the police." His laughter is cold and grating. "An interesting choice. It makes this all rather easy for me, really."

I think back to those shelves lined with jars of crimson pills. "This is all for…sea trumpets?" I ask in disgust. "You're, what? Trafficking drugs?"

"I'm delivering on a business transaction," he says calmly, "and a lucrative one at that. My buyers are eager for their merchandise. I'm eager for my payout."

Is that what he'd been doing all this time—dealing drugs overseas? Waiting for the right moment to slip back onto Halcyon Bay, collect what remains of his trove, and disappear again?

My gut tells me this isn't the full story. If the sea trumpet pills I found are all that's left, then Florian's supply is terribly limited. But my uncle doesn't strike me as a near-sighted man. Why would he risk his neck for product so scarce, when his insatiable greed demands so much more?

Unless…there *is* more. More sea trumpets stored elsewhere on the island. More product for my uncle's criminal clientele. More money to finance his cushy new life.

"Again, this look of shock and surprise!" Florian's coal-black eyes flash predatorily. "Are you struggling to keep up?"

"I'm keeping up just fine," I hiss. "I still haven't heard what any of this has to do with me."

"My team will need safe passage through the tunnels to move my product off the island, undetected and without incident. That's where you come in."

Where I come in…

Aiding and abetting in the transport of illegal narcotics.

Over my cold, dead body.

"I won't help you," I say. "It'll never work, anyway. Tristen has security watching the exit point."

"Tristen has security watching *one* exit point—the sea trumpet fields," Florian corrects me. "The other exit remains clear and unattended."

He must mean the tunnel that ends at the cavern. The one that floods with seawater.

I shake my head. "There's no pass-through that way."

"Imbeciles, all of you…" My uncle rolls his eyes, looking so much like his son that it twists up my stomach. "When king tide rolls in every spring, the water levels of the bay reach an all-time high. To the same degree, they recede to an all-time low for a brief window. When this happens, the cavern exit will drain, enough for a small convoy of boats to pass through."

The Jon boats.

Shit.

"Dumbfounded, are we?" Florian taunts.

"It won't work," I whisper again.

"Hogwash! *Of course* it will. In about a week, my son will host his first ever charity ball. That same night, king tide will be in full effect. You, in that dashing gown of yours, will stand guard in the parlor, ensuring my people make it through the tunnels safely while diverting any prying eyes. My men will slip inside, retrieve my supply, and, if all goes as planned, we'll be gone before midnight."

"No," I say firmly. "Shoot me now if you'd like, but I'm not helping you."

I won't facilitate my uncle's escape, or aid in the trafficking of drugs. I won't give him free rein to reap more chaos on some other unassuming continent. I'd rather die than let that happen.

"I hoped you'd be reasonable, Meridel," Florian replies. "That we could work together civilly, as family should. But, if you want to be obstinate about this…"

He pulls a cell phone from his back pocket and, with a few swift taps, holds up the screen for me. It takes me a moment to process what I'm seeing—video footage of a modest island home painted a vibrant green.

Green as Hatch's eyes.

No.

The porch lights are on. His mother's sedan is parked in the drive. Dread seeps through me when I look at the time stamp—2:17. This is a *live* recording, happening in real time.

Seconds later, headlights pierce the frame and Hatch's truck pulls to a grumbling stop before the house. He disembarks slowly, smiling a dreamy smile, still in a haze after the magical night we'd shared. I'd felt the same way *moments* ago—swaddled in a euphoric blanket of love and possibility—only to have it ripped away at the snap of my uncle's fingers.

Florian grins as my eyes widen. "You wouldn't want someone you love to get hurt on account of your stubbornness, would you?"

I shove down my terror, assuming a mask of composure. "I have no idea what you're talking about."

"Come, now. Don't you recognize this place?" His tone is soft and calculating, luring me into a predatory dance. A cat toying with a defenseless little mouse.

A little field mouse, just like Payne had taunted me.

I never should've stayed out here in the guest house alone, never should've refused all of Tristen's security measures. In doing so, I'd made myself the weakest link. The easiest crack for Florian to break through.

Filled with an instinctive need to protect the Seaborns, I clench my teeth again, my gaze hard on my uncle. "No. I don't recognize it."

"It doesn't look familiar to you at all?"

"For the last time, *no*. I don't know that house, or anyone that lives there—"

"Don't lie to him, Dell."

Acid roils in the pit of my stomach at this second voice.

Prescott emerges from the shadows of the bedroom, slithering through the dark doorway like a snake in search of a meal. He shakes his pale head, looking almost sorry for me as he does. "Lying will only make things worse for you."

I warned Prescott to stay away from me. I tried to be the bigger person, the *better* person. Tried not to give in to the hateful monster thrashing within. But I should've dealt with him properly days ago.

"I'm afraid Mr. Savage is right." Florian leans back into his seat, an ankle hooked over his knee, the gun still leveled on me.

"Are you hiding anyone else back there?" I hiss.

"Actually…" Florian chuckles. "Come on out, Moriah."

A woman emerges from the shadowy bedroom—the slippery, smart-mouthed journalist. She winks at me as I choke out a gasp.

"Thanks to these two, I know all about your dalliance with young Mr. Seaborn," Florian explains. "Hatcher, is it? I'm sure you'd hate for any misfortune to befall him or his family. What's his mother's name again? Kara, if memory serves? And his brother…Hayden? Harden?"—Florian snaps his fingers once, twice—"Holden! Yes, that's it. And, of course, there's that sweet little nephew of his too—"

"Leave them alone," I grit out, causing a triumphant grin to dawn across Florian's face.

"Well, well! How quickly things change with the right motivation." Florian laughs. "Rest assured, I have other contingencies as well, in case the Seaborns prove not motivating enough."

My uncle flips his phone to me again, showing me all-new video footage. It's darker here, but I can make out a rustic wood cabin, tucked cozily against a dense pine forest.

My parents' cabin in Woodbridge.

How? Tristen already had people watching the cabin. Surely they'd know if Florian had others scouting the home.

"It's not all that perplexing, really," Florian chimes in, as if reading my thoughts. "Tristen's surveillance team didn't take much convincing to turn in my favor. It seems I pay more handsomely than my underachieving son."

He'd usurped Tristen's team. Paid them to do his bidding.

Meaning my parents aren't being protected—they're being *surrounded,* primed for an ambush. Sheep at the mercy of bloodthirsty wolves.

And I'd done nothing to warn them. I'd kept them in the dark, thinking that'd be for the best. Just like my mother did to me with Willow.

"There's no greater motivator in life than money," Florian says, taking deep satisfaction in my dismayed expression. "You'd do well to remember that, Meridel."

"Not everyone is like you," I toss back. "All you have is money, but you're bereft of everything that truly matters. Destitute in all the ways that count."

His scowl is as keen as a razor's edge. "And what ways are those?"

"Morality. Decency. *Love.* You'll never know what it means to love someone, or to be loved in return."

My uncle jumps to his feet and, in two swift steps, fists my hair and yanks my neck back. I cry out at the sudden, jarring movement. "Watch your tongue," Florian snaps down at me, spittle flying from his mouth.

My fingers dig into the couch as he dips my neck at a painful angle. "Stay away from them," I bark back, trying to imbue my words with guts and grit despite my trembling.

"What happens to your parents and the Seaborns depends entirely upon your compliance. Do as you're told, and no one will be harmed. Disobey me, and your loved ones will pay with blood. Who lives and dies is in your hands."

And though he doesn't say it, I'm sure that if I prove too difficult, Florian will kill me and find someone else to extort. June. Palmer. It won't matter. He won't relent until he wins.

"My patience is wearing," Florian says testily. "Do we have an accord?"

Hatch will know something's up if I try to mislead him. He'll see through my lies, and Tristen certainly will too.

But maybe I can use that to my advantage.

If I get to them first, warn them somehow, maybe we can stop my uncle together. Sabotage his plan before it gets underway.

What choice do you have but to try?

"Yes," I whisper, not having thought out my strategy yet. Details will have to come later. For now, all I know is I need to get word to Hatch. To Tristen. To my parents.

With one final tug on my hair, Florian releases me. "Splendid," he chirps. "Moriah, would you retrieve Meridel's cell phone for me, please?"

Before I know it, Moriah is at my purse, snatching my cell phone up in one easy motion, along with any chance I have at beating my uncle at his game. She drops it softly into his waiting palm. It feels like a cleaver embedding in my chest.

"All communications will go through me now," Florian emphasizes, wagging the phone in his hand. "We'll have to do away with any potential in-person disturbances as well."

"She spends every afternoon and evening with Seaborn," Moriah reports. My fingers itch to dig bloody trenches down her face. "She also spends several hours a day working at the library. And quite a lot of time with the pregnant cousin as well."

"Oh, I almost forgot! Palmer must be about ready to pop!"

I grate my teeth, interpreting my uncle's words for what they are—a threat. "Leave her out of this."

"Palmer's of no use to me, darling. But I still can't have you running your mouth about town…" His lips do a little twitch, as if gauging what bomb to detonate next. "Let's keep eyes on the Marins," he says to his underlings. "See to it that Meridel keeps her distance from them. I can't imagine they'll think much of her absence when the baby comes. They'll be so busy, after all."

I swallow down a whimper. He'll keep me from seeing Palmer, from meeting the baby…

"Seaborn will be harder to neutralize," Prescott says, hints of jealousy written across his face. His sleepy eyes flash with quiet fury, his lips curled up to expose two rows of white teeth—part boy, part villain.

"Yes, the boyfriend presents an entirely different problem," Florian muses. "I think it best I leave that to you, Meridel."

"Leave what to me?" I spit.

"Terminating your relationship with Mr. Seaborn," he answers unfeelingly, as if I'm stupid for not drawing that conclusion myself.

"No," I choke out. "I won't do it."

His dark eyebrows lift slowly. "Either you convince Mr. Seaborn to stay away from you, or I will kill him and every last person he holds dear. One phone call, and that hovel he calls a home will go up in flames. It will look like a perfect accident."

Terror grips me at the thought of Hatch burning alive in that house, suffocated by smoke, no escape in sight. Dying in the same brutal manner his father had…

"Please," I rasp, wracking my brain for a way out of this, for a loophole that refuses to materialize. "Don't hurt him."

"You don't have to beg me, darling," Florian replies. "Mr. Seaborn's fate lies entirely with you. You will either spare him his life, or you will be his undoing."

"And if I do what you ask," I say, my voice as broken as the hollow feeling in my chest, "then…you won't touch him?"

"I'm a man of my word."

The way I fold into myself like paper, my face drooping into my hands, tears streaming in endless rivers, is answer enough for my uncle.

He clasps his hands together, entirely satisfied at watching me shatter before him. "Moriah, send Seaborn a message as Meridel, please. Tell him she wants to meet him later this morning. Say, seven-ish? Make it sound *enticing*. Urgent."

Moriah nods at my uncle, snatching up my phone again to draft the text.

My one saving grace is that the cell service at Cliffmoor House is reliably unpredictable. Maybe Hatch won't get the message. Maybe I'll manage to avoid seeing him. Delay this meeting for a few more hours. At least until I can figure out how to cut myself free of this mess.

"What about my job?" I ask weakly.

"You're going on temporary leave, I'm afraid." A smile carves deep into Florian's hellish face. "It appears you've fallen quite ill as of late."

"Why not have me quit?"

"Your access to our esteemed island library may prove beneficial to me. But more on that later. Let's see how tomorrow plays out first. Our arrangement is based on mutual trust, after all. If you cooperate fully with my demands, no one needs to get hurt. Once I'm gone, you may reunite with your family and reconcile with Mr. Seaborn to your heart's content. Do we understand each other?"

"Yes," I reply haggardly, needing my uncle to stop talking long enough for me to think. *What do I do next? How do I circumvent him?*

My phone chimes in Moriah's hand—a text tone, but it sounds more like a death toll. She beams at us, holding up the lit screen. I can't read the conversation from this distance, but I can see the little text bubble…

Hatch responded.

"*Can't wait,*" Moriah reads aloud smugly.

I burst into a fresh flood of tears.

CHAPTER FORTY-FOUR

Hatch stands at the bow of the *Willow's Wind,* eyes scanning a bright morning sky that peels itself back, strip by strip, to reveal colors I can't summon the words for, so brilliant they deserve new names—new words worthy of their fire and limitlessness.

It hurts to take it in. The beauty. The spectacle. A magnificent stage for my inevitable heartbreak…and his.

The well of this island's cruelty is bottomless.

On dragging feet, I approach the *Willow,* hyper-aware that Moriah lingers nearby, armed to the teeth, with eyes and ears trained on my every move.

She puts on a convincingly innocent show for onlookers—peering curiously at the silver tarpon splashing beneath the docks, snapping photos of the hungry pelicans floating by in search of a meal, squinting out at the rising sun and seeming only to admire the beautiful day. But I know better. If anything goes awry—if she were to sense that I've done or said anything to compromise my uncle's plans—it will all be over for me. For Hatch.

The megawatt smile he bursts into when he sees me is a knife plunged through my chest.

"There's my girl," Hatch breathes, his squinty eyes shining with love for me. The sun pales in comparison.

I hope he knows that despite what I'm about to say, I will *always* be his girl.

"Hey," I say.

He takes my hands and helps me onto the boat, his gaze immediately keen on my face—my eyes red-rimmed and puffy, my skin tight and stippled in whorls of pink. Products of a sleepless night, endless tears, and Florian's threats.

"Are you okay?" he asks with a furrowed brow. He tries to touch my cheek, but I shake myself free of him.

"I'm fine."

If I say too much, I know I'll break down. If I look at him too closely, I'll plummet to my knees.

"You know, I love seeing you every night"—Hatch takes a step forward, smiling—"but I could *really* get used to seeing you every morning too."

He reaches for me again, but I put my hands up.

"Hatch. Stop."

He does, and the air between us thickens. His smile falters a little. Dims.

"Look, I, um…I think…I made a mistake last night."

I've never hated myself more than I do right now.

"What do you mean?"

"I mean it was a bit…rushed."

I'm sorry, Hatch. I'm so, so sorry. I'll fix this. I swear it.

"Oh?" His whole face falls, but not from anger. All I read from his expression is pain. A deep-rooted hurt I've ripped to the surface.

"Yeah, so…I'm thinking that…we should take a step back for now."

"A step back?"

Moriah plants herself on a bench along the docks, inconspicuously staring out at the horizon, fanning herself with her hand. Large sunglasses shield her eyes. She smiles at the sailors scampering past.

"A break," I amend.

"A break." He repeats the words as though he can't comprehend them, like I'm speaking a foreign language he never dreamed he'd have to learn. "What kind of break, Dell?"

Moriah's face is no longer turned to the scurrying sailors, but to *me*. She plucks her glasses from her face and tucks them into her collar. Her eyes sear through me.

Make this believable. Protect Hatch at all costs.

"This just isn't working for me right now," I say.

"It was working fine last night," he counters, taking another step closer. "What happened since then?"

I step back in turn. If Hatch touches me, I know I won't be able to resist him.

He pauses, registering my dismissive body language, absorbing it like a blow. Feeling every mile of distance I'm wedging between us.

Please forgive me.

"Nothing happened, Hatch. I just gave it some thought, and I realized we're being stupid. How can we make this work when we don't even live in the same state?"

"We can figure that out," Hatch responds. "Just like we said we would—"

"I'm not moving to Halcyon Bay," I interrupt him, though I know in my heart I'd been coming around to the idea. If it meant being with Hatch forever, I could do it.

"I wouldn't ask that of you, Dell." His tone is so earnest, so damn resolute, it's enough to make me weep. "I'll go to you. I'll move to Maine."

"I don't want you to move for me."

"But…I want that. For us." He blinks.

God, I want it too. That's all I want.

"It's just too soon." I shake my head, averting my lying eyes. "Too complicated."

"Love is only as complicated as you make it," Hatch argues, a shiny gleam of emotion in his eyes.

Just do it. Now. Do it quickly and let it be over.

"Um, about that…"

Hatch freezes.

"I don't think we should have said that." My words are shaky and lacking conviction.

"Why not?" he asks fiercely. "*I love you, Dell.* I meant every word I said. Didn't you?"

My voice is crushed in the back of my throat, my heart sinking down to a miserable, vacant place in my core.

"Dell." In two impossibly fast steps, Hatch is chest-to-chest with me. His hands find my arms. I'm not strong enough to pull away. "Did you mean what you said last night?"

Tears begin to flow.

I'm sorry, I'm sorry.

"No," I croak.

"No?" Hatch repeats, as if unable to grasp the true meaning of the word. "No, you don't love me?"

Yes! I shake my head, the word beating at my lips, practically clawing its way out. *Yes yes yes yes yes.*

"Say it," he insists, his voice trembling. Afraid of me and everything I'm doing to us.

I grit my teeth, the words refusing to come, all while Moriah watches shrewdly from a distance.

"Hatch, please—"

He dips into those precious few inches of space that were keeping me together, the sweltering air between us tingling at our proximity, his lips hovering over mine. I put my palms to his chest to maintain some distance. The throbbing echo of his heartbeat makes me sway.

"Tell me you don't love me." His lips graze my tear-soaked cheek. "Say it and I'll leave."

I'm undone. Wrecked. Irreparable.

My insides seize up, grief squeezing the life from me.

I'm sorry, Hatch. I love you. I'm sorry.

"Don't make me do this," I rasp, losing sight of everything before me. Hatch, the boat, and the marina beyond are all just smears of salty tears and hurt and the sense that life is going on for other people, while for me, it's fading to something like death.

My life is ending. Right here. This instant.

"I've laid it all on the line for you, Dell," Hatch says, his eyes as stormy as a war-torn sea. "I'd lay my life down, if you only asked. Because I love you so damn much. I'll never not love you, with everything I have. And I know you love me too. I feel it in my bones…"

I do, Hatch. I do. I love you more than anything.

There's no way I can tell him anything different. I can only try to convince him not to love me.

"C'mon," I breathe, pulling myself free of him. "Don't you see it? You're like…a ship, free and fearless. But me?" I throw my hands up. "I'm a freaking anchor. All I've ever done is drag you down."

"You were never an anchor to me," Hatch fights back. "I was lost, completely fucking lost, before I laid eyes on you. So don't tell me you're an anchor, Dell. Don't…" His voice breaks a little. "If I'm a ship, you're the lighthouse shining out from the coast. You bring me home. I need you, okay? *I need you.* So, please…please don't tell me I have to figure life out without you."

"I'm sorry," I mumble, shielding my tear-soaked face.

"If something more is going on here," he says shakily, "something bigger that you can't talk about, give me a sign. Don't leave me thinking this is real if it isn't."

My eyes flick back to Moriah, reclining on that bench. Two men I've never seen before flank her on either side. They're both dressed casually, like tourists taking in the sights, but I know they belong to her. To my uncle.

I can't let them hurt Hatch.

If I give him any inkling that this isn't real, he'll be relentless in his drive to help me. I'll be putting him directly in harm's way. Tossing him in shark-infested waters.

"It's real," I whisper. "You should probably go now."

I'll fix this, Hatch. We'll find our way back. I promise. I swear…

When he finally retreats from me, I bite hard on my bottom lip, stifling the innumerable "I'm sorry's" and "I love you's" threatening to blow this charade out of the water. I'm crying profusely. I can't stop.

"Okay," he rasps. "I guess I'll…leave you to your boat, then."

Our boat.

Ours.

Yours and mine.

He swings over the edge and lands dockside. It takes every ounce of restraint in me not to fling myself over that wall, wrap myself around his body, and swear on pain of death that I'll never leave his side.

Instead, I watch him leave.

I watch him walk away from me and all the love we've made. The love that I've fractured into millions of pieces. Invisible shards pierce every inch of my skin, slitting open each vein, leaving me to a quiet and unrelenting death.

I fall to my knees on the boat that was ours and watch as my world slips away.

CHAPTER FORTY-FIVE

I thought the pain of last summer was the worst I'd ever feel.

I couldn't have been more wrong about that.

Last summer was marked by the sting of betrayal. Of truths that had been withheld from me, buried deep in the murky waters of my childhood. That pain was an old one, a wound that wouldn't fully heal, but could still be softened—alleviated—by time. The hurt would linger, but it would lessen too.

That's *nothing* like the pain of breaking up with Hatch.

This pain is the repeated blast of a gunshot to the chest, a thousand swift stabs to my slow-beating heart. This pain amplifies, like blood leaking from a broken body. I know it will echo until my dying breath, every moment without him reminding me of the life I'd given away. The love that had been robbed from me.

This will be my life's defining pain—the one I'll wear like a scarlet letter, doomed to dwell in the anemic shadows of a future that never was.

Unless I can find a way out.

Salty streams pour down my face as I pedal my bike back to Cliffmoor

House, hyper-aware of the black car with tinted windows trailing slowly behind me—Moriah and her henchmen.

When I get to the estate, I stop for no one, blazing across the grounds and locking myself inside the guest house. Florian's mole could be anyone—Payne, Nova, any number of guards or house staff. My uncle has likely tapped into the security cameras too. His eyes are all-seeing, his reach immeasurable. So I'm better off isolating than mistakenly confiding in the wrong person.

I cry myself sick as the morning stretches into afternoon. A raging headache curls up behind my eyes, grating against my skull like a cat nuzzling a windowpane. It takes every ounce of willpower in me not to fold up in the fetal position and give up altogether...

But I won't.

I'll use this pain to my advantage, like a whetstone sharpening the blade of my vengeance.

First on my list of tasks is getting ahold of Mom and Dad.

If I can make a quick phone call, or steal five minutes alone at a computer, I can warn them about the danger they're in. I can convince them to go somewhere safe, some place far away from Woodbridge. They can check into a hotel in a more populated city, somewhere crowded and bustling and altogether more complicated for my uncle's crew of vigilantes to penetrate. Maybe then, my parents can alert authorities and send for help.

But the guest house phone was disconnected long ago. God knows whether the landline at Cliffmoor House still works. And without access to the library, there's no way I'll get an email out...

I'm thinking myself into pretzels.

The only person on these grounds I can trust right now is Tristen—ironic, considering how often I've questioned his motives. But how do I get him alone and away from the house? It'd be near impossible for us to slip away discreetly...

Maybe I don't need to get him alone.

Maybe I just need his cell phone.

Is it worth the risk?

I spring to my feet and head for the front door. When I swing it open, I nearly jump out of my skin when I'm confronted by Payne, perched on the stoop with an enigmatic smirk. "Going somewhere, little field mouse?"

It has to be him—my uncle's informant.

"I told you not to call me that again, creep," I hiss.

"Careful," Payne teases. "You'll fool me into thinking I'm growing on you. 'Creep' is a major step up from 'dickbag.'"

"Both of which are far too endearing for you."

"Uh-oh. Someone's thinly-veiled hatred is showing." Payne's smirk widens. "You can lower your hackles, Dell. I come in peace."

"What do you want?"

"Your cousin asked me to pop in to see if you liked your present." He peers around me into the guest house, his gaze settling on the open box atop the coffee table—on the glittering, gossamer fabric cascading over the edge like a waterfall of stars.

"It's fine," I deadpan. "Now you can leave."

Payne's steely eyes flash with amusement. "You sound positively thrilled."

"It takes more than a sparkly dress to whip me into a frenzy."

He chuckles. "Have you tried it on? Nova had to guess your size. Tristen wanted to know whether it needs altering—"

"Since when are you my cousin's messenger boy?" I snap. "Why doesn't he come ask me himself?"

Payne's playful expression tightens, lips puckering as though he's tasted sour fruit. "He's at a meeting downtown with his event coordinators making final arrangements for the ball."

"Why didn't you go with him?" I ask, my suspicion growing.

"What, and miss out on all this great fun we're having? Not a chance."

I narrow my eyes to slits. Payne rarely separates from Tristen. Why would he stay behind? To keep me in his sights, I suppose. Keep my uncle abreast of my movements.

"Well, playtime's over." I grab for the door again. "You can slither back under your rock now."

Payne shakes his head, placing a hand on the door to keep it open. "I thought I made myself clear, Dell. I'm not your enemy here."

"And I thought I made *myself* clear that I don't let stupid men do my cognitive work for me." I yank at the door with force, swinging it hard. "*Adios*, dickbag."

It slams shut in his face, but Payne's disquieting cackle still bleeds through the thin walls.

I crawl under my sheets and pray for a miracle.

"Wakey, wakey."

A lamp flicks on, and I startle awake to find two shadow-cloaked figures at the foot of my bed.

I lurch up from my reclined position, only to be greeted by Prescott and Moriah's gruesome smiles. My stomach shoots like a cannonball into my mouth. "What the hell do you want?"

"It's showtime," Prescott announces.

"What does that mean? What time is it?"

"Right around four AM," Moriah says. "It's an early day, but you should feel pretty well-rested. You've been out for hours now."

My body stiffens against her violating words. How long had they been standing over me, surveying me like a zoo animal?

"You people are sick," I growl.

Prescott's smile grows somehow more iniquitous. "What's sick about watching you sleep? I think I like you best this way. All soft and warm. Susceptible…"

If I don't look directly at him, maybe I can keep from vomiting. Not that I have much in me to puke up. The last time I ate anything solid was well over twenty-four hours ago.

"Florian has a task for you," Moriah announces. "You'll be going with Prescott to—"

"I'm not going *anywhere* with him."

"Are you sure you want me to make that call?" she sneers, pulling my cell phone from her pants pocket and wiggling it by her face. "Your uncle will be most disappointed, and whenever that happens, heads tend to roll."

My eyes shutter closed, a tremble on my lip.

"Wonderful!" Moriah chirps. "Now get yourself cleaned up and meet Prescott outside in five minutes. Chop, chop!"

"Where are we going?" I croak.

The sadistic pair exchange a knowing glance. "Somewhere you know better than any of us," Prescott explains. "Your humble place of business. The island library."

CHAPTER FORTY-SIX

"You may as well hop on, Dell," Prescott calls over the purr of his motorbike. I can hear hints of a smile tugging up his face, but I refuse to turn my face to look at him. "It's a long walk to the library. You're going to wear yourself out."

The morning is young—still hours from sunrise—suffused with a cool, salty mist from the sea. I march down the moonlit sidewalks of Old Town, with the ancient oaks casting deep shadows over the road, hellbent on ignoring Prescott's every word.

He rolls beside me on his motorbike, trying to coax me into climbing on behind him. "I know it wasn't cool of Florian to trash your bicycle, but what do you say we make the best of it?"

Someone from Florian's camp had discarded Virginia's bike overnight, assuring themselves that I couldn't slip away easily. Hell, it might've been Prescott for all I know, anticipating this very moment.

"I'll let you use my helmet," he offers, needling me for the nine-hundredth time. "Just like last summer, remember?"

As if that's a game changer.

I forge ahead on my own, thinking back to Moriah's instructions. Get to the library before dawn—before Dex arrives, or any meddling patrons—and locate a certain book. To say this confused me is an understatement, especially since she refused to mention *which* book I'd be looking for. But she'd sent Prescott along to escort-slash-supervise me, and I can only assume the prick comes armed with a title.

"C'mon, Dell," he whines, as though I'm being unreasonable. "Am I really that repulsive? We used to be friends!"

This book must be a pivotal piece to fit a much larger puzzle, one Florian doesn't want anyone knowing about. But I'm determined to thwart his plan somehow. To get to the book before Prescott does, and hide it so it can't be found. I have no idea how, but I have to try.

"It's the crooked nose, isn't it?" Prescott asks, unwilling to let up or give me a goddamn second of peace. "Not pretty enough for you? Nothing like that precious boyfriend of yours."

I make no response, give him no satisfaction.

"Look, if I can get past the fact that you broke my face, I think you can get past the whole kidnapping thing. It wasn't my call anyway! I didn't want to drug you, or pull that gun on you in the fields. I was just following orders. Can't blame a guy for that."

The hell I can't.

"I know it was cruel of me to turn on you like that." Prescott veers his bike this way and that, weaving closer and farther from the sidewalk, as slow and meandering as this one-sided conversation. "I regret it, Dell. I really do."

Do not answer him, I silently coach myself. *All he wants is to get under your skin. To torment you.*

"I thought not pressing charges for the incident at my place the other day was a step in the right direction. An olive branch, you know?" His eyes are trained on me, eager for some reaction, but I give him none.

"It gets to me sometimes," Prescott adds ruefully, "the thought that I might've ruined something special between us…"

Something special?

I clench my teeth, my skin stretching taut over every part of my face.

It takes everything in me not to sink my nails into his.

He sighs loudly, growing bored of my unwillingness to play. "At this rate, we'll never make it to the library before dawn," he complains. "Your uncle won't be happy that you deviated from schedule. Regardless of how you feel about me, we need to pick up the pace—"

I break into a sudden sprint.

"Whoa, hey!" Prescott revs his motorbike to catch up.

He's right about the time crunch, and I can't risk upsetting Florian. One phone call to set his thugs loose, and I'll never see Hatch or my parents again.

"What the hell are you doing?" Prescott asks when he reaches me, keeping speed with my pounding footsteps.

I haven't run with any degree of seriousness since my high school track days almost seven years ago. I'm rusty, but I still feel myself soaring across the pavement, barely skimming the sidewalk's surface. The burning in my legs is part pain, part release, as Prescott's protests drown into background noise. Eventually, he speeds ahead in the direction of the library, leaving me in a cloud of gray exhaust.

I never believed myself capable of hating someone the way I do Prescott Savage. The lingering miasma of those teasing invitations—his sly and unwanted advances toward me—leaves me disturbed to my core, goosebumps rising through my clothes as I work up a sweat. The rhythmic striking of my feet on the concrete helps, each step driving Prescott's gross insinuations farther and farther from my mind.

The sleeping island falls away as darkness presses in, like a balm spread thick over my hemorrhaging wounds, numbing me to the pain. For fifteen merciful minutes, it's just the salty air and me. Fifteen minutes where I don't feel like myself. Don't feel confined to this body, or trapped by this mind. Nothing feels out of reach. Nothing is impossible.

I'm a seabird mid-flight.

A rushing wind.

The surging tide.

Invincible.

So I imagine it into being—will it to life with every strike of my sneakers. When I cross that finish line, it won't be Florian waiting for me. It won't be Prescott goading me. It'll be Hatch. My parents. Palmer and Mojo. June and Leif. Tristen. All of them, everyone I love, safe and sound. This terror will be behind us. *Finally.*

Fifteen minutes…

I turn off Plumbago Street onto the library's roundabout.

Prescott stands near the newspaper receptacles. His hoodie is drawn low over his head, his motorbike noticeably missing from view. I can only assume he hid it behind the building, keeping our presence here under wraps.

I walk past him like he isn't there, making for the door.

He's at my heels in seconds. "Moriah really went for the jugular with some of those tabloid articles," he comments, that wormy voice working its way into my ears again, disrupting the tiny peace I'm clinging to.

I concede nothing, pulling out my key to unlock the door. I let it swing fast after I slip inside, hoping to smack Prescott dead in the face—maybe fracture a couple more bones—but his hand is there in an instant to catch it. He creeps in swiftly and shuts the door with a click.

Moving carefully in the pitch-dark, I head for Dexter's office, knowing not to hit the light switch. Lighting this place up like a Christmas tree would be too risky. The last thing I need is some HBPD rookie showing up here hungry for his ticket to glory.

Prescott keeps disturbingly close, barely a step behind me, his stale breath on my neck setting my teeth on edge. I ball my hands into fists, silently daring him to touch me, my anger just this side of combustion. Whether by sheer, dumb luck or a heightened sense of spatial awareness, the prick never does.

I refocus on my task.

Once outside Dexter's office, I feel around for the lock and jam a second key into it, twisting and pushing until the door cracks ajar.

"Why can't you use the computer behind the desk in the lobby?" Prescott whispers.

I clench my teeth. I'll have to speak to him at some point, at the very least to get the title of the damn book. Might as well start now. "The other computers don't work unless the main hub is powered on. Now shut up and let me work."

He does as I say, lingering inside the doorway while I pick my way around Dexter's desk. Dropping to my knees, I feel around the carpeted floor until I locate the power strip. Switching it on, I hear the whirr and hum of electricity. The computer screen flicks to life, illuminating my face in blue light. I enter my password to access the library program.

"What's the title?" I ask aloud, not bothering to lift my eyes, impatient fingers hovering above the keyboard.

"*Legends that Built Halcyon Bay* by Douglas Barnaby."

Every ounce of blood drains from my face, seeping down, down, down to my toes.

Legends is currently sitting in the backseat of Hatch's truck.

If I run a search in the system, it won't come up as 'Available.'

It'll appear as 'Borrowed.'

By *Hatcher Seaborn.*

"Did you hear me?" Prescott asks.

"I have ears, asshole," I bark, thinking hard against the clock. I can't involve Hatch in this. Can't give my uncle any more of a reason to target him.

"Then what's the problem?" Prescott moves around the desk toward me.

"The computer's frozen," I lie.

"Let me see it," he says.

A surge of fiery panic shoots like a rocket to my brain. I slam my toe on the power strip and the screen goes black, the room swallowed in darkness once more.

"What happened?" Prescott asks a little too loudly. I can't see him, but I can tell that he's paused mid-step.

Noiselessly, I unplug the strip from the wall, pulling the computer cord along with it. "Power outage," I say. "It happens constantly here, sometimes for hours at a time."

"You're kidding."

I tuck the equipment under my shirt, praying my story is convincing.

"No, I'm not. This whole island is technologically impaired. You live in a goddamn time warp out here."

"But it was on just a second ago," he protests.

"You want to waste time fiddling with a dead computer? Be my guest. I know where the book is, so I'm going to go find it." I skitter around the desk, brushing past him as I go.

"How do you know where it is?" Prescott asks, suspicion thick in his voice.

"Because I work here, dumbass," I retort, hoping it will suffice.

After a brief second of hesitation, I hear a patter of footfalls swiftly trailing me.

We make our way towards the *Regional* section, as I mentally plan out my next steps. First, put on the greatest acting performance of my life pretending to search for this book. Then, upon not finding it, explain that it must be misshelved or checked out. Look in the surrounding sections. With the ongoing 'power outage,' we won't be able to search for it in the system. Inevitably, we'll have to leave before the sun rises, well before anyone sees us...

It won't get Florian off the warpath—he'll likely force me right back here later tonight—but it'll cause a delay, at least for a few hours. That's all I need. A little more time to map a way out of this.

For the next hour, Prescott and I use our cell phone lights to skim every book in the *Regional* section, as well as the surrounding bookshelves on the first floor. At one point, when his head is turned, I slip the power strip and cord underneath a leather chair.

I can sense Prescott's agitation growing with each passing minute, matched only by the stress I'm trying hard to keep at bay. What could Florian want with a book on island mythology?

"Incredible," Prescott mutters under his breath. "Of all the books in this place"—he runs long fingers over a shelf, touching each spine—"what are the chances *this* one is missing?"

I glance at the nearest tapered window, at the dapples of pink sprinkled across the sky. It takes everything in me not to cry with joy. "Sunrise," I point out, tamping down my excitement.

"Shit," he says. "We need to go."

No need to tell me twice, bitch.

Without further prompting, I make for the library doors, the aisles slightly easier to navigate with slivers of muted color pouring in through the windows. Prescott follows suit, but more at a distance, likely consumed with thoughts over how he'll explain this to my uncle.

My heart drums forcefully in my ears, a feeling of triumph pulsing through my limbs. Even the tiniest setback in Florian's plan is a massive win for me. I need to figure out how to get the book back from Hatch without raising suspicion. Once I have it, I'll need some time alone with it, to extract whatever information my uncle might want.

Once we're in the lobby, I make a bee-line for the door, flipping the lock, when I notice Prescott reading something on the circulation desk. I linger there, eager to leave but desperate to know what piqued his interest.

When I see a smile dawn across his face, I know I've made a terrible mistake somewhere. Forgotten something crucial. Sealed my fate.

"Seems your boyfriend also enjoys the offerings of our local library," Prescott comments, holding up a notepad with handwritten scribbles.

It's Dexter's visitor log.

The one Hatch signed when we came days ago.

"A sailor *and* a scholar." Prescott smirks, wielding this snippet of information like armament for battle. "You've caught yourself quite the unicorn there, Dell. I wonder what he came here for…" An indelible threat is buried in those words. "Do you have any ideas?"

I'm quiet. Caught. Backed into a corner with no way out. All I wanted was to keep Hatch out of this, and that's precisely what I failed to do.

"Oh, you don't have to tell *me,* of course," Prescott says a bit wistfully, picking at his nails. "But once your uncle Florian finds out, I'm sure he'll be on pins and needles to have a heart-to-heart with you. Or, better yet, with fishboy himself."

My face is as hard as stone as Prescott approaches, moving in the waning darkness with distinctly feline prowess.

"You know I've always had a terrible soft spot for you, Dell. And I want to give you the benefit of the doubt here. I don't want to believe you'd lie to me. I mean, this could all be an unfortunate coincidence, right?" He reaches a hand toward my face—I assume to dust his fingers over my cheek, upgrading his psychological torture to physical.

My fists tighten as I step off to the side, about to snarl at Prescott to *keep his filthy hands off of me,* when he says in an eerily soft voice, "Only one way to find out."

His hand stretches past me to the light switch, flicking it on.

The space bursts white.

Prescott's eyes burn with silent victory.

CHAPTER FORTY-SEVEN

Prescott uses the library incident as a bargaining chip. He promises not to tell Florian about my attempt to foil their plan, so long as I go straight to Hatch and procure the book. Part of the deal is that Prescott gets to watch. Gets to see the ache in Hatch's face when I darken his doorstep and break his heart all over again.

I don't see a way out of it. If Florian learns what I've done, he might remove me from the equation and decide to send someone else to retrieve the book. Someone with no intention of letting Hatch escape unscathed. Someone who'd rather see him dead than leave a loose end unaccounted for.

I walk up the sidewalk to his driveway, a pang in my heart at the sight of that vivid green house that had begun to feel familiar and safe—an extension of *him*. Now it's just a bright reminder of all that I'm missing out on. Of the love I'd shunned, and the family that will never be mine.

Prescott is tucked into the opposite corner of the street, shielded in the long morning shadows of a neighboring house. I feel his vigilance at my back as if he were breathing over me. He's visibly thrilled by this turn of events—at getting to see me twist the knife I'd lodged deep in Hatch's ribcage.

I'll never forgive myself.

Before I've taken two steps onto the property, the front door swings open and Hatch emerges. His shoulders are slumped and he's moving fast, his eyes unusually dark, a backwards baseball cap tucked over his waves.

He doesn't notice me standing dead in my tracks at the foot of the drive. Just makes for his truck with singular focus and an aura of melancholy.

I can't move, can't speak, barely sucking in strangled breaths.

Once at the Ranger, Hatch yanks open the driver door, about to jump inside…but then he catches sight of me standing there, open-mouthed and dumbfounded.

When our eyes connect, I gasp out an irrational, "Oh!"

"Dell?" He pauses, blinking, as if extracting himself from the hazy stupor of a dream. He shuts the driver door and shoves his hands in his pockets. Swallows. "What are you doing here?"

I'm sorry. I love you. I take it all back…

"Book," is all that tumbles from my lips.

"Book?" Hatch's eyebrows pull tight as he takes in my haggard, sweat-soaked appearance. "Dell, how'd you get here? Where's your bike?"

I don't know how to answer his questions, so I revert back to the lie I'd practiced over and over the entire walk here. "The library book we borrowed," I blurt. "Dexter needs it back for an online course he's teaching."

"Oh," Hatch says, shock registering that I'm only here to collect a stupid library book. "I didn't know the library makes house calls now…" His eyes are sunken in, a wash of purple shadow smeared beneath the lower lids. "It's in my backseat."

He opens the door and grabs it, examining it in disbelief before walking the several paces down the driveway to where I stand. He holds it out to me.

I stare at the book in his hands for a long moment, wishing for some way to freeze time. To put the world on pause and tell him the truth. Tell him how much I love him, and that I never meant to hurt him. Tell him how deeply I'm hurting too. That it's worse than any pain I've ever experienced.

"Here you go," he says sadly.

I reach a hand out, and when our fingertips brush—just the barest hint of a graze—I feel my mouth slip, my throat squeeze, stomach clenching.

Hatch makes a small, choking sound, as if our brief touch affected him just as deeply, the ache of loss pummeling into his chest like a mack truck.

"Thanks," I murmur, dropping my eyes to keep from crying.

We stand there in silence, things unsaid wringing at my gut. Eventually, I turn down the sidewalk and take off walking. I can't stand another second of this. It's too much, too hard…

"That's it?" Hatch calls at my back, unable to keep the hurt from his voice.

I freeze, wilting where I stand like a flower in winter. I knew this was coming—the encore to a breakup I never wanted. Salt in a fresh wound. The performance Prescott was craving.

"That's all I get?" Hatch asks again. "I'm not okay with this, you know."

If I give in to him—if I let myself stay any longer—things will only be worse for us. I *can't* compromise Hatch or his family. Can't give Prescott any more ammunition to report back to my uncle.

I hear Hatch's footsteps coming fast down the drive.

When I turn, there he is—*unbearably* close—his hands curling around my elbows. "I can't lose you, Dell," he says fiercely. Everything about him pulls me in, tugging on the unbreakable rope he's lassoed around my heart. He scans my eyes deeply, in search of some clear-cut reason for why I'm acting as I am. "Talk to me, please. Don't block me out."

I want so much to melt against him, but the book in my hand could burn a hole through my fingers. Florian is waiting. Prescott is watching.

"I don't know what's going on with you," Hatch says, "but I'm not giving up. I'm not walking away from this."

That's precisely why I have to.

"Please. Let me love you." He drops his forehead to mine. I close my eyes, relishing in all the places our bodies connect, allowing myself this final, fleeting pleasure. This is how I'll always keep him. This timeless moment tucked in the locket of my heart. His chapped hands rubbing tender circles on my arms. The scents of clean cotton, salt air, and Coppertone on his skin. His forehead pressed against mine, hair soft, noses brushing. So close that when I open my eyes, I can't see him clearly. In place of his features, all I see are warm smears of color. A perfect haze of gold and green.

My Hatch, infinitely.

I pull back from him, a sharp and foreign motion that feels like ripping my heart in two.

Hatch looks as if I've slapped him across the face.

"I'm sorry," I say roughly, turning away in a cold, unfeeling swoop.

Hatch doesn't chase me, doesn't call my name, but I feel his burning gaze on my back, sure as the sun warming my face. I make sure to hold myself together, if only on the outside. I keep the mess buried deep within.

The early morning sky ahead of me glows, bursting with cloudless orange flame. It's nothing compared to the light I leave behind.

CHAPTER FORTY-EIGHT

The next few days slip by in a blur.

I withdraw from the outside world, a ghostly fixture of the guest house, like Eribeth before me. A prisoner in mind and body. Barely eating, barely showering, my existence narrowed only to sleep and tears.

I hear from no one.

Speak to no one.

I keep heavy furniture lodged in front of the door to keep me from walking off in my sleep. And to keep my uncle's minions out.

Hatch doesn't come by, a fact for which I'm both happy and sad.

Happy, I convince myself. *You're glad he's safe. Even if it hurts.*

So long as he's kept far from this—so long as my parents remain unharmed—I'll adapt to life in this dungeon. I'll accept that perhaps I'm destined for the darkness.

It welcomes me back. Envelops my soul in despair.

I let myself drown in that ocean all over again.

An unexpected rap at the door pulls me from a weepy half-sleep.

I jerk up, panting, instantly on high alert.

Streams of hazy sunlight spill in through the window.

It can't be my uncle, or his sadistic band of flunkies. They wouldn't risk being seen here in broad daylight.

The impatient rapping continues as I slide from the warmth of the bed, padding into the main room to peek through the curtains.

Palmer stands there, glaring at me through slitted eyes. Her flaxen hair is swept into a messy top knot, and she's balancing a large Pizzana pizza on her belly. The red and white checkered box reads: *Cheesy nirvana at first bite!*

I drop the curtains and shove the furniture out of the way. When I open the door and step outside, I'm blinded by a hot, grating sun.

"What's up with you?" Palmer asks suspiciously. "I've called you, like, a dozen times."

"Sorry, I lost my phone," I lie, my voice oddly sluggish. I haven't conversed with anyone in several long days.

"Were you still sleeping at this hour?" She grimaces. "You look terrible."

That's light years ahead of how I feel.

"What time is it?" I don't bother asking what day it is. That would transform Palmer's look of disgust into one of concern, and I don't need the extra scrutiny.

"Noonish." She scans me up and down with shrewd eyes. "Dex says you've been sick?"

"Yeah…I caught a bad cold."

"You look like you haven't eaten in days."

"I haven't been able to keep a whole lot down."

"Well"—Palmer drums her nails on the pizza box—"nothing a little Pizzana can't fix. Hope you like Hawaiian."

I try to protest, despite not recalling when I last had a proper meal, and a rumbling in my belly loud enough to startle the birds. But Palmer rolls her eyes, unimpressed. "Don't give me any of that purist 'pineapple-doesn't-belong-on-pizza' crap."

"I wasn't—"

"Good. Come join me by the pool, then. I'm famished, and, quite frankly, you could use the vitamin D."

She marches off before I can say anything to the contrary.

I shuffle behind her in my pajamas, wincing against the blazing sun as I peer across the grounds for the first time in days, in awe over what I see.

The grungy, unkempt gardens have been remade into a lush island oasis, freshly landscaped and bursting with color. Gone are the wayward branches and the unpruned bushes and the long, wispy grass. The old dilapidated gazebo has been replaced by a shiny wooden structure. The mucky pool water has been cleaned and treated and now glistens a crisp, crystalline blue. Romantic amber lights are strung along the stone path up to Cliffmoor House, and scores of stunning blue and orange blooms are newly planted across the lawn. Tristen has pulled out all the stops for this ball.

"Come on, slow poke!" Palmer calls as she settles down poolside, dipping her tanned legs into the sparkling water. "I literally feel myself aging over here."

I desperately wish I could tell Palmer the truth, but that would mean putting two more lives at risk. I can't chance her and the baby getting hurt over my poor judgment. If any of my uncle's peons were to catch wind of my subterfuge, they'd scurry like rats back to his lair to tattle on me.

I sit crossed-legged at the edge of the pool, staring as my cousin pulls a container of red chili pepper flakes from her purse. She sprinkles a liberal layer over her side of the pizza.

"What?" she huffs, sensing my eyes upon her. "Spicy food is supposed to help get things moving. This baby's gotta come out sooner or later."

"You haven't even hit your due date yet."

Palmer grabs a slice and takes an emphatic bite, unaffected by the greasy cheese strings dripping from her chin. "It's been long enough. Time to get this show on the road."

I grab a piece for myself and take a small bite, nearly crying out with pleasure when it first hits my tongue. It really does taste like I'm in pizza nirvana, especially after unwittingly starving myself for days.

"So what's bugging you besides the cold?" Palmer asks between bites.

I chew extra slowly and hope she forgets the question.

"Something with your parents?"

I swallow. Deny in silence.

"Something with Florian?"

Too close for comfort. Must deflect.

"Have you had any more visions since leaving the hospital?" I ask, deviating hard. "Are you still hearing whispers?"

Palmer blinks, momentarily caught off guard, but quickly picks back up again. "I hear the whispers, but the doctors prescribed me some mild antipsychotics to keep the visions at bay. I still see the woman in my dreams sometimes, though. It feels like she's trying to tell me something, but can't get the message through. Like we have a language barrier." She rips off a hunk of doughy pizza crust and pops it into her mouth.

"You seem less concerned," I note.

"I'm sort of used to her now, odd as it sounds," Palmer admits. "She doesn't scare me so much anymore."

"What does she look like, in your dreams?" I ask.

One of Palmer's blond eyebrows spike up. "All right, Captain Runaround, enough with the deflection. I bring the rations, I get to ask the questions."

I flinch under the heat of her stare.

"What's going on with you for real?" she implores.

"Why does something always have to be 'going on' with me?" I fire back. "Is it so improbable that I might actually just be sick?"

"Please," Palmer retorts, pulling another melty, chili-coated slice from the pie. "I can read your face like a book. It's a gift. So either you come clean now—as *painlessly* as possible—or I'll slowly break you down until you have no other choice. Unless, of course, you'd rather I call Hatch and drag the truth out of him instead?" She wags her eyebrows as she takes another massive, drippy bite.

My heart plummets at the mention of Hatch's name. "You probably wouldn't get too far on that front."

Palmer's smug expression slips. "Why not?"

"Because I told Hatch I needed some space."

She almost chokes on a glob of cheese. "You *what?*" Her wide, saucer eyes are even more accusing than her tone.

"Things weren't…working between us—"

"So you *broke up* with him?" Her face blanches, a portrait of disbelief.

Prickling emotion radiates from my nose, climbing to my eyes, threatening to undo me. If I cry, it's all over. Every bit of this charade falls apart.

"I don't need you making me feel worse about it," I mumble.

"But *why,* Dell?" she asks, her tone growing more shrill and mistrusting by the second. "Why in the world would you do that?"

"I already told you—"

"No!" she cries. "You haven't told me anything. You treat everyone around you like a stranger, but I'm not just some stranger anymore!"

The workers and guards peppering the grounds turn and stare. I see Payne at a distance flanked by two landscapers. He waves at me slowly, a cryptic smile on his lips. Too many eyes on us.

Shit.

"If you went so far as to end things with Hatch, there's obviously a reason," Palmer continues, incensed by my evasiveness. "I've confided in you about so much this past year, but you never reciprocate! I always have to weasel the truth out of you—"

"I don't want to be stuck here, okay?" I blurt, not knowing how else to get her to stop. I need Palmer to leave this place *now.* I need her to forget about Cliffmoor House. Forget me.

"Stuck?" she repeats.

Make it hurt. Make her leave.

"Yes. Stuck here like you."

Betrayal pulses in her sky-blue eyes, sculpts into the space between her brows. "Like me?" Her voice cracks.

"Yeah. Stuck on this shitty island. Stuck with your high school boyfriend. Stuck in life. Just…stuck."

Her face twists up. "You don't mean that."

"Don't I?" I level my eyes on Palmer's. "You really think I want all of *this* for myself?" I brandish a condescending hand over my cousin, as if to suggest something about her is inherently wrong, or silly, or not worth aspiring to.

"Screw you," she grits out.

That's right. Screw me.

Palmer scrambles to her feet with some difficulty. I know better than to attempt to help. "The freaking nerve," she mutters shakily.

Slinging her purse over her shoulder, she slams the pizza box closed, gripping it to her side. I watch each of her angry, staccato movements, feigning a face of unfeeling composure. I have to pretend not to care, though my heart is shattering into millions of raw, jigsaw pieces.

"When you pack up your bags this time, make it for good," Palmer snaps. "I've had enough of you jerking us around."

"Fine." *So long as you're okay, Palmer, I can live with knowing you hate me.*

She tosses me a withering look. "And you can forget the stupid godmother thing too. I wouldn't want you to feel *stuck* with Mia."

I clamp down hard on my bottom lip, biting back a swell of rising emotion. "Understood."

Palmer shakes her head, utter devastation written across her face. "I don't know why I ever thought I could count on you."

She pivots, making like a raging bull for the garden gate…

Only to freeze in her tracks seconds later.

She groans loud enough for me to hear. For all the workers to hear.

The pizza box crashes to the ground.

"Palmer!"

Before I can think better of it, I'm moving toward her. She's staring down the front of her shorts, her mouth gaping.

"Palmer?"

Catching her breath, she looks up at me, trembling, all traces of her former anger erased.

"I think…my water just broke."

CHAPTER FORTY-NINE

The waiting room at Halcyon Bay General is incomparably cold and bleak. I sit alone by the far window—wary not to draw attention to myself, nor to disturb Leif's cartoon-viewing or Dex's magazine-flipping—digging my fingernails into the pleather seat to keep from screaming till my blood vessels pop.

I messed up big time.

When Palmer's water broke, she flew into a panic. The workers, guards, and landscapers of Cliffmoor House flocked to us. One of them asked if they should call for an ambulance. Another extended his landscaping truck as a getaway car. Payne's slithery voice chimed in, offering to drive her to the hospital himself.

I snapped.

Palmer was going into *labor*. I couldn't allow these men near her, any number of whom might be depraved acolytes of my uncle. I shoved my way between them, barking mad and insistent that *I'd* be the only one driving Palmer anywhere. It was no small miracle that she let me, after the kind of fight we'd had, but in light of the situation, she had more pressing matters to contend with.

We jumped in her car and sped away from Cliffmoor House. It was only after we screeched to a halt before the hospital doors—after two orderlies carried Palmer onto a wheelchair and rushed her inside—that I realized what I'd actually done…

How would my uncle retaliate?

I'd left the grounds unsupervised, and had ample time alone with my cousin—ample time to run my mouth. Florian wouldn't take kindly to that. I hadn't said a word to Palmer, outside of frantically coaching her to breathe, but my uncle wouldn't care. He wouldn't pause to ask questions, or listen to my excuses.

I parked Palmer's car in a daze, zombie-shuffled through the hospital lobby, and slumped into a chair, all the while asking myself, *What on earth have you done?*

Mojo hurtled in not ten minutes later, outfitted in a lavender button-down and fitted gray slacks, with a large overnight bag in hand. He'd been working for a local tourism company—making extra money between The Knotty Talismen gigs—and from the looks of it, that's where he was when Palmer called.

Upon arriving, Mojo's cheeks were flustered-pink, his eyes swimming with an *everything's about to change* glaze. My heart pinched tightly as I pointed him toward the maternity ward. He tossed me a nod, a halfhearted smile— as if still torn over whether to be mad at me—before shooting off like a pinball.

June flew in with Leif and Dex soon after. My aunt planted herself at the front desk, begging every nurse who passed by for updates about Palmer until they reticently allowed her into the delivery room. Leif and Dex settled in by me, busying themselves with their respective activities, both of them quiet, calm, and unperturbed.

This is where I find myself now. Nails-deep in my pleather seat, gripping on for dear life. Teeth clenched to the point of aching, every muscle in me braced for impact. Peering out the filmy hospital window like it's a crystal ball, searching the clouds for answers as to how Florian might react to my disobedience. Would he strike out against my parents?

Against Hatch?

Over the next few hours, Mojo's family trickles in. A kind-eyed woman I recognize as his mother arrives with a big-bellied man. Then, a troop of young men with deep skin and mop-like hair—Mojo's brothers and cousins, I suppose—show up in a tumult of grins and boisterous jokes.

Soon after, Sasha slips in with a wave, taking a seat several spots over, falling into easy conversation with the others. Her eyes veer my way on occasion, taking interest in whatever defeated, broken expression she finds on my face. It's all I need right now. To be scrutinized in a moment of strain and exhaustion. When I'm at my absolute lowest. Very clearly without Hatch by my side.

An hour later and still anxiously awaiting news, Sasha strides over, sliding into the seat next to mine. "Hey," she says, her greeting oddly chipper.

"Hey," I respond too quickly, flicking tired, jumpy eyes in her direction.

"Are you doing okay?" she asks.

Since when does Sasha care about my wellbeing?

"Why wouldn't I be?" I toss back.

"You're the one that brought Palmer to the hospital, right?" Her full, brown eyes are less austere than usual. Softer than I've ever seen them.

I nod.

"Well, I mean, that must've been stressful," she says, sounding almost…kind.

I stare back at her with as much conviction as I can muster. "I'm just glad I was there to help."

She shoots me a tightlipped smile, debating her next words. "Outside of Mojo and her mom, I think you're the only person Palmer would've wanted with her in that moment. She's not one to show vulnerability or weakness. But I know she trusts you. I'm sure it was comforting for her to have you there."

I don't respond, certain I've shattered all of that—Palmer's trust, our bond. The truth of it tears at my gut.

"I think, maybe, that's the reason I hated you so much," Sasha adds.

I blink in surprise, taken aback by her admission.

Sasha waves a flippant hand, as if to downplay what she'd said. "Not anymore, Dell. Just at first. I'd like to think I've evolved a little since last summer." She laughs sheepishly, her fingers twirling around a glossy strand of her hair. "I guess it hit me hard, seeing how you were affecting these people. *My* people. Friends I'd hurt and exploited through the years. It's like you waltzed onto the island—"

"More like tumbled in head-first," I mumble.

She snorts. "But you instantly captured Palmer and Hatch's attention, both of whom I've loved for the better part of my life. And it made me feel bitter, the way they seemed to like you more."

"That's not what happened."

"I know, but that's how it felt." Her smile is sad, heavy with remorse. "I masked so much pain behind all the gossip and petty lies. I wreaked emotional warfare on everyone that meant something to me. But I didn't equip myself for the fallout."

Sasha pauses to swallow, collecting herself in that tiny space of silence. "I was losing them, and I didn't even know it," she admits. "I never thought these people I've known and loved forever might actually tire of my antics and wash their hands of me. You showing up here was the ass-kicking I needed to realize that. And, God, I hated you for it…" She laughs again, then bites down on her bottom lip. Nibbles it nervously. "But I have to thank you, Dell, for waking me up. For forcing me to see all I was putting at risk. I'm still a work in progress, but I'm fixing what I can. Learning to look at myself in the mirror and not see a colossal mistake staring back."

Empathy blooms in my chest. I can relate to feeling like one giant error. Like a walking, breathing faux pas. And I sense a real shift in Sasha. A clear dose of accountability, and a quiet surrendering of weapons.

"You're not a colossal mistake," I say.

"Thanks. I appreciate that." Her shoulders relax a little. "And—not that my two cents really matter here, but—I think you'll make an awesome godmother to Palmer's baby. Even if I am just a *tiny bit* jealous."

The sad truth is, I don't know if I am Mia's godmother anymore, and I can't bring myself to speak on it without crying. I decide to ask Sasha a personal question instead—an indication that I'd like to see her do better, *choose* better, for her life going forward.

"You're not really getting back with that spring break douchebag, are you?"

Sasha's eyes widen. "Um. No, actually. I'm not."

"Good." I nod.

"Yeah, it sort of dawned on me the other day that guys that 'smash and dash' aren't worth my time. Much less a place in my bed." She smiles uncertainly. "I'm a little surprised you asked. I thought all this time, maybe, you hated me too?"

"Oh, I did. Past tense." The corner of my lip lifts involuntarily.

Sasha snorts with relief, but before she can say anything more, the sound of sprinting feet bounding down the hallway snaps us to attention.

Mojo is there seconds later—a teary-eyed, sweaty, incandescently-happy mess. Every single person in the room shoots to their feet. Sasha squeezes my wrist.

"She's here!" Mojo cries before falling into a heap of loving arms.

I decide to slip away among the ruckus of celebration. I can't imagine I'll be welcome to meet the baby after everything I said to Palmer. It's enough to know that she's recovering well. To see the incomparable joy swimming in Mojo's eyes. To know that Mia is home, healthy, and safe.

I'm halfway down the road when I hear Mojo calling me from behind.

"Yo, Dell!"

I turn to see him flapping his arms in windshield-wiper motions, that habitually goofy grin curving up his face. Back to his exuberant, bubbly self again. "Where are you going?" he laughs.

"I can't stay," I say, waving back animatedly to shield the pain on my face. "Tell Palmer I love her, okay? Give Mia a big kiss for me."

"Kiss her yourself," Mojo says as he approaches. "You're her *madrina*, right?"

"Oh, um…I don't think Palmer would—"

"Look, Dell, I seriously overreacted the last time we talked," Mojo cuts in. "I was torn up with worry over what was happening to Palmer. It's not a valid excuse, but it was easier to be pissed than to admit how scared I was. You took the brunt of it. I feel awful for blowing up on you. Please, don't go."

"No, Mojo, don't even worry about that," I say quickly. "I just don't think Palmer would want me to—"

"Palmer asked me to call you in *specifically*," Mojo counters, cupping my shoulders and jostling me back toward the hospital. "So get marching, soldier! General's orders."

He ushers me back inside the lobby and up the elevator, all the way to Palmer's private room. I don't have the heart or the willpower to fight him. I'd be lying if I said I don't want to see my cousin and her baby.

With a perky knock, Mojo swings open the door.

June, Leif, and Mojo's parents hover over the bed, gushing with muted *oohs* and *aahs*. They turn to welcome us in with misty eyes.

"Sweet cheeks?" Mojo purrs. "Look who came to see you."

Everyone steps back to reveal Palmer reclining in bed, swathed in a puddle of snowy-white sheets, blond tresses swept over her shoulder in a tousled braid. Her cheeks are slick and flushed, her eyes gleaming as bright as her smile. A tiny pink bundle lies nestled in her arms.

Mojo nudges me. I stagger forward, a knot lodged in my throat. "What do you say we give the girls a minute?" he suggests, gesturing for the others to exit the room with him.

"Just a quick one!" June whisper-chirps. "I'll go see if I can convince the nurse to let Palmer sip on some juice. Anything other than those damned ice chips."

Chattering among themselves, they hustle from the room. The door clicks shut as I meet Palmer's eyes, noting how they widen slightly to expose a naked, curious expression. A rawness that feels like a shot to the heart.

"Hi," I say weakly. "How are you feeling?"

"Like I've been hit by a bus." She tilts her chin toward the pink-faced infant in her arms. "But look what I got out of it."

Taking a step closer, I peek at Mia for the first time. Her eyes are shut, yellow-white lashes dusting her cheeks, her ruddy lips pursed up tight as a rosebud. The barest tufts of fine, golden hair adorn her head. Stork bites speckle the skin around her button-nose.

"She's beautiful, Palmer," I breathe.

"Do you want to hold her?"

I bite my lip, whispering, "Are you sure?"

"I guess that depends on whether you meant all that bullshit you said earlier," Palmer says, watching me through eyes clear and devout.

I shake my head slowly, eaten up with regret.

"Yeah. Didn't think so." Her face softens. "Now come hold your goddaughter before it's feeding time again and you lose your chance."

Cradling Mia in my arms is *bliss*. She smells of milk and nature and perfect sweetness, feels as light and squishy as a doll. Her eyes briefly flutter open, exposing the deep ocean-blues behind those thin, powder-pink eyelids.

I press my lips to her forehead, kissing that silky baby skin. "Welcome to the world, Mia," I whisper. "We're all so lucky to have you."

"Dell…" Palmer licks her lips. "I have to tell you something quick, before the others come back."

"What is it?" I nestle Mia back in her arms.

"It's about your psychic friend, Freya. She was right. About everything." Palmer's throat bobs. "Remember how she mentioned that the spirits tend to relay messages when we surpass our human limits? When we're between worlds?"

"Yeah."

"It happened, just like she said…while I was in *labor*."

I suck in a sharp breath.

"I blacked out for a short time during Mia's delivery," Palmer explains. "My obstetrician thinks that the anesthesia made my blood pressure drop. That there wasn't enough blood getting to my brain. The nurses had to rush in with an oxygen tank. It was a whole thing."

"My God. That's terrifying."

"It felt like I was dreaming," Palmer says. "Dreaming about *her*—the spirit woman. Only this time, she was in crystal-clear focus. Every other time, she'd been dim and hazy, like in old film noir. But today she was in full color, and I felt like I knew her. She looked so familiar."

"Like Tristen?" I surmise.

"How did you know?"

"He had the hair and bone fragments tested from the tunnel," I say soberly. "The results showed that they were his mother's remains—"

Palmer gasps, clutching Mia tight to her breast. "His mother?"

"Sereia."

"Holy crap! They look so much alike."

"What'd she show you?"

"Flashes of her life," Palmer says. "It was *wild*. As a baby, Sereia was adopted by this couple who found her in a lobster trap at the seaport—"

"They *found* her?"

"In a freaking lobster trap!" Palmer squeals, before catching herself. "Spooky, isn't it?" she asks, quieter this time so as not to startle Mia.

Disturbing is a better word.

"The couple had an older son too, and from the looks of it, he was pretty cruel to Sereia. Growing up on the island, she was a total outcast. Stunningly beautiful, but excluded for it. Unwanted. The local women hated her. The men adored and feared her.

"She struggled to blend in and find her way, though she did have many courtships and affairs. Did some pretty hardcore drugs too. I think she needed an escape, but didn't know who to trust. She gave birth to a son—Tristen, I guess. And not long after that, she, um…she died."

"I'm assuming she didn't kill herself," I say. That's the story Tristen had been told. The lie his father professed.

"No, Dell. She was…strangled."

"By Florian?"

Palmer shrugs. "It happened in the dead of night. It was hard to see much of anything, to be honest. But based on what I could hear, the attack was personal. Florian would be my best guess."

Even if Sereia hadn't died by Florian's hand, I'm certain he'd been the one to put out the hit. "And she was pregnant?"

Palmer nods. "And there's another thing too…but, fair warning, this is going to sound batshit in every conceivable way."

"Tell me."

Her worried eyes drill into my face. "Sereia wasn't like us."

"What do you mean?"

"I mean…she's not, like, a regular human person."

"Well, yeah. She's dead, so—"

"No." Palmer shakes her head gently. "I don't mean that she's dead, or that she's a ghost, or whatever." She bites her lip, trying to weave a tapestry of the nebulous threads and strands she'd witnessed. "What I mean to say is…Sereia…well, she…she never was…"

"Never was what?" I implore.

"*Human.*"

Palmer leaves it at that—one word, stressed for emphasis.

"Hold on," I say in disbelief. "If Sereia wasn't human, then what *was* she?"

"Something else," Palmer says. "When Sereia was killed, she didn't perish as humans do. It doesn't work that way for *beings* like her. When she died, she was split in two. Bone ripped from soul."

"Meaning?"

"Meaning part of her is very much alive right now. The only reason she's been trapped in the tunnels all this time is because a ritual act was performed to bind her spirit to her body. To trap her down there."

"How is that even possible?"

Again, Palmer shrugs. "She spent years trying to escape it. Whispering into the darkness, sweeping along the walls, desperate for anyone to hear and liberate her. For someone to empathize with her energy. She tried with you, but the connection wasn't strong enough."

The whispers. I'd heard them once, then never again.

"Later that night, when we went down into the tunnels together, do you remember the light we saw?"

I nod.

"That was Sereia trying to make contact. She clung to me, and I brought her to the surface. That's why I've been hearing and seeing her ever since. And now that she's shown me this part of herself—these memories—she's free again. She can go back where she came from."

"Which is?"

"The sea, Dell," Palmer deadpans. "Back to the sea."

"But, then…that would mean…"

Palmer lifts her eyebrows as I try to come to terms with this near-absurd revelation. This is unlike *any* of the myths I've heard about the sea girls—unfortunate souls that died at the hands of the Brine, fated to drift along the shallows of Halcyon Bay. Those were girls turned specters of the sea. Humans mutated into creatures. But Sereia's origin story is something else entirely.

According to Palmer, Sereia was—*is*—an inhuman being sprung from the ocean.

Not made.

Born.

"So…is she a…"

My throat constricts, stifling the next word before I'm able to utter it. It's too surreal. Unfathomable.

But this is Halcyon Bay. A strange and unassuming spit of land miles from the rest of the world, shrouded in a swirling mist of folklore and legends, overlapping and converging and bleeding into present-day life.

"Mermaid?" I whisper once I've built up the courage.

Palmer screws up her lips. "Well, it sounds *dumb* when you put it like that," she argues, as if the word is too crass and unsophisticated to be taken seriously. Secretly, she looks relieved that I had the guts to voice what she's thinking.

"Can you come up with a better term for what we're discussing?" I ask.

A litany of mythical, humanlike sea creatures fills my mind. *Siren. Nymph. Selkie. Merrow. Nereid.* None of which are more believable than mermaids.

Palmer is notably quiet, her eyes on Mia's sleeping face.

"Well?" I prompt her. "Is Sereia a 'you-know-what?'"

"She's…something like that," Palmer admits.

Meaning Tristen—our outcasted, broody, black-sheep cousin—has a more colorful ancestry than any we could've imagined.

And his conniving father may have an even greater reason to want the hell off this island.

CHAPTER FIFTY

A sleek black SUV pulls up beside me on my walk back to Cliffmoor House. The tinted back window rolls down to half-mast. My uncle lowers his dark sunglasses, enough for those pit-black eyes to bore into me. "Get in," he mutters, his voice a deadly rustle.

I do so without argument.

The car reeks of cigar smoke, buzzes with silent threats. I shut the door and flatten myself against it, as far from Florian as humanly possible. He sniffs the air once and his nostrils flare with disgust, as if I dragged in some abhorrent stench with me.

"At what point did I say that you could leave the grounds unescorted?" he asks softly, rolling up his sleeves to the elbows. "Or that you could speak with *anyone* without my explicit consent?"

"I didn't say anything," I blurt quickly. "Palmer was going into labor. I wanted to make sure she got to the hospital safely—"

His hand whips out to strike me, his knuckles colliding with my mouth. I yelp at the impact, blood pooling beneath my tongue, oozing from a small cut on my lip.

Florian is silent as I recover my breath. He pulls a crisp white handkerchief from his pocket, wiping each slender finger, erasing the evidence of his violence. He tosses the handkerchief at me when he's done, but I don't bother wiping my face clean. I let the blood run as I stare into the eyes of evil.

"Ooh…" he taunts me. "If looks could kill."

What I wouldn't give to kill this man. I would go down trying right now if I could. But if I step another toe out of line, he'll come for my parents and Hatch. He'll make them suffer. Whether I'm alive to see it or not.

"I don't think you realize the level of destruction I'm prepared to inflict on the people you love, Meridel," Florian says. "On the living *and* dead."

Those words make my skin prickle.

"What do you mean by that?"

"Your sister Willow was recently interred at Evergreen Hills Cemetery in Woodbridge, was she not?"

All the fire and heat drains from my face. Florian had been sniffing around Willow's gravesite weeks ago. Why is he bringing this up now?

The slight smirk on his lips is both vicious and victorious. "It just so happens that the night guard at that cemetery is a personal friend of mine. Small world, isn't it?"

"Monty?" My heart thrashes in my chest.

"Who?" My uncle's dark eyes narrow a touch. "Ah, you mean the former guard. No, not that one. Poor bloke had a heart attack and passed days ago, I'm afraid."

I gasp. *Monty's dead?*

"Terrible news, that," Florian laments, though the cruel smile never slips from his face.

"You did it," I rasp slowly. "You killed that innocent man. For what?"

"I needed someone on the inside who would prioritize my interests. Your friend Monty stood in my way." My uncle lifts an unaffected shoulder. "Nothing personal. Just eliminating a problem."

I shiver—bone-chilled—at the callous, easy manner with which my uncle 'eliminates' his problems. My heart breaks for Monty and his family. More collateral damage from this senseless tirade.

"I hope you understand how easy it would be for me to procure your sister's remains," Florian warns. "It would be a shame to have to unearth her bones and litter them like garbage across the Atlantic."

Hot, hateful tears glide down my cheeks, his words unlocking a brand new fear in my mind.

"I have quite a knack for making things disappear," Florian says. "Like that old walking cane you took such an interest in last year…the one with the wolf's face?"

My breath hitches at the mention of the weapon Ambrose used against my sister. When Florian escaped, the cane vanished with him.

A breathy chuckle escapes his lips, his teeth sharper than any weapon. "Make no mistake, I can do the same for people. I can make their remains cease to exist. Make it so they're nothing but a pile of waning memories."

"Is that what you did to Sereia?" I ask, anger throbbing in my veins.

My uncle runs a thumb along the grizzly hair of his jaw.

"You killed her, didn't you?" A shudder ghosts down my spine. "Your own son's mother."

His silence is deafening.

"Did you know she was pregnant?"

I sense the tiniest flick of his eyebrow, his black eyes brimming with poison.

"Where is she, Florian? Did you discard her bones at sea? Did you bury them somewhere here on the island?"

"You should be more concerned with all the ways I will desecrate Willow's bones, should you not fall in line," he hisses.

My throat cinches tight. Mom would never recover if she lost Willow again. If her remains were stolen—her final resting place defiled—I can't begin to fathom what something like that would do to our family.

"Tomorrow evening is the ball," Florian says icily. "You will attend and comport yourself like a perfect lady—a lovely adornment meant to be seen and not heard. You will flutter about in your silly gown, giggling and grazing and blending in with the scenery. At my behest, you will ensure that my men pass through the tunnels without discovery. Once your task is complete, you will wait for further orders from me. Do you understand?"

I give him the smallest, most begrudging nod known to existence.

"A final word of warning, Meridel…" My uncle drums restless fingers on his thigh. "If I catch even the slightest wind that you've defied me, I will hunt down every person you love and force you to watch as I have them skinned to the bone. You will have no one left. No survivors. Only oceans of blood on your hands."

He repositions his sunglasses over his eyes. "Think long and hard about that before you choose to disobey me again." He reaches over me to grasp the door handle. I wince at his proximity as the door swings open. "Now get out of my sight."

CHAPTER FIFTY-ONE

Panicked cries in the distance rouse me from sleep.

It's the morning of the ball.

I'm not in my bed.

Instead, I'm sprawled along a vacant shoreline, half-submerged in foamy water, cradled in its soporific embrace.

Sleepwalking.

I'd forgotten to barricade the damn door yesterday. I'd been too distraught over Florian's threats to think clearly. Too worried that he might dig up my sister's remains for sport.

A low-lying sun winks down at me from a gray, wisp-coated sky. Flustered voices drift across the beach on the wind.

Someone shrieks, and I bolt up.

Something's wrong.

Pulling myself onto clumsy feet, I scamper up the damp sand, back to the grounds and toward the sounds of terror. When I get to the gate of the footbridge I'd left open in my wake, I see them.

Dozens of dead seabirds littering the pristine gardens of Cliffmoor

House. Boneless, feathery masses—heaps and smears of brown and white—strewn across the crisp, manicured lawn.

One misshapen seabird floats atop the surface of the pool, wings fanned out morbidly at either side of it.

My eyes drag from one bloating body to the next.

My God...

I sway a little, seeking purchase on the wooden handrail.

Some distance away, Briggs pushes past the wall of slack-jawed event staff to get a better look. He blinks through his half-moon spectacles at the multitude of plumed casualties before him. Then, clearing his throat, he springs into action.

"There are contractor bags in the shed," he says to no one in particular. "Clean up this mess and get on with your duties. No time to dilly-dally! The gardens must be in shipshape for tonight's festivities."

Nervous whispers slip between the workers as they weave across the grounds. Their worried words catch and cling to my ears as they move.

Klynes. Cursed. Omen. Doomed.

My stomach coils as they shovel up the bird corpses, dumping their limp bodies into trash bags. Bile climbs into my mouth and I hurtle inside the guest house, making like a bullet for the bathroom.

I empty my stomach into the toilet, then curl up like an injured animal against the claw foot tub. Shivering, I press my face to the cold porcelain—too drained to think or cry or see—and await the inevitable hour of my summoning.

The giant ballroom doors are swung open invitingly. Soft candlelight and elegant waltz music seep into the corridor, like two warm, welcoming hands to usher me in...or to slowly wring my neck until I suffocate.

It's nine o'clock—half hour past the start of the ball. Minutes ago, I'd heard a stealthy one-two knock at the guest house door, but when I peered outside, no one was there.

I could only assume it was a covert message from my uncle.

Time to make my grand entrance.

Droves of lavishly-dressed invitees arrive along with me, extravagant skirts rustling as they greet one another, stilettos click-clacking on the hardwood floors. I recognize some of their faces from town, and promptly dip my chin to avoid eye contact.

Outfitted in the dazzling gown Tristen selected for me, I swish to the ballroom with my heart in my throat. The fit of the dress is adequate considering all the weight I've lost. My chest doesn't fill up the bodice completely, but it's so impeccably embellished—the V-shape neckline so plunging—no one would ever notice.

Silver and gold thread weave across the bodice in delicate whirls of starlight, each one encrusted with thousands of tiny, winking crystals, dripping against a deep, midnight-blue chiffon. Sheer, off-the-shoulder sleeves cascade past my wrists in shimmery ruffles. Those star-like patterns of twinkling thread and crystal fall in dainty streams down the long, draping skirt, spilling down my legs into a sparkling puddle, with a slit up one side that nearly grazes my hip bone. My every step bares an eye-catching slip of my thigh, so provocative it'd make any red-blooded male blush.

It's an exquisite gown, beyond anything I could ever dream of…
Wasted on this abhorrent sham of an evening.
I catch a glimpse of myself in a gilded mirror in the hall. My dark hair falls in undulating waves over my shoulders, reflecting the lustrous blue hues of the gown, and the sea glass I wear like armor over my heart. My makeup is basic—all I could manage with trembling fingers. Just a swipe of smoky gray over my lids, a wash of mascara to distract from my bloodshot eyes, and a daub of nude lipstick, the only one I packed for this trip. My cheeks hadn't required rouge. They glow pink with inner heat—a fearful flush that radiates up my nose, and down my neck and cleavage. The effect is almost pretty, at least from the outside.

I feel like an utter farce.
A snake with two faces.
Compelled to execute my uncle's demands.
Betraying myself in defense of the people I love.
Thank goodness they won't be here tonight.

Palmer and Mojo are due to spend another evening in the hospital with Mia. June and Leif steer clear of Cliffmoor House as a matter of course. Hatch surely won't be making an appearance. Not after the way I'd wrecked things between us, effectively uninviting him from all my family's affairs.

Still, some selfish part of me wishes I could see him tonight, my heart calling desperately for that knife-like pleasure. Everything about me feels wrong without him. The colors of my world are paler, the flavors weak, the sounds muted. Utterly, insurmountably, hopelessly wrong…

Don't go there, I think, girding myself for battle. Better to pine for the ghost of him than to jeopardize his safety.

Blinking back the burning sensation from my eyes, I inhale deeply and step inside the ballroom.

A gasp escapes me as I'm swept into a glistening nightscape. Into a scene plucked from the pages of an enchanted, moonlit fairytale.

Broad swaths of shimmery, indigo silk are draped across the coffered ceiling in waves. The three-tiered chandeliers are dimmed to a sensual low, drizzling like starlight over the space. Hundreds of pillar candles of varying heights line the far wall—a flickering white flame gleaming from each wick, reflected in the glassy mirrors and the arched windows alike—creating the illusion of innumerable stars winking back through the night-dark cosmos.

Party guests whisk along the dance floor in bejeweled shades of sapphire and midnight, onyx and dusk, their smiles and finery glistening with every twist and twirl. The whole ballroom appears to shift and ripple with their movements, as if animated by the burning stars and the all-seeing moon and the salty night wind.

A soaring champagne tower occupies a table near the dance floor, each tier of brimming, bubbly flutes spilling generously onto the next. Lush dining tables with inky linens, gilded dishes and cutlery, and dewy white flowers encircle the dance floor. An ensemble of musicians perform a honeyed, lilting melody that might've been procured from the heavens. Sharply-dressed servers weave through the ballroom, their faces partially concealed, dipped in twinkling black masks, as they glide about with trays of champagne and hors d'oeuvres.

It's all so mesmerizing…

Spellbinding.

Treacherous.

I glare at each server as they pass me by—their pearly grins bared, platters outstretched. My uncle's minions surely hide among them. Disguised as staff, their true identities shielded. Blending in easily with the swarms of unsuspecting, starry-eyed guests.

"Dell."

Nova appears at my side, looking radiant in a champagne slip—not nearly as showy or opulent as the other gowns, yet somehow more stunning in its simplicity. The shimmering, satiny material slides across her slim figure in a way that leaves little to the imagination. If Tristen hasn't yet built up the nerve to confess his feelings, perhaps seeing Nova in this dress will do the trick.

She's collected her auburn hair into a soft updo, secured in place with a dainty shooting-star barrette, her face framed by those two chunky pink tendrils. She wears no makeup save for a sheen of icy eyeshadow, her natural bronze complexion as luminescent as her dress. Tossing me a halfhearted smile, she takes up a spot at the edge of the dance floor.

Together, we stare in silence across the blanket of stars and light and magic, until eventually, Nova mutters under her breath, "What the hell am I doing here?" She studies the party crowd with squinted eyes, as if perhaps they're an invasive species—an alien breed warranting careful observation. "This is *so* not my scene."

"He wants you here," I say, noting the blandness in my voice. The robotic articulation. The absence of emotion. I sound broken. Broken to the point of numbness.

Nova doesn't pull her eyes from the dance floor, but her lips twitch in response. She's never struck me as the nervous type—always firm and full of conviction, her every move calculated and weighed against the odds—but the woman beside me is a ball of nerves tonight. She squirms in her dress, fingers kneading over the fabric.

"Can't imagine why," she mutters solemnly.

"You know exactly why."

When she looks at me then, her cheeks are rosier than before. She looks so innocent with that deep flush of color, that unguarded expression, brown eyes swimming with candlelight. Totally innocuous. Almost fragile.

But looks can be deceiving.

Alarm bells ring in my head, the sound akin to a prophetic death toll. *She could be the enemy.*

I pray it isn't true.

Deep down I know I'm not equipped for that betrayal. Against all odds, Nova has slipped beneath my skin. And Tristen…well, I can't *begin* to divine what he'd do. The infinite, brutal ways he might spiral out of control. God knows this deception might send him over the edge for good.

"Broken people seek brokenness in others," Nova says sadly, as if it's the only way she can reconcile Tristen's confusing affections.

You know she isn't the enemy, a voice inside of me whispers. *She's your friend.*

I wish I believed it. Wish I could reassure Nova that everything would work itself out. That something good awaits us. That true love conquers all. But I'm not so sure it does anymore…not since losing Hatch. How am I supposed to believe in anything good after that?

"Welcome, everyone!"

Tristen's deep voice cracks like thunder across the ballroom. The guests, musicians, and servers quiet down.

"I'd like to take a moment to say a few words…"

Payne wheels my cousin to the center of the dance floor, and everyone steps back to give him a wide berth.

Tristen's dark eyes feast on the glittering room and vast assembly of guests. He's dressed in a sharp, well-cut tuxedo with a subtle midnight-blue sheen. His black hair is freshly sheared and shiny with product, swept back from his dark eyes. His face is clean-shaven, devoid of its usual five o'clock shadow. He offers the crowd a debonair smile, one I'd never imagine him capable of.

My breath hitches in time with Nova's when we notice he's holding a microphone to his lips.

Holding it in his own slender, pale hand.

"I'd like to thank you all for joining me this evening for the inaugural Stars at Sea Charity Ball," Tristen announces. "It's my great pleasure to see so many of you here, partaking in this starry, philanthropic evening."

The guests break into polite, yet tentative applause.

"I'd also like to express my deepest thanks for your generous donations benefiting the Stand Against Paralysis Foundation," Tristen adds. "This organization provides comprehensive rehabilitation and cutting-edge treatments for paralyzed persons, with the goal of achieving total paralysis recovery. I will personally be matching all of your charitable contributions, and together, we'll help change countless lives for the better."

Applause, again—more enthusiastic this time.

"As most of you know, I suffered a spinal cord injury last year, which left me completely quadriplegic," Tristen says. "After several surgeries and tireless therapy, I'm slowly recovering mobility in my arms and hands."

He lifts the mic a little, and cheers break out among the crowd.

"Thank you very much!" he says with a chuckle. "Already this night feels like a massive success. Would someone please bring me a glass of champagne?"

The cheers soar to a crescendo as a server rushes forward with a flute. Tristen takes it, eating up the attention. "Champagne for everyone!"

Sometimes, he really is his father's son.

The servers swiftly pass champagne to every empty-handed guest. Nova takes one for herself. I do too, though I won't be drinking tonight.

Tristen's eyes land on me for a brief moment, then slide to Nova at my side. His stare turns to a longing gaze—gentle sparks flickering to life in that abrasive darkness. The corners of his smile hike up a touch more. A softness washes over him that looks like admiration. Or, perhaps, adoration.

Nova wriggles in place like there are flames smoldering beneath her skin.

"Cliffmoor House has always been an illustrious fixture of our island community," Tristen says when he finally pulls his eyes away, "though its prestige has been tainted by some unfortunate happenings as of late." The room goes dead-silent at this, hundreds of bubbly flutes held high—sparkling but untouched. "My hope is that, together, we will usher Cliffmoor House into a brighter era, one as eminent as the stars in our sky. To an unforgettable evening—cheers!"

The crowd roars and clinks their flutes, and when the music starts up again, people flock to the dance floor. I lose sight of Tristen as everything devolves into a lively whirlwind of blue and amber light.

"I'd better make my rounds," Nova says. "Tonight's a bit complicated, with so many people coming and going."

"Aren't you supposed to be off the clock?"

"Technically, yes." She shrugs, offering me a feeble smile. "But I'm never really off the clock. Work helps keep the demons at bay."

I don't have the heart to tell her the bleak truth. That there's no way to keep the *real* demons at bay. They're already here, crawling among us. Swarming beneath the makeshift nightscape of this very ballroom. We're nothing but puppets tied to invisible strings. Florian possesses all the cards.

With a wink, Nova vanishes into the throng.

In her absence, a server swoops in close beside me, holding out a platter of goat cheese balls drizzled in honey.

"No, thank you," I mutter, despite being so hungry I could launch myself—feral cat style—at the tray. I can't trust that the food and drinks aren't laced. I need my wits sharp, my senses alert.

"Eat, Dell," the server commands.

My jaw clenches.

That voice.

Sleepy-gray eyes are hooded beneath the server's mask. A crooked nose that never healed quite right pokes out underneath it. White-blond hair is slicked to one side with gel, making it appear darker—more sinister.

"You wouldn't want to pass out in the middle of a dance," Prescott taunts.

"Stay away from me," I warn as I back against a table, a scream crushed in the depths of my throat.

"Or you'll what?" he provokes.

My fingernails dig half-moons into my palms. I bite down hard on my tongue to keep from howling, cursing Prescott's unsettling confidence.

His smile flashes against the hypnotic, star-soaked backdrop. "What exactly are you going to do, Dell?"

I'm going to lose my goddamn shit, that's what…

No. I stop myself, gritting my teeth.

He isn't worth endangering my parents, Hatch, or anyone else at this ball. He's just a pawn in Florian's game. A lowly instrument of chaos. Irrelevant in the larger scheme of things.

But he'd still be the one I obliterate first.

Just not tonight. Not with so much at stake.

Scowling, I push along the fringes of the dance floor, desperate to carve out some breathing room for myself. I'm only as free as a bird in a gleaming cage tonight, but surely I can find some distant corner to escape him.

Yet, everywhere I turn, every simpering guest I glide past, I feel the claustrophobic weight of Prescott's eyes on my back.

Is he following me? I wonder, refusing to give him the satisfaction of turning to look. Will we play this deranged cat and mouse game all night long?

Just keep moving.

Don't stop.

A strong hand finds my waist, and the leash I had on my anger shatters. "*I said*"—I whirl around, teeth bared—"*stay the fuck away from me—*"

My mouth falls open, my words trampled at the sight of the man before me.

Not Prescott.

Hatch.

CHAPTER FIFTY-TWO

This is bad. Very bad.

But Hatch looks…

Good beyond belief.

My breath catches at the sight of him. He's thrilling to look at. A dreamy blur of sparks and watercolor and night-blue shadows, bundled up in sleek tuxedo packaging.

"Who are you so angry with?" Hatch asks, a crease forming between his eyes.

The ball still whirls and flickers with life around me, but I barely process any of it. All I can focus on is his twinkling gaze mirroring the starry candlelight. The slight inflections of his eyebrows, his lips, his chiseled jaw. His wind-tousled hair streaked in an amber glow.

His eyes are intent on my face, reading whatever cocktail of pain and fear and lust he must find there. Because even though I can't speak the words aloud—can't express my feelings, or touch him the way I'd like to—I also can't disguise the plain truth of it on my face. My consummate need for him. My grief over having discarded him like garbage.

"You shouldn't be here," I breathe, glancing around as discreetly as possible, in search of eyes that might be watching us.

His gaze follows mine with a guarded expression, burning with quiet fire. *What must he think of me?*

To my surprise, he offers me his hand. "I'm pushing my luck tonight." His lips part slightly, and all I can think about is seizing them in mine. "Dance with me, Dell."

"Uh…" My jaw falls a bit, my mind void of the clarity and the willpower to say no, though I *know* I should.

"Please." His voice is a low, seductive rumble that transfixes me to my core.

Shit. No. I can't. I'm not thinking straight.

But, good God, *look at him.*

"Indulge me."

The same two words he uttered last year, when we danced briefly at Palmer's wedding.

Just like that, I'm a goner.

Despite all logic—every voice in my head screaming bloody-murder for me to run in the opposite direction—my hand slips into his, and he steers me onto the shimmering dance floor.

We move warily at first, setting a gentle pace, uncertainty marring each of our steps, but that only lasts for a second. Our bodies recognize each other, have even *missed* each other, it seems. Soon we're reacting in a way we shouldn't…

Like objects pulled by strange gravity, we glide in close until our eyes lock, our chests graze, our shaky breaths synchronize. His hand on the small of my back slips downward, gripping me harder through the silky fabric of my gown. My tentative hand on his shoulder slides up into his hair. He presses himself against me, and the feeling of his body molded to mine makes me tremble. I cling fast to him, worried my legs might betray me, his eyes flooding me with feelings I'd done everything in my power to cast aside.

He leans in, our faces inches apart. The sunshine-warmth of him pours over me, those green eyes thick and full of winking stars. It would be so deliciously easy to give in. To dip my head back and let him take me. Take whatever he wants. Consume me. Devour me.

"Can we go somewhere private?" he rasps. "Please. I just want to talk." Then, I swear he holds his breath.

A flicker of movement catches my eye over his shoulder—someone stepping out of sync with the other dancers.

Prescott storms away from us, pushing through the ballroom and out into the hall.

I untangle my arms from where they're wrapped up in Hatch. This needs to stop. *I* need to stop. Stop our dancing, stop this moment, stop everything from spiraling out of control.

"You have to leave," I insist, raising my voice. Not enough to cause a scene, but enough to make sure a few servers hear me. To make an impression on whomever here is part of Florian's crew. "You shouldn't have come. We're over, remember?"

I expect Hatch to back away from me, stung by the harshness of my rejection, but he doesn't. Instead, his fingers bury deeper into my dress, one hand slipping down the side of my body. I'm powerless to stop him. Don't want to. When he presses his thumb into my hip, I jerk instinctively, the fear in me matched only by the yearning, my body engaged with his again, a hungry gasp caught in my throat.

My fingers tingle against his chest as I struggle to compose myself, torn between pushing him away or grabbing his lapels and dragging him closer. The scent of his skin—of sea spray, sun, and man—assaults my senses. "Hatch..." My voice is softer now. Helpless. "You can't be here. Please..."

"You think I'm such a good man," he rasps, our lips a breath away from touching, "that I'll just fold and let you go?"

The pressure of his hands on my body makes me question everything, turning the ballroom into a shimmering, raucous blur. "I know you are," I whisper.

His jaw pulses. "No."

The word drops in me like a weighted object, plunging to the soles of my feet. *No.*

He won't leave.

He knows something's wrong.

Knows I'm concealing the truth.

Refuses to accept it.

"You have to," I beg, forcing myself to push out the words, even though they're weak and unconvincing. My hands ball to fists on his jacket.

"I won't leave you," he insists.

I clench my teeth, drop my hands, and step back from him. He watches on stonily as I fashion my face into something angry—something forceful—when I know that my eyes are mushy and desolate and soft with love for him.

I'm sorry.

"Get out," I command. Louder. More vulgar. Whatever it takes to keep him safe.

The waltzers closest to us glance our way, necks craned to better hear the sparking embers of our dispute, no doubt hoping it swells into a full-on blaze. Hushed rumors start to spin among them like the filmy thread of a spider's web—Halcyon Bay's infamous gossip-mongers at work.

Hatch's face hardens, brows drawing together, as he shifts his sights from me to the ballroom beyond. Eyes narrowed, he takes his time surveying the space—the immaculately-dressed guests partaking in an elegant dance, the masked servers donning sparkling trays, the chandelier-drizzle pouring over the polished floor, the instrumentalists making sweet melodies. He's utterly concentrated, trying to decipher some explanation for why I'm acting as I am.

"Go," I beg him again. "Please. Just go."

His lips flatten into a furious line.

My stomach sinks as he turns and strides out of the ballroom.

It takes about two milliseconds of hesitation for me to decide to follow him. I press through the glittering crowd, my gown chasing every footstep, desperate to keep Hatch's broad shoulders in my sights. But he's too far ahead of me, pushing through with force, seething and swiftly weaving down the dim corridor.

You asked him to leave, I think angrily. *Let him go, dammit.*

But I convince myself that I only want to see him out, want to see him exit the estate in one piece. The last thing I need is Prescott swooping on him by surprise.

An indescribable, unrelenting need blooms in my chest, warning me that something terrible will happen if I don't find him.

Zigzagging through the boisterous corridor amid scores of laughing, champagne-ridden faces, a gloved hand wraps firmly around my elbow. I yelp as I'm jerked into the underlit drawing room, the door clicking shut behind me.

An older server I don't recognize glares down at me, his face shielded in a glinting black mask. "It's time," he sneers through yellow teeth.

I wrench my arm away from him. "Time for what?"

Three more masked servers materialize from the shadows, Prescott among them. "Your uncle requests that you secure the parlor," he says, unsmiling, as though I'd given him reason to be annoyed with me. "We'll need at least fifteen minutes to get our group through without interruption."

"And what am I supposed to do if there *is* an interruption?"

"Figure it out," he says derisively.

"We'll be watching," warns the first man, his dark eyes flashing. Then, like specters, they disperse from the room, leaving me to grapple with my inevitable circumstances.

Locating Hatch is going to have to wait. He seems to have up and vanished anyway, eaten up in the glimmering, star-drenched atmosphere. I'll do this one thing, then sneak out and make sure his truck is gone. Make sure he made it out safely.

I pick my way through the house, eager for my part in this scheme to be over. The bustling congregation seems to stem in the foyer, no guests taking interest in the dark, opposing corridor. I slip quietly past, fading into the background, as I venture deeper into the recesses of Cliffmoor House.

When I arrive at the parlor, I'm surprised to find the doors shut.

Quietly, I twist a handle and pull one open a crack, enough to peer inside with caution.

By a low, crackling fire, I spot Tristen in his chair with Nova curled in his lap, engaged in a passionate—and very private—kiss. They claw at each other desperately, as if in fear that some unknown force might rip them apart. Her gown cascades over the harsh edges of him, groans of pleasure escaping their lips. The sultry shadows of their intertwined bodies dance like flames over the curtains and wall.

I back up instantly, shutting the door again.

Warring parts of me want to squeal and scream. I can't spoil this moment for them, but I can't ignore my uncle's bidding for long.

Glancing back the way I came, I spot sullen, looming figures watching me from the foyer—the black-clad servers, waiting for a sign that I've secured their path inside.

Pressing myself into the shadows, I struggle to catch my breath. If I don't clear the parlor like Florian demanded, he'll make good on his deadly promises against my parents and Hatch. He'll defile my sister's remains. He'll destroy everything I love. And he'll make sure I'm tortured by it till my dying breath.

Panic rushes in.

I squeeze my eyes as my throat cinches tight, chest wracked with palpitations. I let my head fall back against the wall. I'm not sure I'm breathing. A wave of terror threatens to send me tumbling, feet over head, into full-scale, nuclear-level hysterics.

"Is *he* in there?"

I snap my eyes open, black stars popping in my vision.

Hatch.

A vicious, glistering tempest brews in his eyes, at once brutal and brilliant and—

"Hatch, wait!"

He brushes past me to fling the parlor doors open. They crash loudly against the furniture as he bursts inside. I fly in after him.

"What the—?"

Nova disentangles herself from Tristen, jumping like a startled cat from his lap. My cousin scowls at us, his cheeks and neck peppered in whorls and pecks, his eyes so piercing they could sever a limb. He's a man untamed—love-rumpled and *furious*.

Back on her feet, Nova runs shaky fingers down her gown, attempting to smooth the wrinkles from the sleek champagne fabric, adjusting the delicate straps that toppled from her shoulders. She looks at me with melted chocolate eyes, rubbing her swollen, just-kissed lips.

"What the hell are you two doing here?" Tristen barks.

"What the hell did you do to Dell?" Hatch growls back defiantly. "Are you threatening her? Forcing her to do this?"

"Threatening her?" Tristen repeats, his face a feverish medley of bewilderment and pent-up frustration. Those black, knife-sharp eyes come to land on me. "What's he talking about, Dell?"

Hatch glares at us both with furious expectation.

I effectively lose every drop of my cool.

"We broke up!" I scream, hating the words that explode from my lips. "We broke up, and Hatch is looking for someone to blame."

Tristen's eyes shrivel up, a stunned hiss spilling from his teeth like a deflating tire.

"Not we. *You.*" A ragged breath shakes loose from Hatch's lips. "You broke up with me. You ended things, out of the goddamn blue. And nothing you've done since has made any fucking sense!"

He looks so heartbroken, I'm inclined to throw everything out the window and collapse in a heap on the floor, sobbing out the truth and letting the chips fall where they may.

"You're playing mind games with me, and I don't understand why…" Hatch waves a hand in Tristen's direction. "Is it because of him? Did he put you up to this?"

"No!" I insist, shaking my head so forcefully, my brain matter seems to scramble up in my cranium. This is all going terribly, terribly wrong. If Florian sics his watchdogs on my family, on the Seaborns…

"Then what's going on?" Hatch implores again, his eyes drooping and weary. "I know this isn't you. It's not! We're supposed to be together, Dell. We fought for this. We said forever."

I choke back tears, desperate to give up, give in…

No.

I won't break. *Can't* break.

I won't give my uncle an excuse to attack the people I love.

I will do what's required of me to keep them alive.

Even if it rips my heart to pieces.

I draw on all of my anger, pull on every last scrap of hate I carry with me, like the tides dredge up seashells buried in the sandy shore. I pack all those emotions into a tight ball, and then I lob it at him.

"This *is* me, Hatch!" I shout, letting my fear fuel me. "I'm allowed to change my mind about us. I'm tired of fighting a losing battle! When is it going to click for you? I don't want you to be here. *I don't want you anymore.*"

The room stills but for the low spit of fire. Pin-drop silence and uneven breaths pack the air.

"What the hell are you playing at, Dell?" Tristen asks. He has an eagle-eyed look about him, as if he's caught a whiff of something nasty. "Hatcher's right. You wouldn't do this."

It's dangerous to arouse suspicion in my cousin. I can't have him examining my reasons too closely.

"I don't remember asking for your opinion," I snarl at him, desperate to course-correct. "Much less your two cents about my relationship. We both know your track record in love is abysmal. Absolutely pathetic."

My cruel words reverberate across the room. Nova's eyes narrow. Tristen doesn't answer, which only tells me his mind is calculating faster than he can speak. That he's seeing clearly through my charade.

Fine. Let him speculate. All that matters is getting Hatch away from this house.

I turn on Hatch again. "You shouldn't have come—"

"I heard you the first time," he interrupts me. "I've heard every crappy thing you've said tonight. Every crappy thing you said a few days ago too. I've replayed your words hundreds of times in my head. But the one thing I haven't heard you say is that you don't love me."

I do I do I do I do. The truth drums in my chest like my own heartbeat.

"So?" I ask, delaying the inevitable.

"*So?*" Hatch shakes his head—perplexed, insulted. He swallows thickly. "So do you love me, Dell?"

My tongue is swelling up in my mouth. I'm having a physical allergic reaction to this question.

The only way to love him is to give him up.

I close my eyes, focusing on the rise and fall of my chest. I try not to think too hard about what's actually happening. What I'm having to do to him all over again. What he's forcing me to verbalize.

"Do. You. Love. Me?" Hatch punctuates each word.

Lie to him. Drive it home. Make it so he can't feel the pounding insincerity behind every word.

I meet those glistering, seagrass eyes for what I'm sure is the last time. Hot, salty tears fill up my vision. The parlor smears. His face ripples.

I love you, Hatcher Seaborn.

"No."

My universe teeters on the edge of that *no*, tipping into a steep and starless oblivion.

"I don't...love you."

I am nothing. No one.

A fleck of dust wafting through nonexistence.

Ruined.

His face—my sun—collapses into shadows, a solar eclipse that will mar the rest of my days.

Maybe this is finally enough.

Maybe now he stands a chance at true happiness, far from the destructive reaches of this family. From me.

"You don't love me..." He stumbles over the words, nodding a little, each sober bob of his head seeming to drive the point further, the nail deeper in our coffin.

"Do you get it now?" I choke out, dying inside.

Again, he nods—a slow, seeping realization. "Yeah, I get it." Darkness pushes like smoke into his gaze. "You know, I really did mean it when I said I'd follow you anywhere. That I'd always come, so long as you let me. But where you're going is...far beyond my reach. I see that now."

Something snaps in the depths of my chest. An irreparable break on a tether. My lifeline to love—a jugular vein—slashed and bleeding.

As Hatch slips from the parlor, pain slams into me. I grip the edges of a table with both hands, rivers streaming down my face.

"I don't buy this for a second," Tristen mutters in his absence, mistrusting eyes keen on me. "You're hiding something."

"You don't know a goddamn thing!" I cry, blinded by the burning of my tears.

"I know your heart," he says.

My heart. The thing scared shitless in my chest, bleeding like hell, but still hammering anyway—relentless in its cage of bone. The pain is excruciating. I think it might punch through my body and hurl itself onto the floor, pulsing like a fish in need of water.

"And I know your heart's with him," Tristen continues. "He isn't someone you'd throw away like this. You're desperate, cousin. Desperate to keep love at a distance. But why?" His mouth puckers, questioning, probing.

I can't muster the words to rebuke him, too afraid of what I might let spill, or how I'll break apart. Of who might be listening, or watching us from behind security cameras.

"Nova," Tristen says after a long minute, "would you wheel me out, please? Guests will be wondering where I am."

Nova drifts to Tristen's chair, avoiding my watery gaze as she takes hold of the handle grips. Together, they glide from the parlor, leaving me to tread through an ocean of self-loathing, trapped and floundering in the net of my uncle's schemes.

CHAPTER FIFTY-THREE

Fifteen servers disappear through the bookcase in the parlor.

They slip through like phantoms while I stand guard at the door, sneering as each one passes me by, determined to commit defining details to memory, in case I ever cross paths with them again. They're all masked, but I take note of the dark and blond hair, the pungent aftershave, the acne-scarred, sun-leathered skin peeking out. Anything I can possibly remember…

Fifteen men under Florian's command, though I'm sure more remain at the ball. Prescott never resurfaces, for one. Moriah hasn't shown up either. I can only imagine there are others merrymaking among us. Keeping a leery eye on affairs aboveground.

I have a sinking feeling my uncle isn't finished with me yet.

After about twenty minutes, the men stop coming. I abandon my post, bolting quickly to the empty foyer to peek out the front door, hoping against hope that Hatch's truck is gone. That he hadn't been cornered by Prescott or any of Florian's minions.

The iron gates are swung open to welcome guests inside, but there are none out front right now. Everyone arrived hours ago, it seems, and is happily tucked away inside the starlit ballroom, swept up in the music, champagne, and spectacle. The salty night atmosphere is still and quiet, the deep blue skies hanging low overhead, dappled in streaks and flickers of light—consistent with the night's festivities, as if Tristen himself had coaxed the stars to shine.

My eyes land on two figures at the foot of the drive, engaged in a low but heated discussion.

Illuminated only by a dim streetlamp, I see a burly guard geared up in all-black, standing with his hands in his pockets. It's Tank, Nova's second-in-command. My heart gallops when I realize who he's arguing with.

Hatch.

Had he done something rash after our fight? Had he made a scene in the ballroom? Was he being kicked out?

Something about their stance—the way Hatch is growling at Tank, and how Tank seems to be shrugging away, almost too casually—tells me I've misread things…

Hatch isn't being kicked out or cornered. *He's* the one doing the questioning. But what about? And why do I get the sense that this isn't the first time they've met?

I step onto the porch to investigate, but a kindly voice pops up behind me, stopping me in my tracks.

"Miss Dell?"

It's Briggs.

He smiles. "Why aren't you inside enjoying the festivities?"

I glance back at the two men at a distance, their conversation escalating. "Something's going on out there."

Whatever it is, it has to be stopped. Hatch can't be drawing attention to himself tonight. He just needs to be gone. *Safe.*

Briggs peeks around me, his brow wrinkling at the strange sight. "Isn't Mr. Seaborn your guest this evening?"

"No," I say. "He isn't. Actually, I'd, um…I'd like for him to leave."

"You want him to leave?" Briggs studies me through his spectacles, gray eyes leadened with surprise.

I avoid his judicious stare, keeping my voice steady. "Please, Briggs, can you ask him to leave for me? He doesn't seem to be…getting the message."

"Very well, Miss Dell." He nods dutifully, putting aside his better instincts to do what's been asked of him, ever devoted to his role. "You head back inside. I'll handle it."

With a tilt of his chin, he takes off down the driveway.

I don't head back inside.

Instead, I press myself into the shadows of the slightly-opened door, shielded from the beams of porch light. Here, I can see without being seen, and hopefully make sense of what the heck is happening some sixty yards away.

Briggs quietly advances on the men in the darkness. Neither of them notice his approach.

Hatch barks something inaudible at Tank before turning to leave, storming down the street.

Tank pulls something sleek from his pants pocket, taking a few long steps in pursuit of Hatch. I can't tell what he has in his hand, but it makes my gut squeeze nonetheless.

Why is he charging Hatch like that?

Briggs reaches Tank, grabbing his shoulder from behind, taking him by surprise. The guard pivots on a dime, and Briggs falls plumb into his arms. It looks like they're giving each other…a bear hug? Tank is practically holding Briggs up.

After a moment, Tank stumbles backwards and, in slow motion, pulls something from Briggs' body. Something long and thin that had been lodged in his stomach.

What the…

Wrapped in Tank's hand, I see—

Oh, my God.

A knife.

Tank is holding a *knife.*

The light from the streetlamp above shines on the uppermost part of the blade, closest to the hilt.

The pointed end is bloody.

I gasp.

He stabbed him.

Briggs crumples to the ground.

My head explodes.

He stabbed Briggs!

Tank looms over the body…over my friend…

A hand slaps across my mouth, muffling my cries. I'm jostled quickly inside of Cliffmoor House, the front door locking after me. Down the corridor, classical music ramps up—a nightmare unfolding with a full orchestra.

Nova's brown eyes bore into mine, her face inches away. "Don't scream," she urges me in a whisper, her hand still firmly pressed to my lips. "I saw everything…"

No.

It's her.

I shake myself free and try to back away, but my feet get tangled in my gown and I teeter. She catches me by the arm, keeping me from spilling onto the floor. "Dell, listen to me, I'm on your side," she insists. "I need you to tell me—"

"Everything all right, ladies?" a slippery voice asks nearby.

It's the older server with the yellow-stained teeth, the one who ambushed me along with Prescott and the others. One of Florian's men that stayed behind. He grimaces from under that glittering mask.

Nova plasters a coy smile on her face, giggling almost drunkenly. "*This one* had a little too much champagne!" She pats my shoulder, rolling her eyes in amusement. "I'd better get her to a bathroom. Wouldn't want her getting sick out here for everyone to see!"

With that, Nova drags me away from the server, darting down the corridor and into a vacant bathroom. She pulls me inside, slams her back against the door, locks it, and inhales a breath.

I cling to the edge of the marble vanity for support. An earthquake of tremors rages through me, as the image of Briggs' collapsing body replays on an endless loop in my head.

"Dell…" Nova starts hesitantly.

Briggs can't be dead.

He was fine a minute ago.

We were *speaking* a minute ago.

My breath seizes as another realization thunders over me.

That knife was meant for Hatch.

Briggs snuck up on Tank—took him by surprise—but he wasn't the target of his assault. *Hatch was.* And he's out there somewhere, clueless to the danger he's in. Because of me. Because I did nothing to warn him…

"I need you to talk to me, Dell," Nova commands, her voice a steady hum cutting through the fog of my mind, her eyes wide and pleading. "Tell me what you know. Tell me so I can help you."

"You can't help me," I grit out, trying to form a plan to sneak away and get to Hatch. I don't have a car or a bike at my disposal. I don't even know where he is…

"Why not?" Nova asks.

"Because your friend just knifed Briggs!" I spit back.

"Tank's no friend of mine." She shakes her head. "I've had my suspicions ever since the day that journalist 'snuck' past him and onto the grounds. He's clearly gone off the deep end."

Off the deep end? That's *how she's choosing to classify this?*

"He. Fucking. Stabbed. Briggs."

"I know. Tell me who he's working for. Let me help you."

"No. We need to help *Briggs.* We need to get him to a hospital, to a doctor that can—"

"He's already gone." Nova's eyes and words are heavy. Sober.

"N-no." I choke on my saliva, tears flooding down my face. "He's not. He c-can't be…"

"I need you to listen to me," Nova says. "Tank is lethal, and he doesn't leave loose ends. If the first strike didn't kill Briggs, he'll make sure to finish the job. I'm sorry, but it's true—"

"So we're just supposed to leave him out there?"

"I promise I'll get Briggs back as soon as I can, but time is of the essence," Nova says. "I need to know if Tank is working for your uncle."

"Yes," I croak. *Yes yes yes yes.* I've been dying to scream the truth for days.

"Is Florian here?"

My whole face convulses with the lies that have been eating me up, fear invading every cell in my body. "He'll kill my parents if I talk," I half-sob.

She doesn't question it. "I'll have Tristen get in touch with them. He'll get them somewhere safe. They'll be okay, Dell—"

"No, you don't understand!" I cry. "The men watching them— *Tristen's* men—are under my uncle's control. By the time you warn my parents, it'll be too late."

"We'll figure something out," she promises. "What does Florian want?"

If I tell her, he'll make good on his threats. He'll go after everyone I love…

"Tell me what he's after," she says urgently.

But who's to say he won't do that anyway? Who's to say this isn't the start of a massive killing spree, regardless of my quiet compliance?

"Dell!" Nova insists.

Fuck it. If there's even the slightest chance Nova can help me, I don't really have a choice.

"He's smuggling drugs off the island through the tunnels. I helped his traffickers gain access to them from the parlor. They're moving everything offshore through the caves as we speak."

"But the caves are flooded—"

"Not at king tide," I say. "When the water's at its lowest point, the caves drain for a few hours."

"So he's been extorting you," she says, the pieces clicking into place. "Making you do his bidding. Threatening your family. Is that why you were so adamant about pushing Hatch away?"

I nod. "A lot of good it did. Tank still went after him. And Briggs…he just…got caught in the middle…" My voice trails off, snuffed out by the sting of emotion. My eyes burn and burn and burn.

Nova blinks rapidly as she thinks. "Why would Tank go after Hatch?"

"They were having a disagreement, I don't know what about. But it seemed personal somehow. I need to find him before my uncle does."

"Take my car." Nova slips a hand up her leg to a thin, skin-colored holster wrapped around her thigh, pulling a key from it. "There's an old Mustang Cobra parked a block over on Sable Palm Drive. Maroon with black racing stripes. Take it. Find Hatch and get somewhere safe."

"What about my parents?"

"I'll get in touch with some friends of mine in Maine. They'll get to them in time—"

"No, they *won't* get to them in time!" I retort, flying into a panic. "My uncle has a small army surrounding their cabin as we speak! Five minutes from now, they could be hog-tied on the kitchen floor. Florian already threatened arson. He'll have them burned alive."

"Can you call them?" Nova asks. "Convince them to vacate?"

Call them—and go directly against Florian's orders.

Fuck it. All bets are off anyway. I've already spilled my guts to Nova. Hatch is being hunted. Briggs is dead. My uncle is out for blood. Soon enough, he'll call for my decapitated head on a stick. I may as well phone my parents. And fast.

"Give me your cell phone," I demand.

"What happened to yours?"

"What the hell do you think?"

She plunges a hand down her cleavage, retrieving a sleek silver cell phone from the depths of her bra. Eyebrows raised, she offers it to me. "Call Tristen once you find Hatch and let us know you're okay. Do you still have the gun I gave you?"

I shake my head, taking the phone. "*He* took it."

Nova winces. "I only have one on me right now…"

"Don't worry about it." A weapon of my own would be handy, but Nova *cannot* go unarmed in this house. Not after what we'd just witnessed. Not after Briggs.

"What are you going to do?" I ask.

She rattles off a list of tasks. "Inform Tristen. Clear the ball. Disarm

Tank. Find Briggs. Stop your uncle. In that order."

"Is that all?" I ask, breathless.

An empty smile tugs up one side of her face. "We can do this."

Twisting the knob on the door carefully, Nova cracks it open, peering into the corridor…

A large man charges into the bathroom, sending us tumbling backwards.

The server.

He shoves Nova aside, and she nosedives into the toilet, some part of her thin body making a jarring *crack!* at the impact.

I hurl my fist against whatever part of him I can reach, connecting hard with the space between his ear and jaw. He grunts, absorbing the blow, before flying at me with outstretched hands. They come around my neck, that breath-crushing sensation all too familiar.

He pummels me into the wall, my skull knocking against a gilded sconce. I yelp, certain from the pain that it broke skin.

"Unruly little bitch!" Spit sprays through the man's teeth as his fingers squeeze harder, pulping my throat, ripping the very breath from me. "Your uncle asked that I keep a close eye on you. He had a feeling you might have some wild thoughts tonight."

I claw at his torso, jerking my legs, hiking my knees in hopes of connecting with his groin, but he overpowers me easily, especially in this gown. With a sneer, he lifts me up the wall by the neck. I gasp as dark clouds swirl into my vision, the heavy blackness of death creeping in.

"Mr. Klyne gave me free rein to do with you as I please, should I sniff out any insubordination." The man steps closer, dropping his nose to my bare shoulder. "And you, my dear, *reek* of insubordination."

I writhe and thrash, desperate to get free of him, but he only holds me tighter—captive, impotent. The music swells through the walls of Cliffmoor House, taunting me with its jovial, euphoric notes. All while my life is slowly siphoned away, breath by broken, choking breath.

"So it falls to me to dispose of you. But first"—the server nuzzles into my hair—"I want to hear you scream…"

Click.

I blink against the stars and the clouds and the darkness, honing in on the black muzzle of a gun thrust against the server's neck.

"Put her down."

Nova's on her feet, a trickle of blood oozing from her collarbone. By the way she's carrying herself—her champagne dress slipping to one side, one shoulder drooping limply, the shriveled pinch in her expression—I can tell she's hurting.

"You're not going to shoot me in a house full of civilians," the man laughs. "You'll create mass hysteria."

"I've got one word for you, shithead."

His dark eyes veer toward her. "What's that?"

Nova grins. "Silencer."

A soft, muted *pew* reverberates in the bathroom—no louder than the soft trill of a bird. Blood spatters fountain-wide. The server folds like paper, dropping lifelessly to the floor. I fall along with him, fighting for breath.

Nova is there in an instant, helping me to my feet. Her bulbous eyes match the shock spilling through me. Crimson blood coats my chest, my gown. I smell it saturating the air, taste the harsh metal of it on my tongue.

"Are you okay?" Nova asks, assessing the damage to my neck. "You're bruising fast."

I nod, taking several long, heaping breaths. "I'm okay," I reply hoarsely, though my trachea would beg to differ. "Is your clavicle broken?"

"Fractured, I think." She shrugs her good shoulder. "Bones can be mended later. For now, we need to move. There will be more like him coming, I'm sure."

"Count on it."

I grab a towel to wipe the blood from my neck, my breasts. All it does is smear the evidence—a wash of warrior-red painted across my chest.

"That color looks good on you," Nova comments.

"The blue?" I ask, peering down at my shimmering gown.

"No. Not the blue." She winks through the pain and twists the doorknob, murmuring a quick, "Good luck, Dell," before vanishing down the corridor toward flickering lights and distant laughter.

"Good luck," I whisper back, turning in the opposite direction with her car keys and cell phone in hand—and a prayer on my lips.

CHAPTER FIFTY-FOUR

I bolt like a blustery ocean wind across the grounds, swaddled in the deep shadows of night. My bloodstained gown snags in the rose bushes and thistles as I slip unseen through the garden gate.

An armed guard is posted outside of it, one of Nova's team. I freeze when his eyes sweep over me, terrified that he might be one of Florian's spies. But the man only nods at me briefly—the blood smears on my skin and dress undetectable in the thick darkness—and within seconds, I'm on the move again.

Once in the cul-de-sac, I zigzag between hordes of tightly-packed vehicles, ducking low as I weave across as nimbly as possible in this awkward, puddling skirt. When I make it to the street corner, I break out—heels and all—in a sprint toward Sable Palm Drive.

There.

Parked in the shade of a wayward-leaning palm, Nova's maroon Cobra glints in the moonlight.

Adrenaline surges in my brain. I race to it, unlock the car, and mash myself into the driver's seat, swatting down the poofy, uncooperative layers of my gown. The engine rumbles to life under me, and I slam too hard on the gas pedal. The sharp screech of tires pierce the night and I'm off, the island sliding past my vision at rapid speeds.

Frantic, I snake through the winding streets of Old Town, searching for any sign of Hatch's weathered Ranger…but there is none. He's gone.

Where are you?

I head to his house, calling my parents on the way. Twice I dial Mom's number. Both times she doesn't pick up.

I dial Dad next, knowing he's more likely to answer a call from a random number than she is. *Please pick up,* I pray as each ring stretches eternally. *Please be okay.*

"Hello?" My father's familiar, gravelly voice hits me like a heavenly choir of angels.

"Dad!" I exclaim.

"Dell? What phone are you calling from?"

"Thank God you're all right! Listen, where's—"

"Ope, hold on! Your mom's flagging me to hand her the phone. She looks like she might dislocate a shoulder. Just a sec."

"No, Dad, wait—"

"Dell!" Mom sounds as ecstatic to hear my voice as I am hers.

"Mom! Listen—"

"We haven't heard from you in over a week," she says, her excitement quickly giving way to anger. "Why don't you pick up your phone when I call? Whose number is this?"

"Mom, I need you to listen to me, okay? I don't have much time. Where are you right now?"

"Why are you panting like that, Dell?" A sense of urgency is sewn into her question. Her maternal radar is flawless. "Have you been crying? What's going on?"

"Mom!" She falls silent at my explosive tone. "Stop talking and listen to me for five seconds. Where are you?"

"Driving home from *Cucina di Napoli.*"

That's my parents' favorite Italian restaurant, located in the center of Woodbridge's teeny-tiny downtown strip. My mind races, mentally drawing a map of their route home. The drive is easily less than ten minutes long. Utterly secluded. Unlit at night.

"Do *not* go home," I say. "As a matter of fact, get off Hemlock altogether. Definitely don't turn onto Elk Road—"

"Why not?"

"I need you to trust me on this, okay? *Don't go home.* You and Dad need to get out of Woodbridge right now. Hop on the interstate and drive somewhere populated. A big city, like Portland or Lewiston or Bangor. Don't pull over, or make any stops until you get there. Then, check into a hotel and—"

"What are you talking about, Dell? Tell me what's wrong!"

A pang beats in my chest when I think of the comforts of Woodbridge—of the home I'd grown up in, and my parents, who'd carved out such a small, peaceful life for us there. It was their promised land, their slice of heaven, far from the hellscape of Halcyon Bay.

Guilt consumes me as I deliver this news, my words about to raze every inch of their honeyed dreamland to the ground. "There are men in the woods outside the cabin waiting for you," I say quickly. "They have orders to *kill you.* So you cannot go home."

Silence grips the phone line. Then, a sharp intake of breath.

"Did you hear me, Mom?"

"How do you know that?" she asks in shock. "What men?"

"Florian's been watching the cabin—"

"*Florian?*"

"Yes, and if you go home now, his men will kill you and make it look like an accident. Do you understand me? You *cannot* go back, no matter what. You and Dad need to get somewhere safe—miles away from Woodbridge—and when you get there, I need you to call the police. Tell them to search the woods behind the house. Tell them Florian is shuttling drugs out of Halcyon Bay. Can you do that for me?"

"Where are you, Dell?" I hear panic dripping from every shrill syllable she utters. "Are you still on the island? *Are you in that house?*"

"Will you do that for me, Mom?" I scream over her questions.

"Yes, yes!" she screams back. "I'll do it! Now tell me where you are!

Tell me—"

"I need to go," I say, choking back tears. "Whatever you do, Mom, *please*…don't come back to Halcyon Bay." My breath catches at the sheer irony of that statement. The brazen audacity that I should make such a request.

I feel like the butt of the biggest cosmic joke in existence.

"Dell, wait! What are you—"

"I'll call you as soon as I can, I promise."

"What does that mean?"

"I love you so much, okay?" The tears pour in earnest but I clear my throat, wiping them back. "Please tell Dad I love him too."

"No, wait! Don't hang up! Dell—"

"Goodbye, Mom."

"Don't—"

I end the call and power off Nova's phone.

The Seaborns' house is still, their porch light humming in tune with the cicadas tucked stealthily among the trees. Through a curtained window, I see a flickering of blue—a TV turned on. Kara's car sits in the driveway, undisturbed. All seems well. Normal.

Hatch's truck is nowhere to be found.

I speed toward the seaport next, thinking he might've taken to Captain Patton's ship. Once there, I tear across the near-empty parking lot, eyes squinting into the depths of the quiet marina, but there's barely a sign of life out there—just the gentle lulling of sleeping ships at their moorings, the moon and her stars dripping white flecks over dark water.

No Hatch. No Ranger.

Where are you?

'Cuda's, maybe? The well-loved dive bar would be Hatch's first choice for a drink. But I doubt he'd want to be in that atmosphere tonight. There's no place more bitterly lonely than a bar full of rowdy drunks…

Think, dammit!

He'd likely want some solitude—a place to clear his mind.

Somewhere with a view to numb the night's events.

Something good to cling to.

That's it.

I peel a quick U-turn, blazing toward the coast.

There's only one more place I can think to try.

Idyll Point rises before me, steadfast against the infinite sky, welcoming me back with silent grace.

Though there's no sign of Hatch's truck, I have to believe he's here. Maybe he'd parked farther up the beach and walked.

I park Nova's car along some nearby dunes, leaving my heels behind as I rush up the beach toward the graffitied entrance, squinting at the tower, scanning the wrought iron balcony overhead. I'm desperate to lay eyes on him—I can already envision his face pressed to the howling wind—but all I see up there is darkness, and a sky brimming with stars.

I feel every stomp of my feet through the sand, reverberating up my legs to my throbbing chest. Every drag of my dress weighs me down like bricks, but I keep moving.

Finally, I reach the entrance.

The door is ajar.

Hatch.

My heart soars, tears blurring my vision in anticipation of seeing him. Goosebumps coat my flesh, every bone in my body screaming, tortured by the distance, the desperate need to hold him again. To tell him how sorry I am. To assure him that I never stopped loving him. That I never could.

I push through the dark, musty insides of the lighthouse, flying up the spiral stairwell as though I'm being chased. All I can think is that he's here. *He's here.*

Up, up, up. I can't move fast enough, tripping over the hem of my ridiculous skirt, my hands grasping the railing, propelling me forward.

When I reach the landing at the top, I see the side door swung open. An impetuous wind whooshes through the space. A thick cloud of sea spray packs the air.

I shoot for that door, a sudden dose of worry spilling into my veins.

What if it isn't him up here? Or what if it is, and he doesn't want to see me? Doesn't believe me?

I step onto the balcony, my eyes adjusting. "Hatch?" I pant his name into the night, my chest impossibly tight from the sprint.

Where are you?

I walk several paces into the blackness—an imposing and terrifying presence to face on my own. The wind lashes across my skin, tangles its cold fingers in my hair…

I half-sob into the darkness again. "Hatch!"

"Dell?"

I whip around and there he is, peering around the other side of the door. His tie is loose, his collar unbuttoned, hair dripping wildly over his forehead. A dark expression swims in his gaze—fractured and fraught with confusion.

My soul levitates from my body.

He steps around the door and walks toward me. I breathe out his name. I'd worship it if I could. "*Hatch.*"

"Dell, what are you—"

I crash into him like the surf, slamming my mouth against his, our bodies stumbling into the lighthouse wall.

At first, he kisses me back hungrily, giving in to the tidal-pull of my lips, grasping fistfuls of my gown. But then his hands are on my waist, shifting me away from him, forcefully breaking us apart. "What the hell—" he starts.

"I'm sorry!" I cry. "You were right about everything. I'm so sorry. I didn't mean it…"

I stretch up onto my toes again, desperate to taste him, to leave all the pain in our past, but his hold on me tightens, fingers digging into my sides to keep me down. He roughs a hand around my back and drags me closer, but doesn't lower his lips to mine. We remain that way—frozen in suspense, with the wind swallowing our breaths—for a long moment. His eyes rage in the twinkling night, those green seas shaken and brutal.

"I'm so sorry, Hatch…" I loose a breath, a sob. "Please, believe me…"

"Tell me what's going on," he commands.

"My uncle's back," I breathe over the thundering of my heart. "He's been threatening me, forcing me to stay away from you—"

"What?" The fierceness in Hatch's expression subsides a little. "For how long?"

"Since the night you gave me the *Willow*." My eyes burn at the memory. It had been the perfect evening—the start of a future I'd felt so hopeful for. "He was waiting in the guest house when I got back."

Hatch clenches his teeth. "Why didn't you say anything?"

"They've been watching me nonstop. Florian told me he'd kill you and your family if I spoke up. He said he'd kill my parents too. That he'd dig up Willow's grave."

"Did Tristen know about this?"

"No." I shake my head. "No one did."

"So, everything you said before"—he searches my eyes—"that was all just…what exactly?" He asks the question as if his whole entire world hinges on my answer.

"An act," I say, trembling. "It was all an act, Hatch."

"And what a riveting performance it was!"

We turn to find my uncle smiling at us from the doorway.

CHAPTER FIFTY-FIVE

"Your grandmother Ginnie would be so proud to have another actress in the family!" Florian croons. "Pity she isn't here to witness all that you've become."

I grab for Hatch's shoulder, scrambling to wedge myself between him and my uncle, but Hatch is faster, his arms already reaching around, shifting me closer to the lighthouse wall while he stands like a concrete barrier before me.

"Ah, young love—so delightfully *unoriginal*." Florian chuckles, leaning against the rickety door frame. "Set a frantic, caged bird free, and she'll lead you right back to her nest. Isn't that right, dearest?"

Had he been trailing me all this time? Watching to see where I'd go? Hoping I'd lead him here…to Hatch?

I glimpse the exposed iron railing surrounding us—dilapidated in some areas, weakened by rust. We're in a terribly vulnerable position, nearly four stories above solid ground, with the wind whipping in every direction. It would be too easy for my uncle to run at us. To catch us off guard, send one or both of us plummeting…

Just like he did to Tristen. To Eribeth.

I swallow hard, my fingers latched onto Hatch's arm.

"As quaint as this rendezvous point is, I'm afraid we all have somewhere else to be." Another predatory smile curves up Florian's bearded face. "I'm hosting a little after-party back at Cliffmoor House. Very exclusive. The guest list wouldn't be complete without the two of you."

Neither of us make a move, my mind racing to figure out some way out of this…but there isn't one. Florian's blocking the only door, barricading the stairwell. There's no way down—no way out—except through.

I can sense Hatch's wheels turning too, waiting for the right moment to strike. Physically, my uncle is no match for his strength. If Hatch charges him at precisely the right angle, we can both make a clean break inside, and lock him out on the balcony…or send him plunging over the edge. But if my uncle's concealing a weapon, I doubt we'd make it two steps.

"Don't attempt any heroics, Mr. Seaborn," Florian drones, almost bored. Right on cue, he pulls a gun from his jacket. "I'd hate for you to have to watch your beloved become a human shooting target. She won't be half as becoming riddled in bullet holes, I assure you."

Hatch stiffens beside me, every muscle engaged. He backs up a step, shielding me.

"A wise choice," my uncle sneers, interpreting Hatch's body language. "Now off you go."

"Take me," I plead over the wind. "Just me. Hatch has nothing to do with this—"

"It's too late for that," Florian says cuttingly. "Mr. Seaborn is *intricately* involved now. So get moving, both of you. Time is of the essence." He gestures toward the open door with his gun.

Hatch wraps an arm around me, keeping me sandwiched between him and the wall so Florian can't get a clear shot at me. We glide forward together and squeeze through the doorway to the platform, all while my uncle grins at us, utterly amused.

Two large men—guards—wait for us inside, grabbing us both from behind. A shriek escapes me, the hoarse echo ricocheting through the lighthouse, before my guard puts me in a chokehold.

"Don't touch her!" I hear Hatch growl, before his voice is silenced to muffled, panting grunts.

They force us down the dark, spiral stairs, the man's grip on my neck growing more constricting with every step. We move quickly, my feet stumbling and twisting up in my dress, my hands desperate for purchase on the handrail. When we make it to the landing and through the door to the beach, someone else is there with a roll of duct tape in hand.

Prescott.

He slaps a long strip of tape over my mouth, grinning as he moves on to wrap my wrists behind my back—tighter, tighter. When Hatch sees this, he turns wild with rage, somehow managing to dislodge himself from the guard restraining him. With one strike of his fist, he knocks Prescott to the ground, sand granules spraying up around us. A snarling guard is on him in seconds, yanking Hatch's arms around his back, kicking him in the thigh to force him to his knees. Hatch thrashes, putting on the fight of his life…but then Florian is there, and—in one swift motion—backhands Hatch across the face with his gun.

Hatch goes limp, dropping into the sand.

I howl through my restraints, launching myself at my uncle. He sidesteps me, and I hurtle into the arms of Hatch's guard.

The guard jostles me back to my feet, smiling with wicked, gold-lined teeth. "This kitten's got some claws," he jeers, wetting his fleshy lips. Drooling like a starved man who's been offered a decadent feast.

Hate and revulsion wage war inside of me, but Hatch's shallow breathing a few feet away pulls at all of my attention.

Get to him.

Rip the world apart to get to him.

I lash out against the guard, kicking and writhing, but all he does is chuckle, pressing my body disgustingly close to his. So close I can feel each bulky fold of skin through his shirt. Can smell the sour, garlic stench on his breath.

Let me go! I scream, but through the thick tape, all that emerge are disembodied moans.

Prescott is back on his feet, swaying as he presses a hand to his bloodied mouth. His eyes latch onto the corpulent guard holding me close.

"I'll take her," Prescott says, reaching for me.

"Why?" the guard teases, squeezing his fat fingers into my arms. "I like it when they put up a little fight."

"Play later, boys," Florian cuts in. "To Cliffmoor House. *Now.*"

The guard throws me over his shoulder, while Prescott and the third assailant drag Hatch along, leaving a body-sized trench in the sand. I'm shoved into the backseat of a black sedan, and Hatch is pushed in beside me—unconscious, mouth taped, head slumped back at an unnerving angle. A cut gapes open across his eyebrow, blood streaming in rivulets down the side of his face.

I inch as close to him as I can, nuzzling into his chest, barely able to see through the sea of my tears.

Wake up, Hatch. Wake up, baby. Please…

The two guards drop into the driver and passenger seats, and we speed off in the direction of Cliffmoor House. I glance back through the window to find my uncle in a separate car with Prescott, trailing close behind.

We're trapped.

Trapped.

I lay my head against Hatch's shoulder, wishing I could wipe the blood from his face, offer him some comfort, coax him awake…

I'm sorry. I'm so sorry.

Hatch remains unconscious, his breath barely there.

So still it scares me.

White Magnolia Court welcomes me back with quiet, breezy sighs, rustling live oaks, and eerie slivers of moonlight.

The cul-de-sac is empty, the crowded assembly of vehicles dispersed. Nova must've managed to clear the ball somehow. To send everyone home and, hopefully, minimize my uncle's carnage.

We glide up the drive with Florian's car in hot pursuit, and the iron gate creaks shut behind us. Peering back, I spot a guard I don't recognize standing off to the side of it, his dour face illuminated by the hazy streetlamp.

Florian must have control of the house, I realize as the front porch comes into view, and I spot yet another guard I don't recognize.

What does that mean for Tristen? For Nova?

My heart nosedives.

Where's Briggs?

We roll to a stop and Prescott flings open Hatch's door, grabbing him roughly by the underarms. I launch myself over Hatch's body to protect him, but someone opens the other door, grabbing me by the waist and hauling me out.

I scream through the tape plastered over my mouth, desperate for someone to hear me as I'm dragged into the night. But then a hard punch is delivered to my side, knocking the wind from me, and my screams subside into whimpers.

Prescott and another guard drag Hatch up the porch. My captor throws me over his shoulder and follows, every inch of my body shivering with shockwaves of pain.

Florian trails us in silence—a grim reaper come to collect.

The muted blast of a gunshot rings out.

I jolt, forcing my trembling body to still. To listen.

It came from inside the house.

Once we make it indoors, the men lock the door behind us. The guard holding me drops me onto the floor. Hatch is dumped nearby, sprawling unconsciously onto his side. I drag myself closer to him, my wrists burning and raw from the tape.

Prescott steps between us.

The foyer clarifies before my blurry, watery eyes.

Any hope I'd prayed for is swiftly ripped away.

Nova is bound, her eyes shut, and sprawled across the wooden floor. Her tanned skin shimmers in the low light, her brown hair undone and spilling angel-soft around her. Her gown fans out prettily from her lithe body.

Blood puddles beneath it.

No.

I choke out a pained cry.

Just past her limp body, I see Tristen. He howls through the tape that covers his mouth. He's unrestrained, splayed on his stomach, his wheelchair abandoned behind him. His pale, shaking hands trace desperate lines over Nova's blood-soaked body, face, and hair. It's as if he'd catapulted himself from his chair, flung himself at her to try to shield her from the bullet. To try to save her, however he could.

Another lifeless body is curled in the far corner, partially cloaked in the shadows of the corridor. It's a man, cold and unattended. Tossed aside like rubbish.

Briggs.

A sob wracks through me, panic expanding like a balloon in my chest.

Payne is on his knees dead-center in the foyer, positioned execution-style beneath the drip of chandelier light. His mouth is taped, his wrists are bound, his sinewy body is slick with sweat. Moriah holds a gun to his forehead. A devious smile cracks her bony face in half when her blue saucer eyes connect with mine.

My gaze roves over the others in the room. Tank is there, along with several other faces I don't recognize. More of my uncle's acolytes.

"First thing's first," Florian announces, eyeing Payne with vague disinterest. "Why is this one staring down the wrong end of your barrel, Moriah?"

"He killed three of our men, sir," Moriah replies. Her eyes flit to Nova, lying eerily-still in a bloody mound. "She killed another five."

Payne locks eyes with me. Stone-still. Unflinching.

He isn't one of them.

The truth of it sinks to my bones.

"Ah." Florian nods. "Proceed then, but avoid the head. So messy." He turns his face dismissively.

Moriah lowers the gun to the base of Payne's neck, in direct line with his heart. Payne nods at me, a silver tear lining his eye. His stare holds me captive, transfixed in time. I gulp down another sob.

If I'm to be the last thing this man ever lays eyes on, it won't be the back of my head he sees. I won't turn away from him.

Moriah smiles—a sinister, gruesome thing—and pulls the trigger.

Payne's body slumps forward. Blood blooms on his shirt like a fresh sea trumpet.

Missiles explode in my brain as I double over, my head bursting from a pain so deep, I wonder if *I'm* the one who got shot.

"Buh-bye, mall cop." Moriah delivers a pointed kick to Payne's shoulder. His body curls and slides several feet across the floor.

"Splendid." My uncle rolls his neck, unaffected by the grisly scene before him. "What about the others?"

"All accounted for," Tank reports. "We waited for the guests and staff to vacate, then Moriah, Jax, Porter and I took out everyone that was left, and destroyed the security camera footage. We, um"—he clears his throat gruffly—"we left the invalid alive for you, sir."

Florian ignores that last comment, ignores the presence of his son altogether. "Marvelous," he hisses, those black-stone eyes blazing like hot coals in a fire. "You barely managed to execute the work I paid you for, Mr. Sullivan. Bravo! Any other bumbling thug off the street could've accomplished as much."

Tank's brow furrows. "Sir?"

"Did you expect a gold star for your clumsy performance this evening? A pat on the back for your gross mishandling of affairs?"

Tank's ears burn bright red.

"You're an amateur at best," Florian spits. "I should be miles offshore by now. Instead, I've spent the last hour chasing Meridel through town hoping she'd lead me to Seaborn, all to remedy your grievous error!"

"I'm sorry he escaped, sir."

"You certainly will be." Florian points down at Hatch. "Here he is, Mr. Sullivan. Have at him."

I fight harder against my binds. I need to stop this. Need to keep Hatch safe.

Tank hesitates, not venturing to step closer.

"I said, have at him," Florian repeats sharply, his anger magnifying with every passing second.

"Nova killed one of our yacht engineers, sir," Tank explains. "We need to find a suitable replacement—"

"So find one."

"Well, I was thinking…Seaborn repaired all the outboards for the Jon boats. Left them in near-mint condition." Tank lifts a shoulder. "He might not be a bad option."

My mind races to process this information.

Seaborn repaired all the outboards.

Hatch had casually mentioned some outboards before. He'd said that an out-of-towner had come around the seaport, looking to hire a tradesman to repair a bunch of crappy old boat motors…

I gasp, realizing what this means.

Hatch had unwittingly facilitated Florian's plan.

He'd made the necessary engine repairs to get the Jon boats up and running. The same boats currently being used to smuggle narcotics off the island.

"Seaborn knows electrical and marine mechanics, sir," Tank continues. "Knows boats like the back of his hand. He's a real lifer-type, I could tell when we talked."

Tank was the one who hired Hatch on the seaport.

Had they never run into each other at Cliffmoor House? Did Hatch only recognize him for the first time at the ball? Did he question his motives? Confront him?

That must be why Tank tried to stab him. To keep Hatch quiet. To snuff out any trail that might lead back to my uncle.

My mind spins and spins with each new revelation.

"Well, well." My uncle's eyes narrow as he squats down to Hatch's level. "What a fortuitous turn of events. Looks like you may be more useful to me alive than dead…" He shoots cruel eyes at his guards. "Someone revive him."

"With pleasure," Prescott replies. He steps away to snatch up one of the many gilded candelabras lining the foyer.

No.

I scrape across the floors toward Hatch.

In three steps, Prescott is back, holding the dripping candelabra over Hatch's body. Ever so slowly, he tips it over.

No no no!

I scream as fire-hot wax falls over Hatch's back and shoulders, scalding him through his thin dress shirt. Hatch jerks to life with a muffled yelp, then groans and groans as Prescott lets more wax drip over him. Hatch struggles to right himself, to get his bearings…

I can barely breathe, my nose covered in snot, tendrils of sweaty hair plastered to my face.

"Mr. Seaborn!" my uncle says, smiling. "How kind of you to join us."

This finally prompts Prescott to pull back. Hatch shudders as he hauls himself up, catching his breath. Through the film of blood and sweat, his eyes find mine. They flare painfully. I think I might die.

"According to our mutual acquaintance here"—Florian waves a hand in Tank's direction—"you have a certain skill set that would be beneficial in our travels. In short, we need your assistance. Are you willing to cooperate?"

Hatch thrashes in place, consumed by pain and wrath, his eyes a raging storm expressing what his lips can't say.

My uncle stands again, scratching his chin as he ponders some quiet thought. "I see…" He purses his lips. "You'll need some convincing, then?"

Without turning, he snaps his fingers and two men are at my back, thrusting rough hands under my arms, dragging me to the center of the room where my uncle stands. They dump me in a tangled heap at Florian's feet—a flash of limbs, tears, and shimmering stars. Payne's freshly spilled blood seeps up my dress.

Hatch writhes as two guards hold him back by the arms.

I wince when Florian lightly pats the top of my head. "I'd originally promised Meridel to the people of Ula Cove. But, because I'm feeling generous, I'll give you a chance to save her, Mr. Seaborn."

Ula Cove? As in, the land of the blue sea trumpets?

I peer up at my uncle, my entire body tingling.

"Did I forget to mention that?" Florian asks. "Come now, Meridel!

You didn't *really* think your work ended with the ball, did you?" He clucks his tongue in disapproval. "Foolish girl. You know me better than that."

Fucking liar.

He said that if I helped him, if I stayed quiet, he'd depart with his drugs and never look back. He said that he'd leave my loved ones in peace. That I'd get a chance to sweep up the shattered fragments of my life.

Fucking. Liar.

He was never going to let me stay here.

He was never going to let me *live.*

"Meridel has long been pledged to the Ulan people," Florian announces. "As I've come to learn from my dear friends in the Brine, for the sea trumpets to flourish, *Mother* must be sated. A sacrificial lamb is vital. And who better than my darling niece to fit the bill?"

My blood runs cold, all of this sounding eerily familiar.

It's happening all over again.

A variant of the Brine is underfoot in Ula Cove.

And I'm destined to be their first sea girl.

That's why Florian needed me to procure *Legends* for him. So he could learn how to propagate a fresh crop of sea trumpets. Or, possibly, to help him locate the ones in the Vale of Azurine that haven't been spotted for decades. All to manufacture and traffic more drugs. To slake his unabating greed.

"However"—Florian's jaw feathers—"should my demands be met, I could easily persuade the people of Ula to claim another's blood. The choice is yours, Mr. Seaborn. Travel with us and ensure that our journey runs smoothly, and Meridel goes free. Refuse my offer, and she dies. Simple as that. Do we have an accord?"

Hatch glowers at him, hard and unyielding.

"Would someone please remove the tape from Mr. Seaborn's mouth?" Florian drones. "This is a gentlemen's agreement. I need to hear him speak."

Prescott swiftly reaches around Hatch, ripping the tape from his lips in one brusque swoop. Hatch sways, grunting in pain.

"Do we have an accord?" my uncle repeats.

"Let Dell go and I'll do whatever you want," Hatch rasps.

Florian flashes his teeth like a wolf who's spotted his next meal. "I'm afraid that's not an option."

"Either Dell goes free *now*, or there is no deal."

"Or"—Florian pulls the revolver from his jacket, pressing the muzzle to the bare, bloody skin of my chest—"I shoot Meridel right here in front of you, and employ other means of coercion."

"I'll kill you," Hatch threatens.

Florian arches a brow. "Love really does make fools of us all. Oh, well. *C'est la vie.*" He cocks back the hammer, ready to shoot.

"No!" Hatch yells. At the other end of the foyer, Tristen slams his fists on the floor, his face a feverish red, just like the puddle of liquid crimson before him.

I squeeze my eyes tight, bracing myself. One pull on that trigger and it will all be over. I'll fall into an unending blackness. Plummet over the cliffside of this life into the abyss of the next.

"My patience is waning, Mr. Seaborn," Florian warns. "The slaughter won't end with Meridel. I'll pick off your family members, one by one. I'll do ungodly things to them that will have you begging me for mercy. Begging me to give you another opportunity like this."

Agony flickers across Hatch's face. I wish so much that I could take his pain away.

"So, you see, I still win. I *always* win." Florian sneers. "Make. Your. Choice."

I shake my head, my moans and muffled screams echoing low in the foyer as my eyes meet Hatch's. *You can't do this! Don't give him what he wants!* But I don't see the same ferocity in those sea green eyes. Don't see the flame of anger or brutal determination. All I see is endless love. A man that would do anything to keep me from harm.

My Hatch.

"I'll do it," he croaks.

"Sensational!" Florian grins. "It's settled then. The young lovers will join us on our voyage to Ula Cove."

"What about the others, sir?" Moriah asks.

Florian eyes the bodies littering the foyer as if they're stinking trash in need of disposal. "Leave them. With any luck, authorities will think my son went on a murderous rampage after the ball and killed his own employees."

"And what are we to do with your son?"

Florian sighs with boredom, as if this particular issue isn't worth his attention. "Drag him along," he says, already prowling toward the parlor. "I will *personally* deal with him on board the yacht."

That's where the Jon boats must be converging—on a yacht offshore. A yacht meant to transport my uncle and his cronies the rest of the way to Ula Cove.

Guards pull me to my feet and begin shuffling me toward the hall, veering close to Briggs' body. I can barely stand to look at him. His spectacles are shattered, glass shards sprinkled over his face. His skin bears a hue of jaundice, mouth dripping open to one side. His crisp shirt—ever-spotless and immaculately starched—is suffused with blood, too much blood to survive. There isn't one stab wound, but multiple, sprinkled all across his chest and stomach.

Grief grips me, wraps its fist around my heart and clamps down.

That's when I see it.

The knife.

It's lodged in Briggs' side, the thin hilt exposed and prime for the taking. Small enough to fit in the folds of my hands. Tank had left it there—*overconfident bastard*—and moved on to other means of destruction.

It's my one chance.

When they've dragged me close enough, I plunge to the ground before the guards can stop me, hurling myself over Briggs' cold body. I'm overcome with tears, gutted by the loss of my friend.

You didn't die in vain, Briggs. I won't let you die in vain.

The guards shout and curse as they haul me up by the arms, jostling me toward the parlor. No one notices that I've ripped the knife from Briggs' side and tucked it between my bound hands, pressed discreetly to the back of my gown.

CHAPTER FIFTY-SIX

The night is a black vacuum of nothingness. A swarm of storm clouds creep in slowly from the sea, gobbling up every last wink of brightness in the sky. There are no stars to be found anymore, nor a sliver of moonlight, as we spill stealthily onto the shore.

The tunnels at our backs were a scramble of rushing bodies, packed with black-clad traffickers shoving through to collect their trove, and guards roughly shuttling the rest of us—Tristen, Hatch, and I—through the caves to the beach.

I can just make out the rock formations around us, the strip of shoreline marked by limestone outcrops. *Whispering Rocks.* Another heavenly memory, ruined.

The beach is already flooded. The saltwater reaches my ankles, soothing my aching feet. In an hour or so, the caves will be impassable, no way in or out.

I'm grateful for the darkness, the muddle, the rush. It keeps the knife—the blood dripping from my fingers where the blade nicks my palms—concealed.

I'm yanked forward by Prescott to a waiting Jon boat. His clammy hand curled around my upper arm churns up painful memories of last summer, when he'd grabbed me so aggressively outside of June's house. When he'd pressed against me in the sea trumpet fields, and rammed a gun into my ribs.

I steady my breathing.

The past is done.

All that matters is right now. Every agonizing second.

The knife tucked between my hands sings a song of revenge. A melody of bloodlust weaves like the salt breeze through the darkness—a siren song, hungry for flesh. For debts to be repaid.

For Briggs. For Nova.

For Hatch. For Tristen.

For my family.

There's no time for fear. Only action.

Prescott hauls me up and over the boat. I drop onto a narrow metal bench with a thud. Tank shoves Hatch in behind me and jumps inside too. The four of us settle in for a ride—Prescott and Tank at either end, Hatch and me in the middle with our backs to each other.

Tank starts up the small engine. It purrs to life with velvet ease. *Hatch's handiwork.* The irony is sickening.

Tank pushes off from the shore and soon, we're cutting across the shallows, the boat slicing a foamy trail through the coming waves.

I begin working on the tape at my wrists. Small, thin cuts. Barely making a dent. But slowly, steadily, I am, with as little motion and fuss as possible.

Water rocks against the Jon boat, beating the sides of it in bumps and splashes. Between the rollicking waves and the low whirring of the engine, the quiet sounds of my cuts and slashes are drowned out.

"What're the odds that *you*, the random boat whiz I found on the seaport, would become Florian's man of the hour?" Tank asks suddenly, the question directed at Hatch, though his mouth is taped shut. "You're lucky to be alive, you know. I was gunning for you when I killed the old butler."

"Too bad," Prescott mumbles, seething in his hatred. "Would've been nice to finally have him out of the way."

"No love lost between the two of you, is there?" Tank asks.

"You could say that." I can *hear* Prescott's scowl ringing through the darkness. "You might say we have similar tastes in women, but that's where our parallels end."

Before long, I've gained some leverage, some more wiggle room. I get a firmer grip on the knife. My strokes become longer, stronger. I've almost cut myself free.

"Oh, I get it." Tank chuckles, as if he's riddled out something that greatly amuses him. "This is about *the girl*."

"Isn't it always about a girl?" Prescott asks rhetorically.

The tape breaks, freeing my wrists. A jolt of triumph courses through me.

Immediately, I reach back in silence to touch Hatch's arm. My nails gently scrape his forearm and he tenses. But then he appears to loosen a breath, realizing that somehow I've gotten my hands free…and that I'm attempting to do the same for him.

I guide my fingers down to meet his and start slicing away at the tape, keeping my nicks small and short, careful not to cut too deeply, keeping a safe distance from the soft, veiny skin of his wrists.

"That's some shitty luck, man," Tank says, "to fall for someone you can't have. Someone marked for death."

Despite the turn in conversation, I concentrate only on my slow progress, snipping back layer after layer of the thick tape. *Get him free.* That's all that matters.

"Shitty luck," Prescott repeats under his breath, ruminating on those words. Then, as if he's had a change of heart, he says, "But who knows? We'll have some time together on the yacht. Anything's possible." His hand lands on my knee. "Isn't that right, Dell?"

The violation makes my fingers slip. I start sharply. Hatch grunts in pain—I must've jabbed him with the tip of the blade. *Crap.*

I draw my legs up and away from Prescott, desperate to get him off of me. Upon sensing my panic—my very clear desire not to be touched—he digs his fingertips in to keep me still. "Just a matter of time," he croons.

I tense up at the sordid undertone of his threat, matched by the squeeze of his grip on my knee. His smile perforates the darkness, his teeth a wicked flash of white. Drunk on the thrill of exerting power over me. On making me feel scared and helpless and entirely at his mercy.

When that hand starts to slide up my thigh, I see red.

Kicking up, my heels connect hard with his shin.

Prescott groans, dropping his hand from my leg as he doubles over, but I still feel the searing pressure of that greedy hand on me, slithering up the length of my thigh…

"Someone should teach you some manners," he snarls.

My fingers form a fist around the knife's hilt at my back. *Someone should make sure you never lay a hand on a woman again.*

Once he's caught his breath, Prescott leans forward, hands on the tops of his own thighs now. "You shouldn't fight me so hard on this, Dell. Fishboy's your uncle's puppet now. You think you'll be allowed to cozy up with him on the yacht? Think again. You'll be kept in isolation. And once fishboy serves his purpose, your uncle will off him. You'll never see your precious—"

I plunge the knife into his hand.

The blade glides easily through the soft tissue between tendons, biting down deep into his thigh.

Prescott screams, the agonized sound ripping through the night like the screech of a bird.

I hear Hatch struggling behind me—exhaling a harsh, guttural noise, as if exerting a great amount of effort—and then, the sudden snap of tape.

Tank yelps as Hatch launches onto him, his hands now free, having broken the last bit of tape from his wrists by sheer force. The crack and thud of fists colliding against bone fill the air. I can feel the men brawling behind me, causing the boat to teeter as we push farther out to sea.

Prescott thrashes in place as he screams, trying to lift his wounded hand, but it's affixed to his leg, immoveable. If the knife is dislodged, he'll surely bleed out.

I rip the tape from my mouth and spit at him.

"You bitch!" he howls, swiping at me with his free arm. He strikes me hard on the shoulder, fingernails clawing across my chest, carving deep enough to draw blood.

I gasp, reaching forward to yank the knife from his leg.

Prescott inhales sharply when I get it free…

And drive it straight into his stomach.

I hear him choke in surprise, producing a strange gurgling sound. In slow motion, he reaches down and paws at the hilt in desperation. The blade slides out smoothly, and his mouth gapes wide, realizing too late what he's done. Blood pours from between his lips. He drops the knife to the floor of the boat.

He's not dead yet, but I know I've killed him.

Hatch groans behind me, the sound more smothered than fierce. Turning, I see him frozen in place, the silhouette of a gun pressed against his temple.

"Hatch," I whisper, frightened beyond measure.

Tank wheezes behind him, shoulders rising and falling with exhaustion. "I should kill you both for this stunt," he grits between his teeth. I think he's bleeding from his face.

"Do it!" Prescott burbles out through his sobs. "Shoot them now!"

"But Mr. Klyne's orders were—"

"Screw his orders!" Prescott cries. "Kill them now! She stabbed me twice!"

"We need Seaborn alive," Tank insists. "Hang tight, Savage. They'll get you cleaned up on the yacht."

"I'm not going to make it to the yacht, you idiot!"

"Tie the girl up," Tank instructs Hatch, pulling some rope from his tactical vest. "Try anything funny and I *will* shoot her. You have my word on that."

Hatch doesn't take it.

Tank lobs the rope at his face. "*Now*, Seaborn."

The rope dangles over one of Hatch's shoulders, but still, he refuses to budge.

Tank heaves a breath, his frustration growing. "Then I guess there's no reason for her to keep breathing." He turns the gun on me, but Hatch blocks his shot. "Do as I say," Tank repeats. "Tie her back up, or she dies tonight."

Slowly, Hatch does an about-face in his seat, turning toward me. I can't keep the tears from pouring at the sight of him. Even through the darkness, I can tell that one beautiful, green eye is disfigured. Swollen. A bloody trickle races from a black cut on his nose.

My Hatch.

He leans in close, warm hands cupping mine. I carefully peel back the tape from his lips, then sink against his chest. "What do we do?" I breathe out, shivering.

Hatch is unflinchingly still, holding me close. I can tell he's thinking hard about what steps to take next.

"Hurry up, Seaborn," Tank commands, growing impatient. "Savage, you doing all right up there?"

Prescott is eerily silent behind me.

"Savage? How you holding up?"

No response.

I keep my eyes trained on Hatch. "What do we do?" I ask again, terrified that he won't have an answer. That there *is* no answer. That this is the end.

He exhales a shaky breath, something brewing beneath the surface I can't get a read on. He drops his gaze to the hunk of blue sea glass pressed to my heart. I look down too, only to find it *glowing*.

Tank barks out a cautionary "Seaborn!"

In an unexpected maneuver, Hatch grips my arms so hard, it steals what little breath I have away. "Hatch?"

Tank yells something at us, but I can't make out what he says.

"I love you," Hatch rasps, his large hands clamping down on me. "Until the very last sunset. Never forget that."

In one fell swoop, he lifts me up by the arms.

"Hatch!" I scream.

He pitches me over the side of the boat.

A gunshot blasts in the night.

And I'm swallowed up in the sea.

CHAPTER FIFTY-SEVEN

Black water cradles my body as I plunge, wrapped in the sea's cool, bubbly embrace, as if in an attempt to shield me from the bullets whizzing past.

Tiny torpedoes cascade from the surface, hungry for skin and blood. The inky tides twist me this way and that, whisking me down, deeper still. Each bullet narrowly misses its mark…

Until one breaks the skin of my shoulder. A graze.

I wince as I fall into the void, my eyes closing involuntarily. If I scream, the water will rush into my lungs and I'll choke. The small wound burns, but not enough to debilitate me. Only to galvanize me. To set me on fire.

Hatch.

He's still up there.

It's a lightning rod to my disoriented mind—kindling to flame.

I open my eyes to greet the darkness again, determined to push myself up, up…

Inhuman, white-orb eyes pin me in place.

A woman's face gleams at me through the water, her stare cold enough to drown men and flood continents. Her pearly skin ripples, a frown on her waxen, barely-there lips. Hair like drifting seaweed and unraveling rope fans wide around her. She radiates a ghostly light where there is none, as if fashioned from the very substance of the moon.

She's magnificent and terrifying, ethereal and paralyzing.

She circles me like prey.

A whispered name pushes forth in my mind—

Sereia.

My sea glass glows and glows…

In the distraction of seeing her, I don't notice right away when the chaos above me ceases. The sea is quiet, deadly calm. The torrent of bullets has stopped. The hum of the boat engine is dull. Distant.

Hatch.

Get to Hatch.

I flail in place, terror chilling me to my bones. Not because I'm enveloped in water so black I can't see my fingers in front of my face, nor because this ghostly sea woman has materialized from nowhere, and may have every intention of drowning or dismembering me…

But because of him.

Because he's still on that boat.

Still making for that yacht offshore, trapped by our enemies.

Without me.

The fear gives way to anger. Anger that he'd pushed me over the edge and stayed behind. That we're not together, the way it's supposed to be.

What if Tank shot him after he threw me off?

My throat pinches tight at the thought of Hatch lying motionless, bleeding and broken, his green eyes sealed shut forever…

NO.

With every relentless thrum of my heart, I know he's okay.

He has to be okay.

He's alive.

The sea woman's strange expression ruffles, curious and brutal and keenly intelligent, interpreting my emotions as easily as one might read a newspaper.

She's not one of the sea girls…but she's no mermaid either.

Stop wasting time, I think. Every second without him is an ocean stretching between us.

I push up to the surface. My chest squeezes tightly from the lack of oxygen and the icy drip of panic surging in my veins. With every stroke of my arms, every kick of my feet, I know how easily I could be attacked by any number of animals. I carry the scent of blood on me. Within seconds, I could be mauled and dragged to a watery grave, decapitated by killer jaws, or lose a limb and bleed out. Even once I hit the surface, my splashing will echo far and wide. It'll sound like a dinner bell. Like feeding time at the zoo.

Still, I push up through the water, needing to breathe, to assess where I am and how to get back to him.

I will get back to you, Hatch. Even if it destroys me.

I breach the surface and gulp a mouthful of night air. Waves splash around my shoulders, rocking me as I tread in place. The purring of the boat engine is inaudible, the world heaving with vacancy. There's no sign of Hatch anywhere, no trail to chase. No breadcrumbs on these rolling waters to follow.

Smears of distant light beckon me back to land.

I make for the shoreline, forming a plan.

I know where they're going.

I'm just a few paces behind.

But I'm coming.

I swim to the beach, almost too absorbed in my thoughts to realize I'm *surrounded* in electric blue water. Everywhere I touch, the ocean glows in response—glows as brightly as my sea glass necklace.

I've heard of bioluminescent plankton before—organisms that create a mesmerizing, neon effect when the water they occupy is disturbed, warding off predators—but *this* feels like something more. Like a safety net. An otherworldly gift. A promise that I'm not as alone as I feel.

I'm coming, Hatch.

Sure as the night ends and the sun rises, I'm coming.

CHAPTER FIFTY-EIGHT

The shore is inundated, the entrance to the cave practically consumed. I swim on relentlessly, though my body screams for rest, my stupid, sopping gown weighing down my limbs.

I duck beneath the pitch-black water, slip through the jagged crevice, and into the cave. When I surface again, I realize there's only a small breath of airspace left inside—mere inches at most. The sea is rising quickly, rushing to fill up every nook and cranny.

I spiral onto my back, kicking steadily through the darkness, the tip of my nose grazing the roof of the cave. A few times, it scrapes against the rock a little too hard. Tears sting my eyes, but I don't stop for a second. I have to focus all of my energy on getting across, pouring my strength into every brisk stroke, before the dark water swallows me up for good.

Just keep moving, keep breathing.

The water climbs higher, fighting my every effort. I can barely keep my head above it. It slides into my nostrils and I kick out faster, jamming my fingers into the uneven rocks overhead to help me propel.

Faster, faster.

My thoughts race frantically. I'm too far from the entry point to turn back now. I'll drown before I ever make it out to open water. I need to keep going…need to get back to the tunnel…

But I'm disoriented by the heavy darkness pressing over me, and the gurgling saltwater pouring in from every angle, creeping into my nose, my mouth, my ears. I tilt my neck back, inhaling deeply, sucking back one last breath, and—

My head slams against a rock.

I gasp and slip under the surface. The bubbling water overwhelms me—twirls and spins my body like a death-wielding dance partner. My skirt ruffles up like wings at my back. I have nowhere to fly to, no manner of escape…

Focus.

I blink feebly into the vast, swirling darkness, my chances of survival dimming by the second…

A haze of blue light sparks in my periphery.

My sea glass, I realize. It still glows at my chest, that tiny, radiant blue battling the prevailing gloom.

I wrap the shard in my fingers and yank, breaking the thin, silver chain around my neck. I hold the glowing stone at arms-length, following that flare of blue-flame through the water. It leads me like a beacon, infused with a strange, inexplicable magic. A piece of my sister entrusted to me, to *save* me.

My heart fills with resolve, my legs pumping hard and fast beneath me, hardwired to get me to safety.

Hatch Hatch Hatch. His name is my mantra—the vital drum of my heartbeat.

Through the murky water, I see shapes materializing at a distance.

Yes.

I must be close now…I must be—

There!

A flight of crude stone steps takes form.

Hell yes.

I launch myself across that final stretch, desperate to fill my lungs with air again. *So close, so close.*

When I reach the steps, I grip one and start crawling, scraping up on hands and knees, dragging my gown like a sodden corpse behind me.

That first gulp of air when I breach the surface is heavenly.

I flip onto my back, hacking and sputtering water through each strangled breath. Once I'm well enough to move again, I rise to my feet, trying to pinpoint what hurts most and where.

Lightning-pain shoots down my skull from the top of my head. I touch the spot gingerly, wincing when a warm substance douses my fingertips. *Blood.* That rock got me good. My left shoulder is bleeding too, burning from the bullet graze. The skin of my chest is raw and tender, slashed with deep trenches where Prescott clawed me…

Shock twists at my gut as I remember.

I killed him.

My legs wobble under me.

Prescott is dead.

I actually killed a man.

Not a man. A monster.

And I'm not sorry.

But still. This changes me. Marks me forever.

A looming wave of disgust threatens to cripple me—to force me to my knees, overwhelm me with doubts about my own brutal nature—but I thrust it aside and start moving. No one and nothing will keep me from Hatch. Not my fears and not my weaknesses, mental or otherwise.

My equilibrium is off as I break into a sprint. I hold my hands out at either side of me for balance, keeping me from knocking against the rock walls as I slip through the tunnel. I fall into a quick rhythm, retracing the steps I've forged countless times before, my bare feet aching, *screaming* for relief. But I don't take a second to pause.

Once I've made it to the safe room, I run up the steps and burst into the parlor. I force myself to walk past the utter destruction in the corridor—the littered bodies and spilled blood. I don't have time to inspect them now, nor to dwell on which side of this war they fell on. I only have one goal—to find Tristen's car keys.

I careen down the corridor, my sights set on the door…then freeze when I hear someone *moving* in the foyer. I press in close to the wall, shielded in shadows, my ears perked.

"T-Tristen?" a gravelly voice calls out softly. "T-Tristen, where are you?"

It can't be.

I rush forward, my hopes soaring.

In the foyer, a woman in a blood-soaked gown clings to a bannister near the foot of the staircase. She's torn a strip of fabric from her dress, and is pressing it firmly to her hip, staunching the flow of blood.

"Oh, my God, Nova!" I fly to her side, hands shaking when I grip her arms. "You're alive! I can't believe you're alive…"

"Where…" She looks disoriented, struggling to speak. Her face is blanched and sickly-white. "Where's T-Tristen?"

"He's gone." My lip trembles. "My uncle took him."

Nova's eyes flutter. "Gone?"

"I'm going after him," I promise.

"You know where Florian's headed?"

I nod. "A place called Ula Cove, near the Cayman Islands. He's planning to grow sea trumpets and build a drug empire there."

Her mouth gapes. "Why'd he take Tristen?"

"I don't know," I say, refusing to give in to the despair in my bones. "I can only assume he wants Tristen to pay for betraying him last summer. Killing him would've been too easy."

Nova's eyes close as she feels the weight of my every word. "What about Hatch? Did you find him?"

Hatch. My voice breaks, a whimper bubbling up in my throat. "Florian took him too, to work on his yacht."

"What?"

"Apparently, you or Payne killed one of their engineers. Hatch is their replacement."

Nova's eyes slide over me, taking in my drenched hair, the bloody marks on my chest, the wound at my shoulder, the ruined gown clinging to my body. "What did they do to you?" she whispers.

"Hatch and I were on the same boat heading offshore," I confess, ashamed to admit that I'd been there—*right there*—and I'd failed to save him. I'd failed the love of my life. "Tank and Prescott were with us, holding us captive. I stole a knife and cut us both free, but it wasn't enough. Hatch threw me overboard to try to save me. To give me a chance to get away."

Fire rages in my soul, a battle cry ringing through my shaking body. *This isn't over.* Far from it. "I'm going to get them back."

"How?" Nova asks.

"I know a captain. He'll get me off the island." I say it as though it's explanation enough, but I know it isn't. Not even close. "I'll drop you off at the hospital first—"

"No," she interjects, refusing my offer. "I'm going with you."

"You're absolutely not."

"Yes, I am," she insists. "I'm going, Dell."

"Look, I can't delay this trip until you're better, and you're not in any condition to travel—"

"I'll stitch myself up." She adjusts her grip on the cloth against her hip, tamping down the pain, contorting her face. "When do we leave?"

"Nova, I can't let you—"

"What you can't do is leave me behind." Her voice is small, but assertive.

"You're not going to make it," I whisper. She'd survived the gunshot, but I don't think she can withstand much more.

"Takes more than a wonky shot to take me out. That Moriah girl's aim is crap." Nova peers down at her hip, inspecting the damage. "I've had way worse than this, trust me."

She seems to have staunched the blood flow for now, but who knows what kind of mess she's dealing with on the inside.

"So, I take it we're going to go see this captain friend of yours?" Nova asks through a wince.

Is it really my place to tell a grown woman what she can't do? If roles were reversed, would I let her stand in my way? Keep me from Hatch in his moment of need?

I exhale. "Yes. I need the key to Tristen's car."

"Payne should have a set," Nova says, not turning her face to look. I can't blame her.

Bracing myself, I kneel beside Payne's cold body, checking his pockets, wracked with regret over all the vitriol I'd slung at him. He'd been difficult and arrogant, sure—he'd even crossed the line and teased me in ways he shouldn't have—but he was always on our side. Always looking out for Tristen.

The key is in one of his back pockets. I slide it up and out, breathing deeply once I've created some distance from him.

"Got it," I pant, standing up too quickly, woozy from being surrounded by so much blood. "Let's go."

Nova nods, releasing the bannister and reaching for me.

We hold each other together—Nova's arm dangling over my shoulders, mine wrapped around her waist—and limp through the door into the night.

CHAPTER FIFTY-NINE

I speed to Freya's storefront with Nova curled up in the passenger seat, shivering in her ruined gown, her face a deathly shade of white. She's lost a lot of blood—an unsettling amount of blood. Every time she closes her eyes for a brief rest, I feel my heart plummet, terrified they won't open again.

For now, they do.

I park streetside and fly out of the car, making Nova promise to stay inside and *stay alive* until I make it back. She smiles through the pain—a sharp wince in her expression—before waving me on.

Within seconds, my fists are banging on the door. "Freya! Cap'n!" My hoarse voice carries on the wind down the vacant street. The sound is utterly out of place here—in the quiet, bar-less, tourist-free side of downtown—especially at this hour. "Freya, please! It's Dell!"

After several long minutes, I hear grumbling at the other side of the door. It creaks open slowly to reveal Captain Patton wrapped in a terry-cloth robe, his gold teeth exposed in a wide yawn, pudgy fingers scratching at his bare, hairy chest.

"Cap'n, please—"

"What on earth!" He takes in my drippy eyes, my waterlogged gown, my skin awash in blood. "Are you all right, Delly?" Blinking, he peers around me, his one good eye searching the tranquil, night-shrouded street beyond. In a foreboding tone, he asks, "Where's your other half?"

My other half.

The question coils up in the pit of my stomach, pulls a screw loose on my legs. My knees buckle under my weight and I collapse, a feeble hand sliding down the peeling door frame as I fall.

He's gone gone gone.

"Whoa there!" the captain cries, immediately grabbing for my arms. He lifts me up with care, holding me steady. His crystalline eye catches on the car—on Nova's limp form through the window—and it widens, aghast. "There're *two* of you like this?"

"No, I'm…I'm all right," I croak, clinging to the crook of his elbow for dear life.

"Freya!" he calls inside suddenly, cutting me off. "I need help out here, quick!" His good eye flits back to me, then to Nova. "Who is that woman, Delly?"

"Her name is Nova." I swallow. "She's my friend. But she's badly injured. Gunshot wound to the abdomen."

"What happened?" the captain asks.

"My uncle came back." A sob wracks through me. "Hatch is…gone. Florian took him."

His lips pucker tightly, the creases deepening around his mouth. "Took him where?"

"To an island off the Caymans where he's planning to cultivate sea trumpets." The captain looks at me with blatant confusion. "Florian took Hatch and my cousin Tristen. I'm going after them, but I need a captain to take me. I need *you* to take me."

The captain gapes at me, stunned by my request, but also, inevitably, enticed by it. The promise of a new adventure at sea is too tempting for an old sailor to ignore. The glint in his good eye tells me he's interested, even as he shakes his head.

"I can't sail the schooner by my lonesome, Delly, even with the engines running. I'd still need to hire a crew, or at least a couple deckhands. 'Specially for a longer trip like that—"

"I have a boat," I blurt, my thoughts immediately going to the *Willow*. "It's smaller than yours. More manageable." God knows if that's true, but I need him to say yes.

"What kind of boat?" One of the captain's bushy silver eyebrows lifts curiously.

"The…fishing kind?" I don't know how to describe it. 'Boat' is not a language I speak fluently. "It used to belong to Abraham Urban."

"Hmm. I remember Urban's boat," Cap'n Pat says thoughtfully. "On that sort of vessel, all the way to the Caymans, I'd say it'd be at least…oh, five or six days of travel, weather permitting? Could be longer if we get caught in a storm or two. A week or more, maybe."

Five or six days? A week or more?

I only have the vaguest sense of where we're going. I certainly haven't given any thought to how long it would take to make the trip, or how much fuel we'd need, or what the weather conditions would be like.

Freya emerges from the dark insides of the establishment. Her mouth falls open when she sees the ghastly state I'm in. "Meridel, child! What happened to you?"

"Her snake of an uncle came back to our little island," the captain pipes up. "Seems to have wrecked all sorts of havoc over at Cliffmoor House. Took some hostages with him too."

"Who?" Freya asks, her gaze keen on me.

"Hatch," I choke out. "And Tristen."

"Where is he taking them?"

"To an island called Ula Cove," I explain. The psychic squints at me uncertainly. "It's the only other place in the world where sea trumpets are known to grow."

"I see. And what does Florian aim to do in Ula Cove?"

"Revitalize his drug empire," I say. "He's been trafficking sea trumpets for years from Halcyon Bay. That's why he came back—to collect his remaining supply. But he's greedy. He plans to grow a new crop."

"Did you inform the police?" the captain asks.

I shake my head. "I can't trust them. My uncle has operatives in the department. They've completely bungled the search for him on purpose. They won't care about getting Tristen or Hatch back, much less about sea trumpets growing on foreign land." I stare between the both of them. "Look, I know it's a huge ask, but I'm begging you, from the bottom of my heart, *please*…come with me, Captain. Help me bring Hatch home."

They look at each other, neither venturing to respond.

"Please." My eyes well with endless tears. "*Please*. I have nowhere else to go."

The captain's mouth twitches with resolve. "A trip like this won't be an easy one, Delly."

Hope soars through me. "I'm not afraid of that."

"I'll need help on the open water," he says. "You'll have to learn quickly—"

"Yes!" I nod, crying, unable to keep down the flood of emotion. "Yes. Whatever it takes."

"Who else will travel with you, child?" Freya asks.

I turn to face the waiting car. Nova's head is pressed to the glass, her hair flat and lifeless against her pale face. Even those streaks of peachy-pink look like they've lost their color. She winks at me, forcing another half-smile. It looks as though it takes every ounce of strength she has.

"Your friend, I presume?" Freya furrows her brow. "She doesn't look so well…"

"That's because the poor girl's been shot," the captain replies. "What she needs is medical attention, Delly, *not* a rough ride on a leaky old trawler. Neptune knows how long it'll be before we see land again. Tell me you're not entertaining this idea?"

"She could succumb to infection, Meridel," Freya chimes in quietly.

"And I ain't keen on nobody dying on my watch," the captain says.

"She won't let me take her to the hospital," I say. "She cares for my cousin. I think she might even love him."

"She can't love your cousin if she's dead!" the captain argues. "She's better off staying right here."

"I can't leave her."

"Bah!" The captain roughs a frustrated hand through his scruffy, sleep-mussed hair.

Freya's molten eyes scan mine, reaching deep within my soul. I bare everything for her—all the love lost and the pain endured, the tears that had become an ocean of grief. There's nothing left for me to hide anymore. No pretenses to maintain, no lies to preserve. My life is forfeit without Hatch in it, and I don't care who knows.

"Please," I whisper.

Help me to convince him.

Help me get them back.

Help me...

"I will join you on your voyage, Meridel," Freya offers, taking both the captain and me by surprise.

"You will?" we ask together.

Freya nods. "I will tend to your friend, and see to it that she recovers." She exchanges a look with the captain I don't fully understand.

I have no idea what kind of medical training Freya has, but I've seen firsthand how capable she is. I trust the sage woman implicitly. At least for the time being, I'd say she's Nova's best chance.

"Thank you," I say, my voice shaky with gratitude.

"I don't like it," Captain Patton complains.

We both stare at him with pure determination, neither of us budging on the matter, and he can sense it.

"Oh, what the hell!" He throws his hands up in resignation.

Freya sheds a small, roguish smile.

"Don't say I didn't warn you," the captain snaps, his clear eye jumping between us disapprovingly.

"Thank you so much, Captain." I breathe a sigh of relief. "Thank you, thank you, thank you—"

"Don't thank me yet, Delly," he says soberly. "How soon do we need to leave?"

"Tonight. Immediately. As soon as possible."

"I'll need a few hours to gather supplies. Gotta load up on fuel bladders so we aren't forced to make any untimely pit stops—"

"Fuel bladders?" I ask.

"Your average fuel tanks won't cut it for a longer trip like this," he says. "We'll also need plenty of food and water. Do you have enough money to pay for all this?"

"I have money," I say, thinking back to my duffel bag, flung haphazardly under my bed in the guest house. I'd hidden my wallet inside a pair of clean socks days ago—along with my apartment keys and Blackbane's lighter—right after Florian confiscated my cell phone and Nova's gun. My inheritance from Virginia is currently sitting untouched in my checking account. I just need to get the captain my debit card, and—

A nagging thought tugs at the fringes of my mind.

Countless lives were claimed at Cliffmoor House this evening, lives of both criminal and innocent men alike. If I leave the island and do nothing about that, how long will the bodies rot in that cold, empty mansion before they're discovered? Before they're properly buried, if that ever happens at all?

I can't leave Briggs that way.

"There are some casualties back at Cliffmoor House," I rasp. "I should try to do something about them before we leave…"

What the hell are you going to do? I think hopelessly, my grasp on the situation rapidly slipping away. *Bury a slew of dead bodies in the yard? Drag them out one by one to sea? Spend all night mopping blood from the hardwood floors?*

This is worse than anything I could imagine.

Move the corpses, and I'm screwed. I'll never finish by daybreak. My prints will be everywhere…

Leave them, and I'm most certainly screwed too. Eventually, someone will come searching—a family member, or a friend. On the off chance that no one does, the bodies will start to smell…

Call the police, I'm screwed. God knows if they'll pin the whole catastrophe on Tristen. Or me.

But if I don't call them—screwed. Now I'm covering up a crime. A mass murder scene.

Shit. *Shit.*

"Anyone you know?" Captain Patton asks gently.

The knot in my throat tightens. "My friend, Briggs—"

"*Colin Briggs?*" they ask at the same time, an audible tenor of worry in their voices.

I nod slowly, devastated to have to deliver this news.

"Is Briggsy…" The captain's words trail off.

I gulp down a whimper. "He didn't make it."

I press my fingers to my mouth, swallowing back the acid on my tongue—the sudden, compulsive need to throw up.

Freya's beautiful face shutters into one of sorrow. The captain clears his throat. "I'll, um…call Goldwin down at the mortuary," he croaks. "He'll pick Briggsy up. Keep him on ice till we get back."

The captain shoots me a tenebrous look, silently willing me not to ask questions about his shadier connections. Truthfully, I don't want to know the details. "Goldwin prides himself on his discretion," he emphasizes.

I know this won't fix anything permanently, but it seems to be the better of all evils right now.

"What about the others?" I ask. The captain hesitates. "Some of them were good men. They don't deserve to be left that way."

The captain grunts. Sighs. "Fine. Goldwin owes me a few favors anyway. Guess it's time I cash those suckers in."

CHAPTER SIXTY

A nondescript gray van peels up the drive to Cliffmoor House. Out pops Goldwin—a shriveled, sallow-looking individual with a hooked nose and a bad comb over.

"Well, if it ain't ole Goldilocks in the flesh," Cap'n greets the tiny mortician. "Though I reckon I should scrap the 'locks' part and stick to Goldy now? Things are looking a little sparse up top, if you know what I mean." He whistles mockingly at Goldwin's balding head.

Goldwin scowls, running a jittery hand over his thinning hair. "You're one to talk, Fortuna," he squawks. "No one's seen you without that filthy hat for years! You're not fooling anyone."

The captain frowns, tugging down his yellow bucket hat.

My eyes slide tiredly between the old men. *Bickering about hair loss at a time like this?* I think whatever's left of my brain might actually implode.

"Little late for a house call, isn't it?" Goldwin jeers.

"Aye, but the devil's hour is most fitting for a job like this." Captain Patton wraps an arm around Goldwin's gnarly shoulders, but the embrace doesn't seem particularly friendly. He escorts him inside, whispering low all the while.

I don't strain to listen, or bother following them in. The gory sight and hulking stench of death has already burrowed under my skin. Pierced through my organs, rooted deep in my bones. I'm not sure I'll ever be rid of it. I don't care to expose myself to more.

Over the next hour, the men move in practiced tandem—a well-oiled, corpse-transporting machine. Goldwin backs the van right up to the front porch, concealing their actions from outside view. They both don shin-length aprons and medical masks, latex gloves and shoe covers. They shuttle cases of supplies inside the mansion…and, within minutes, slip back out with body bags in tow, easing them carefully into the trunk.

I sit under the porch, fully expecting my heart to give out—to succumb to this painful, thunderous beating—thinking myself nauseous while I watch them work. My head grows heavy, a deadweight in my hands. I weep in silence and wonder over where Hatch is, and what's being done to him, and how I'm going to reach him before…before…

Stop.

Don't even think it.

When the men finish, they peel off their regalia and dump it in a biohazard bag. Goldwin tosses the bag in the van and turns to the captain with one final scowl. "Now we're square, Fortuna."

"Goldy, you and I will *never* be square," the captain warns, his tone alluding to some dark, unfinished business.

Goldwin curses under his breath, his face puckered and red as he hobbles away. I spring to my feet, remembering a lingering detail I hadn't yet addressed. "Wait!"

The mortician twists to face me, his beady eyes narrowing.

"Can you mail out a letter for me?" I ask him, breathless. "Please. It's important."

Goldwin gripes in protest, but Captain Patton swiftly interjects, "Oh, he'd be *happy* to, Delly." He pulls a wad of crumpled napkins from his back pocket, handing them to me. "You got any pens in that death truck of yours?" he spits at Goldwin.

The tiny man grunts and totters away to search his glove box, returning a few seconds later with a stumpy yellow pencil. "Make it snappy," he squawks, dropping it into my palm.

I settle on the porch again and unfurl the captain's cache of napkins. They're all from Barracuda's Teeth, a caricature of the dive bar's namesake fish smiling wide in sunglasses. I pick one up and read the groovy lettering. *'Cuda's—Hooking You Up Since '55*. The C is curled into a hook.

It's been so long since I last saw this. I've lived and died a hundred times since. But that first night at 'Cuda's—my first back on Halcyon Bay after so many years—was the start of a journey. The start of everything.

I write with unsteady fingers:

Palmer,

Florian has Hatch and Tristen. I'm going after them. This isn't me packing my bags up for good. I'm coming back. I need you to know that.

See you soon so you can yell at me.

Dell

P.S. I'll miss you.

I consider mentioning where I'm headed, but the last thing I want is Palmer endangering herself by coming after me…or worse, tipping my parents off. I can't risk losing anyone else I love.

I fold the napkin up and hand it to Goldwin, along with Palmer's address. Within seconds, he's off in his truck, vanishing into the misty night air so swiftly one could wonder if he'd ever been there at all.

I join Captain Patton in the foyer at last.

In the hazy chandelier light, the room looks almost normal…except for the rich smears of blood on the floor, the crimson spatters on the walls, the staircase risers, the marble sculptures…

"Not much we can do about this mess, I'm afraid," the captain laments. "Not if we want to embark before daybreak."

The black wave of sadness that failed to drown me subsides, leaving only scattered fragments—ashes—in its wake. A soft, smothered anger flickers to life from those ashes, rising up like a phoenix in my chest. It gains momentum with each flap of its scorched wings, growing stronger, more violent, and sharp as the tip of a knife.

That phoenix—my rage—takes the form of an impulse. A desire that had been there all along, right from the very first moments spent at Cliffmoor House last summer.

A yearning to watch it crumble.

To make it all *burn*.

"Delly?" the captain asks, touching my arm gently.

This is how I'll put an end to my family's reign of terror—by destroying this symbol of Klyne prestige and depravity. By chopping the head right off the snake.

"Delly girl?" Captain Patton's tentative voice sounds distant and echoey.

When Tristen and I visited Blackbane in prison, the madman insinuated that this would end in smoke and sacrifice. That I was destined to be the tragic victim of my story.

I couldn't have known then all that would transpire—how much those evil words would stick with me, how they'd cast a looming shadow over my every move. But I'd kept the lighter ever since that fateful day, a reminder of all that I'd endured. For what reason, I didn't know…

Until now.

The captain clears his throat. "Delly, we really should get moving—"

"You go ahead," I say. "I want to collect some supplies before I go. There's a safe room underground with non-perishables. It only makes sense to bring them along."

"How will you get back to the seaport?" the captain asks.

"Don't worry about me," I insist. "Use my card to fuel up. I'll meet you at the *Willow* in a couple of hours. With any luck, Freya and Nova will be ready by then too."

The two of them had stayed behind so Freya could clean Nova's wounds, remove the bullet lodged above her hip, and stitch her back up. I hope the procedure is going smoothly. That Freya's surgical skills and curative herbs are strong enough to keep Nova from death.

"Are you sure?" he asks.

"Trust me." I nod reassuringly. "I'll be right behind you."

My mother's foreboding words fill my mind as the captain waddles out the front door—

"You can only linger in hell for so long before you become flame or demon yourself."

Mom was right.

I had lingered in hell for too long.

Cracked myself open.

Let the darkness creep in.

But I am no victim.

I am the flame.

The incendiary.

And I will burn this house to the fucking ground.

It has to look like an accident. A kitchen fire, or a short circuit, or a...

Gas leak.

Yes, that's it.

That'll give me plenty of time to get away, maybe even off the island, before the explosion.

But first thing's first.

I dump my duffel bag with all my belongings in the parlor. Changing into fresh clothes, I ball up my bloody ball gown and shove it in the fireplace with the log stacks. It's safe to assume the shimmery material is flammable. It'll burn hot and fast. *Perfect.*

I load up my large travel backpack with several days' worth of water bottles, jars of peanut butter, and canned beans, tuna, and fruit. I squeeze even more in my duffel where they fit. *We need more water than this,* I think bleakly, as I carefully arrange everything to maximize space. Hopefully, Captain and Freya are packing some too.

With all that assembled, I grab a flashlight from the table in the corridor and cram it in my jeans pocket on my way to the foyer.

My eyes fall upon the statues—on their elegant forms and vacant stares, their blood-speckled faces turned away in disgust, as if they can sense what I intend to do. I hone in on a target: an exquisite marble bust. The youthful male looks like a flawless Renaissance jewel. Anatomically precise with chiseled features, smooth muscles, and lush, swirling hair.

One hard push sends him toppling from his stand and crashing to the floor. The sculpture splinters at the neck. The head rolls off into a corner. *Excellent.*

I collect the decapitated statue head in my arms, clutching it to my chest. Then I race back to the parlor, through the bookcase, down the steps into the safe room, through the paneled wall, and into the briny tunnel.

Flicking on my flashlight, I lean it up against the far wall, illuminating the gas line that runs out to the sea trumpet fields. If I break this pipe, natural gas will slowly trickle into the tunnel. With all the other access points sealed shut—the caves flooded, the door to the fields locked—the only place the gas can flow is up to Cliffmoor House. If I start a raging fire in the parlor, it's only a matter of time before the gas reaches the hearth, ignites, and…*boom.*

No more Cliffmoor House.

I grip the statue head and, bracing myself, swing it around with all of my might. It slams hard against the pipe—*bang!*—creating a visible dent. I bring the head down three more times—*bang, bang, bang!*—only to make more superficial damage.

This isn't working.

Think, Dell. Think.

I need to locate a weak spot. An area prone to breaking…

A joint.

Picking up my flashlight, I move deeper into the tunnel until I find a junction point—two rust-bitten pipes fitted snugly together. A strong enough impact could surely force them apart.

I angle the flashlight against the rock wall again, holding my breath as I clutch the statue head. *Please let this work.* Stepping back, I throw all my weight into a hard swing, grunting as I bring the head down, and—*bang!*

The joint cracks.

A whistle spills from the broken line, just as a sickening, rotten-egg smell hits my nose. In the white beam of light, I see an invisible ripple fill the air.

Gas is leaking.

I sprint back up to the safe room, wedging the wooden panel open with a chair. On my way out, my eyes catch one final time on that beautiful painting of Cliffmoor House—a vast, dream-like rendition of a mansion that will soon be nothing but rubble.

I jam a second chair in the doorway before ascending the narrow steps to the house. I leave the bookcase aperture open too, so the gas can flow freely into the parlor.

Fingers clenched around Blackbane's lighter, I stand before the ornate fireplace. *This is it.*

I flick it once, twice, three times, anticipation surging in my veins. The device lights up—a bright lick of flame against the inky, peacock-blue room—casting a spooky luster over Virginia's stunning portrait.

I'll always associate my grandmother's face with this room. The first time I ever walked these magnificent halls, I remember I couldn't wrap my mind around the image of her, or the swirling emotions it dragged up from me. She was an utter stranger to me, yet she felt so oddly familiar.

My stomach twists at the memory. Briggs escorted me through the house that night. The thought of his kind, silver eyes swimming behind half-moon spectacles punches me square in the gut.

Those eyes will never open again.

Without another thought, I drop the cigarette lighter onto the gown. Fire catches quickly, the flames gobbling up every one of those glittering stars and crystals. I watch, mesmerized, as the fabric turns to kindling for the logs. Soon, the wood blazes orange, the smell of smoke permeating the room.

It won't be long now.

I know full well what I've done, though my mind is unburdened by worry, unconcerned with repercussions. I find peace in knowing that, after tonight, this place won't hold the power to hurt anyone else.

For the first time in a long time, I feel I've done something right.

I haul the backpack over my shoulders. It's bone-breakingly heavy, but I barely even feel it. My whole body tingles, coursing with adrenaline.

I take one final glance around, certain I've taken all I need from this place. My mother's box. My grandmother's journal. My trove of dreadful memories. Nothing else is worth saving. Nothing remains of true value. The rest is just…stuff. Pretty artifacts. Shiny vestiges of evil.

Let it all burn.

Grabbing my duffel, I slip out the back of Cliffmoor House, letting the French door latch behind me with a whispered *good riddance.*

CHAPTER SIXTY-ONE

Between the three of us, we carry Nova below deck and onto the single mattress in the cabin of the *Willow's Wind*. She's wrapped up in gauze, medical tape all along her lower stomach and back, her tanned skin clammy and paler than pale.

"Don't worry," Nova whispers, mustering a tiny wince of a smile. "We'll get them back."

"But what about you?" I rasp, too scared to form the question I really want to ask—*will I lose you too?*

"I'm a hard woman to kill," she says simply, her eyes fluttering shut as she drifts off to sleep.

Freya and I assist Captain Patton on deck, silently untying ropes while he charts a southbound course. We work under cover of darkness, leaving all the boat lights off. There's only an hour or so left before daybreak. Soon, the seaport will be crawling with early-risers eager for their morning catch.

The captain pokes his head out of the wheelhouse. "Ready?"

I nod, and the boat engine purrs to life, rattling the otherwise calm waters of the harbor.

The *Willow* crawls slowly through the sleeping marina. I train my eyes on the distant Halcyon Reef Light—the new one they'd built to replace Idyll Point, six miles out to sea. It shoots beams across the ocean, guiding our path as we leave a foggy Halcyon Bay in our wake.

It feels different this time, leaving the island. I'm not running, for one—neither from a tragic past, nor the spark of unlikely love. Those days are long over, those fears long past.

There's nothing and no one for me to run from anymore.

There are a million things for me to run *to*.

One in particular.

I feel him here, amid the wide expanse of blue. I see the moments we've shared as though I'm reliving them—nostalgic, flickering pictures playing on the big screen of my mind. Memories flood me as we push out of the shallow, cradling arms of the bay.

With Hatch, I've had some of the greatest times of my life—endured the hardest trials and the most incredible joys. The film reel of memories rolls on and on, of times when he was with me, and the world was a distant murmur...

I blink and there we are, tangled in his truck bed, his caramel-brown hair sweeping across his forehead, ever dampened by the ocean's spray. I laugh as I push it back from his face, letting my hand slide to the nape of his neck, burying my fingers in those soft, unruly waves, like strands of gold and bronze sifting through my fingers.

Blink, and we're lying together atop Idyll Point, holding our breaths in the soft glimmer of candlelight. I admire the tanned, sinewy landscape of his body, hewn of hard labor and relentless sunshine. My fingertips blaze new trails over that manly terrain, mapping the lines of him, every crest and valley marble-smooth and fire-warm.

Blink, and we're pressed into the shadowy corners of the *Willow*, shielded from the moonlight. That roguish mouth curves up one side of his face, a dimple carved into his stubbled cheek. And then we're all hungry lips and tongues and teeth, utterly drunk on some indefinable substance, a singular taste we find only in each other.

Blink, and we're tucked inside a murky dive bar, heads hunched together like little kids conspiring. Brilliant eyes of seagrass-green rake over me. I study the kaleidoscopic rings of that gaze, my heart pierced by his arrow, certain I'll ever know a more beautiful thing.

"We're almost out of the bay!" Captain Patton calls from the wheelhouse. I don't turn my head, standing my ground at the bow, looking ever farther, out, out…

Those glimpses of memory are more real than anything. Real as the tide and the stars and the wind, blowing cold against my tear-stained face. Memories are my lifeblood, keeping me alive, sure as the waves rush to the shore. I let them surge in me, let them sustain me, like life-giving drugs to my veins.

The sea remembers, and so do I.

"I'm coming for you, Hatch," I whisper, my promise winding its way to the inky sky, and hopefully, to wherever he is. I inhale a salty breath, and another, and another. "I love you. I'm coming."

Behind us, an explosion erupts in the distance, like a thousand fireworks come alive at the edge of the sea. But those are no fireworks, and this is no celebration.

Flames consume the sky behind me.

The moonlit horizon lies ahead.

And Hatch beyond it.

AUTHOR'S NOTE

Thank you so much for reading *Isle of Brine and Bone!*

This book—the second in the Halcyon Bay series—was both incredibly challenging and rewarding for me to write. I had to push my storytelling to new heights, tapping into many raw and sometimes difficult emotions in order to authentically craft this part of Dell's story. It's a deeply human chapter, full of grief, loss, and darkness, but also joy, recovery, and light. At the core of it all is Dell's perseverance, which, funnily enough, is exactly what this book required of me.

I hope you're as excited for the next installment as I am!

If you enjoyed *Isle of Brine and Bone,* I would greatly appreciate it if you would consider leaving a review online! And if you'd like to be the first to hear about my upcoming releases and bookish updates, sign up for my newsletter at www.nataliamlucia.com.

Thank you again for reading!

ACKNOWLEDGMENTS

I credit this book to every single person who helped drag me over the finish line.

To Ryan, first and always, for reassuring me that tomorrow will be better. I wanted to throw in the towel more than once, but your daily encouragements kept that from happening. Thank you for holding my head above water. I love love love you.

To Mom, Dad, and Niki, for informing everyone we know (and some we don't know) that I'm an author. Thank you for always cheering me on the loudest. For being my greatest supporters at every age. I can't express what it means to me to know you all are proud of me.

To Maria, for designing another drool-worthy cover. Working with you is the best, thank you.

To Rachel, for being the most incredible friend and lending your hawk eyes to this manuscript. Thank you doesn't even begin to cover it.

To my team of early readers/beta besties: Alyssa, Daphne, Emily, Hailey, Shannon, and Vanessa. Your enthusiasm made all the difference with this one. Thanks for championing this story (and me) like you do. I truly couldn't have done it without you.

To my street team, for being such a bright and positive force. Your energy for these characters (particularly one swoony-eyed fisherman) is infectious. Thank you all for everything you do to promote, celebrate, and love on my books.

To the countless author friends who inspire, advise, and laugh with me every day: thank you for your friendship and wisdom. Navigating the publishing world can be tough. I'd be lost without you.

To the readers, for giving my stories a chance. I know you all have TBRs for miles, and reading time is precious. I'm honored you've chosen to spend some of yours on my books. Thank you so much for being here.

To God, for always paving a way. I write because You make it so.

Two published books under my belt, and I'm still amazed that I get to do this…

Onto the next one!

Natalia Macias Lucia was raised on ghost stories, Cuban food, and sweltering summers in her native South Florida. She loves the sun, surf, and swampland almost as much as she loves writing, and when not dreaming up new book ideas, she can often be found by the ocean with her husband, family, and neurotic Jack Russell Terrier.

An avid reader with a lifelong dream of becoming a novelist, Natalia earned a bachelor's degree in English Literature from the University of Miami. She enjoys writing dark fairytales woven into contemporary life, filled with swoony romance, thrilling twists, and things that go bump in the night.

Visit her online at **www.nataliamlucia.com**.